Falling Into Us

JASINDA WILDER

FALLING INTO US

ISBN: 978-0-9891044-2-5
Copyright © 2013 by Jasinda Wilder

Cover art by Sarah Hansen of Okay Creations. Cover art © 2013 by Sarah Hansen.
Copyediting and interior book design by Indie Author Services.

If you've been hurt the worst by those meant to love the most,
if you've sought release from agony through the bliss of pain,
if you've been rejected because of a perceived imperfection,
then this book is for you.
You are loved;
you are not alone;
you are beautiful.

One: A Beginning; Or, a Dare
Jason Dorsey
September, sophomore year of high school

"QUIT BEING A PRICK, MALCOLM." I gave Malcolm Henry a hard shove, and he stumbled away.

"It's a legitimate question, Dorsey. You've had a crush on Nell Hawthorne for-fricking-ever. When are you gonna man up and ask her out?" Malcolm was the only black guy on the varsity team, our fastest runner, our star running back, and the third part of our team's All-State power trio, along with Kyle, the QB, and me, the wide receiver.

Malcolm was built like me, short and stocky and muscular, and he had a huge seventies-style afro that he cultivated carefully, figuring if he had to be the only black guy on an all-white, rural community football team, he might as well look the part.

"You're too fucking chicken," he goaded me. "You won't do it."

I gave him a glare. "Shut the hell up, Malc." We were tossing a ball back and forth on the field as we waited for the other guys to dress out. We'd both gotten out of class early since we had phys ed sixth period, and Coach Donaldson was the gym teacher. "I'm not chicken. I just haven't had the right opportunity. She's Kyle's best friend, for one thing. I'm not sure how he'd take it. And besides, you know what happened with Mr. Hawthorne and Aaron Swarnicki. He'd have my balls on his desk if I had asked her out. She literally *just* turned sixteen like a week ago."

"Which means you've had a week to plan this shit. Come on, Jay. Don't puss out on me now. You've been whining about how bad you want a shot at Nell since seventh grade. Now's your chance." He tossed the ball to me, then took off running, sprinting in a zigzag pattern. I hurled the ball at him but missed him by a mile. "Good fucking thing you're not the QB, Jason. You suck."

"Like you could do better? You couldn't hit the broad side of a barn."

He threw the ball to me, nailing me hard in the chest. "I bet I could hit the broad side of Nell's ass from fifty yards away."

I knew he was riling me, but it worked. "Don't talk about her that way, you turd." I threw the ball back to him, then mimicked his earlier move, cutting right and sprinting several yards before turning to catch the ball.

"Then man the fuck up. Ask. Her ass. *Out.*" Malcom threw the ball and it landed flush in my arms; Malcolm could throw better than I could, but I'd never admit it to him.

"I will," I said. "I will. When I'm ready."

At that moment, Blain, Nick, Chuck, and Frankie all trotted out onto the field, tossing their gear in a haphazard pile on the sidelines. I threw the ball to Frankie, who charged at me, tucking the ball in the crook of his arm. I let him zip past me, then easily caught up to him and tackled him to the ground, nailing him hard in the side. We both went down laughing, but when we hit, it was Frankie who took longer to get up, gasping for breath.

"You're too chicken, Dorsey." Frankie pressed a fist to his ribs, wincing. "Fuck, man. I think you bruised a rib. I don't have my gear on, dude, take it easy."

"Pussy. Can't take a tackle? Maybe you should try running a few plays, take a few real tackles. Might help you man up a bit, you fucking tub." I grinned at him as I said it, because we both knew Frankie was the offensive lineman responsible for keeping my ass safe from getting nailed as I cut out for a run. He was a hell of a player and one of my best friends, after Kyle and Malcolm.

"Yeah, yeah, I'm the tub, you're the twinkle toes little fairy." He feinted at me, then wrapped a burly arm around my neck and squeezed; Frankie was huge, truly mammoth, seventeen and already standing over six feet tall and weighing in at nearly two-fifty. He was the kind of guy who looked overweight at first glance, but if you felt him tackle you, you'd realize he was two hundred and fifty pounds of solid muscle. "Maybe you should quit prancing around the field like a fucking twinkie and try blocking for your baby little ass."

I gasped for breath as he squeezed and had to drive my fist into his ribs to get him to let go. Blain, the safety and the team peacemaker, shoved both of us aside. "Knock it off, guys. You know how Coach is about horsing around."

"Shut up, Blain," Malcolm, Frankie, and I all said in unison.

"Let's get back to how you're too chicken to ask Nell out," Malcolm said.

"How about let's not." I threw the ball sideways across the field to Chuck, the second-string receiver, who caught it and threw it to Nick, another offensive lineman.

"I dare you," Frankie said. "I double-dog dare you."

I laughed. "What is this, second grade? You double-dog dare me? Seriously?"

Frankie didn't laugh with me. "Yeah, I'm daring you to ask out Nell Hawthorne. I'm sick of you acting like your crush on her is some big secret. Everyone knows but her and Kyle. Make a move or shut up about it."

"I'll sweeten the pot," Malcolm said. "I'll bet you a hundred bucks you won't do it."

"That's stupid. I'm not taking bets or dares about this. She's my friend. I'll ask her out if and when I'm ready." I busied myself putting on my pads in an attempt to try to hide my discomfort

"Yeah, she's your friend…because you've been friend-zoned." This was Malcolm.

The bastard.

"I have not been friend-zoned." I tightened my cleats unnecessarily, jerking the laces so hard my foot twinged, and I had to loosen and retie them.

Malcolm could always see right through me. "Yeah, you have, and you know it." He stood nose to nose with me. "A hundred bucks. Put up or shut up."

I shoved him away, but he got right back in my face and shoved me back. "I'm not fucking betting your asses about this," I said.

"That's 'cause you're a scardey-twat," Frankie said.

This elicited a round of laughter from the entire offensive line, now gathered around us.

"'Scaredy-twat'?" I mocked. "Did you really just say that?"

Frankie lumbered toward me, puffed up and ready to throw down. "Yeah, I did. 'Cause that's what you are."

I faced him down, but we both knew I'd never dare actually step up to Frankie: We would both end up in the hospital. "I'm not afraid," I said, lying through my teeth.

The truth was, I really was afraid. I'd been friends with Nell Hawthorne since third grade, and I'd had a crush on her nearly that long. Frankie had been dead right when he'd said everyone knew except Nell herself and Kyle. And Kyle might have known, but chose to ignore it; I wasn't honestly sure.

When you've spent nearly ten years crushing on someone you don't dare ask out, the idea of asking her out on a date is terrifying. I also knew if I didn't take the bet, I'd be the laughingstock of the entire football team.

"Fuck. Fine. I'll ask her out tomorrow." I hated being pressured into it, but I also knew I'd probably never do it otherwise. "You'll all owe me a bill by practice tomorrow."

Frankie and Malcolm both shook my hand, since they were the only ones actually participating in the bet.

I went through practice on autopilot, running the plays and catching the ball without really thinking about it. My brain was running a million miles a minute, by turns planning out what I'd say and freaking about getting it wrong.

By the time I got to school the next day, I was a nervous wreck. It didn't help that Dad had gotten home from work early and worked me over pretty hard. Practice would be rough today with the bruises clouding my ribs and back, but I was used to it by now. It made me tough, he said. It was for my own good, he said. He was right, in a way, though; it did make me tough.

No tackle would ever hurt as much as his fists.

I had fourth-period western civ and fifth-period U.S. government with Nell, and I was planning on making my move between classes. I'd walk her to her locker and ask her as we exchanged books. I stood outside Mrs. Hasting's first-floor classroom, waiting for Nell to show up for fifth period. I had to bite on my cheek to hide the wince when Malcolm playfully half-tackled me from the side, driving his brawny shoulder straight into a bruise. I shrugged him off, forcing out a laugh as we wrestled until Happy Harry the Hippy Hall Monitor strolled past, calling out a cheerful "Knock it off, you crazy ruffians."

Happy Harry was everybody's friend. He looked like John Lennon, with long shaggy brown hair, a scruffy beard, and round glasses. He'd smoked way too much pot in the sixties and hadn't ever really left that decade, mentally. He was Principal Bowman's brother, and was perpetually placid, nice to everyone almost to a fault, and always smiling. He never had to ask anyone anything twice, since even the most hard-ass goth liked Harry.

"So, you're gonna do it after class, right?" Malcolm asked me in a confidential mutter, flashing a triple-folded hundred-dollar bill between his index and middle fingers.

I reached for the bill, but he danced out of the way. "Yeah, I am," I said. "Hang out by the our lockers between fourth and fifth period."

I rubbed my side where a purple-yellow bruise the size of a grapefruit shadowed my ribs and around to my back, the same spot where Malcolm had hit me with his tackle.

Kyle's voice came from behind me. "Your dad go after you again?"

Kyle was the only person other than my mom who knew Dad beat me. I'd made Kyle promise to never tell anyone, though. Telling wouldn't do any good, since Dad was the captain of our town's police force. He'd bury any reports, intimidate any social workers who tried to get in his way. It had happened before. I'd made the mistake of telling a gym teacher in eighth grade that the bruise on my stomach was from my dad hitting me, and the teacher had gone to a social worker. The gym teacher had been transferred to a different district within a week, and the social worker had been fired.

I'd missed a week of school, out "sick." In reality, I'd been in too much pain to get out of bed. The bruises on my body had taken over a month to disappear. I'd never tried to tell anyone after that. I spent as much time at school, at football practice, or at Kyle's house as I could. Anything to stay out of Dad's way. It suited him, since he'd never wanted kids in the first place. I was a disappointment to him, he claimed. Even when I made varsity my freshman year, I was a disappointment. Even when I broke the district record for most receptions in a single season that same freshman year, I was a useless piece of shit. I hadn't beaten Dad's record, and that was all that mattered.

See, Dad had been All-State three years in a row during high school and then had gone on to play as a starting WR for Michigan State, and was widely praised as one of the best players in college football. He'd then been scouted by the Kansas City Chiefs, the Minnesota Vikings, and the New York Giants. He'd torn his ACL his first game with the Giants, though, and it had been a career-ending injury. He'd returned to his hometown here in Michigan and joined the police force as a bitter, angry man. When the first Gulf War happened, he'd joined the Army and done two tours with the infantry, and had come back even more fucked up from the things he'd seen and done.

He liked to get drunk after work, and he'd tell me horror stories. Unlike most combat vets I'd heard of, Dad liked to talk about his experiences. Only with me, though, and only when he was at the bottom of a fifth. He'd tell me about the buddies he'd seen shot, blown up by IEDs, hit by snipers and RPGs. If I tried to leave, he'd lay into me. Even drunk, Dad was formidable. The ACL injury had ended his career as a professional wide receiver, but it hadn't made him any less physically intimidating. He stood several inches taller than me, wide through the shoulders with thick biceps and corded forearms, his short-cropped salt-and-pepper hair beaded with sweat as he swayed in front of me.

He had quick, hard fists, and even drunk he was accurate. He knew where to hit to cause the most pain. I'd gotten better at blocking and dodging, which Dad encouraged. He wanted me to be a *man*, a *warrior*. Men don't feel pain. Men can run plays with bruised ribs and battered kidneys. Men don't cry. Men don't tell. Men break records.

Kyle knew all this—he understood it as much as anyone who didn't live it could, and he never told.

"Yeah, but I'm fine." I hated sympathy.

Kyle just met my eyes, staring me down, assessing. He knew I'd never admit to being in pain, so he'd gotten better at gauging how bad off I was. "You sure? Coach wants to run tap-dance drills today."

"Shit," I muttered.

Tap-dance drills were usually run with the coach or the QB throwing a ball and the receiver practicing catching it near the sidelines, tap dancing to stay in bounds with one or both feet. Coach liked to run these drills with full interference, so I'd learn to make the catch while a defender tried to stop me. What this meant was I'd spend most of the practice getting tackled over and over again. With already-bruised ribs, I'd be lucky if could walk off the field under my own power.

"No, I'm fine," I said. "We're playing Brighton on Friday, and they like to double-team me. I need the practice."

Kyle just shook his head. "You're such a stubborn asshole."

I laughed. "Yeah. But I'm the best motherfucking wide receiver in the state. There's something to be said for Dad's 'training program.'" I made air quotes with my fingers as I said the last part.

"What was that word Mr. Lang used yesterday? Talking about the Spartans and how they trained their warriors?" Kyle dug a Powerbar out of his bag and opened it, handing me half.

"*Agoge,*" I answered.

"That's it," Kyle said, chewing noisily. "Just pretend you're a Spartan, training in an *agoge.*"

"It wasn't a building, I don't think," I said, eating my half. "It was more of a lifestyle, a program. And yeah, that's basically it. Mike Dorsey, Spartan agoge trainer."

"Am I gonna have to drag you off the field again?" Kyle asked, only half joking.

"Probably," I answered.

"We'll hit up the hideout after practice, then." Kyle took off for his fifth-period science class on the other end of the school, hustling so he wouldn't be late.

"Sounds good," I said, calling after him.

The hideout was a spot out in the woods behind my house. There was an old lightning-struck oak tree with huge spreading branches bending low over the ground, forming a cave-like canopy. Over the years Kyle and I had turned the spot into a clubhouse of kinds, weaving branches together and old boards and pieces of tin from the junkyard around the thick trunk so that we had an enclosed area. We'd dragged old chairs, some crates, even a ratty old couch in there. It was our secret, and even now, when we were old enough that we should be embarrassed about having a secret clubhouse, we still kept it secret. My cousin Doug had once somehow looted several cases of cheap beer from a liquor store, and he'd given me a couple of them, so Kyle and I often went to the hideout to drink together.

For me, though, the hideout was just that, somewhere I could go to get away from my dad. I'd spent the night there on several occasions, to the point that I kept an old wool blanket in one of the crates.

My conversation with Malcolm and then Kyle had taken most of the seven minutes before fifth period, so I was surprised when Nell still hadn't shown up for class. I thought I'd shit myself if I got myself all psyched up to ask her out and then she didn't show up for class.

Then she appeared, hair loose around her shoulders, smiling and laughing. Becca was on one side of her, Jill on the other. Those three girls were, in my opinion, the three hottest girls in the entire school, and I could never decide how to rank them in terms of who was the hottest. It depended on my mood, most days. I knew Nell the best, since I'd spent most of my life daydreaming about her like a little puppy, but Becca was just as hot in a different way. She was shorter and curvier than Nell, and Becca had long curly black hair, so tightly curled that it was a thick mass of springy ringlets, whereas Nell's hair was a perfect shade of strawberry blonde. Becca's skin was the color of dark caramel, where Nell's was like ivory, white and pale. Nell was outgoing and cheerful, whereas Becca was quiet and painfully shy, but brilliantly smart.

Jill was almost lost in the shuffle when she was with Becca and Nell. She just couldn't compete, if you ask me. If you looked at her when she was on her own or with other people, Jill was hot for sure, but she just wasn't in the same league as Nell and Becca. Jill was a Barbie doll, like, for real. Tall, impossibly proportioned, naturally shock-blonde hair and blue eyes. She was the sweetest girl you'd ever meet, and yeah, I know, guys shouldn't use the term "sweet," but it just fit. Jill was sweet as a spoonful of sugar. She was also a stereotypical bubbly blonde in that she was almost unbelievably air-headed and kind of shallow. She was loyal as hell to her friends, though, and I liked that about her.

It was a *High School Musical* moment: the three hottest girls in school, striding side by side down the middle of the sun-bathed hallway, Nell in the middle, everyone watching her, admiring her, talking about her. And then she stopped right in front of me, smiling at me, saying hi to me, and I was frozen, gaping, stunned.

Someone bumped me from behind, hard, knocking me out of my reverie. Malcolm stumbled past me, coughing. "My bad, bro. I didn't see you there." He nodded at Nell and the others. "Hey, whassup girls? Lookin' fine today, I see. Lookin' real fine, don't you agree, Jason?" Malcolm liked to "play up his blackness," as he put it, especially when he was trying to be funny, which was most of the time.

I glared at him, then turned my attention to Nell. "Hey, Nell. What's up?" Lame. Lame. *So* lame.

She grinned at me. "Hi, Jason."

Becca and Jill had kept walking, stopping at their lockers a few feet away. This spot, the humanities hallway on the first floor near the lunchroom and the adjacent outdoor courtyard, was the prime focal point of our high school's social world. It was where everything happened. You asked girls out there, you challenged guys to fights there, you broke up there. If you were popular, it was where you hung out and got seen, where the leaders of the various cliques held court. So, of course, being one of the stars of the football team, I had to ask her out there. Nell was popular, but she was the kind of girl who didn't have a clique. She was cool with everyone, popular because she was beautiful, smart, and the daughter of the second most influential man in our town, second only to Kyle's dad, and she was Kyle's best friend. Kyle, of course, was the god of the high school. He was the star quarterback, All-State at sixteen, the son of a senator, and so good-looking it was stupid. He had the perfect life. Best friends with the hottest girl in school, rich, good-looking, popular, athletic, awesome parents. He even had a badass car, a classic Camaro SS his older brother had rebuilt and then left behind when he ran off at seventeen. The only reason I didn't hate Kyle was that he was my best friend and I'd known him since kindergarten, and I could tell everyone the story of when he peed his pants in third grade and I'd covered for him.

Everyone was watching me. They knew something was going down. Malcolm and Frankie had probably told everyone they knew, which was everyone, that I was asking Nell out, so the whole crowd of "cool kids" was standing in the hallway, not even pretending not to watch.

I couldn't puss out now. Damn it.

I swallowed the ball of dry nerves and clenched my trembling hands into fists at my sides. "So, Nell. I was thinking. You wanna go out with me tonight? Seven o'clock?" My voice hadn't shaken or squeaked, and I'd sounded suitably nonchalant.

Nell's eyes widened and she sucked in a surprised breath, then let out an excited squeal before chomping her teeth together to stop it. "Yes! I mean, yeah, sure. I'd love to. Where are we going?"

I had actually done some prep for this, thank god. "I was thinking Bravo."

She grinned again. It was an expensive place for high schoolers, and you had to have reservations, especially on a Friday night. I had an agreement with my dad: I would focus on my grades and football, and he'd make sure I didn't need to work. I got a two-hundred-dollar bonus for every game we won, plus twenty dollars for every touchdown I scored. Our team was undefeated so far this year, and I'd already scored six touchdowns in the four games we'd played.

Yeah. My dad really pushed me to succeed at football. Winning was everything, second only to being "a real man."

"Don't you have to make reservations to get in there on Fridays?" Nell asked.

I just grinned cockily and shoved my fist in my hip pocket. "Yep."

She narrowed her eyes at me. "How could you be so sure I'd say yes?"

I grinned even more widely, mainly to cover my hammering heart. "Well, you did, didn't you?"

She couldn't hold the serious look for long. "I'll see you at seven, then."

I nodded and pushed past her into our classroom, ignoring the hushed whispers. I slumped into my seat in the back by the window and pretended not to see Nell doing the girly whispered freak-out with Becca and Jill. I wanted to have a whispery freak-out myself, but I couldn't, because I was a man, and men didn't show emotions.

Nell settled gracefully into her seat a few rows over and in front of me. She set her backpack on the floor beside her foot and bent over to open it, using the opportunity to steal a glance at me, blushing and smiling when she saw me looking right at her. I wondered in the back of my head if she would let me kiss her.

Probably not, but it sure would be cool if she did.

Fortunately for me, Coach made us watch a film instead of running drills. He let Kyle skip the film, knowing Kyle would study it at home on his own. The rest of us weren't so lucky, so we were stuck watching Brighton games until almost six-thirty.

I'd planned on picking Nell up right after practice anyway, so I'd smuggled some jeans and a but-
ton-down shirt in my backpack. The shirt was wrinkled, but there wasn't much I could do about that. I
showered after the guys all left and then hopped into
my truck. I'd bought the truck myself, saving my earn-
ings from all of last year's football season plus my end-
of-year straight-A bonus to buy it. It was a ten-year-old
F-150, black, long-bed, manual transmission, four-by-
four. It was my baby. It wasn't much, but it was mine.
Dad couldn't and wouldn't take it away from me no
matter what I did, since I'd saved and paid for it myself.
He respected that.

He had his own kind of honor, in a warped way.
He had no qualms about beating me until I pissed
blood, but he respected my space and my things, and
he paid my way as long as I earned it. He'd cut short
his *lessons* if I fought back. Of course, the lesson would
be shortened via me getting knocked out, but it would
be less of a beating, so I'd started fighting back more
regularly.

I drove to Nell's house, my tires crunching on the
gravel road. My nerves were wreaking havoc on me
now. It was finally happening. I was going out on a
date with Nell Hawthorne. I could picture her wearing
a demure but sleek knee-length skirt, some kind of top

that couldn't disguise her incredible rack. Long straw-berry blonde hair loose around her shoulders, just the bangs pinned back behind her head like always. She liked to paint her fingernails bright colors, usually red or orange or pink. Sometimes blue or green, but never black or gray or any dull colors.

I stopped in the middle of the road a mile from her house and tried to pull myself together. It was just a date. We were just two friends going on a date. Nothing else. There was no reason to think I'd get to kiss her. I wouldn't even try to hold her hand. Just… hang out and talk. No need to get excited.

But I was. I was wired, I was so excited.

I let out a long breath, slapped my steering wheel with both hands, and whooped as loud as I could, releasing some of my built-up excitement. I was pumped, so worked up at the prospect of going on a date with Nell that I didn't even feel my bruises.

I put the truck back in drive and pulled up to Nell's driveway. My cell phone rang just as I was stopping in front of her house. I glanced at the screen, sliding the "answer" key when I saw Kyle's name. The digital clock readout at the top of the screen read 6:54 p.m., so I was a bit early. I'd been ignoring the fact that I'd have to tell him I was going out on a date with the girl who was closer to him than a sister. Now that he was calling, minutes before the date, I almost didn't want to tell him.

"Hey, Kyle, my man! Whassup!" I faked enthusiasm to cover the rush of nerves.

The hesitation on the other end was louder than a shout. "Actually, Jason, this is Nell. I'm calling from Kyle's phone…I—I forgot mine." Nell's voice hit me in the chest like a ton of bricks.

Then her words registered. "Forgot yours? Where are you? I'm pulling up to your driveway right now."

An even longer hesitation. My stomach shriveled and sank at her next words: "Listen, I'm sorry, but I can't go out with you."

Shit. I should have known it wouldn't be that easy. "Oh, I gotcha." I tried to cover my disappointment, but I was sure she could hear it anyway. "Everything okay? I mean—"

"I just—I may have said yes too quickly, Jason. I'm sorry. I don't think…I don't think it'd work."

"So this isn't a rain check, is it." I couldn't disguise my hurt at this point.

"No. I'm so sorry."

"It's fine, I guess." I laughed, realizing how stupid that sounded, especially since she could obviously tell I was upset. "Shit, no. It's not. This is kinda shady, Nell. I was all excited." I had to get it together. I clenched my fist around the steering wheel and squeezed my eyes shut.

"I'm so, *so* sorry, Jason. I just realized, after really thinking about things…I mean, I'm flattered, and I was excited that you asked me, but—"

I interrupted her. "This is about Kyle, isn't it? You're with him, on his phone, so of *course* this about him." I should have known. I really should have. Everyone always thought they were together anyway.

"Jason, that's not—I mean, yeah, I'm with him right now, but—"

"It's fine. I get it. I think we all knew this was coming, so I shouldn't be surprised. I just wish you'd told me sooner." I sounded like a dick, but I just couldn't help it.

"I'm sorry, Jason. I don't know what else to say."

"Nothing to say. It's all good. I'll just…whatever. See you in chemistry on Monday."

I was about to hang up when her voice stopped me. "Jason, wait."

"What."

"I probably shouldn't tell you this, but…Becca has had a crush on you since seventh grade. I guarantee she'll go out with you."

"Becca?" Shock laced my words. "Wouldn't that be weird? I mean, what would I say? She'd think she was my second choice or something. I mean, I guess that's true, but not like *that*, you know?"

Nell answered after a short pause. "Just tell her the truth. I backed out on you, last minute. You already have reservations, and I thought she might like to go with you instead of me."

"Think it'll work? Really?" Becca? She was cool, but she wasn't Nell. Out loud, I said, "She is pretty hot."

"It'll work. Just call her." She rattled off Becca's number, and I repeated it back to her, scribbling it on a receipt from a gas station.

"Thanks...I think. But, Nell? Next time you're gonna break a guy's heart, give him a bit more notice, would you?" I tried to inject some playfulness into my voice.

"Don't be ridiculous, Jason. I didn't break your heart. We hadn't even gone out yet. But I *am* sorry for standing you up like this."

"No worries. Besides, maybe something will work out with Becca and me. She's almost as hot as you. Wait, shit, that didn't come out right. Don't tell Becca I said that. You guys are equally hot, I was just—" God, I sounded like a moron. Someone stop me.

Nell laughed, cutting me off. "Jason? Shut up. Call Becca."

The line went dead, and I stared at the rectangular bit of receipt paper with ten digits scrawled messily across the back. Becca? I wasn't sure if asking her out was a good idea. I didn't know much about her, now that I thought about it. I had the feeling she came from a pretty strict household, but I was just judging by the fact that she always dressed super-modestly, never showing much skin beyond short-sleeve shirts and knee-length skirts. Nothing low-cut, nothing up past her kneecap. She never hung around guys, never acted flirty, never showed up to parties. She was quiet, studious, kind and polite when spoken to, and people tended to leave her alone or be nice to her simply because she was Nell Hawthorne's friend.

She'd had a crush on me? Really? How had I never noticed that?

I sat in the driveway for another few minutes, thinking. I nearly peed myself when someone knocked on my window. I rolled it down. Mrs. Hawthorne's gentle, pretty face was scrunched up in confusion.

"Jason? Is everything okay? Nell isn't here. She went out running with Kyle." Mrs. Hawthorne was the kind of woman you wanted to be *your* mother. Slender, with fine blonde hair and pale skin, she was the epitome of wonderful, always smiling, showing up to football games to cheer us all on, and she usually had baked goods. She knew almost everyone in town by name, and she liked to hug people. She usually smelled like cookies and faint perfume.

My own mother was barely a person, hiding out in her room and watching soap operas and reality TV, staying away from the battleground that was the living room. Dad knocked her around sometimes, but as soon as I was old enough to take it, he turned his fists on me and left her alone except for the twice-weekly thumping of the headboard against the adjoining wall between my bedroom and theirs.

"Oh, yeah," I said. "Everything's cool. I thought we were hanging out, me and her and Kyle, but I got the times wrong."

Mrs. Hawthorne frowned at me. "Now, it's not nice to lie, Jason Dorsey."

I grinned at her. "Me? What would I have to lie about?"

She frowned ever more at that. "I've known you since you were in diapers, Jason. I know when you're lying." The corners of her lips turned up in a smirk that reminded me a lot of Nell. "I also know Nell and Kyle had some kind of argument, and I suspect I know what it was about."

"They argued?" This was news to me. "I just talked to Nell on Kyle's phone. They didn't sound mad at each other, I can tell you that much." I think I might have sounded slightly bitter.

She glanced at the ground, almost awkward, if such a graceful creature as Mrs. Hawthorne was capable of awkwardness. "I think they made up." She met my eyes. "You've always liked Nell, Jason. I know that, but she doesn't."

I blew out a breath of frustration. It seemed like Frankie really *had* been right when he said everyone knew I liked Nell but Nell. "Well, it doesn't matter anymore. I have a feeling she's with Kyle now."

Mrs. Hawthorne nodded. "Yeah, that's my thinking. It wouldn't surprise me. I'm sorry, Jason. I know that must hurt."

I shrugged. "It's fine. It always did seem kind of inevitable that those two would end up together, though, you know?"

Mrs. Hawthorne nodded again. "Yeah, I've always thought so." She turned a sharp gaze on me. "What are you going to do now?"

I fiddled with the gearshift knob, tracing the white lines and numbers. "I dunno. Nell said I should ask Becca out, but I don't know about that. I don't want Becca to think I was just doing it because I had no one better to ask, you know?"

"Hmmm. That's not a bad idea, actually. I think if you told Becca the truth, she'd respect that. It might be

awkward at first, but she's a very understanding girl.
She'd understand where you were coming from. Make
it casual, though. Just go and talk to her."

"Are you sure?" I asked.

"I'm sure. It's worth a try, isn't it?" She touched my
hand. "Jason? You know if you ever need anything, you
can come here, right?" There was an edge to her voice,
something deep and sharp. As if she knew something
no one but Kyle would know.

I just stared at her, unsure how to respond.
"Thanks, Mrs. Hawthorne. You rock."

She smiled at me, and I was sure there was a hint
of sadness in her eyes. As if she suspected. But it wasn't
like she could do anything, even if she did know, even
if I did tell her what happened in the Dorsey living
room.

I knew Becca lived in one of the newer subdivi-
sions a few miles away, so I headed in that direction
after leaving Nell's house. I stopped near the entrance
to the subdivision and dialed the number that Nell had
given me.

Two: Second Choice a First Date
Becca de Rosa
September, sophomore year of high school

I SWORE UNDER MY BREATH as I tried to hurry through the last ten questions of my calculus homework. I hated calculus. It was tedious and difficult, but I had to be in all advanced classes to please Father. Or, rather, to maintain his approval, since pleasing him was all but impossible. The loud bass thumping of my brother Ben's stupid rap music made it even more difficult to concentrate, especially since he'd turned it up louder after I'd asked him to turn it down. I loved my brother, but he was so very difficult, especially when he was in one of these moods, the depressed, angry times.

I *had* to finish this calculus, because if I didn't, I knew I would never do it, and that meant I couldn't leave the house. My parents were hideously exacting when it came to my academics. They demanded a weekly progress report, including all upcoming tests and exams, completed homework assignments and those due, and any possible extra credit. I was allowed three hours of personal "free" time every day, but only after all homework was completed. Which, seeing as I was in all AP courses, meant that I often did not get even as much as a single hour to myself. I usually labored over homework until nine or ten every night, and after ten I was not allowed to leave the house. I spent much of my time in my room, away from my constantly bickering parents. When I was not doing homework, I would write, read, or watch a television show on my laptop. I had precisely zero social life outside of school.

I had never been on date, nor would I ever, I often despaired. My life would be consumed by studies, words, numbers, tests, and exams. Even as I hurried through the last problem and then opened my notes on required terminology, I found my mind wandering. Calculus terms became something else, became what most things became in my mind:

Poetry.

I watched my mechanical pencil scribble across the page of my journal, which was always open near me, no matter where I was. I did not try to understand the things pouring onto the page. When my pencil stopped moving, I read what I'd written:

THE CALCULUS OF BOREDOM
The average rate of change
Seems to define my axis of rotation.
The area of an ellipse
Definitely defines the constant term
Of my life.
My daily pattern of being
Is the end behavior of my
Bounded function.
Degenerate, derivative, differential,
Essential discontinuity,
Explicit differentiation,
Explicit function:
Exponential Decay.
I have no me,
I have only
The conditional convergence
Of their constant term
Of continuous function
Of disapproval.
Each decision seems to be
Part of a chain rule,
An annulus,

Or,

The region between two concentric circles which have
different radii; or,

In other words…

My

Fucking

Parents.

I sighed, feeling a whisper of pleasure at the words. They expressed a part of me. I had four notebooks filled with poetry from the last few years, and the current one was two-thirds filled already. Poetry was my only pleasure in life, the only thing that allowed me any personality, any expression. Everything else was school and speech therapy and piano lessons. I liked the piano, and I knew I was good at it, but it wasn't for me. It was expected of me, demanded of me.

I shook myself out of my reverie and returned to memorizing the terms for the current lesson, as well as the ones for next week. If I got next week's homework at least started, if not finished, I might even manage some kind of free time. I finished the calc terms and moved on to economics, which was easy enough that I could put on headphones and listen to music. The first song to come up on my Pandora playlist was "Demons" by Imagine Dragons, and god, it was so apropos. So perfect.

I finished econ and was halfway through my reading assignment for my eighteenth-century Lit class—which actually counted for college credit—when my phone rang. My cell phone was the one concession my parents made toward me having some kind of social life. I was allowed to have a cell phone and an unlimited text and data plan, so I could text as much as I want. The only catch was, my parents would, without warning, take my phone and read through my text messages to make sure there was nothing untoward occurring in my life—where untoward equals fun or exciting or in any way interesting.

Even my private thoughts sounded like calculus equations.

The only thing that I kept private from my parents was my poetry, and I hid those notebooks in a shoebox buried in the depths of my closet. The notebook currently in use was never out of my sight, either in my purse or my backpack, disguised between textbooks and notebooks filled with school notes. I would rather burn my notebooks than let anyone read them; they expressed my every thought, my every emotion, all my deepest, darkest demons. To read my notebooks would be to read the very substance of my soul.

I answered my phone without looking at it, since only Jill and Nell had my number. "Hello?"

"Uh...hey. Becca, it's Jason...uh...Jason Dorsey."

Jason Dorsey was the very last person on the planet I'd ever expect to call me at seven-thirty on a Friday night, especially when I knew for a fact he had a date with Nell tonight.

"Jason? How did you get my number, and why are you calling me?" I couldn't help sounding a little bitchy; I'd been in love with Jason Dorsey since we were in fourth grade and he punched Danny Morelli in the nose for making fun of my stutter. I'd been in love with Jason Dorsey since forever, but he didn't even know I existed, except as Nell's awkward friend.

I might have been a little angry at Jason, just in general.

"Well, I...you see..." He sounded unlike himself, meaning he sounded hesitant and not at all his cocky, arrogant self. "Um, god, I'm making a mess of this."

"I do not even know what it is you are making a mess of, Jason. Just say what you called me to say." I was nervous and trying not to be a bitch, so I sounded formal and stilted from my effort to not stutter.

"Okay, it's like this. You know how I asked Nell out today?"

"Yes."

"Well, the thing is, the date never happened."

"So I surmised from the fact that you are speaking to me instead of Nell." I just couldn't figure out what he wanted. Why was he calling me?

"Well, she's with Kyle. I think they're, like, together."

I couldn't have been more shocked if I tried. "But she agreed to a date with you. I don't understand."

"Yeah, me, either. I showed up at her house to pick her up, and she wasn't there. She called me from Kyle's phone and cancelled the date."

"You mean she wanted to do it another time." Why would Nell agree to a date with Jason if she was with Kyle? And since when was she with Kyle? Nothing made sense. And I still didn't know why Jason was calling me about this, of all people. We were hardly friends.

"No," Jason said, sounding obviously frustrated. "I mean, she told me it wouldn't work out, meaning ever."

"I'm sorry to hear that. I know you liked her a lot." I didn't know what else to say. All through elementary school, junior high, and high school, I'd wanted Jason to see me, to pay attention to me, but all he could see was Nell.

"God, does *everyone* know? I didn't realize it was that obvious." He sounded irritated.

I couldn't help laughing. "It is kind of obvious, Jason, yes. You've had a crush on her for a very long time. Anyone who knows you and her both can see it."

"Except her."

"Yes, except her," I agreed. "Again, what does this have to do with me?"

A long silence from the other end of the conversation announced to me that Jason was clearly uncomfortable or nervous about whatever he'd called me to say.

"I—well, I have reservations at Bravo," he said, "and I was wondering if you wanted to go with me."

The penny dropped, finally. "Y-you what? Oh, hell n-no, Jason! You did not just-just ask me out as Nell's sloppy se-seconds! Ugh!" I groaned in anger, at Jason for both insulting me like he just had, and for making me so angry I had reverted to incoherent stuttering.

"No, Becca, it's not like that, I promise!"

I took several deep breaths and focused on forming my words clearly. "Please explain your reasoning to me, Jason. I am afraid I do not see how you arrived at your conclusion that this was a good idea."

Jason moaned, a distant, muffled sound as if he'd buried his face in his hand with the phone held away from his face. "Listen, Becca. This wasn't even my idea. None of it."

"Well, that absolutely helps me feel better about this. Do continue."

Jason laughed. "God, Becca. You're funny when you're pissed."

"I'm funny all the time. You just never knew until now."

He laughed again, which wasn't helping my attempts to stay mad. "See? Funny. Maybe you're right. Maybe you are funny all the time, and I just never knew. Give me a chance to find out."

"Why? Do you even understand how insulting this is?" I spoke in a mocking deep voice. "'Oh, hi, I got dumped and you're my consolation prize.' Wow, Jason. I'd be so *honored*. Or not."

"I thought you were going to give me a chance to explain?" Jason asked.

"Okay, fine. Go."

"I'm in your subdivision already, so how about you tell me which house is yours, and I'll pick you up. I'll explain the whole sordid affair over dinner."

"Wow, you used a big word, Jason. Good job."

He sounded a little hurt, actually, and I felt a twinge of guilt. "Damn, Becca. That wasn't cool. Not all jocks are dumb, you know." He paused and then continued. "Besides, sordid isn't that big of a word. Anyway, come on. I know how this seems, but it's not like you're thinking, really. Give me a shot. Please?"

I laughed despite myself. "Fine. Give me a few minutes to check with my parents. And stay where you are."

He sounded confused but agreed. "Sure, okay. See you in a minute. I'm sitting in the entrance to the Harris Lake Estates."

"I'm not sure I want to know how you know where I live."

He chuckled. "I gave Jill a ride home after school one day, and she mentioned that you live in the same neighborhood. Nothing...*disreputable* going on."

I laughed again. "I'm hanging up."

"Fine. I was done talking to you anyway." He laughed and hung up before I could.

Now came the tricky part: lying to my parents. They'd never in a million years let me go to dinner with a boy, any boy, much less one neither they nor I knew. Jason and I had grown up together, gone to the same schools, been in a lot of the same classes together, but I didn't really *know* him.

I stuffed my journal in my purse along with my cell phone and skipped down the stairs. My parents were sitting at the dining room table, arguing in a complicated mixture of English, Arabic, and Italian. "I'm going out with Nell."

My father looked up, a lifted eyebrow stopping me in my tracks. "You have finished all of your homework?"

I nodded. "Yes, Father."

He dipped his chin in a shallow, regal nod. "Very well. Check in at ten."

"I will. *Grazie.*"

I slipped out the front door, checking my purse for my keys before I left. If I dared come home past curfew, he'd lock the doors whether I had a key or not. I had my driver's license, but Father wouldn't allow me a car until my junior year, provided I kept a 4.0 GPA through the rest of this year, at which point he would buy me a car. I'd honestly rather buy my own, but that wasn't allowed, either. I couldn't get a job, because it would distract me from my studies.

I hated being dependent on my parents, but I had no choice.

Nell and I often met at the intersection, since if there were boys in the car and they picked me up from my house, my father would have an aneurism. Even if it was harmless, just friends all hanging out, he would lose his mind. I'd gotten good at deceiving him when it came to hanging out with Nell and Jill—which meant Kyle and Jill's boyfriend Nick—and often Jason as well. We'd go to the mall and hang out, and when it came time to check in, I would make sure it seemed like I was alone with Nell and Jill. This date with Jason would be trickier, though.

I decided I'd handle the check-in call later. For now, I had to get my nerves under control. I only lived half a block from the entrance to my subdivision, so it wasn't a long walk, but I saw Jason's truck sitting at the side of the road, and Jason's spiky blond hair and tanned skin, and the walk suddenly seemed endless. Every step echoed in my ears, hammering like thunder. Each step seemed to make every bit of me shiver and jiggle, and I wondered if he would think I was overweight. I knew I wasn't, logically. I was short and well-endowed, but I was in shape and ate well. I knew it, and most of the time I was fine with how I looked. But every once in a while, usually around Jason, I'd feel self-conscious about my shape. I knew he was attracted to Nell, which made me wonder if he'd ever even see me, since I looked nothing like Nell. I was shorter than she was, heavier than she was. I had dark skin and dark hair. Nell was tall and slender and had pale skin and perfect blonde hair. Nell was energetic and talkative and popular and confident, and I was... not. I was quiet, and shy, and I stuttered.

God, I knew I was going to stutter around Jason. I just knew it. He'd make me nervous or excited, and I'd forget myself and start stuttering. I was already nervous, and I wasn't even within ten feet of Jason. I took several deep breaths and tried to call up my ire at his nerve. He still owed me a hell of an explanation, but I knew I'd let it go after a while. I'd give him shit about it, but I'd forgive him. Eventually.

I approached his black pickup truck and smoothed the front of my gray cotton skirt. Jason jumped out of his truck and circled around to open my door for me; points to Jason for manners. He didn't speak until he'd swung the truck around the short boulevard at the entrance and out onto the main road.

"So," I said. "Explain."

Jason just grinned at me and turned on the radio, tuning it to a country station. I grimaced and changed it, but Jason frowned at me, tuning it back. "I like that song."

I glared at him. "I hate country music."

"Have you ever really listened to it?" he asked.

I sighed and shook my head. "No, not really," I admitted.

He turned the volume up so the music filled the car as a new song came on. "Listen to this song. It's one of my favorites. It tells such an amazing story."

I closed my eyes and focused on the words... *Eighty-nine cents in the ashtray, half-empty bottle of Gatorade*...I was hooked immediately by the simple, vivid imagery. I lost myself in the song. Every line, every verse, and every repetition of the chorus was sung with wrenching emotion. *I drive your truck…*god. It hit so hard. I didn't know why, because I'd never lost anyone the way the singer had, but I felt the song so poignantly.

When it ended, Jason clicked the stereo off. "So? What'd you think?"

"Who was that singing?" I asked.

"Lee Brice. The song is called 'I Drive Your Truck,' if you couldn't tell from the chorus." He grinned at me. "So was I right?"

I nodded. "Yes. You were right. That is a very touching song. It wasn't so twangy like I thought it'd be."

He laughed. "You're thinking of the older style of country. The stuff coming out these days isn't all like that, it's more like country-influenced rock, I guess you could call it. I like country music because it's…I don't know. It's about stuff. Most of the songs tell a story, or deal with something you can grab on to, you know? Something you can understand. I mean that song, obviously it's about a guy who lost a close friend or a brother or his dad or something. It's right there in the lyrics."

"The lyrics were very poetic." I smiled at him. "Play something else for me."

He grinned and turned the radio back on. He listened for a few beats and then nodded. "This is another good one." Glancing at me, Jason pointed in my direction as if dedicating a performance to me. "This one's for you, Becca."

I couldn't help laughing. "You're weird."

He cranked it up and shouted over the guitars. "I'm dedicating it to you! Listen up!"

He rolled the windows down and stuck his hand out, bobbing his head with the music and slapping the side of the truck with his palm in time with the beat. It had the same feel, the music in the background to the singer's voice. It was more pop-influenced, I thought, and the singer had less of a country accent, but it was still definitely a country song. Then I started paying attention to the lyrics, in which the singer told the subject of the song, a woman, that she didn't have to do all sorts of sweet and sexy things, but it sure would be cool if she did. It was a cleverly written song, romantic and heartfelt.

When the song ended, Jason turned the volume down a bit as another song came on. "Like that one? That was 'Sure Be Cool If You Did' by Blake Shelton."

"Isn't that the guy on that TV show? *X-factor* or *The Voice* or something?"

"Yeah. He's on *The Voice*."

I glared at him. "Why would you dedicate that song to me, anyway?"

He blushed and looked away, glancing at me sideways as he drove. "I don't know. I just did. It seemed… fitting, I guess. For you and me, out on a date?"

I sighed. "You still haven't explained anything to me."

He rolled his eyes and rubbed the side of his face. "I know, I know. I just…you're out with me now, and I'm having fun. Why ruin it with serious talk?"

I gave him a *really?* kind of look. "Because the only reason I agreed to come out with you is because you promised to explain."

"Fine." He turned the radio down. "It's like this. Apparently every single person in the whole damn town knows I had a crush on Nell." I noticed his use of the past tense, but I didn't interrupt. "Well, at practice yesterday the guys were making fun of me about it."

"That's not very nice. Aren't they supposed to be your teammates?"

He stared at me as if I'd said something he didn't understand. "They are my teammates. It's a guy thing, I guess. We give each other shit. It's just…it's just what you do." He held up his hand when I opened my mouth to ask a question. "I thought you wanted me to explain? Then shut up for a second. They were giving me shit about having had a crush on Nell for my whole life but never doing anything about it. So, yeah.

Frankie and Malcolm each bet me a hundred dollars that I wouldn't ask Nell out the next day. Well, you can't turn down a bet like that, so I asked her out. I mean, I wanted to anyway, but this way I got money in the process."

"So would you have asked her out had your friends not made that bet with you?"

Jason didn't answer right away. "Probably not."

"Why not?"

He sighed. "It's scary, you know? I mean, asking someone out is scary enough as it is, but...when you've liked the person from a distance for so long, and they never even knew? It's terrifying."

"Are you admitting to being afraid?" I asked, teasing him.

He glared at me. "Damn straight I am. But I did it anyway. That's what courage is, you know: being afraid and doing what you have to do anyway. That's what Dad told me, anyway, and it strikes me as true." His faced darkened when he mentioned his father, and his fist tightened on the steering wheel. "But shit yeah, I was afraid when I asked her out. I was shaking."

I laughed. "You sure could have fooled me. You looked like you were as cocky as ever."

He looked at me with interest. "Cocky? Do I come across as cocky?"

I nodded. "Yeah. You act like you own the world. Like you're not afraid of anyone or anything." I picked at the chipping robin's-egg-blue fingernail polish on my thumb. "I don't know how you can do that. Act like that."

He shook his head. "I don't mean to come off as cocky. I don't feel that way most of the time, to tell you the truth."

I glanced at him. "So it's an act?"

He shrugged. "Some of it, yeah. A lot of it, actually. I'm just like anyone else. I've got things I'm afraid of, secrets, insecurities, whatever. Everyone's got that stuff. Maybe I just hide it better."

I didn't answer right away. The idea of Jason Dorsey being insecure or afraid seemed almost comically absurd to me. He never hesitated, never questioned himself. He was always self-assured and in control and confident. He knew who he was and what he was good at, and he knew people liked him. Not like me, in other words.

"Maybe you do," I said. "Now, back to the subject at hand. How did you end up asking me out?"

Jason shifted in his seat. "So I showed up at Nell's door for the date, and I got a phone call. I answered, thinking it was Kyle since it was his number on the I.D. It turned out to be Nell, backing out of the date.

Apparently she and Kyle had some kind of argument that led to them realizing they belonged together or some melodramatic horseshit like that. I don't know. All I know is, I was kind of upset, you know?" He looked at me, then away, as if about to say something that embarrassed him. "So then Nell tells me I should ask you to go out with me in her place. Now, for the record, I told her you'd react exactly the way you did. She was all like, 'oh, just tell her what happened and it'll be fine.' So, it's not like I got dumped by Nell and thought, 'Oh, what about Becca, she's almost as good as Nell.'"

I sucked in a sharp breath. That's exactly how it felt to me. "No? Then what did you think?"

He didn't answer for a long time. After almost five minutes of uncomfortable silence, he parked the truck in a slot in front of Bravo. He slid out and opened my door for me, and then the front door of the restaurant. My heart stopped when his hand settled on the small of my back, guiding me in through the inner foyer door. Neither of us spoke until we were seated at a round four-person table, a basket of bread and a dish of olive oil in front of us.

After we'd ordered, I leveled a serious look at Jason. "You never answered me. What were you thinking?"

Jason wouldn't look at me. "I don't know. A lot of things. I was thinking I was hurt, for one thing. I mean,

I've liked Nell since we were kids. She never knew, and she never will, now. She and Kyle are, like, perfect together, you know? And she just stood me up without a second thought. It hurt. Then she told me to ask you instead, and it opened up a new line of thought. At first, it was kind of like just 'why not?' And yeah, I know how that sounds, and I'm sorry. You wanted the truth, so there it is." He dipped bread into the olive oil and popped it in his mouth, chewing and swallowing before continuing; I was mesmerized by the way his jaw moved, by the strong lines as he chewed, the sure movement of his hands, the constant roaming of his eyes, flicking from the table to the door and then settling on me. "But the more I thought about it, the more I realized something. I realized I was holding on to the idea of having a crush on Nell. And really, a crush? What does that even mean? She's never noticed me because she's always been into Kyle. They're just... so wrapped up in each other. They might not have put a romantic spin on it till now, but they've always been together. So I think I was just in love with the idea of having her notice me because she never did and never would."

"And now?" I sipped my Coke and waited for his answer. If I didn't like it, I was ready to bolt and walk home. This whole situation was skirting the edges of my ability to handle it.

It almost seemed like he was actually seeing me for *me*, and that was dangerous for my sanity. I almost didn't want him to want me, because that would mean doing something about it.

"And now?" Jason swirled the ice in his glass with his straw. "Now I'm seeing things a bit differently. I thought about you, and I guess I realized I didn't really know you. We've moved in the same circles our whole lives, you know? And I mean, you're one of Nell's best friends, but with Nell, pretty much anyone is going to come second after Kyle. Anyway, I realized I don't know you, and I'd kind of like to. I mean, I know you're really smart, like, smarter than pretty much everyone I know. And I know you're really beautiful. But I don't know much else. I think your parents are immigrants, but I'm not sure. I know you stutter sometimes. But really, that's it."

He thought I was beautiful? I had to focus on breathing to keep calm.

I laughed. "I'm not sure the term 'immigrant' is politically correct, Jason." I was proud of myself for getting that out sounding casual, and without stuttering. I was still reeling from his throwaway comment about me being beautiful.

He shrugged. "You know what I mean. They moved here from another country." He waved with a piece of bread. "Immigrants. Not a bad or good thing, just a thing."

"My father is from Italy. He's from a port city called Brindisi, which is in the region of Puglia—"

"Is that by Rome?" Jason asked.

I laughed. "No, it isn't. It's on the opposite side of the country, and farther south. He moved here when he was thirty, and he met my mother as he was leaving LaGuardia Airport."

"Where's your mom from? Italy?"

Our server dropped off our plates at that moment, and I dug in with pleasure before answering. "No, my mother is from Beirut, Lebanon. She moved here at the same time as my father, but she was much younger, only twenty-three. They fell in love, and got married within a year. They ended up moving here just after I was born. My older brother Benjamin was born in New York and lived there for three years."

Jason had stopped eating to stare at me. "You're Arabic?"

"Half." I set my fork down. "Why do you seem so surprised?"

He shrugged. "I dunno. I guess I just didn't realize it. Do you speak your parents' languages?"

It was my turn to shrug, turning my face away. "Yeah. It's complicated, but we all speak all three languages. My mom speaks Italian as well as Arabic and English, and my dad speaks Italian plus the others. Ben and I both speak all three. My parents insist we know their languages, plus we take vacations every year to Lebanon and Italy to see family."

He gaped at me. "Wait. You speak *three* fucking languages?" He said it so loud the people around us looked at us.

"Do you have to shout?" I demanded, my voice quiet but intense.

"Sorry," Jason mumbled.

"And yes, for the record, I do speak three fucking languages." Jason's eyes bugged out at my curse word, which apparently surprised him. "And yes, I can drop the F-bomb in all three. Can, and do. Just because I'm quiet and have a stutter doesn't mean I don't like to swear."

Jason frowned at me. "That's not why I'm surprised. You just seem...good. Like, not the kind of person to drop F-bombs at all. Not that you *couldn't*, but that you *wouldn't*. I'm actually kind of insulted that you'd think I'd think that about you."

I felt myself blush with embarrassment. "I'm sorry. That was a rude assumption. It's just how most people think. They never hear me talk, or when they do, it's when I'm upset and stuttering. So then they assume I'm stupid or something, despite the fact that I've got a 4.0 GPA, speak three languages, and have college credit already."

Jason stared at me again. "College credit? How?"

I waved my hand. "AP courses. Instead of skipping grades, my parents have me staying with my peers in the same grade, but they've worked out a plan with the school board. I'm in all kinds of advanced classes. I'm in a senior-level lit class right now, and that also counts as college credit. I'm also doing a co-op at the local community college. I go there every Tuesday morning instead of the high school and attend a class there. It's complicated and boring to talk about. It just means a shit-ton of homework."

"That's impressive, Becca." He sounded genuinely impressed.

I tried to wave it off, uncomfortable with his attention. "It's not. My parents believe in using what you're given. I'm apparently very smart, so I have to push myself as hard as possible. The best isn't good enough. If I succeed at being the best, I have to go up to the next level."

Jason's face darkened. "I know how that is, be*lieve* me."

"Your parents push you in school, too?" I asked. He never really seemed like the studious type. Not that he was stupid, just not an academic type of guy.

He laughed. "Well, don't sound so surprised. But no, not like yours do you. My dad expects perfection from me in everything. I mean, *every*thing. I have a 4.0, too, but I'm in normal classes, so it's not as impressive as you. It's just part of the deal. What I meant was, it's like that with me and football. It's not good enough that I make the varsity team my freshman year, which is really unusual, by the way. I have to break school records for most receptions and most touchdowns. And that's not good enough, either. No, I have to break district records. So I do all that, and I'm only a sophomore. Now he's after the state record. 'Go bigger, Jason.'" His voice went deep and his eyes glazed over as he seemed to channel his father. "'Stop settling for second best, you piece of shit. Play harder. Break the state record, Jason.'"

I felt something clench inside me at the obvious torment on his face. "He says that to you? Your own father?"

"My father." He seemed to find the term "father" funny somehow, but it didn't lessen the darkness in his eyes. "Yeah. He says that shit all the time. Whatever. He's a dick, but he's the reason I'm gonna set the national high school record for most career receptions."

"You are?"

He laughed outright. "Yeah. The record was set by Davis Howell between 2009 and 2012, with 358.

That's according to the National Federation of State High School Association Sports Record Book, which my dad checks nearly every day. I'm not even halfway through my second season, and I've already made over 150 receptions. I need to average at least six receptions per game to break the record, and I do that easily. I'm only a sophomore, so I've still got the rest of this year and all of junior and senior years. But that's just that particular stat record. Dad has his sights set on receiving yards, too. Which, by the way, is set by Dorial Green-Beckham from Springfield Missouri, at 6,356. To break that, I have to average at least 115 receiving yards per game. Which is absurd. Those are pro stats, Becca. These kids setting these records, they go on to be first-round NFL draft picks. They're future Heisman winners. I'm...well, I'm good. I can do it. I have to." I could hear him actually psyching himself up as he said it, convincing himself.

I didn't know the difference between receptions and receiving yards or what a draft pick was, but I could see the panic in his eyes, and I could recognize the hardened determination of someone who's been given a goal and no option but to achieve it; I saw it in him because I saw it in myself every day. "What happens if you don't?" I asked.

His face shut down, went hard and cold. "That's... not an option."

"I don't like how that sounds, Jason. What do you mean, it's not an option? You *have* to break the national record, or what?" He didn't answer, just picked at his chicken parmesan. "Jason? Or what?" I leaned forward, tried to get him to meet my eyes.

He looked up suddenly, and the hate in his eyes had me scooting back in fear. "Or *nothing*, Becca. I will. Because I *have* to, okay? That's it." He looked away, and I wasn't sure what to say, what to think. "I'm sorry. I— that was—I'm sorry. I'll be right back." He shot to his feet and retreated to the bathroom, leaving me with a half-eaten plate of pesto and no appetite.

He wasn't just driven, he was being pushed so hard it was consuming him. I would never have guessed. I watched him play every game, since Nell and Jill dragged me to games all the time. Kyle was the quarterback, and the star of the team, flashy and beautiful and godlike in his near-perfection, and Jill's boyfriend Nick Nagle was on the team, too, but he was one of the guys in the front line who wrestle with the other team's front line. I watched Jason play all the time, and he always seemed to have fun, like being on the field was his element, as if there was nowhere he'd rather be. I was seeing a different reality now, it seemed.

Jason came back and seemed to be in control once again. He sat down and touched the back of my hand with his, sending lightning shooting through me. "I'm sorry I blew up, Becca. It's no big deal, really. Yeah, my dad pushes me hard, but it's for the best. It makes me better. Don't worry about it, okay?"

I recognized a blow-off when I got one. "Okay, well, that's bullshit, but I'll let it slide."

He grinned, and confident, cocky Jason was back. "So. Enough about me and football. Tell me something about you."

"Like what?" I asked, nervous.

"Like, I don't know. Something no one else knows."

I searched for something unimportant to tell him. "I'm double-jointed in my hands?" I bent the fingers of one of my hands back with the palm of the other so the tips of my fingers touched the back of my forearm. Jason winced, and then again when I bent my thumb back double. "It helps with piano, since I have nimble fingers."

"You play the piano, too?" he asked.

"Yeah, since I was four. I have to practice at least two hours every day."

"Plus all AP classes and courses at a community college."

"And don't forget speech therapy."

"What?" He paused with his fork halfway to his mouth.

"My speech impediment? The stuttering? I didn't just wake up one day and decide not to stutter anymore. I go to speech therapy twice a month. I have to work at it, all the time."

He tilted his head to the side. "Work at it how?"

I shook my head. "You don't want to hear about this."

He smiled, and this wasn't a flashy, cocky grin, but a slow, sweet smile that melted something inside me. I'd been working the whole dinner to keep my pattering heart under control, to just enjoy the time I was getting to spend with Jason and not expect anything, but this smile…it made me feel like he liked me. Like this could be something.

"I do too want to hear about this," he said, taking my hand in his and rubbing the back of my thumb with his.

It was an intimate gesture that had my every pore tingling, my scalp tightening, my heart hammering. I pulled my hand away and twirled a curl of hair around my index finger.

I composed my thoughts and tried to answer him in a way that would make sense. "Well, there's a lot to know, honestly. I've had my whole life to figure all this out. Some kids have stutters when they are young, but they grow out of it. For them, it is just a difficulty in the process of learning correct speech. For others, like me, it is a lifelong battle, something I will never completely be free of."

Jason was focused and interested, toying with his straw as he watched me. "So do they know what causes stutters?"

"*They*, which will someday be me, don't know exactly, other than that it is a combination of elements. It is thought to be both genetic as well as environmental, and there is evidence showing a difference in brain structure as well. It isn't an indication of intelligence, nor is it the same as childhood apraxia of speech, which is a different kind of developmental disorder."

Jason sat back in his chair, seeming stunned. "You really know a lot about this. You sound like...I don't know. Like a doctor or something."

I smiled shyly. "Well, since I suffer from stuttering, I decided a long time ago that I should know about what it is I'm dealing with. I plan to major in speech therapy in college and eventually pursue it into post-graduate studies to become a researcher. I want to help find new ways to help children with stutters overcome it, if finding a cure isn't possible."

"So you really are going to become a doctor."

I nodded. "Yes, definitely. I've known since I was eleven that I wanted to be like Mrs. Larson, my speech therapist. She's helped me more than I can ever express. Not just in fluency techniques, but in learning to be confident and to like myself despite my stutter." I paused, not sure I should share the next part of my speech, but something about Jason drew me to him, made me trust him. "Mrs. Larson was the one to suggest I write to express my feelings."

"What do you write?" Jason asked.

I shrugged, spinning a tight curl between my fingers. "Just stuff. What I'm thinking, what I'm feeling. The things I can't necessarily say, or wouldn't say."

"So is it like a book? Or poetry?"

I squirmed. Nell knew I had poetry journals, but even she had never seen them. I barely knew Jason, and this was getting intensely personal and very difficult. His bright green eyes like pools of sunlit jade pierced me, drawing my secrets from me, drawing words from me that I hadn't intended to speak.

"Poetry," I said in a barely audible voice. "But not like rhyming, Shakespearean sonnets about flowers and things. It's different. Free-verse, I guess you'd call it. Just words on a page that come from inside me." This was more than I'd even told Nell about why I write. My heart hammered, and I felt nauseous.

He just smiled at me. "I think that's cool. I wish I could do that. Write poetry or whatever. Words aren't something I'm good with, especially writing. I get the thoughts sorted in my head, but then they just don't end up on the paper like I'd thought them." He tossed his napkin on his plate and pushed it away, but his eyes never left mine. "Could I read something you wrote sometime?"

I shifted in my seat. "I don't know. It's kind of like a diary for me, you know? It's…really personal. It's not that I don't trust you, Jason. It's…" I felt my nerves rising, threatening to erase my fluency. "It-it's…no one has ever read it before. Not even Nell. Ssss-so I don't know. Not yet. I'mmmmm—I'm sorry." My entire face was hot with embarrassment, my eyes shut and my head ducked down.

I felt a hesitant finger push away a tendril of hair and then I felt my face rising, gently lifted by Jason's hand. "Hey, it's fine. No big deal. If it's private, it's private." I heard the smile in his voice, how much he wanted me to understand that it really was okay. "For real, Becca, don't worry about it. I didn't realize it was a diary, or I wouldn't have asked."

I could only shrug and focus on breathing. Once I had myself calm enough to speak without embarrassing myself, I forced my eyes to his. The understanding and compassion in his green eyes was so palpable I could feel it radiating off him and into me.

"Thanks for getting it," I said.

He just waved his hand. "Nah, I shouldn't have asked." He looked around and flagged the waiter down. "You want some tiramisu or cheesecake or something?"

"I'd love some cheesecake," I said with a grin. Cheesecake was my weakness. I just couldn't say no, even if it meant an extra twenty minutes on the elliptical in my basement.

Jason smiled happily. "Will I sound like a tool if I say I'm glad you're not the kind of chick who eats like a bird? The fact that you like to eat and seem to enjoy your food makes me happy. I'm a foodie, and dessert has always been my favorite part."

"A foodie?" I asked. I'd never heard the term before.

He shrugged. "I love food. I love to eat. I work out so much that I need a lot of calories. My dad will eat pretty much anything put in front of him, and my mom could burn water, so I do most of the cooking at home." His eyes hardened at the mention of his father, and I realized that was probably the reaction he'd have every time.

"What's your favorite thing to make?"

He thought about it for a moment. "That's a good question. I make a lot of pasta, because it's good for carb-loading, but I can put different kinds of meat in it for extra protein, plus veggies go great in pretty much all kinds of pasta. I love to grill, too. I've been known to grill burgers in the snow, all bundled up in my coat and gloves and everything." He laughed at himself, and I laughed with him, easily able to picture Jason bouncing up and down in the snow with a knit cap and thick gloves while burgers sizzled on a grill.

Our cheesecake came, and we stopped all conversation, demolishing the big wedge of strawberry-topped deliciousness within minutes. Jason paid the bill and held the doors for me again, waiting until I'd tucked my skirt out of the way before shutting the truck door. He pulled out of the lot, cranked up the radio, and rolled down the windows to let in the warm late summer air.

"This is my favorite band," Jason shouted over the music and the wind. "Zac Brown Band. Song's called 'Whatever It Is.'"

I dug in my purse for a hair tie and put my hair back so the wind wouldn't tangle it, then closed my eyes and let the music wash over me. He didn't dedicate this one to me, thankfully, but I could feel his eyes on me, flicking over to me as he drove and then back to the road. We weren't headed back to my house, I realized after a few minutes. We were zipping down a two-lane blacktop road, away from everything, the late evening haze shifting from dark gold to deepening gray.

"Where are we going?" I asked.

He just shrugged. "I don't know. This way." He pointed at the road ahead of us with a snarky smirk. "Just driving."

I nodded and let my right hand hang out the window, and settled my left hand on the console between us. The song shifted to some slow and sleepy ballad, and Jason left it on but didn't tell me who it was or the song title. I didn't care, I realized. It was perfect music for a date, romantic and sweet. I felt Jason's proximity like an inferno beside me. His hand was out the window like mine as he drove with his right, slowing down and turning us onto a narrow dirt road with trees growing up at the very edge. Fields stretched out into the distance beyond the trees, and the road twisted and turned, gravel bouncing off the tire wells and dust kicking up in the side-view mirrors.

My heart palpitated when Jason switched hands on the steering wheel, settling his right hand on the console inches from mine. I wondered if he would take my hand, and what I would do if he did. I bet his hand was warm and rough and strong, and I could almost picture my small dark fingers nestled between his larger, tanned white ones. My heart hammered, and I couldn't take my eyes off his hand, which was somehow closer to mine than it had been. I watched as Jason's eyes shifted to mine, then to our hands, then out the windshield again. His left foot was bouncing crazily, and his hand was beating a rhythm on the steering wheel in time to the Carrie Underwood song playing on the radio.

I wanted to hold his hand. Nothing else mattered. I wasn't sure where we were or where we were going or what time it was, and I didn't care. I turned my head and met his eyes, and then, with a deep breath, slid my hand underneath his. His eyes widened and his breath hitched, but he didn't hesitate to wind his fingers between mine. He smiled, and everything was better than fine.

We drove until darkness had fallen, taking turns listening to country music and talking. Jason told me about his dreams of going pro, and I in turn told him about my proposed career path in speech therapy. We talked about school, about the various cliques, and realized we were both only really part of the "in crowd" because of who we were friends with. I didn't believe Jason at first, but then he explained that he'd learned to be outspoken just so he didn't get completely lost in Kyle's shadow.

"See, Kyle doesn't mean to steal the spotlight," Jason said. "It's just how he is. He's just one of those people who takes the center of attention without trying. I've been his friend since I don't even know when. First grade, maybe? Forever. It's always been that way. I'd get so frustrated, because everyone would want to be around Kyle, want to be his friend, want his attention because Kyle's just *that cool*. I wasn't that kid. I had to learn to put myself out there, talk loud enough to be heard, you know? Just so I didn't get lost in the glow of Kyle's golden-boy brilliance."

"Do I sense bitterness there?" I teased.

He laughed. "Nah, not at *all*." His voice was laced with sarcasm. "For real, though. Kyle is my boy. I'd do anything for that kid. No matter what's happened, he's always made sure we're in it together. But it can be tough being best friends with the star of the town."

I nodded. "I know what you mean. Nell is like that. She doesn't even realize it— she's just naturally cool. Everyone likes her. She's popular, and she doesn't even know it."

Suddenly it was full dark and we were still spinning around corners on dusty dirt roads, Jason's headlights cutting a swath in the darkness. Panic hit all at once as I realized I had no clue what time it was.

I dug my phone out of my purse frantically, then let my head slam back against the seat as I saw the readout: 10:10 p.m. "Shit, shit, sh-sh-sh-*shit*!" I felt tears welling up. "Stop the truck, Jason. Stop, please. Right now."

Jason skidded to a stop and turned to look at me in concern. "What's wrong?"

I swallowed hard. "I—I didn't tell Father I was leaving with you. He thinks I'm with Nell. I was supposed to check in at ten. If I call him now, he'll demand to talk to Nell, and he'll be mad. I'm in s-so-so much trouble, Jason."

"It's only ten minutes, what's the big deal? It's not like we're doing anything wrong. We're just driving around." Jason genuinely didn't understand.

I shook my head, breathing slowly to calm myself down. "You didn't hear what I said. I told him I was with Nell. I *lied*."

"Why'd you lie?"

I shrugged, not quite sure I could explain. "He wouldn't let me go if he knew I was with you. I'm only allowed to go out with Nell and Jill, and even then, we're not supposed to be hanging out with boys. If he knew I was alone with you? He's gonna kill me. Besides, he wouldn't approve of you. I just know he wouldn't." I didn't think about how that last part would sound to Jason, but I felt awful as soon as I saw the hurt on his face.

"He wouldn't, huh? Guess I get that. Not really the kind of guy you bring home to Daddy, am I?" His voice was bitter.

I touched his arm. "It's not like that, Jason. I didn't say *I* didn't approve of you, just that *he* wouldn't, and he won't approve of anyone. I'll die an old maid if he has his way. Don't be angry."

Jason relented and shoved the gearshift into park. "Well, let's make sure you don't get into trouble. Call Nell and then make it a conference call. Maybe your dad will think you're with her."

I nodded. "That just might work."

I called Nell and quickly explained the situation and what I wanted her to do, not letting her get a word in edgewise. She readily agreed, and I dialed Father's cell phone number, merging the calls before he answered.

"You're late, *figlia*." His voice was low and angry. "Where are you?"

"*Mi dispiace*, Father. I'm w-w-w-with Nell. We lost track of time. I'm so sorry. It won't happen again, *prometto*."

"Let me speak with Nell."

Nell's voice came over the phone, sounding canned and far away to me; this wasn't going to work, I just knew it. "It's my fault, Mr. de Rosa. We were watching a movie, and we just got carried away. Don't be mad at Becca, please."

"What movie are you watching?" He sounded suspicious.

"*Far and Away*," Nell answered without a hint of hesitation. "It's about—"

"I know what it is," Father cut in. "Be home in twenty minutes, Rebecca. We shall discuss this when you are home." He hung up, and silence filled the car.

I jumped when my phone rang again.

"Ohmigod," Nell said, half-laughing. "Your dad is so scary. Do you think he bought it?"

"I don't even know. I'm still in trouble for checking in late."

"So. You're not with me, and it's almost ten-thirty. I'm guessing you're with Jason?" She sounded sly and pleased with herself.

"Yeah. You could have warned me, you know." I let a little of my irritation with Nell show through.

She didn't sound sorry at all. "Would you have gone if I'd called you first?" I didn't answer, which was answer enough for Nell. "Exactly. You'd have chickened out."

"So what happened with you and Kyle?" I asked.

"Don't you have to be home in twenty minutes?" She was avoiding the question, and we both knew it.

"You're not getting out of this, Nell."

"Call me when you're home, if you can."

"Fine. 'Bye."

"'Bye."

I turned to Jason. "Can you take me home?"

He nodded and put the truck in gear. "Sure. We're not that far from your place, actually. I've been driving in a big circle, more or less."

True to his word, he was slowing to a stop just inside the subdivision entrance. "Stop here," I said before we reached my house.

As I got out, Jason reached over and snagged my hand, stopping me. "Can we go out again sometime?"

I stared at his strong fingers circling my wrist. "I don't know, Jason. I want to, but I'm not sure it's possible."

He nodded. "Sure. I heard how he was. I'll see you at school on Monday?" He released my wrist, and I shut the door behind me.

I stopped and glanced at him through the open window. "I had a great time, Jason. I didn't think I would, but I did."

Jason grinned. "I guess we can thank Nell, huh?"

I frowned at him. "I wouldn't go that far."

He just laughed. "I'm joking. I had a great time, too. Thanks for giving me a chance."

I turned away and waved at him with my hand over my head. "Don't let it go to your head."

"Call me!" he said, slightly too loud.

"Not going to happen," I said, walking backward.

"Then text me?" He was leaning out the window, his entire upper half visible.

I grinned at him. "That I might do. Now go before you get me in even more trouble."

He slapped the roof of his truck and ducked back in, peeling out and fishtailing the truck in semi-circle with a slight squeal of tires. I shook my head at him, laughing.

When I turned around, however, I stopped laughing. Father was standing on the sidewalk, arms crossed over his broad chest, silver hair slicked back, dress shirt open one button and his tie loosened.

My heart dropped. Judging by the dark scowl on his face, he'd seen Jason.

Not good.

Three: Romeo & Juliet Redux
Becca
October, that same year

"Y-Y-YOU CAN'T KEEP ME L-L-L-LOCKED UP in my room forever, Father!" I stood in the doorway to my room, fury pounding through me, taking all my fluency with it.

He stood impassive in the hall outside my room, arms crossed over his chest. His eyes were narrowed, dark, angry. "Yes. I can. And I will. You lied to me. You were out with that football player. I'll keep you in here for as long it takes for you to learn your lesson."

I closed my eyes and counted to ten, breathing deep with each number. "This isn't fah-fah-fair. We just went to dinner. Drove around. I know I lied, and I'm sorry. But p-p-plea-please, I'm going crazy. I already don't have a life, but now you won't let me do anything."

"Your sanity is at no risk, Rebecca. Stop exaggerating."

Another ten-count, ten more deep breaths. Father never rushed me; he always waited until I was ready to speak. He had a stutter as a child, and didn't completely shed it until he moved to the States and did some fluency shaping therapy. He understood that much about me at least.

"It's not an exaggeration, Father. School, my room, homework, piano, speech. That's all I ever do. Even before this, that's all I ever did. Now? You might as well enroll me in online school and literally lock me in my room. I'll be seventeen in two months, Father. When will I get to make my own decisions?"

"*Basta, figlia.*" He didn't yell, because he never yelled. The words were delivered quietly, intensely.

I clamped my mouth closed around my screams of protest. I clenched my hands into fists and refused to cry. "You'll regret this, Father. Remember that." I closed the door in his face and sat at my desk, staring out the window at the trees waving in the afternoon sunlight.

I stuck my earbuds in my ears and scrolled through my iPod until I found the song I wanted, "Flightless

Bird" by Iron & Wine. It was a song from the *Twilight* soundtrack, and I'd since devoured every song by Iron & Wine I could find. I liked the poetry in the lyrics, the slightly off-kilter sound and deep-felt meaning in every song. "Singers and the Endless Song" came up next, and I let myself go, let myself stare out the window and listen, just breathing and not speaking, not stuttering, not failing to properly express myself.

At some point, my pen began a frantic scribble across the page, giving vent to my thoughts.

ANYWHERE BUT HERE
Trees wave and tease
Blown in the long free breeze
Urging me out and into the blue
Into the sunlit green spaces
Where no words trip over clumsy tongues
Where no tensions drip like rain from eaves
I don't even wish I was a bird
I only wish I was out there
Walking in the grass or climbing in the trees
Heated by the sun or chilled by the wind or wet in the rain
Anywhere but here
Chained to this stagnant shore
A prisoner of perfection
An enemy of state

For no more crime than being
A teenaged girl
In like with a teenaged boy
For no more crime than driving
In lazy dusty endless circles
Listening to country songs
And my own nervous heartbeat
My pulse pounding and my nerves twanging
Like the banjos on the radio
I can't even shout my anger
Can't even scream my frustration
Can't even curse
It would only come out a jumble
"Fu—fu-fu-fuck you!"
Fu fu fu fu
Bu bu bu bu
Duh duh duh
Childish stumbling words
Tripping syllables and slippery syntactic screw-ups
That's me
The silent girl
The stutterer
The prisoner
The smart girl
The valedictorian scribbling maledictions to no one

I heard my doorknob twist and the door banged open, revealing my older brother Ben. He glanced around my room, found me at my desk, and nodded at me, his long, stringy black hair hanging in tangles in front of his face. He kicked the door shut, stopping it from slamming by catching the knob at the last second.

"'Sup, Beck?" He plopped onto my bed and kicked his feet out on my comforter, shoes and all. "Still locked in your tower, huh?" He tossed his head to clear the hair away from his mouth and eyes.

His eyes were cloudy, hazed, reddened. I sighed and turned away from my desk, closing my notebook. "Are you high again, Ben?"

He shrugged. "Yeah, so? I'm havin' more fun than you."

"Dead people have more fun than me," I deadpanned.

Ben laughed. "True. *Old* dead people, at that."

I laughed and lay on the bed next to Ben, crawling over him to lie on the inside next to the wall, shoving him over with my hip. "You better not get mud on my comforter, Benny."

"I won't. And don't call me Benny. I hate it." He dug in his pocket, pulled out a glass pipe and a lighter, then lifted up and shoved open my window. He lay back down and dug in the cargo pocket of his baggy shorts and pulled out the brown tube from a paper towel roll. Each end of the tube had fabric softener sheets rubber banded over the opening. He sparked the lighter and put the pipe to his lips, lit the pot and sucked it into his lungs, setting the pipe and lighter on his chest before settling back onto the bed.

"You're really going to do that right here in my room? In the house?" I asked, pissed off.

He shrugged, grinning a closed-lipped smile at me. He lifted the tube to his mouth and blew the thick, acrid smoke through the dryer sheet and out the window, the pungent smell now masked enough to not be readily noticeable.

"If Father catches you, he'll send you to military school, Ben. You know that, right?"

Ben shrugged again. "He can try. I'm eighteen anyway, Beck. He can't do shit but have me arrested." He glanced at me, gesturing to me with the pipe; I shook my head, like I always did, and he took another long drag. "Why do you call him that?" he asked around his lungful of smoke.

"Call who what?" I felt loose, and realized I was getting a slight contact high from the fumes.

He blew out the smoke before answering. "Dad. You still call him 'Father' like we're in the fucking eighteenth century or some shit."

I shrugged. "I don't know. I just do."

Ben glanced at me in irritation, brushing a strand of hair away from his eyes with the end of the clear yellow plastic lighter. "I call bullshit on that. You're a certifiable genius, Beck. You've got a reason for everything you do."

I sighed. "Fine. You want to know? I call him *Father* because it creates distance. He's not *Dad* to me, much less *Daddy* or anything else. He's my father, so that's what I call him. It's a formal word, and it connotes a formal relationship."

Ben laughed. "'It connotes a formal relationship,'" he repeated, half-mocking. "Only you, Becca. Only you would say something like that. I just don't get why you still put up with his crap. I stopped a long time ago."

"But you don't care. I do. That's the difference."

He glanced at me. "Meaning what? What don't I care about?"

"Yourself. The future. I have plans, and need Father's money to get there. I can't afford the universities I need if I'm going to get my doctorate."

"That's shallow and short-sighted," Ben said. "You could get scholarships. Take out loans. You don't need his bullshit. He's a fucking tyrant, a dictator. I hate his ass. Soon as I get a job and save enough for an apartment, I'm moving my ass out."

"It is not shallow or short-sighted," I argued. "Do you have any clue how much it's gonna cost to get my bachelors, masters, *and* doctorate? Depending on the university, hundreds of thousands of dollars. I'll still have to take out loans, but with Father's help, it'll be manageable."

Ben just stared at me. "Listen to you. You skipped your childhood, I think. What sixteen-year-old is thinking about this stuff? Just be a kid, man. Sneak out. Make out with a guy behind the bleachers or some shit. Get into trouble and make me beat some dude's ass for you. Quit being so goddamn serious all the time." He took a long drag on his pipe and then leaned over and blew it straight into my face before I could roll away. "Smoke some pot and loosen up. We're young. We've got time. Just chill and don't be so serious."

I coughed and waved the smoke away. "Goddamn it, Ben. Don't be an asshole. Now I'm going to get high. I tried it with you once, remember? I hated it."

Ben nodded, staring at the ceiling. "Oh, yeah. I remember now. You freaked the fuck out, thought Amma was going to come back from the dead and yell at us, even though Amma was alive and living in Beirut at the time."

I laughed. "You said yourself you thought it was laced with something."

He nodded again without looking at me, tamping down the ashes in the bowl with his thumb. "Yeah, dude, I remember. That shit was potent. You were so wasted I had to carry you up to your bed."

"I really hated that, Ben." I snatched the pipe and lighter from him and shoved them in his cargo pocket. "I hate it now. I hate what it does to you. It messes with your moods, and you know it. The doctor said—"

Ben stood up, suddenly angry. "I don't give a fuck what the doctor said!" he yelled. "I hate all those stupid meds they want me to take. They make me feel like a freaking zombie, like I'm half-dead. I'm tired all the time, and I lose a ton of weight 'cause I can't fucking eat. I hate it. You don't know what it's like. This stuff helps me more. Keeps me level, you know? When I get all whacked out and crazy, smoking brings me down, and when I'm depressed, it brings me up. It works better than any of that shit no one can pronounce. Fucking Zoloft and Wellbutrin and Xanax and Clonazepam and Valium and Ativan. It's all bullshit. Doesn't work. *This* shit works." He grabbed the paraphernalia from his pocket and shook it at me.

I could already see the down-shift in his mood happening. "Ben, you know that's not true," I said, my voice soft and careful. "I know I don't know what it's like for you, but the way you're dealing with it isn't healthy."

Ben blew out a frustrated breath, pocketing his things again and heading for the door. "You're not a doctor yet, Becca, so quit trying to fix me."

"Ben, wait. I'm sorry. I just—just—I want you to be happy. Th-that's all."

He stopped in the doorway and glanced at me through a curtain of stringy hair. He gave me a look that was deeper than I thought Ben capable of. "The problem is, when I *am* happy, no one can handle it. And when I'm not happy, they can't handle it. It's not that I don't care about my life or my future, Becca. I do. I just know that I'm limited, okay? What happens up here," he tapped his temple, "inherently limits what I can do in my life. Drugs, no drugs, pot, no pot, there's just no good way to handle my shit. I'll never accomplish important stuff like you will, Beck. I know that. I've accepted it. I'm just gonna live it up and enjoy my life as much as I can for as long as I can. Eventually it'll all catch up to me. I know that, too. But it's my life, my choice, and no one else's."

"Just be careful, okay?"

He nodded, smiling at me. "Sure thing, Beck." He turned away and closed the door, then poked his head back through. "Hey, by the way, if you ever want help sneaking out to see Jason Dorsey, let me know. I'll cover for you." He winked and was gone before I could reply.

Jason

I'd barely even seen Becca twice in a month, and those were both fleeting glimpses in passing at school. We didn't have any classes together this semester and we had different lunch periods, too. She caught up to me at my locker right before I was heading out to practice one Friday in mid-October. It was cool outside, so she was wearing a floor-length blue wool skirt, a white V-neck T-shirt, and an unbuttoned gray sweater. Her clothes were cut so that they clung to her curves without being overtly revealing, and I found this the sexiest thing ever. Any girl could put on a push-up bra and a low-cut shirt so she spilled out. It took class and style to look deliciously sexy without looking skanky, and Becca pulled this off with every outfit she wore.

"Hey, Jason." She leaned against the locker beside me, mere inches away, so close I could smell the conditioner in her hair and the body lotion on her skin.

I wanted to bury my face in the hollow of her neck and smell her, bury my face in her springy hair. I didn't, though, because that might come across as slightly forward in this stage of the game. I tossed my history book in my backpack and zipped it shut, then hung it off one shoulder before pivoting to lean against the locker, facing Becca.

"Hey, Becca." I crossed one foot over my ankle and my arms across my chest. I felt a glimmer of pride when her eyes followed my arms and traced the bulge of my pecs. She liked what she saw, which meant I'd be pounding the weights extra hard today.

"I'm sorry I never got a chance to see you again. Father has me on lockdown." She tugged on one of her curls, making it bounce up and down.

I made an irritated face. "He really keeps you on a short leash, doesn't he? Damn, that sucks."

"I did lie to him, Jason."

I huffed in irritation. "You're a teenager. It's par for the course. We're supposed to sneak out and lie to our parents. We weren't doing anything bad. You shouldn't have gotten grounded for this long."

"Yeah, that's what Ben told me, too. I just…I'm not sure I'm ready to openly defy him. Besides, my bedroom is on the second floor. I'm not sure I'm brave enough to sneak out that way." She hiked her backpack higher up on both shoulders. "Ben said he'd help me sneak out, but…I'm just not-nnn-not sure."

I was realizing she only really stuttered when she was nervous about something, and I hated hearing her struggle. I could see how she berated herself mentally after every fumbled word. "Hey," I said. "It's fine. I'm not trying to encourage you to, like, become a delinquent or something. I want to see you, yeah. But I don't want to be the cause of adding more trouble to your life."

She smiled at me. "You're sweet. I'm in no danger of becoming a delinquent. I'm just considering a few white lies so I can hang out with a friend."

"Is that all I am to you?" I said, only half-teasing. "A friend? I'm wounded."

Becca either didn't catch the humor in my voice, or chose to ignore it. "What did you have in mind, if friends isn't enough?" Her eyes were wide and fixed on mine, serious and so brown they were all but black, shot through with streaks of lighter brown around the pupil.

I tried and miserably failed to pull my gaze from her mesmerizing eyes. "I don't know. More?" I swallowed the ball of hot embarrassment in my throat and went for broke. "My girlfriend?"

Her eyes went even wider, and her mouth dropped open slightly. She sucked in a long, hard breath, and I couldn't help but admire the way the sudden inrush swelled her breasts in the soft cotton of her white shirt.

"Y-your g-ggg-girlfriend? Ww-we wwwww—*damn* it." With each stuttered word, she blinked hard, as if a circuit in her brain was catching on a loop; she closed her eyes and seemed to be counting mentally. "We went on one date, Jason." Each word was carefully enunciated and nearly monotone, as if she was reading something out loud.

I made sure to not show any reaction to her struggle, just waited until she said what she had to say. It was painful to watch her struggle with both her words and her embarrassment.

"But it was a really awesome date," I said.

When she responded, her words were smoother and more natural, but some beginning syllables were slightly drawn out, like a stutter corrected midway. "True. But shouldn't we go on another date before we make anything official?"

I shrugged. "Sure, if you want to do it that way. Won't change anything for me, though. I really like you."

She didn't speak for so long I wasn't sure if she was going to. She seemed to be either scripting out her next words, or considering whether to say them at all. Eventually, she did speak, and it all came out in a rush, as if she was spitting out the words before she could take them back or chicken out. "I've had a crush on you since fourth grade." She looked away, her dusky skin pinking slightly with a blush of embarrassment.

"Fourth grade? Nell told me seventh."

Becca huffed and sputtered in anger. "She told you? I'll cut a bitch!"

I laughed so hard I snorted, which only made me laugh harder. "You'll cut a bitch? Oh, god, Beck, you shouldn't try to talk street. Make it stop!" I sucked in a breath, then made the mistake of glancing at Becca, who had her arms crossed beneath her breasts and was glaring at me with a complex mix of emotions on her face. "I'm sorry, I'm sorry. It's just too funny."

"Are you done yet?" Becca spat out the words.

I breathed deeply and tried to compose myself. "Yes, I'm done. I'm sorry, that was just the funniest thing I've heard in a long time."

Becca couldn't stop a smile from creeping over her lips. "Ben says that all the time, and it's funny. I guess I can't pull it off as well as he does, though." She sobered a bit. "I still can't believe Nell actually told you I had a crush on you."

"In her defense, it was only to convince me to ask you out. I wasn't going to, mainly because I had a feeling you'd react pretty much exactly the way you did."

"How else was I supposed to react?"

"I don't know. I can't imagine there was much else you could do. It was a pretty odd situation."

Becca inched slightly closer to me, close enough that she had to stare up into my eyes. Her breasts were brushing my chest, and I had to use every ounce of willpower to not crush her against me and kiss her. She searched my eyes, and then I saw a decision flow over her features.

"Pick me up at the entrance to my sub at midnight," she said, her voice sounding at once excited, worried, and determined.

"Midnight?" I frowned. "What the hell are we supposed to do at midnight in this podunk town? Everything closes at eight."

She glanced around us briefly, saw that the hallway was empty but for us, then lifted up on her tiptoes and kissed me on the cheek, right on the edge of my jawline. "I'm sure you can figure something out. Even if we just drive around and listen to country music again, I'm sure we'll have fun."

"How are you gonna get out of your room? Please don't fall out of your window and break something. That would for sure put a damper on our plans." I was trying to playing it cool, but my entire body was on fire, trembling and wired from the electric feel of her lips on my cheek.

She grinned. "You leave that to me. But it will probably involve my brother. God knows he's had plenty of experience sneaking out. He's half the reason my parents are so hard on me."

"Call me or text me if you end up needing help. I have a ladder I could bring."

She snorted. "I think a ladder might be kind of noisy. The idea is to draw less attention to the fact that I'm sneaking out under my fun-Nazi father's nose, not more."

I shrugged. "Just a thought. I could make you a grappling hook?"

"A grappling hook?" Becca laughed outright at that. "Where are you going to get a grappling hook?"

"I don't know. I haven't thought that far ahead. Maybe I could just steal the anchor from my dad's fishing boat? I could toss it into your window, and you could shimmy down it."

Becca laughed even harder at that. "Because that's not conspicuous at all."

We both pushed away from the lockers and strolled down the hallway toward the front office and the exit. Somehow, my hand ended up tangled in Becca's, our fingers twined together. We both looked down at our joined hands and then at each other.

"Yep," I said. "You're my girlfriend. Don't even try to deny it."

Becca slapped my bicep with her free hand but didn't take her hand out of mine. "I agreed to no such thing. I might be, but then again, I might not be. Nothing's official. The jury is still out."

"You're just trying to play it cool, Becca. Don't lie." I tugged her so she stumbled against my side, and then I wrapped my arm around her waist, careful to keep it in the kosher-zone above her waistline but beneath her bra strap.

She seemed to have stopped breathing, but she didn't pull away. She might have burrowed a little closer, actually. "Have you met me? I'm the furthest thing from cool." She murmured the words as if she believed them but didn't want me to.

I frowned down at her. She wouldn't meet my eyes, so I pulled her to a stop and twisted her to face me. Her body was flush against mine, soft and fitting perfectly. Her chin rested on my chest, and I knew she could feel my heart crashing against my ribcage.

"I think you're cool, Becca," I said. "I always have."

She wrinkled her nose in confusion. "You have? I always kind of figured you barely knew who I was."

I made a face at her. "That's not possible. You're too beautiful to fade into the background."

She tilted her head to rest her cheek against my shirt, then shook her curls in denial. "I'm not, but thanks."

"You're not supposed to disagree with me. I can think whatever I want about you, and it's true because I think it."

She turned her face up to look at me, a comical expression of puzzlement on her features. "That is very dizzyingly circular logic. You think what you think, and it's true because you think it?" Her arms slid up my back to grip my triceps.

"It's kind of like 'I think, therefore I am.' Wasn't it Marcel Proust who said that?"

Becca snickered, not quite derisively. "Descartes, actually. Proust is someone totally different."

I laughed. "See, that's what I get for trying to be smart."

"I was just impressed that you knew that phrase, and that you knew who Proust was."

I grunted. "Well, obviously, I don't know either. I've got no clue who Proust was. And I'm not even sure I understand the phrase much better."

We started walking again, and our hands resumed their twined grip around each other.

"Marcel Proust was a French novelist best known for his work *In Search of Lost Time*. He was one of the first writers to openly discuss homosexuality, which was a really big deal when he lived, around the turn of the century." Becca seemed to lose herself in reciting the facts, her words coming out effortlessly, although she sounded like she was composing an essay. "The phrase *cogito ergo sum*, which translates from the Latin into 'I think, therefore I am,' was a philosophical statement proposed by the French philosopher René Descartes in the seventeenth century. And actually, the phrase was written in French, as *Je pense, donc je suis*. All it really means is that the process of doubting whether or not you exist is proof of your existence."

"Why would anyone doubt their own existence? It seems pretty self-explanatory, you know? I'm here, I see things, I feel things. I am, therefore I am."

Becca tilted her head and nodded slowly. "Very good. That's a good point. And a lot of laypeople gave that exact same answer to the philosphers. To them, though—the philosophers, I mean—the idea went deeper than that. It went back to Plato, who talked about 'the knowledge of knowledge.' Think about it like this: Who told you two plus two equals four?"

I answered immediately. "My kindergarten teacher. But she showed me, with blocks. Two blocks plus two blocks means I have four blocks."

"Right, that's a concrete example. But apply that doubt, that 'who told you so?' mindset to more insubstantial, metaphysical ideas, like one's place in life, in the universe. Like the conundrum, if a tree falls in the forest and no one's around to hear, does it make any noise?"

I snorted. "That one is stupid. Just ask the squirrel who jumps out of the falling tree if he heard the damn thing crash to the ground."

Becca laughed. "You're taking all the fun out of the argument. But you see my point, or rather, their point. That's what Descartes was saying. The fact that he could outline physical reality as perceived by himself proved his own existence, in his perception of reality at least. 'I must finally conclude that the proposition, I am, I exist, is necessarily true whenever it is put forward by me or conceived in my mind.' That was his ultimate argument."

I chewed on my lip and thought about it. "I guess I see his point. Like, how do I know what you see, how do I know what you're thinking? I don't. I only know what I know. If there's no one around to hear a sound, the sound exists, but it doesn't necessarily exist in the sense that it has…I don't know…it doesn't have any purpose if no one's around to receive the sound waves."

She chuckled. "Yeah, sort of."

"Meaning I've totally missed it, but you're too nice to say so." She ducked her head, and I knew I was right. "See? Trying to get into a philosophical discussion with you is an exercise in futility. My brain just don't work that way."

She pushed at me with her hip. "I'm just a freak that way. I had to write a paper on Descartes for a philosophy class I took at the college last semester."

I grinned down at her. "It's scary how smart you are. You sounded like a damn professor, all lecturing me and shit."

She ducked her head. "S-sorry. I didn't mean to le-lecture you."

I swung my backpack around to my front, ducked down into a squat in front of her, and swept her onto my back in a piggyback ride, bursting into a full-out sprint down the hallway. She squealed and wrapped her arms around my neck, burying her face in my shoulder and laughing, demanding that I put her down. I just wanted to get her mind off being nervous so she wouldn't stutter, not that it bothered me, but because it did her.

"Put me down, you lunatic!" She slapped my chest. "This is scary!" The fact that she didn't stutter and said it laughing told me was having fun, so I kept running down the empty front hallway, past the main office, where Mrs. Jones, the secretary, looked up and peered at us over her glasses in disapproval.

We approached the doors that led to the parking lot, and I slowed enough to kick the crash bar and open the door, ducking through and skipping down the steps. My backpack jounced against my stomach, my books hitting my bruises painfully, but I didn't care. I had her legs wrapped around my waist, her arms around my neck, her breath in my hair, and her sweet laughter in my ear.

I made it halfway across the parking lot before she started wiggling in my grip, so I slowed to a stop and let her down. There were no cars in the parking lot, so I looked around in confusion. "Where's your car?"

She twisted a lock of hair around her finger. "I don't have one." She said it carefully, clearly upset by the admission but determined not to show it.

"So how are you getting home?" I asked.

"Ben is probably waiting for me at the circle. He picks me up after school since Mom and Dad are both working."

"Well, shit, that's on the other side of the school. Why didn't you say something?"

She gave me an incredulous look. "I tried! You were carting me through the school like a caveman dragging his woman to his cave!"

I laughed. "So you admit it! You're my woman." I grabbed her wrist and jerked her against me, and faked a deep, gruff voice. "Me Jason. You mine."

She seemed to melt, just a bit. Her eyes widened and wavered, dark and luminous like black coffee glinting in the rays of sunshine. "Fine. Me Becca. You mine." She said it barely above a whisper, as if she couldn't believe her own words.

I felt my stomach flipping, my heart rabbiting. Her lips were parted, waiting. Shit. I was gonna kiss her, wasn't I?

Yep.

I slowly, carefully lowered my lips to hers, giving her plenty of time to back away. She tasted like vanilla lip stuff and smelled like citrus and melons and cleanliness and an indefinable, intoxicating something else. Her lips were soft and wet against mine, still at first, but then as moments passed and the kiss continued, her lips began to move, tilting to gain a better fit. I lost my breath, lost track of everything except her body flush and soft against mine, her hands sliding slowly up my spine to rub against my close-cropped spiky blond hair.

A car horn blared from a few feet away, and we both jumped guiltily.

"Becca! Whoo-hoo! That's how you break the rules, girl!" It was Ben, Becca's brother, skidding his battered red Trans Am to a stop next to us. "I've been waiting for you for ten minutes, Beck. I guess I see why."

"I wasn't breaking the rules, Ben. Shut up." Becca had my hand in hers, a kind of declaration to her brother. Clearly she trusted him not to say anything to their parents.

Ben just laughed, black hair hanging loose around his shoulders in a glossy, messy tangle. "Sure you weren't. I wouldn't rat you out, but you know you wouldn't want *Father* to know I caught you making out with this punk in the school parking lot."

I watched Becca's eyes narrow at her brother. "You wouldn't dare. Don't forget I know about your little dryer-sheet trick. I bet *Dad* would be interested to know about that."

They were both emphasizing the different words they used for their dad, which made me think even her brother thought it was odd that she called him "Father." I was curious about the dryer sheet trick, though.

Ben ran his fingers through his hair, flipping it back over his scalp. "I just said I wouldn't tell, didn't I? And wasn't I the one who offered to help you sneak out so you could see this kid?" He pointed at me with his thumb.

I knew of Ben de Rosa. He was kind of a legend around our high school, notorious for skipping classes, getting into fights, cursing out teachers, and playing high-profile but ultimately harmless pranks around the school, but then always able to talk himself out of the punishment he deserved. He was our town's stoner, the kid you always knew had pot, and was probably high every time you saw him. No one ever ratted him out, though, and he'd never been arrested somehow, despite the common knowledge of his activities. I'd never been able to figure out how he did it, and now that I'd come to understand more about Becca's life, it was even harder to comprehend how Ben could do anything he wanted and get away with it, when Becca couldn't even go out on a date with me without getting grounded for a month.

Becca just shook her head at her brother, then turned to me. "I've gotta go. I'm supposed to be home by four-thirty."

I glanced at my phone and cursed when I saw the time. "Shit! It's after four already! Coach is gonna rip me a new asshole. I better go dress out before I spend the entire practice doing down-ups." I hesitated, then bent down and touched her lips quickly with mine. "Midnight? Right?"

She pulled away with a self-conscious glance at her brother, then nodded. "Yeah. Midnight. If I don't show up, it's because I couldn't make it, not because I didn't want to." She slid gracefully into her brother's car and waved out the open window at me, holding her hair in a temporary ponytail with the other hand.

Coach made me run two miles at full speed with a sandbag across each shoulder, then do down-ups for twenty minutes before letting me run scrimmage with the guys.

Totally worth it for my first kiss.

Four: Midnight in the Garden
Becca
Later that night

I CLUNG TO THE DRAINPIPE, frozen in fear. "It's going to break, Ben," I whispered, my voice a raspy whimper.

He just stuck his head out the window above me and grinned. "I know it seems like it, but it won't, I promise. I climbed up on a ladder last summer and nailed that fucker to the wall real good."

I laughed, picturing Ben up on a ladder, trying to juggle a hammer, nails, and a joint, all so he could sneak out at night without falling. I'd crept into his room at a quarter to twelve and told him I wanted to sneak out to see Jason. He just grinned at me and shoved open his window, pointing at the drainpipe a few feet.

"Look down—I even put some footholds on there and painted 'em white so you can't see them." He sounded pleased with himself.

I glanced down, my stomach wobbling at the distance beneath me, but eventually focused on the drainpipe and saw that, sure enough, he'd nailed a piece of wood crossways between the pipe and the wall so you'd have somewhere to put your feet as you slid down. I wondered that Father had never noticed, but then realized that he never really went outside the house. He came home from work at seven every night and left at six in the morning, and went golfing most of the day Saturday and Sunday. He'd have no reason to make a circuit of the house or to examine the drainpipe for secret escape routes. My brother was hiding his egress route in plain sight, it seemed.

I slid down a bit further, touched the foothold, and then slid down some more. "Is there another foothold beneath me?" I asked.

"Yeah, I put in two. Should be another a few more feet down." Ben watched me descend, his hair hanging loose around his face.

I shimmied down until my hands caught the foothold and lowered myself farther, until my feet found another hold. At that point, the ground was only a few feet down, so I jumped free. I happened to glance up at

Ben as I did so, and he had his hand out and his mouth open as if to protest. I fell a lot farther than I'd thought I would, and hit the ground with a hard thump, my ankles jarring. I tumbled backward and hit again on my tailbone, cursing under my breath as my ankles and my butt began to throb.

"Are you okay?" Ben asked in a whisper-shout. "I was gonna say, that seems like a lot closer than it really is. You gotta keep climbing down and not let go until your hand's on the foothold. I almost broke my ankle the first time I climbed down that way."

I rubbed my tailbone and rotated one ankle and then the other. I'd be sore for a while, but nothing was injured. "I'm fine," I said. "Thanks, Ben."

"I don't want to know where you're going or what you're doing. I need some kind of plausible deniability," he said. He ducked back in his room and then reappeared with a backpack in his hands. "Catch this."

He dropped it and I caught it in my arms, unzipped the main compartment to find a few old ratty T-shirts wrapped around a fifth of Jack Daniels. I glanced up at him, and he winked at me. "Can't have much fun without some booze, can you? I didn't think you and Dorsey would want pot, or I'd give you that."

"You're not supposed to encourage us to drink, Benjamin."

Ben laughed too loud and clapped his hand over his mouth. "God, you are such a goody-goody, Beck. What the fuck's the point of sneaking out at midnight if you're not gonna do it right?" I just shook my head, re-zipped the bag and slung it over my shoulder, and had turned to make my way through the side yard when Ben stopped me with a *pssst*. "I want the rest of whatever you don't drink, so bring the bag back. And...don't drink it all. You'll get sick."

I rolled my eyes at him, even though he couldn't see me. "I'm not stupid, Ben. I know better than to drink an entire fifth at once."

Ben lifted an eyebrow. "Well, maybe some of us aren't as smart as you. It's one of those 'fun at the time but a bitch later' things."

I just shook my head. "I'm leaving now, Ben. Bye, and thanks."

"Plausible deniability starts now. I don't know you." I heard his window slide closed with a faint squeak.

I laughed as I ducked under the low-hanging branches of the huge pine trees standing between our house and our neighbors. The grass was wet with dew and the air had a bite of cold to it, making me glad I'd decided to change into jeans and put on a heavier sweater. The sky was clear of clouds and dotted with stars, a thick wedge of white-glowing half-moon rising midway through the silver-studded black. My breath puffed in faint clouds of white as I dodged along the trees and out to the road. I saw Jason's truck idling with the headlights off, a cloud of exhaust roiling around the back of the truck. The interior light of the cab was on, bathing Jason in a pale yellow glow. I could see the top of his head bent toward his lap, the hedgehog spikes of his blond hair still held in perfect place by the gel he used, his neck thick and tanned by hours in the sun.

He glanced up as I approached the passenger side of the truck, a happy grin spreading across his features. He hopped out of the truck, and I heard the strains of country music turned down low escaping into the night. Hurrying around the front, Jason had the door open for me before I could even touch the door. I stepped up and slid in across the cloth seats, and immediately felt at home. Somehow I had a feeling I'd be spending a lot of time in this truck. I loved it already.

I thought of the first country song he'd played for me, and took inventory of the inside of his cab. The seats were gray cloth, a console in the middle with two black cup holders between my seat and his, a nearly empty bottle of Mountain Dew Code Red in the holder nearest the driver's side. Scattered across the armrest section of the console were a thick history textbook open to the Civil War section; a notebook filled with a neat, slanted, all-caps scrawl; and a to-go bag of Cheez-Its. On the floor at my feet was a faded maroon Jansport backpack, his green-and-white varsity letter pinned to the outside pocket. Several empty bottles of Mountain Dew and Gatorade were piled up on the floor near the vent at my feet, along with empty packets of beef jerky and sunflower seeds. A zipped-closed CD case sat on the dashboard, wedged against the windshield, fat with discs and faded with age. On the floor between the seats, stuffed between the gear-shift and the seat front, was a thick U of M stadium blanket, and balled up on top of that, a black Carhartt hooded sweatshirt, thick, zippered, and clearly much worn. Peeking out from between the sweatshirt and the blanket was a strap of some kind, like for a camera case or some other protective bag.

As Jason stuffed his books in his backpack, I pushed the sweatshirt aside to get a look at what was beneath it. I discovered an expensive-looking backpack-style Nikon camera bag. Jason had the truck in gear and was pulling around in a U-turn to speed onto the main road, flicking on his headlights. I tugged the camera bag free from beneath the sweatshirt and lifted it onto my lap, unzipped it, and gasped at the enormous, professional-grade camera nestled inside.

"Is this yours?" I asked.

Jason glanced at me, and then a look akin to panic swept over his features. "Yeah, it is. Can you put it back, please?" His voice was calm, too calm. He looked almost angry.

I hurriedly zipped the bag closed, clicked the clasps in place, and re-covered it as I'd found it. "I'm sorry," I said, unsure of what I'd done wrong. "I was just curious. It's a really nice camera. Was it a gift?"

Jason fist tightened on the wheel. "No. Bought it myself."

"How'd you afford this kind of camera? These cost, like, two thousand dollars."

"That's a D800. They're three grand retail. I got that one online for a little over two." He twisted his fist around the steering wheel. "I saved up to buy it."

"You have a job? I didn't know that."

Jason blushed, more from anger than embarrassment, it seemed to me. A vein in his temple throbbed. "I don't have a job."

"Then how?"

He didn't answer for a long time. A traffic light turned red, and we slowed to a stop. "This stays between us, okay? Not even Nell can know." I nodded, and he blew out a long breath. "My dad pays me two hundred per game we win, plus twenty bucks for every touchdown I score. I also get a thousand dollars if I get straight As for an entire year. If I maintain a 4.0 average all four years of high school, he'll go in half on whatever car I want. So that's how I bought this truck. My uncle Rick was selling it, so he gave me a good deal on it. Then I bought the camera."

"So that's your motivation to win all the time?"

He jerked the gearshift violently into second as we accelerated away from the green light. "Partly."

"What's the rest?"

He glanced at me, then away, the shutters drawn across his features. "Not important."

I sensed a deep secret here, and I knew I shouldn't push, but I did anyway. "Maybe it is to me. I want to know about you."

"Drop it, Becca. *Please*." He didn't look at me, and he spoke in a whisper that somehow communicated his desperation.

"Okay, sure. Sorry, I d-didn't mean to p-ppp-pry." I dropped my gaze, upset that I'd upset him, and confused by his sudden shift in demeanor over a camera.

Jason groaned in frustration. "Damn it, Becca, I'm sorry. I didn't mean to snap at you. It's just...there are some things about me that are just...that I can't talk about."

"Is it okay to ask you what you take pictures of? Could I see them?"

Instead of answering, Jason spun the wheel, barely touching the brakes and then tapping the accelerator so the truck skidded across the center line and onto a wide dirt road, the back end fishtailing in the gravel and sliding on an angle before he corrected it straight once more. I was gripping the oh-shit bar above my head and barely breathing as he powered the truck forward, and then I openly shrieked when he took a long curve at dangerous speeds, his brights on, illuminating the narrowing track ahead of us. He seemed to know each and every curve by heart, turning the wheel and touching the brakes before the turn so he could accelerate through the curve in practiced power slides. My heart was hammering in my chest, pounding with equal parts terror and excitement.

"Jason! Please don't crash us!" I was pleased that I said it without stuttering, considering how rampant my nerves were.

He just grinned at me, a cocky flash of straight white teeth. He rounded another corner, then abruptly braked down to nearly a stop and twisted the truck onto an even narrower two-track path through the woods. He took this much slower, reaching down to twist a knob so the four-by-four engaged. The path dipped and rose, and he often had to gun the engine to power the truck over hills, only to speed down the other side.

"Where are we going?"

He pointed ahead of us with a finger flicked from the steering wheel. "Not too much farther. A favorite spot of mine."

The truck dipped precariously sideways as the path twisted and ducked low under a pair of spreading oak trees. Another half mile or so, and the track petered out to nothing, and we were jouncing over grass and between trees. The ground leveled off, then began a slow rise that grew steeper with every foot until the truck was straining upward at a steep angle. At the top, Jason turned the truck to the side and stopped it, cutting the engine but leaving the radio on. He turned off the headlights, dug out the blanket, and hopped out of the truck, gesturing at me to follow. I pushed open my door and hopped to the ground, immediately chilled by the cold air. Jason had the back of the bed lowered and was standing up, waiting for me. I started to climb up, rather awkwardly, but Jason bent at the waist, caught me under my armpits, and lifted me bodily off the ground. I squealed at the sudden loss of gravity, and as soon as my feet touched the ribbed bed of the truck, I stumbled forward and wrapped my arms around him.

"God, Jason! Don't *do* that!" My voice was muffled in the waffled fabric of Jason's long-sleeve shirt.

He smelled like cologne, deodorant, and sweat, and something else spicy and unidentifiable.

"Scared?" He sounded amused and pleased with himself.

I huffed in irritation and glared up at him. "Startled, maybe. Not scared. Give a girl a warning before you haul her off the ground next time, will you?" Jason just chuckled. "You're really strong, aren't you?"

He shrugged. "I work out a lot. For football, and because sometimes I just need the outlet."

"Outlet? What do you mean?"

He hesitated. "Umm...god. Okay, listen. I don't have the best home life, Becca. I told you how my dad pushes me to be perfect, right? He's just...he's not always a nice guy. We fight a lot, and sometimes I just need to...vent. That's all."

Things clicked together, and my stomach sank at the meaning between the lines of what he wasn't saying. "Does he hit you, Jason?" I pulled away and watched his face carefully, sure he was going to avoid the question.

He looked down at me, his features hard and closed. "Don't worry about it, okay? Don't get involved. I don't need saving."

I frowned. "So that's a yes, then. Why have you never told anyone?"

Jason pulled out of my arms and turned away. He squatted and spread the blanket out on the bed of the truck, then un-strung a pair of hook-ended bungee cords holding a cooler in place. Opening the lid of the white and blue Igloo cooler, he withdrew a six-pack of Coke, four wax-wrapped sandwiches, and a bag of potato chips.

"I know it's not, like, a gourmet spread or whatever, but it's food." He separated the four sandwiches into two piles, pointing at each pile in turn. "These are turkey, Dijon, and swiss, and these are ham and sharp cheddar with mayo."

He sat down and patted the blanket next to him, reached behind himself and shoved open the sliding glass window so the soft strains of a country song floated in, a woman's voice singing about gunpowder and lead. I hesitated for a long moment, and then sat down next to him, taking one of the turkey sandwiches.

After we'd both eaten half our sandwich, he set his down on his lap and met my eyes. "Listen, Beck. It's my thing to deal with, okay? Don't make a big deal out of it. I'm fine. It's nothing I can't handle."

"I just don't understand. Why don't you tell someone?"

His green eyes filled with hurt and anger. "Won't do any good. Tried once, and it only caused problems, not just for me, but for everyone who found out. It's not worth it. As soon as I graduate in two years, I'm gone, and I'm not coming back. I'm gonna play football at either MSU, U of M, or Nebraska, and then I'll go pro. I won't ever need shit from my old man."

"I-I-I…*ugh*." I took a deep breath and focused. "I don't know what to say, Jason. It's wrong."

"Nothing to say. Nothing to say, nothing to do." His voice grew intense. "You're the only person except Kyle who knows, okay? You can't say anything, Becca. Promise me. *Promise* me!"

My head was spinning, my heart aching for the boy I was growing to like very, very much. "Jason… someone should know. He can't do that to you. He's your father, for fuck's sake. He should protect you, not hurt you! It's a-a-aw-aw-awful." I felt rage rising up like bile in my throat, images whirling in my head, images of Jason in a corner, cringing away from a shadowy giant with huge fists.

"Does your dad protect you?"

"He's overprotecting and overzealous," I said, not sure why I was defending my father when I spent so much time vilifying him in my own head. "He's unreasoning and hard-headed and stubborn and pushes me to rebellion with his ridiculous rules. But he loves me, in his own way. He'd never hurt me. He just wants me to be the best that I can be. He's overcompensating because of all the trouble Ben gets in."

"And my dad has a world of anger and demons hidden away in his soul." Jason's voice was surprisingly soft, his words poetic. "He got injured playing his first pro game, and it ended his career. The only thing he ever wanted to do was play pro ball, and he couldn't anymore. He had to go crawling back to his parents here in Michigan, and his dad was worse on him than Dad is on me. He ended up joining the police force and moved up pretty fast, but then the Gulf War happened and he saw his chance to be something. He joined the Army and did two tours in Iraq. He was a grunt with no college degree or training. He saw some heavy shit, Becca. Some really awful shit. He *did* some really awful shit, all on Uncle Sam's orders. It…scarred him, on the inside. He has his reasons, too, is my point. Doesn't make it okay."

I was silent for a long time, listening to a different song on the radio and watching the salt-sprinkle of stars across the black-cloth sky. "How do you know so much about what your dad went through?"

Jason answered around a mouthful of chip. "He drinks a lot. When he's had enough, sometimes he talks to me instead of laying into me. Tells me stories like I was one of his buddies from his unit." He swallowed and stared up at the sky. "I hate those sto-ries. Rather get hit."

I shivered then, as a gust of wind blew and cut through my sweater. Jason planted his palms on the lip of the truck bed and hefted himself out to the ground, leaned into the truck, and snagged his sweatshirt. I watched him hesitate, then grab his camera bag. He jumped back into the bed, climbing on the rear tire, and tucked his sweatshirt around my shoulders. It was heavy, warm, and smelled exactly like Jason.

He lifted the camera bag and then glanced at me, a smirk on his face. "You wanted to see a photograph I took?" I nodded eagerly. "Then you gotta trade me. I'll show you one of my photos if you show me some-thing you wrote."

I swallowed hard. "That's—that's...I'm not sure. I've never showed anyone my writing. No one. It's my journal."

Jason nodded, gesturing with the bag. "That's how my photos are for me. They're private. Only for me, because I enjoy it. No one even knows I do it, not even Kyle. It's like a journal for me, too. I'm no good with words, so I use pictures instead."

"Why would you keep something like that a secret?" I asked. "It's not like it's embarrassing. It's cool. It's artistic."

His face darkened. "You don't know my dad. I told you, he's not a nice guy. For one thing, I'm only allowed to do schoolwork and football. Working out, homework, practice, that's it. He's drunk or passed out now, so he doesn't care what I do or where I am as long as I don't get arrested and make a big spectacle or some shit. He's the captain of the police force, so I have to be careful. He won't bail me out, won't get me off the hook. He'll kick the shit out of me if I ever so much as get stopped by one of his men. They're scared of him, too, so they won't dare go against him, either."

"What's that got to do with photography? It's just pictures."

He unwrapped the second ham sandwich and another can of Coke. "Well, that's the second part. Anything that even remotely smacks of art is for fags. His word, not mine. On top of being a plain mean-ass drunk, he's a bigot. Hates pretty much anyone who's not him. If he even knew I had a camera, he'd put me in the fuckin' hospital. Musical instrument? No way. Painting? *Hell* no. I love taking photos, though. I love capturing something in the lens and making something else totally different from it."

He opened his bag and lifted the camera from it, turned it on, and touched a few buttons so the display showed his previously taken photos. He scrolled through them a ways, then turned it to me.

I took the camera gingerly, afraid of handling something that was so important to him, and so hideously expensive. The photograph he'd shown me was breathtaking. It was of a bumblebee, taken in the act of the bee landing on a daisy. It was from up close, so close you could see the wings blurring and the individual hairs on the fat yellow and black body. The sunlight was refracted off the insect's bulbous, multi-faceted eyes, the daisy sharp and bright yellow, the sky a blue blur beyond. It was like something out of *National Geographic*, stunning in its clarity and focus and use of color. The bumblebee looked like an alien creature, made mammoth and impossible.

"Jason...oh, my god. This is incredible. You could sell this to a magazine, I swear to god." I breathed in and examined the photo again, amazed at the way he'd framed it with the flower in the center, taking most of the space, with the bee near the top, caught in the act of hovering downward.

He grinned, and seemed oddly shy for the first time since I'd known him. "Thanks. I got stung about six times trying to get that shot. There were a bunch of big, fat bees flying around a field." He pointed out beyond the tree, to the field beneath us. "Right out there, actually. There must have been a nest or something. Anyway, I followed these bees around for hours, taking picture after picture. I must have taken a couple hundred before I got that one."

"Can I see some more?" I asked, excited now.

He lifted an eyebrow at me. "Nuh-uh. Now it's your turn."

I felt my hands trembling. I knew if I spoke it would come out all jittery and full of blocks, so I just sucked in a breath, reached into my purse, and pulled out my journal. It was a spiral-bound, unlined sketch pad, a piece of brown paper Meijer bag cut out and wrapped around the outside covers. On the front cover, I'd used a Sharpie to copy an inscription of a poem in Arabic:

"What's that say?" Jason asked.

لست وحيدا أبدا
كلّ مافي الأمر
انني
صرت رفيقا لوحدتي

I hesitated, breathing several times and reciting the words in my mind before I said them out loud. "It says, 'I am not alone—the truth is I befriended my loneliness.'" I traced the lines with my forefinger before opening the cover and flipping a few pages idly, looking for the perfect poem to show Jason. "It's by an Arab poet named Abboud al Jabiri. It's actually part of a longer poem, but that's the part I like the most."

"Was he from, like, a long time ago?"

I shook my head. "No, he's alive and living in Jordan, still writing. My mom is a pediatrician, but she's always loved poetry. On top of her medical degree, she has a second minor in Arabic poetry. She kind of turned me on to it, I guess."

"That's pretty cool," Jason said. "So what's your dad do?"

"He's in real estate. He owns several industrial properties, plus he does commercial real estate sales." I glanced at him as I chewed and swallowed. "What about you? You told me about your dad. What about your mom?"

He shrugged. "She doesn't do shit. Works in a dental office three days a week, making copies and shit. Other than that, hides in her room gluing paper cut-outs into a book."

I scrunched up my face, trying to figure out what he meant. "Scrapbooking?"

He shrugged. "Yeah, whatever. Something like that. She's got a 'craft room.'" He made air quotes around the phrase. "She spends all her time in there. Sleeps there, except when Dad makes her sleep with him for...you know. Mainly, she avoids both of us. Me because I take Dad's shit instead of her, and him because he's an asshole."

"What do you mean, you take his shit instead of her?"

He snapped a chip between his fingers and ate both halves. "He used to beat on her, back till I was, like, three or four. Once I got old enough, I started jumping in. I hated seeing Mom cry, you know? She stood up for herself for a while. I remember that. Then she just got tired. Gave up. Let him do whatever he wanted, to me, to her. He wants the conflict, you know? He wants the fight. I started giving him that so he'd leave her alone, and now she sorta resents me for it, I think. Don't know why, since I'm the one getting my ass beat instead of her. Whatever. Stupid bitch." The blasé tone in his voice was awful in its utter apathy.

"Jason! She's still your mother!" I couldn't keep it from coming out.

His eyes blazed green fire, but his voice never rose. "They may have biologically created me, Becca, but they're not parents." He calmed and looked away, his voice growing thoughtful. "Parents love and protect. They shelter, they nurture. All that loving shit that I never got. My old man? He wasn't loved, and he never figured out how to break the cycle. My mom has just spent so long being the victim that she doesn't care anymore, so I get the brunt of his bullshit."

I wasn't sure what to say for a long time. Eventually, I thought of something. "Do you think you can break the cycle, Jason?"

Jason stared down between his knees, crumbling chips into dust. "I *have* to, Becca. I *will*. My grandpa was an asshole, and I'm pretty sure his dad was, too." His voice dropped to a whisper. "I'm scared it's, like, a hereditary thing. What if I can't be different? What if I'm just…genetically hard-wired to be an asshole like my old man?"

I took his hands in mine. "I don't believe that. You already *are* different, Jason. We can choose who we want to be."

"I hope so." He seemed so sad suddenly, and I wanted to find a way to cheer him up, change the subject, but I couldn't think of anything.

We had finished the sandwiches and were munching on chips as we talked, each of us having had two cans of soda. I remembered the bottle in my backpack and reached through the back window to grab the backpack, opened it, and pulled out the bottle. I set it on the blanket between us. Jason stared at it as if it were a venomous snake.

"Where'd you get that?" he asked in the same too-calm voice he'd used before.

"My brother gave it to me. He thought we should party it up, I guess. I don't know. I don't really drink much, but I figured what the hell, right?" I tried to sound casual, but I don't think I succeeded.

"I'm not sure I can drink that," Jason said, in almost a whisper. "That's…that's what my dad drinks. It's… the only way I've ever seen him after seven or eight at night, my whole life. Him, sitting in his leather armchair in front of *SVU* and *Castle* and *Game of Thrones*, and always with that mother*fucking* square bottle on the sidetable, a glass beside him. I watch, every night, as that bottle slowly empties, one glass at a time, until he's meaner than a fucking viper, and twice as dangerous."

His eyes were far away as he spoke, and I sat still and silent, listening intently.

"I don't have anything against drinking. Not everyone is like him. *I'm* not like him, when I drink. I just…I cannot, *will* not ever touch that shit. Ever." Jason stared at the bottle as if it were his father, raw hatred in his eyes. "Please put it away. I have some beer in the cooler, if you want to drink."

I moved quickly, shoving the bottle into the backpack and zipping it closed. "I'm sorry, Jason. I-I didn't n-n-nnn-know." So much for changing the subject.

His hands wrapped around my arms and pulled me closer to him, until our knees overlapped, tangled. "Of course you didn't. Don't be upset. Not for me."

"But I *am* upset for you. You shouldn't have to go through that."

He twisted my shoulders, and I turned in place until my spine was nestled against his chest. Jason leaned back against the cab and wrapped his arms around my stomach beneath my breasts, his knees drawn up next to my sides. I rested my arms on his knees and tilted my head back to lay it against his shoulder, and suddenly, between one breath and the next, I was completely contented. I felt safe. I could feel his heart thumping faintly, and his breath soughed gently onto my nape. I was entirely too aware of his body then, of his hands so close to my breasts, his mouth which I could twist in place and kiss, if I were bold enough, his strong arms caging me perfectly. My heart hammered, and I had to focus on stillness so I didn't panic. I wanted more, more touch, more of his heat, more of his strength. His nearness was intoxicating, and forbidden. I'd sneaked out of my house in the middle of the night, and now I was wrapped in the embrace of a boy. A man? I wasn't sure. Was he a man yet? Was I woman, or a girl? We were stuck somewhere in between. Thoughts like these floated through my head, demanding answers but receiving none, because his proximity and his hardness were intoxicating.

We breathed together in the cool night air, the sky a silver-bathed black above us. We didn't need to speak, and that was an amazing thing in itself. The only sounds were our breathing and the wind rustling in the leaves, and a song playing from the radio, fading into a female DJ's voice announcing the next song: "All right, that was Montgomery Gentry, going back a ways for that one. This next song is for all you late night lovers out there. It's Gloriana, with '(Kissed You) Goodnight.'"

My heartbeat ratcheted up to a frantic patter as I listened to the words of the song, sung sweetly and inciting romance between us in the darkness and the cold of a stolen midnight date. I turned my head, leaned slightly sideways so my shoulder nudged the edge of the truck bed. Jason's eyes were darkest green, glittering in the starlight and the pale luminous moon glow. I felt his heart pounding against his ribs and my side, and I knew he was going to kiss me then. I waited, breath bated, eyes locked on his, my hands clutching his knees for courage. I wasn't afraid to kiss him; no, I was afraid I would be too impatient and kiss him first. Hunger for a second kiss was like desperation in my blood, thundering in my muscles and my heart and firing in my brain.

"Is this okay?" he asked, his voice a soft whisper into the quiet.

I smiled up at him. "Shut up and k-k-k…" I trailed off and closed my eyes, let the word float up and out, "…kiss me already."

He closed the distance eagerly, covering my mouth with his, and the thunder of our hearts was a syncopated crash of need and nerves. I lost myself, and gloried in the welter of touch and taste—soft and wet and hot, soda and salt—and the soaring sound of my pulse in my ears, and music in the spaces between lip-touches—*and I kissed you…goodnight.*

When we pulled apart, Jason's eyes devoured mine. "Kissing you is…god, it's amazing."

"Then do it again." I was amazed by my boldness.

So was he, but he lowered his lips to mine and kissed me again, deeper this time, mouths moving and tongues hesitantly touching and drifting. His palms were splayed on my stomach, and one drifted up my side, stopping at the lower swell of one breast. I lifted my hand and curled it around the back of his head, a move I'd seen in a movie, and knew then the power of my touch, the beauty of a kiss, the wonder of this intimacy. When my fingers caressed the buzzed hair above his nape, he kissed me harder, as if my hand there fueled the fire of his desire. Then his hand slid up just slightly, and his fingers were brushing the side of my breast, a hesitant touch, a quest, a question. I didn't know the answer, the right response. I wanted more. I did. But…was it okay? Was that wrong? Was it too much, too soon? I liked the way his fingers felt, teasing the edge of propriety, the borderline of modesty. Did I dare encourage him to go further?

He took my hesitation for a demurral, and his hand slid upward, away from temptation. I felt the loss of his touch on my breast like a pang of regret, and covered his hand with mine, stopping it near my underarm. Our kiss paused, and our eyes met. His green orbs searched mine, and then widened as I guided his hand down. His sweatshirt had fallen away as I leaned back into him, and his hand drifted up over the swell of my breast. Even through my sweater and my shirt and my bra, I felt the heat of his hand, the rough power in his touch, the gentility in the way he caressed me. No one had ever touched my breast before, and the thrill of it was like a drug in my system.

My sweater was a button-up cardigan, and I reached up to flick open the first button, and then guided his hand across my body underneath the sweater to my opposite breast. His fingers curled around the weight of my breast, testing, touching, hesitant yet eager. I felt so bold, so daring, so…the word that floated to mind was *naughty*, as childish as that word seemed. I shouldn't be letting him touch me like this, much less encouraging it. But it was so thrilling, so intoxicating. I felt my pulse crashing as he explored my breast through two layers of cotton. I felt adult and womanly and worldly as he kneaded me, caressed me, kissed me.

After an amount of time I couldn't begin to measure, we pulled away, and his hand fell from my breast back to my stomach, closer to my hip this time.

"You never read me a poem," he whispered.

My face heated. "You really want to hear one?" He nodded. "You won't laugh?"

"Not unless it's supposed to be funny."

"I don't write funny poems," I said, gathering my courage. "But you can't tell anyone, and you can't tease me about this."

He frowned. "Would you tease me about my photography?"

I shook my head. "Never."

"Then why would I tease you about writing poetry?"

I dug my notebook out of my purse and flipped through the pages, searching for the right one to read him. I found the perfect one, one that spoke to my current feelings, in a way.

I knew I'd never be able to read it out loud without embarrassing myself, so I handed him the notebook and let him read it himself. I could see the words in my mind's eye, feel them as he read them.

GHOSTKISS

You're not here, and I'm not there
I'm a girl, alone in her room
And you're a myth
A possible future
A ghost of my desires to come
I breathe slowly and close my eyes
Tilt my face to the ceiling
And wait for the kiss
Of ghostly lips on flesh
Dream mouth on real
Fantasy tongue tasting mine
Tantalizing and imagined
Because I wonder
What a kiss is
How lips taste
How a tongue feels
Will I know what to do
Without being shown?
A more worrisome question arises
One unique to me:
Can you stutter, in a kiss?
Can you fumble
In the throes of desire?

You're just a ghost
A neverknown fraction of what-if
And you cannot teach me what I wish to know
Until you become real
*And kiss me and kiss me an*d kiss me

Jason glanced at me, then back at the page, amazement in his eyes. "God, Becca. That's...I don't even have words. Magical. That's not just poetry, that's word magic." He looked back at my notebook and seemed to be rereading. "How do you know how to make the perfect words go together? I know all these words on their own, but...but I could never put them all together like this, into a poem."

I ducked my head, heat on my cheeks. "Thanks. I just...the words just come out. I think I write poetry because it's a way for me to be coherent. Eloquent. I have to work to speak clearly. Every single sentence I speak takes effort to not stutter. Poetry? It's just effort-less." All the while he'd been talking about my poetry, I'd been scripting that speech, planning it out, forming the words in my head and practicing them. He started to flip the page, but I took the notebook from him, gently but firmly. "I'm sorry, but I'm not ready to let you just...peruse my private thoughts. Reading that is like reading my mind. I'm just—just—just n-not ready for that y-y-yet." I heaved in a deep breath to slow myself down.

He smiled reassuringly, and showed not one iota of impatience or embarrassment at my stupid stutters and blocks. "It's fine, Becca. I understand completely. Thanks for sharing that with me."

"You showed me yours, so it's only fair I show you mine." I grinned to play up the double entendre.

Jason smirked. "True. They do say that turnabout is fair play." His hand rose up my side again, inching closer, daring higher.

"Tit for...tat..." I could barely breathe as he neared my breast. I wanted his hand there again.

He cupped me through my sweater, and I could breathe again. Then, as if physically tearing himself away, he moved his hand and rested it on my thigh, and my pulse slowly returned to normal. "We should probably go," he whispered.

"Yeah, probably."

"I don't want to, though." He buried his face in my hair and sniffed. "You smell good."

I laughed. "Thanks? I don't want to go, either. I like it here. I can see why this is your favorite spot."

"You should see it in the daytime, when the sun is out. All the way out there," he waved toward the front of the truck, where the hill fell away into an open field, "is all flowers. It's beautiful."

"You should bring me here during the day sometime, then."

He nodded. "I will." He grinned at me, and I was reminded, apropos of nothing but his smile, how beautiful he really was, his face all hard lines and strong curves and perfect angles, and such green, green eyes. "And anyway, this isn't my favorite spot anymore."

I wrinkled my brow in confusion, although I had an idea what he was going to say. "It's not?"

He shook his head and tightened his grip on me. "This is. You, here, with me. In my arms."

I smiled at him, unable to formulate a response other than to burrow closer to him.

After a few more minutes, we reluctantly cleaned up our midnight picnic, and I slid off the back of the truck while Jason bungeed the cooler in place again. I settled in the passenger seat of his truck, cranking the volume up on a fast-paced song with a lot of honky-tonk to it. I bounced in my seat, enjoying the fun, light-hearted music and the feeling of happiness welling up so hot and potent inside me.

Jason drove me home, stopping at the entrance again. "I wish I could just take you home. Walk you to your door and kiss you goodnight."

"Maybe someday," I said. "I don't like it, either. You know it's not that I'm embarrassed by you or anything, right? If I didn't know for a fact Father would ground me for life and actually lock me in my room at night, I'd tell him about us. Introduce you."

He shrugged. "I know. Just be careful getting home, okay? I'll wait until you're in your room. Text me when you're safe, okay?"

I opened the truck door, but his hand latched around my wrist and drew me back. He pulled me closer and closer, shoved the console up and out of the way, the Mountain Dew bottle tumbling to the floor. I wrapped my arms around his neck, stuffed my fingers into the stiff, soft spikes of his hair, let myself lead in to the kiss.

When I was breathless and dizzy, I pulled away.

"God, Becca. Kissing you is...it's seriously the best thing ever."

I touched my lips, knowing they were swollen. "It's dangerous, I think."

"What is?" Jason asked.

"You and me kissing."

"Why?"

I met his eyes, let him see all my roiling emotions. "Because I never want to stop. I could kiss you until I suffocate."

He nodded. "Me, too." He let go of my wrist, trailed his fingers along my cheekbone and down my jaw. "You're beautiful, Becca. So beautiful."

I shook my head at him. "You're ridiculous. But thank you."

He frowned at me as I slid to the ground and held the door in preparation to shut it. "Why am I ridiculous?"

I shrugged, uncomfortable with discussing my insecurities. "You just are. It's sweet of you to compliment me, though."

"It's not a compliment. It's the truth." His gaze shifted a bit, some kind of awareness sneaking into his expression. "Wait. You're not insecure about yourself, are you?"

I twisted a curl around my finger and focused on not stuttering. "I'm pretty sure every girl on the planet is insecure about something, Jason. Some just hide it better than others."

"What could you possibly have to be insecure about?"

I stared at him, boggled. "What could I—? I'm-I'm—I stutter, for one thing, in c-c-case you haven't n-noticed. It's embarrassing. I'm the shortest girl in our class, for another. Plus, I've got hips a mile wide, and I'm freaking top-heavy to boot." I batted at my loose mop of springy curls. "And my hair looks like I sss-stuck a pair of scissors in a power outlet."

Jason glared at me as if I'd insulted him instead of myself. He shoved his door open angrily, left it wide with the bell dinging, crossed in front of the headlight, and stalked toward me. I wasn't afraid of him, per se, but the intense, determined look in his eyes and the purposeful gait of his walk intimidated me. I backed away from him, stumbling as the truck door closed behind me. He pinned me against the truck with his body, and his hands landed on the upper bell of my hips.

"You're not allowed to talk about yourself like that, Becca. You understand me?" His eyes darkened. "You're beautiful. You're sexy. You're so hot it takes my breath away. I don't understand how I could have ever seen anyone else before now. Your hips are perfect, and to a guy, 'top-heavy' is a good thing, and you are top-heavy in the best possible way. You have an amazing body, Becca. A-*maze*-ing. And your stutter? It's just part of who you are to me. It doesn't bother me."

I buried my face against his chest, sure he was just mollifying me. "And my hair?"

He tangled his fingers in my hair, burrowing through the curls as if he was scooping up handfuls of gold coins and letting them run through his fingers. Then he twined his fingers through a hank of curls and tugged my head back, gently but inexorably, so I was forced to look at him.

"I love your hair."

He said the "L" word. About my hair, but he said it.

And then he kissed me. My toes curled in my pastel-purple Keds. Jesus God, the boy could kiss.

He let me go after that, and watched me disappear into the trees. I heard the low rumble of his idling engine and saw as I glanced behind me the pale yellow glow of his headlights. I stood at the bottom of the drainpipe, staring at Ben's window two floors up. There was no way in hell I'd make it up. Getting down was a matter of holding on and letting gravity do its thing. I took a deep breath and focused on the first handhold, nailed through the siding to whatever was beneath it. I grabbed it in both hands and pulled with all my strength. I didn't even get off the ground.

I pulled, jumped, strained, cursed, and only managed to get myself sweaty. That was when I realized I was still wearing Jason's hoodie.

My phone buzzed in my purse at that moment. I pulled it out and read Jason's text: Been a few minutes. You back in your room yet?

I typed my response without thinking about it: No. I climbed down a drainpipe and can't make it back up. Quit laughing IT'S NOT FUNNY.

I was still waiting for Jason's text back and trying to figure out how I was going to get in when I heard a stick snap behind me. I whirled to see Jason gliding toward me from between the trees. He came to stand next to me and stared up the drainpipe that was my current nemesis.

"That could be a problem. I think *I'd* have trouble scaling that." He put his hand on the pipe and wiggled it, testing it, nodding as if satisfied by its sturdiness. "I could give you a boost?"

"I don't know. Then I'd be stuck halfway up. I'm just not strong enough to climb up."

"Do you have a house key?" Jason asked.

"Well, yeah, but Father sets the alarm at night, and I don't know the code."

"Then how'd you get out without it going off? Alarm systems usually include windows."

I was stumped. "I don't know. I didn't consider that. Maybe Ben disabled his window somehow."

"This is Ben's window?"

"Yeah. He's the one who put those pieces of wood there as hand- and footholds."

Jason examined the pipe again. "Oh, I didn't see those at first. Clever." He grinned at me. "Ben must sneak out a lot then, huh?"

I chuckled. "Yeah, he does."

"So how does he get back in?"

I stared at Jason. "Um? I have no clue. I didn't think about that, either. I'm not very experienced at this whole delinquency thing."

"I guess not," Jason said, smirking at me. "I'm a bad influence on you, clearly."

"Yeah, maybe a little," I admitted. "But I like it. I feel free. This was fun. Now, if only I could get back in."

"Does your brother have a cell phone? Could you text him and see if he could help you?" He glanced back at the pipe once more, as if trying to work out some way to get me up it. "I still think you could do it if I gave you a boost."

"You just want an excuse to touch my ass." I went to the pipe and grabbed the handhold a few feet above my head, stretching up on my tiptoes to do so.

Jason sidled up behind me, and my breath caught as his hands grazed over the taut curve of my ass in my jeans. "Do I need an excuse?"

I twisted my head around to meet his gaze. "Yes, you do. We're not at the 'grope Becca's ass whenever you want' stage yet, buster, so hands off." I tried to keep a serious face, but couldn't.

He rested his hands on the swell of my hips, faking a pout. "Fine. Be that way. Deny me the joy of your glorious backside, then."

I gave him a disbelieving look. "Glorious? You really think it's glorious?"

He took this as an invitation, which I guess it was, in a way, to resume touching me on the object in question. "Hmmm. Let me see." He smoothed his hands over my ass, exploring the expanse of it over the denim. "Yep. That's for sure the right word. You, my dear, have a glorious ass."

I felt myself blushing, but I didn't stop his exploration. "I'm glad you think so."

His voice grew serious, and his hands resumed their place at my hips. "Am I…pushing you too fast?"

I leaned back against him. "Yes. No. I don't know. I like it—I like it all. I like letting you touch me, but part of me says you shouldn't. But that's my parents' über-conservative upbringing speaking, I think. I like kissing you. I like sneaking out with you." I sighed. "I've never done anything daring, anything against the rules. I've been *good* my whole life. I like being a little bad with you."

Jason nodded. "Just—I don't ever want to pressure you into anything. I just…I always want more of you. I feel greedy, in a way. I just want to kiss you more, and touch you more. Like you said, it's dangerous. I feel like you're a drug, and I'm getting addicted to you." He pulled my hair away from my jawline and my ear, and pressed a kiss to my skin where jaw met earlobe. "We should get you up there."

He knelt down and made a cradle with his laced-to-gether hands. I hesitated, then put my foot in his hand

and held on to his shoulder with one hand and the drainpipe with the other. Jason gave a whispered count to three and then lifted me up. I had to stifle a squeal as I was rocketed into the air. I bypassed the first hand-hold, balancing precariously with one foot in his hand.

"Stand on my shoulders," Jason instructed. I shifted my weight carefully, holding on to the drain-pipe with both hands, and then found myself standing on Jason's shoulders. The window was closer now, but still far away.

"I'm still not close enough," I said. "The other hold is still a few feet farther up."

Jason moved beneath me, widening his stance. He grabbed hold of my ankles and glanced up at me. "Okay, you're gonna stand on my hands."

"Are you crazy? You can't hold my weight with just your arms! I'll break you in half!"

Jason snorted. "You're a freaking feather, here. Quit arguing and do it. I'll be fine. I won't let you fall. I promise." He lifted one of my ankles and slid his flattened palm under my foot, then straightened his arm so my leg was bent double beneath me. "Now stand up on that foot and then lift the other as soon as you can. Hold on to the pipe for balance. If you feel yourself falling, let it happen. I swear to you I'll catch you."

I swallowed hard, felt my breathing quicken and my heartbeat churn into a pounding frenzy. "I'm scared, Jason."

"I've got you. I won't let anything happen. I promise. Now, on three. Ready? One...two...three!" On three, I pushed up off his shoulders, felt his arms stiffen beneath me, and then my other leg was straightening and his hand was there beneath my foot and I was standing on his hands, twelve feet or so above the ground.

My heart was thudding in my chest, blood pulsing in my ears. I wobbled, and Jason adjusted, and then I was steady. I had the pipe in hand, and then there was the foothold right there at belly level. I grabbed the pipe as far above my head as I could and pulled with all my might, scrabbling at the wall to gain purchase. I felt a moment of panic when Jason's hands fell away and I was on my own, clinging to the wall. Then, miraculously, my feet found the wooden bar and I was slowly, shakily, rising to my feet.

"Holy shit," I breathed. I looked down at Jason, which was a mistake. "Holy sh-shit! I did it!"

"I knew you could, Beck. Now, just a bit farther. Open the window?"

I pushed at it, but only got it open a few inches. "It's stuck." I tapped on the glass with a fingernail, and then within a few moments Ben's face was at the window.

He seemed shocked, half-asleep, just standing there, blinking at me in confusion, and then he sprang into action. He pulled the window open and grabbed me under my arms and tugged me through the window. "Damn, Becca. You scared the blue shitting Jesus out of me."

I tumbled to the thick-pile carpeting face first, feet still hanging out the window with my supposedly glorious ass sticking in the air. I righted myself and stuck my head out the window, waving to Jason. He waggled his phone in the air at me, mouthing *call me* before vanishing into the trees.

I turned back to Ben. "Did you just say 'blue shitting Jesus'?"

He grinned at me. "Yep. Turns out Jesus shits blue. Who knew?" He shrugged as if it was a great secret demystified.

I laughed and shoved him playfully. "Why the hell didn't you tell me it was so hard to climb back up?"

He shrugged. "Guess it didn't occur to me. It doesn't seem hard to me anymore. But then, I've been doing it for a while."

"I don't think I'd have been able to get back in without Jason's help," I said.

"Have fun?"

I nodded, not wanting to spoil the wonder of my night by talking about it with my stoner brother. "It was great. I'm beat, though, gonna go to bed." I tossed Ben's backpack on his bed. "Turns out we didn't drink any of it. We had plenty of fun without it."

Ben fished the bottle out of the bag, then twisted the cap off and took a long slug, swallowing without so much as a wince. "More for me." He tossed the backpack on the ground, lay back on the bed, and took another long slug. "'Night, Beck."

I hesitated at the door, watching him as he took a third drink, by which point the bottle was emptied past the neck, nearly to the top of the label. "Are you sure you should—"

"'Night, Beck." He repeated it more forcefully, clearly closing the topic of his drinking.

I left, my gut heavy with worry. He'd shifted from happy to upset so fast, and he'd downed nearly a quarter of a fifth of whiskey within minutes, acting as if he'd done it frequently. By the time I'd tiptoed to my bedroom, stripped down to T-shirt and panties, and snuggled into my bed, I'd forgotten Ben. I had Jason on the brain, his hands skimming my hips, his lips touching mine, devouring mine.

My last thought was how I'd manage to sneak out to see him as often as I'd want to.

Five: Fight Night
Jason
The following Monday

BECCA HAD TEXTED ME A FEW TIMES over the weekend, but we hadn't managed to see each other. I'd asked, but she'd claimed her dad was acting suspicious so she had to lie low. As for me, weekends were the worst. Dad usually had weekends off unless something big came up, which meant I had to keep busy to stay away from him. Usually I stayed in my room, studying, or in the basement working out. This weekend, I didn't manage to keep out of his way quite enough. He'd tied on a real bender Sunday, mixing in a case of beer with his two fifths of Jack. I'd worked out, done my homework, and had tried sneaking into the kitchen for some lunch. Bad plan. I was pretty sure he'd bruised a few ribs and loosened a tooth, but I'd fought him off enough that he'd gone back to his booze and *Band of Brothers* marathon.

Why he tortured himself with war movies, I'd never figured out, but he was always meanest when he was in those moods. I'd taken my lunch and eaten it in my room. Dinner hadn't happened till after one-thirty in the morning after he was passed out.

I wasn't in the greatest mood by the time school came around Monday morning. I'd had my kisses with Becca running through my mind all weekend, and that was all that had gotten me through those days. But when I saw her between classes, she'd barely given me a smile and hurried on her way. I'd stewed on that the rest of the afternoon, wondering if she was regretting us already.

She found me at my locker again before class. "Sorry I couldn't get out to see you this weekend," she said, sliding up next to my side.

I shrugged. "Are you okay?"

She frowned. "Yeah, why?"

"You barely even looked at me when I saw you between classes earlier."

"I'm just always stressed right then. I've got classes on complete opposite sides of the school, and I've got to go through A hallway, which is a traffic jam, so I'm always running just to be there on time."

I felt better. "Oh. That makes sense."

She tilted her head at me, her frown deepening. "Why? What did you think? That I was ignoring you?" I just shrugged again, knowing it was stupid at that point. "Hey, what's up? You seem like you're in a bad mood. Is it me?"

I slammed the locker closed and wrapped my hand around hers. "I'm fine."

"Bullshit."

I gaped at her. "Becca, it's fine, really—"

She stopped and pushed me against a locker, heedless of the crowds still exiting the building. "Jason. Talk."

I felt her body against mine, her breasts crushed between us and her hips against mine, and I knew I couldn't lie to her. "I just had a hard weekend. Dad was really drunk, and he was watching war movies. He's... it's never good when he's in that kind of mood." I was barely whispering. I'd rather do a billion down-ups than talk about that shit. "I'm fine."

Becca's eyes filled with anger and hurt. "Jason... god. I'm sorry. I—"

I cut her off. "Listen, don't make this your problem. It's not. It's just the shit I got handed. I can deal. I'm fine. Just don't take it personally if I'm sometimes in a shitty mood, okay? Just...smile for me, and maybe kiss me, and I'll be fine."

Becca didn't hesitate, not even a single heartbeat. She pressed her lips to mine and smiled, and the feel of her mouth curving against mine in a smiling kiss lifted the cloud from my head, the weight from my shoulders, lessened the pain in my ribs and the hurt in my heart. I kissed her back, lost myself in her. She let me slide my hands on her hips, pull her closer, kiss her harder, and the silence extended around us as the building emptied. I kissed her, and I thought of that incredible poem she wrote about ghosts kissing her, and I tried my damnedest to kiss her so she knew I was real, I wasn't a ghost anymore. It may have been arrogant or self-centered, but I was convinced that poem was about me; she just didn't know it when she wrote it.

"All right, you two, knock it off. Don't you have practice, Mr. Dorsey?" Mr. Hansen, the biology teacher, barked out as he passed, a handful of goggles hanging from his fingers. He didn't slow down or wait to make sure we split apart, which we didn't.

Becca giggled and rested her forehead on my chest. "We just got busted for PDA. We're *that* couple now, huh?"

"Which couple?" I asked, thrilled that she thought of us as a couple.

"The kind that makes out in the hallways and gets yelled at for it." She had her arms around my neck, and she brushed a finger along my lip where a faint cut was still visible.

I bit her finger gently, and she laughed outright, then burrowed closer and kissed me again. "You'd better go," she said when we pulled away once more. "I wouldn't want to be a bad influence on you."

I laughed, and marveled that she was able to lift my mood within minutes, with just a few words and couple kisses. "Yeah, I should go. Coach'll be pissed if I'm late again."

She pushed away from me, hiked the straps of her backpack higher up her shoulders. "I'll call you. I'll try to get out to see you tonight, if I can."

Practice was a blur. I went hard, that much I knew. My body was on fire, it felt, lit by Becca's kiss. I barely felt the tackles, barely felt the burn in my legs as I strained for the yards. I got home, made dinner, and ate mine as fast as I could, leaving some covered for Dad. Mom sat opposite me, eating with me, quiet as always. She was stick-thin, with lank, long blonde hair usually pulled back in a messy ponytail. I got my eyes from her, I realized, bright green, startling in their vividness. Hers were tired and vacant and somehow sad, though. I sat scarfing the chicken cacciatore I'd made, idly running through things I could do with Becca if she was able to see me, and then I remembered Becca's questions about my mom, and it made me realize I knew nothing about her.

I stopped eating and stared at my mom, wondering.

"What?" Her voice was quiet, scratchy with disuse. "I got something on my face?" She wiped at her mouth.

I shook my head. "I just…how'd you end up with Dad?"

Mom's fork stopped halfway to her mouth. "How'd I what?" She peered at me as if I'd sprouted horns. "Why?"

I shrugged. "Just curious. Realized I never really knew."

"What brought this on?" I shrugged again. Mom finished her bite, washed it down with iced tea. She leaned back in her chair and stared out the window. "He was a patient. He'd just come back from his first tour in Iraq. Even in civvies, he was every inch a soldier. Wore a ball cap, you know the one, the old white Tigers hat? He had that one on, and when he saw me, he took it off and held it in front of himself, standing at attention like I was a general or something."

Her face changed in the grip of that memory, softening, livening. I realized then, for the first time, that she must have been pretty at some point. Odd.

"He was handsome then. Tall, big muscles. Seemed nice. I didn't know anything about war or what it'd be like when he came back. We dated for the two months he had between tours, and it got serious, I guess. I told him I'd write, told him I'd wait. I did." She shifted her glance down to her left hand, to the small diamond on a thin gold band. The softness and liveliness faded, and suddenly she was more the Mom I knew, tired, reserved. "Didn't realize he'd turn into… what he is now. It was gradual, not all at once. Started with a burnt dinner here, a stupid question or a bad day or a bad dream. PTSD, only he never did anything about it, never got help. Just got mean."

I wasn't sure what to say. "Did you love him?"

"Did I love him?" She twisted the diamond around her finger, not looking at me. "Maybe. I don't know. Hard to say, I guess. I mean, it wasn't like in those romance movies." She glanced up at me then, a sly look on her face, the most direct emotion I'd seen in years. "You in love with a girl, Jason?"

I pushed the bits of chicken around on my plate. "There's a girl. Not sure if it's love, but I like her a lot." I wasn't sure why I was telling her this, where this was coming from.

She was quiet for a while. "Well, just be careful, I guess. It can be tricky." She met my eyes. "Wish I could meet her, but I'd understand why you wouldn't want to bring her around here."

I looked away. "Yeah. That's not a great idea. Dad wouldn't understand."

"She know? About your dad?"

I shifted uncomfortably, wishing I was in my truck, away from all this, wishing I'd never opened this up. "Yeah."

"She gonna tell?" Mom's voice was soft, but sharp.

I shook my head. "Probably not."

Mom didn't respond to that. She got up and cleared her plate, finished her tea and set the glass in the sink, then spoke while staring out the window over the sink. "I'm sorry you were born into this, Jason. You're a good kid."

I had no idea what to say.

"Did you ever think about leaving?" The question popped out unbidden.

Mom shook her head. "Wouldn't do any good. You know how he is. Nowhere to go, anyway. I've never lived anywhere but here, wouldn't know where to go, especially with a little boy to take care of." She flipped her ponytail back over her shoulder with a hand, glanced at me. "Now you're almost grown. You'll be gone soon, and all this will be a bad memory."

"You'll stay when I'm gone?"

"Of course," she said, as if it were obvious. "Don't worry about me. Just…focus on your grades and your ball game."

A secret dared its way up and out. "What if I didn't want to play ball anymore?"

She spun in place and stared at me in fear. "Don't say that. Go to college. Play ball on a scholarship. Decide later. Don't cross him now, Jason. Less than two years left now." The fear faded, replaced by curiosity. "What would you do instead?"

I shrugged. "I like photography."

"Really?" She nodded. "Well, I wouldn't tell your dad that. You know how he is."

A phrase to explain away everything: *You know how your dad is.*

Neither of us had heard him come in from the garage. "Don't tell me what?" His voice was low and hard and slightly slurred. He'd stopped at the bar, then. I could hear the alcohol in his words, see it in the narrow glare of his eyes.

I stood up as calmly as I could, hit the reheat button for the plate I'd set in the microwave, then cleared my place. I glanced at Mom, but she was gone, the door to her craft room closing with a *snick* that was loud in the silence. I hunted for something to say.

"Oh, nothing. Just…I…a quiz, in biology. I got C. But it wasn't worth much, so it won't matter." It was a lie; I'd gotten an A on that quiz, but it was better than the alternative.

He took a few steps toward me, and I forced myself to stay in place, lift my chin, and meet his gaze. I tried to convince myself that what I'd said was the truth so he'd see the belief in my eyes. I had my mother's eyes, but I was all Dad physically, broad in the shoulder, close-cropped blond hair, deep-set eyes, brown where mine were green, but our builds were identical. I was shorter, stockier than Dad, broader through the chest, and my cheekbones were higher and sharper than his, courtesy of Mom's quarter-Cherokee heritage.

He stared down at me, standing several inches taller than me, six-two to my five-eleven. "Don't you know any better than to lie to a cop, son?" Another step, this one for pure threat value. "And how am I?"

I knew better than to answer. I kept mouth shut and stared up at him, scared shitless but unable to show it. I never failed to be afraid, at least at first, even after a lifetime of this. The microwave beeped in the background, three beeps in the tense silence.

He struck hard and fast, knocked the breath from me with two lightning jabs to the kidneys. I took them, waited till he drew back for another, and struck back. I'd aimed for his jaw, but he dodged the wrong way and took it on the nose, which broke in a spray of blood. I'd never done that before, made him bleed. He stumbled back, wiping his nose in disbelief. I didn't let him get his balance, though. I hit him again, getting his jaw this time, and then he was upright and I didn't have a chance. He didn't hold back this time.

He cracked me on the jaw, hooked a right to my cheek, splitting it open, and then another right to my face, releasing a sluice of blood from my nose. I stumbled back against the counter, swiping at my face with my forearm. He came at me with a straight left, and I ducked under it, slugging him in the gut hard enough to double him over.

I darted past him, snatched my keys off the counter, and ran out the back door. The screen slammed closed behind me, only to creak back open as Dad lurched after me. I made it to my truck, scrambled in, gunned the engine. Gravel sprayed as the back tires skidded sideways, pointing my hood at the road. I glanced in the rearview mirror, watching Dad's figure diminish, one arm across his stomach, the other wiping at his nose.

I caught myself in the process of the exact same action, right wrist bent down, back of my forearm sliding under my nose. Just like him. I swore under my breath, then cranked the radio and screamed, slamming my palms on the steering wheel. My chest grew sticky, my chin warm and thick with blood. I didn't care. I wasn't sure where I was going. I just drove. I shouldn't have been surprised to find myself at the entrance to Becca's sub.

Can you get away right now? I sent the text before I could second-guess myself.

Give me a few min I'll try.

I wiped at my chin, then saw my forearm was crusted with tacky blood and gave up. He didn't often let himself hit my face, because that always raised questions. I wiggled my jaw, testing it for soreness. He'd gotten me good on the jaw, so it was sore, but thankfully not broken or anything. I'd never had a broken jaw, but I didn't think it'd be fun, or real easy to explain.

I was staring out the window at the deepening evening dark, and didn't see Becca approaching the passenger side. I started when she swung the door open and hopped in. I didn't even stop to think how seeing me bloody would affect her until I turned to smile at her in welcome.

"*Jesus*, Jason! What happened?" She was shoving the center console up and out of the way before I knew what was happening, and her fingers were gentle on my face, a Kleenex from somewhere dabbing at the cut on my cheek and the still-dripping blood from my nose.

"Got in a fight with Dad." I shrugged, going for a nonchalance I didn't feel.

Becca's eyes were watery. "God. You're covered in blood." She probed at my nose, and I winced at the pang of pain. "I think your nose is broken."

"I'll be fine."

She shook her head. "You for sure need s-s-ssss-stitches on your cheek." A tear dripped down her nose as she wiped at the blood with shaking fingers. "You need to go to Urgent Care."

I couldn't figure out why she was crying. All I knew was I hated it. "Don't cry, Beck. Please. I'm okay. It looks worse than it is." That was bullshit, since I could still barely see straight from the pain.

She shook her head, and the tears were dripping faster now. "You're not fine. Don't f-f-fucking lie to me, Jason."

"Sorry. You're right, it hurts like a bitch, but I can't go to a hospital. They know me around here. They'll ask questions."

"Questions th-that should be an-an-an-answered." She was blinking when she stuttered, which I was starting to realize was a sign that she was intensely emotional. "It's not right, J-J-Jason. You shouldn't—"

I pulled away from her touch. "I *can't*. I *won't*. I know you don't understand, but I won't tell. It'd be bad for me. For you. For Mom. For whoever I told." I dug deep and told the truth. "I'm too scared to tell, Becca. Please. Just let it go. I'll be fine."

She shook her head again, wiping at her eyes. "I can't let it go. It hurts too bad to see you like this."

I swore, a long string of florid curses. "I should've gone for a drive instead of coming here. I'm sorry I involved you in my bullshit."

She grabbed my arm in a sharp-nailed grip; I stared down at her fingers digging into my bicep, each nail long and painted with a white strip of polish across the tip, some kind of fancy manicure. "Well, you *did* involve me. I'm involved now, and you can't t-t-ttt-take it b-back. You're my boyfriend, and I care about you."

"What do you want me to do?" I spoke to the window, snapping at her irritably and unable to reel it back in. "I'm not telling. This is my life, and yeah, it fucking sucks ass. But it's the hand I got dealt, and I only got till I graduate. Then I'm fucking gone. If you can't accept that I'm not telling, then...I don't know what. Then this won't work. 'Cause I'm not gonna."

"Why? I just don't get it."

"No, I know you don't. You want the goddamned psychology for why I'm too fucking afraid of what my dad will do if I told someone again? I can't give you that. I'm not as fucking smart as you, okay? I just know he scares me. A broken nose, some bruised ribs, a cut face here and there, I can deal with that. If I tell, what will happen? I'll get taken by CPS and put in a foster home? From what I know, chances are that'll be just as bad or worse. Then he'll start in on Mom 'cause I won't be there, and she won't tell, either—she won't leave. She could've left before I was born and she didn't, because she's a fucking coward, just like me. You don't *know* him, Beck. What we deal with now is better than the alternative. He'd deny it, and he's got credibility to burn. No one wants to cross Mike Dorsey. You want to know why I'm all bloody today? I fought back. That's why. He hit me, and I hit back. It ends faster that way, usually. It's never gotten this bad before, though. I guess because he wasn't as drunk as he usually is when he goes after me. I don't know."

Silence, thick, hard, and for once uncomfortable, rose between us.

"I'm sorry, Jason," Becca whispered.

I knuckled my forehead. "Don't apologize. I'm the one who's sorry. I'm sorry I got you caught up in this. I'm sorry I yelled at you. You deserve better than this shit. Than me."

"Drive."

I glared at her in puzzlement. "What?"

"Start driving, please. Anywhere. Just drive." She sounded mad, which I couldn't figure out.

So I drove. Far, and fast. For once the radio was off, and we were each lost in our thoughts, hers inscrutable, mine a whirl of guilt and shame and confusion and pain. At some point, I hit the freeway and kept driving as evening turned into night. Still, neither of us spoke.

Finally, I couldn't take it anymore. "Why are you mad?"

"Why should you deserve better than me? What's wrong with me that you don't trust me to know what I want?"

That made my head spin. "What? How...?" I stared at her sideways, then returned my gaze to the highway. "How can you turn this back on you? I've got so much bullshit, Becca. You don't need it. You're smart, you're beautiful, you're talented—you can be anything you want. I'm just a jock with Daddy issues. You should be with someone who's...I don't know... who's got less problems than me."

She shook her head, which I realized wasn't a denial, a no, but rather an expression of disbelief or inability to express what she was thinking. "See? That's what I mean. If I want to be with you, then that's my choice. It's *my* choice to be your girlfriend, in spite of the fact that yeah, you've got problems at home that are hard for me to understand or deal with." She was speaking as if she'd scripted this out, sounding rote and monotone, but I knew she meant every word, that this was just how she dealt with strong emotions while struggling to speak fluently. "Who you are is who you are, because of what you go through. I like who you are. I want to help you. I want you to tell me things. I want you to trust me."

"I wouldn't have told you a damn thing about my life if I didn't trust you," I said.

"I know. But now you need to trust me to deal with it."

"Then you need to stop pressuring me to tell someone, okay? I know it doesn't make any sense. It seems like I should want to get away from him, or stop it, but that's not how it works. I don't like it, but...I don't know. I just can't, okay?"

She nodded. "I hate it, and it goes against everything I believe in to let it happen."

"You're not letting anything happen. There's nothing you can do to stop it."

"There *should* be," she whispered, vehement and frustrated.

"But there's not."

Becca just shrugged, and we lapsed into silence. Then her phone rang. She pulled it out and glanced at the screen, and her face paled. "It's Father."

"Can't you ignore it?"

She shook her head. "That'd only be worse." She breathed deep with her eyes closed, then answered it.

"Hello? No, I'm—oh. I—I—I…yes, Father. I'm sorry. I'll be home right away." She hung up and pinched the bridge of her nose.

"What's up?"

"He knows I left with you."

"How? What'd you tell him when you left?"

"That I was going out with Nell. I was going to call her and let her know to cover for me, but when I got in, I saw you and forgot. He figured it out somehow. I don't know. This is bad."

"What's going to happen?" I took her hand and laced our fingers together, ignoring the twinge when her fingers brushed my split knuckles.

"I don't know. Trouble." She visibly retreated into herself, so I just held her hand as I exited the freeway and re-entered going back the other way.

We'd gone farther than I'd realized, and it was a good half hour before we even hit the exit for our end of town. I pulled into a McDonalds parking lot, told Becca to sit tight while I ran in and cleaned up. Half a roll of paper towel later, my face was clean, my nose bent but no longer bleeding, my cheek split wide and ugly. I pulled the truck across the road into CVS, grabbed some Band-aids, and stuck one over the cut on my cheek. I had a spare jersey in my backpack, so I tossed out my bloody T-shirt and slipped the jersey on, not missing how Becca's eyes were riveted to my chest and abs while I had my shirt off.

When we got to Becca's neighborhood, I didn't stop at the entrance like usual.

"Where are you going?" She sounded puzzled.

I shrugged. "He knows, so why bother hiding?"

I pulled into her driveway and got out with her. I wasn't about to let her face trouble alone, not when it was brought on by me. She kept glancing at me sideways as we approached her front door, as if waiting for me to bolt. She didn't realize that no matter how bad her dad was, he couldn't possibly be scarier than mine. I waited at the door while she opened it, then followed her in.

"You don't have to do this, Jason," she whispered to me as we crossed the threshold.

"Yes, I do."

Her father was a big man, barrel-chested with a bit of a belly, mostly silver hair slicked back, and small, dark, hard eyes. "Who are you? Why are you in my home?"

I stepped forward and held out my hand. "I'm Jason Dorsey. I'm Becca's boyfriend."

He took my hand automatically, shook it firmly, then dropped it when I said the last part. "The hell you are. My daughter will not have a boyfriend. You leave now." His eyes burned into me. He was clearly used to intimidating people, and he didn't like that it didn't work on me. "You are the nuisance who has been distracting my daughter from her studies, coercing her to sneak out at night. She will not be seeing you anymore."

"Maybe if you gave her a bit of freedom over her own life, she wouldn't have to sneak out, you ever think of that? I'd be perfectly willing to tell you exactly where we are and what we're doing, sir. With all due respect, I'm not a bad influence. I like your daughter a lot, Mr. de Rosa. The only reason she ever snuck out was because you wouldn't let her leave the house otherwise." He opened his mouth to argue, but I spoke over him. "I don't mean to tell you how to do your job as a parent, sir, but I can tell you this much, that the harder you try to control every little thing Becca does, the more she'll rebel. Give her some freedom, and she won't have to break the rules."

He glared at me, clearly infuriated. "I am her father. I will decide. You are no one."

Becca touched my arm. "Jason, I appreciate what you're doing, but please, let it go."

Mr. de Rosa took a step closer to me. "You leave now. You will not be seeing my daughter again. Never."

Becca stepped between us and stared up at her dad. "Father, please. He's right. We're not doing anything wrong. I'm still studying, still getting good grades. Give us a chance."

Her mother, who had till this point been sitting silently at the dining room table, stood up and crossed the room to stand next to her husband. I saw a lot of Becca in her, with curly black hair framing an older version of Becca's facial features. She spoke quietly in a foreign language that I belatedly realized was Arabic. Becca was clearly following the discussion as her father replied in the same language, arguing heatedly, frustrated. At some point during his argument, Becca's father switched to Italian, and when her mother responded, it was in that language. I even caught a few words of English scattered throughout. It was dizzying to listen to.

After a few minutes of back and forth between her parents, Mr. de Rosa turned his gaze back to Becca and me. "This goes against my better judgement, but your mother has prevailed upon me to give you a chance to prove your responsibility. Both of you." He fixed his gaze on me. "I don't like you, Mr. Dorsey. You seem like a rough character, and I'm not convinced you're not a bad influence on my daughter."

"Well," I began, choosing my words carefully, "I'm sure we can agree that Becca is a good influence on me. But I'm not a bad kid. I have a straight-A average, and I'm first string on the football team. I don't drink and I don't smoke."

"What happened to your face?"

I swallowed and then focused on believing the lie I was about to feed him. "A game of pick-up football with my buddies. A tackle went wrong, and I caught a forehead to the face."

He narrowed his eyes at me. "You're sure it wasn't a fight?"

I nodded. "I'm sure. Coach is very strict about that stuff. I'd be benched for half the season if I got suspended for fighting." Which was true, just not applicable to my situation. "If you get in trouble with the office, you're benched. If your grades drop below a C average, you're benched. I'm hoping for college scholarships on both football and grades."

Her father nodded, seeming to be satisfied. "I will allow you one chance with my daughter. If she's late, *once*, if she fails to check in at the predetermined time, or if she is not where she says she is, then it is over. Do you understand me, Mr. Dorsey?"

I nodded, tamping down the triumphant feeling. "Yes, sir. I do."

He hesitated, then shook my hand again. "What position do you play on the football team?"

"Wide receiver," I said. "I currently hold the district record for most receptions in a single game, as well as the most receiving yards in a season."

He seemed suitably impressed. Glad to know those records were good for something at least.

"What is Becca's curfew?" I asked.

"Ten—" Mrs. de Rosa interrupted him with a single word, and he suppressed a sigh of irritation. "Fine, eleven on the weekdays. Midnight on the weekends. But if her grades slip—"

"They won't, Father, I promise." Becca bounced slightly on her toes, happiness bubbling over but still contained. "Can we go back out, then?"

"Where?"

"Out for a drive, maybe stop and get some milkshakes," I suggested.

"Do you have any points on your record?" he demanded.

I shook my head. "No, sir. No points, no accidents. I own my truck, actually." I wasn't sure why that was relevant, but I wanted to impress him. Stupid, maybe, but if I couldn't get my own father's approval, I sure as hell would try to get everyone else's.

He nodded, then waved a hand in dismissal. "Fine. Go. It's 9 p.m. now, so you have two hours."

I took Becca's hand, and we walked as calmly to my truck as we could. I backed out carefully, feeling

Mr. de Rosa's scrutiny. It wasn't until we were back out on the main road that Becca cut loose with an excited squeal that startled me into laughter.

She unbuckled and slid across the bench to press up next to me, clinging to my arm and burying her face into my shoulder as she laughed excitedly. "How did you do that?" she asked, her eyes bright and happier than I'd ever seen them.

I shrugged. "I don't know. I didn't think it'd work, but I figured it was worth a shot to try and face him directly. Most men respect directness."

She kissed my jaw, and I was finding it hard to focus on the road. Then she kissed my cheek and over, closer to the corner of my lips, and I had to grip the steering wheel and pretend I wasn't suddenly aflame. She didn't stop, though. She kissed my chin, the line of my jaw once again, my neck. Holy hell. My heart was pounding out of my chest, and I hoped to god she wouldn't look down and see how affected I was by her lips against my skin.

Eventually, I had to pull away from her. "Beck, I can't drive when you do that."

"Then pull over and kiss me."

God, that certainly didn't help my condition. I had no choice but to obey. I found an empty parking lot, a park deep in a neighborhood. Swings sat still in the darkness, bathed in the faint yellow-white glow of a single streetlight. A merry-go-round, rusted and tilted to one side, a play structure casting long shadows, a chain link fence, and a distant baseball diamond and soccer field.

I barely had the truck in park when she unbuckled my seatbelt and pulled me into a hot, wet kiss. I wrapped my arms around her, pulled her closer, felt my heart ratchet into a frantic patter at the wondrous crush of her breasts against my chest, her knee sliding between my thighs as she lifted up to deepen the kiss. I felt my breathing catch as her fingers curled behind my head, caressing the hairline on the back of my neck, holding me close, as if I'd try to pull away.

I rested my hands on her hips and couldn't believe she'd let me touch her like this. Yet she wiggled her hips as if begging for more, so I risked taking more liberties, and slid my hands around to cup her ass. Oh, god, surely she could feel how crazy that made me. I didn't know where this was going, but I liked it. It also scared me, because I felt consumed by her, taken over by the need for her. Hormones raged, but it wasn't just hormones. Intellectually, I knew what came next, but I refused to think about that directly. I just knew I couldn't stop kissing her, couldn't stop touching her.

And then her fingers drifted up under the hem of my shirt and touched my bare stomach. Lord.

Oh, god. I let my hand slide up her back and touched bare skin at the small of her spine. So soft, so warm. I caressed up farther, to her bra strap, each shoulder, stealing touches.

She was giving them to me, though, right? So they weren't stolen.

My shirt was up around my diaphragm and her hands were splayed on my chest as she sat on my knees, her back to the windshield. Slowly, so slowly, I lifted her shirt up a bit, revealing more of her dark skin. She traced my chest, the lines of my abs, watching my eyes and staring at my body. The look in her eyes matched what I felt in myself.

Then a hint of pink peeked out from the bottom edge of her shirt and my breath was stopped in my lungs, but she didn't halt my hands as they kept lifting her shirt. Skin, a glorious expanse of breast barely contained in a pink bra. Oh, shit. I was so hard I could explode with a thought. I needed to adjust myself, but didn't dare. Her eyes were on me, full of daring, fear, nerves.

"God...*damn*, Becca." I could barely get the words out. "You are...so hot. So sexy."

"So are you." She brushed a thumb over my lips, eyes on mine from inches away.

I pressed my palms flat against her ribs, just beneath her bra. It was a question, a silent request. She released a pent-up breath and then nodded, a pair of frightened, excited jerks of her chin. I slid my hands up, cupped the weight of her breasts, pink cotton soft against my palms, and then I felt the hardened bumps at the center of the bra fabric against the heel of my hands and I knew what those were, and I was amazed that this was happening, that she was letting me do this.

Oh, god. Oh, shit. So perfect. Up, up, and up my hands slid to the slope of her breasts, skin on skin now, and I couldn't breathe, but I didn't need to because she was kissing me and giving me her own breath, exploring my chest and my sides and down to the waist of my jeans.

And then she was off me suddenly, sliding to the opposite end of the truck against the door. "God, Jason. We have to s-s-slo-slow down. This is going too f-f-f-fast." She tugged her shirt down to cover herself, her breathing ragged.

I rubbed my face with my hand, unable to stop a hiss when my thumb bumped my nose. "Becca, I—I'm sorry. I guess I got carried away. I'm sorry."

She came closer once more. "No, *we* did. It was me, too. I wasn't just *letting* you touch me, I wanted you to. I wanted to touch you. B-bb-bbb-but…" She sucked in a deep breath and visibly composed herself.

"We have to slow down. We're only sixteen. We've only been dating for, like, three dates."

"I know, I know. You're right." I felt responsible, even though she admitted she was as much at fault for getting carried away as me. "I should be the one to slow us down."

She laughed at that. "Um, you're a guy?"

I glared at her. "So that makes me unable to control myself?"

She giggled again. "No, no. Just, guys aren't usually the ones to think about slowing down. The opposite, if I've heard right." Her expression shifted into seriousness. "Have you…have you ever been with anyone else before?"

I wasn't sure exactly what she was asking. "I've never dated anyone before."

She shook her head. "No, that's not what I mmmm-meant." She didn't exactly stutter the last word, more just drew out the initial sound before getting control once again. "I meant, have you been with anyone?"

I just stared at her. "No, Becca. When I kissed you in the parking lot at school, that was my first kiss."

She seemed relieved for some reason. "Mine, too."

"And no, I haven't done anything else with anyone. Everything with you is a first for me."

"Me, too." She glanced at me with her head ducked down. "Are you mad at me for asking?"

"No, just surprised. I guess I assumed you knew I'd never done anything with anyone before."

She shrugged. "You just…you kiss me like you know what you're doing. I just wondered."

I felt a thrill at her words. "So you like how I kiss you?"

She gave a look of utter disbelief. "Well…*yeah*. I…I *love* the way you kiss me. It makes me crazy. I never want to stop kissing you."

"That's how I feel, too," I said. "We should go get milkshakes before I kiss you again, and then we'll both get carried away."

She grinned at me, equal parts shy, joyful, and frustrated. I knew exactly how she felt. We were in unexplored territory for both of us. We didn't know what we were doing, just that we liked it. We knew sort of where it would go eventually if we didn't stop it, and that was a big, scary line in the sand that I know I'd thought about, daydreamed about, but never imagined would be a worry this soon. A worry? That wasn't the right word. I knew I wanted it, of course I did, but it was scary. I drove us to Big Boy for milkshakes, lost in thought. Usually I felt a lot older than my sixteen years, and I knew Becca felt the same way. But in that moment, wondering about how to handle a physical relationship with Becca, I suddenly felt very young and immature indeed.

I had her home at five minutes to eleven.

Six: Lines in the Sand
Becca
December

FATHER HAD LOOSENED UP A BIT with me since October. Ben had straightened up a bit, started going to the local community college and seemed to be getting in less trouble. He wasn't on meds like he should be, but his mood swings seemed to be more in control, which meant less tension in the house for everyone. Jason had started coming over after practice, and we'd study in my room together, as often as not in silence except for music. We both had expectations to manage, but as long as we kept my door open, Father seemed not to mind Jason being over. For Jason, I knew it was a huge relief to not have to go home until late. He never spoke of his father again, and if he was still getting hit, he never showed it. He'd wince at times when I hugged him, but he wouldn't let me see his torso, and he always claimed it was from football. That excuse worked less well after football season had ended, but I recognized his silent plea for me to let it go, so I did.

After we'd finished our homework, my parents would call us down for dinner. Mom seemed to see something in Jason, as if he needed mothering, and she always made sure he ate with us. She never discussed it with me, but I recognized it. For his part, Jason was always thankful, always respectful, and never took dinner with my family for granted. He always insisted on helping clear the table and did the dishes with me most nights. That impressed the hell out of Father, for some reason.

Then, after homework and after dinner, we'd hop in Jason's truck and cruise the roads, sometimes just driving, other times going to the hill, and there we'd kiss until we reached that line in the sand where we both knew we had to stop. For me, that line was when my hands started to roam, when I began to need his hands on my skin, closer and closer. When I felt that need, I'd pull away, and Jason would let me. Sometimes he'd be the one to stop us, but usually it was me.

I went shopping with Nell for Winter Formal on a Saturday afternoon while Jason and Kyle did the same, and we had plans to meet as a foursome for a double date after shopping. We shared a changing room and stuffed ourselves into gowns, vetoing dress after dress, usually without even bothering to zip up the back.

Nell was the first one to bring up the subject of our boyfriends, thankfully, since I'd been trying to work out a way to ask my questions. "So you and Jason have been dating for what, three months?"

I nodded. "Yeah. Since September. October was when it became official or whatever."

She gave me sly grin, her strawberry blonde hair cascading in front of her face as she bent to step into a forest-green sheath dress. "So...how far have you and Jason gone?"

"How far?" I pretended not to know what she meant.

She smacked me on the shoulder. "You know what I mean. I've seen you kissing in his truck after school. So spill. How far have you gone?"

"Like, in terms of bases?" I asked.

Nell snorted, a surprisingly ungraceful sound from her. "Ohmigod, Becca, that's such a stupid way to measure it. Just tell me."

I shrugged. "We just kiss. That's all. We've..." I trailed off as I squirmed into a strapless blue dress with a scoop neck, but the squirm was as much discomfort with the conversation as it was to fit myself into the tight dress. "We've t-t-touched each other a little. Over our clothes. But that's where we've stopped."

"So far." Nell tugged the top of the bodice of my dress up, and then zipped it for me as I stuffed my breasts further down. "Has he touched your boobs? Bare, I mean?"

I blushed and shook my head, turning from side to side to see how the dress fit. It was *tight*, and short, and it pushed my already-in the-way breasts up so far I was sure they'd spill out if I so much as breathed wrong. "No, he ha-hasn't."

Nell giggled, covering her mouth with her hand, then leaned closer to me. "I wonder what it feels like?"

I bumped my head against hers, laughing with her as I tried to imagine how it would feel. "I don't nn-n-know. Pretty amazing, though, I'd think. He's touched me over my bra, and I feel like I'm on fire when he does that. I can't even imagine what it would be like b-bare."

Nell was blushing as hard as me. "I dare you to let him." She met my eyes, serious, but stifling laughter.

I shook my head. "No! I'm not gonna do that on a dare. It's hard enough stopping as it is."

The laughter died in her eyes then, and she nodded her understanding. "It is for us, too. We have to keep reminding ourselves that we have to stop, or we never will." She met my eyes. "Do you think you'll go all the way with him?"

I shrugged. "I can't say I haven't th-th-thought about it. I want to, but I'm scared, too."

Nell nodded, and the conversation switched to other topics as we tried on more dresses. After six stores, we both ended up with the perfect dress. Mine was a deep maroon sleeveless dress, made of soft silk that split between my breasts and came up over my shoulders as straps, but left my chest bare from navel to neck, with a gauzy material stretched between the split so my skin wasn't completely bare. The hem ended right above my knees, and I had a pair of black heels to match a coat that I'd wear over it when outside. It was sexy and daring, but not so skanky that Father would freak out. I knew Jason would love it, and that was all that mattered.

Nell's dress was much like mine, but in dark blue, a shade that accentuated her fair skin. Hers was a bit more revealing, lacking the semi-see-through material that mine had, and the hem was actually two full inches above the knee. I couldn't imagine Father letting me wear something like that, and I didn't dare try.

We attended Winter Formal in January as a group of four, with Nell borrowing her dad's SUV so we could all ride together. Jason was breathtaking in a black suit, cut tight to his impressive muscles. He had a black shirt with a thin maroon tie the perfect shade to match my dress. His hair was freshly cut, spiked and carefully styled, his jaw shaved down a shadow.

After the dance was over, we all four, plus a dozen of our other friends, crashed a Ram's Horn restaurant a few miles from the banquet center where the dance had been held. I couldn't keep my eyes off Jason, even as we both mingled with our friends, our entire school having basically taken over the nonsmoking section. Every once in a while I'd feel his gaze on me, and I'd meet his eyes, startled as always by their vivid green hue. I'd gotten a one-time-only extension of my curfew to two in the morning, but when midnight came around most of the other kids had split off into couples.

Jason had left his truck at my house, so Nell dropped us off there, and we slid into the cold seats, shivering and chattering until the heater had the cab warm.

"So where should we go, sexy lady?" Jason asked me, pulling away from my house.

I shrugged. "The hill?" That had had turned into our code for *let's go make out.*

He grinned at me in anticipation, and I felt heat begin to boil in my blood before we'd even gotten there. He made it in record time, even with the snow. He cut the lights, left the engine on, turned the radio down low, and then unbuckled his seatbelt, waiting for me.

I was nervous, for some reason. I shrugged out of my coat, and felt exposed as his eyes roamed my body. Then I undid the seatbelt and slid across the cloth seat until my thigh touched his. My dress had hiked up a bit as I slid over, and the hem was now midway up my thigh.

I felt Jason's eyes on my thighs, and then his fingers touched my knee. So far, our touch exploration had been from the waist up, but now, with this dress leaving so much of my body bare, I realized all bets were off. It hadn't seemed so revealing in the store, or even at the dance. It was actually a very conservative dress in comparison to some of the barely there things other girls wore. But yet, this close to Jason, knowing how hard it was getting to stop when we reached that line, I felt nearly naked.

"You're shaking," Jason whispered. "You cold?"

I shook my head. "No. Just…nervous."

"Nervous? Why?"

I shrugged, not sure how to put it into words. I was silent for a long time, planning it out, and Jason just waited patiently, one hand on my knee, a finger tracing distracting circles at the exact place where knee began to seem more like thigh.

"I'm nervous about us," I said. "I'm nervous about how kissing you seems to be so hard to stop."

"We can go, if you want."

I shook my head. "No, I don't want to. I suggested we come here because I wanted to. I'm just...nervous about where it's going."

Jason nodded. "We'll stop whenever you want."

"What if...what if...sometimes I don't w-want to stop? But other times I'm afraid of what w-w-will happen if we don't?"

"I know what you mean. I don't ever want to stop, to be honest. But I also don't want to pressure you."

I finally was able to meet his eyes. "Are you ever nervous about...going all the way?"

"I want it to be right. I want it to be perfect." He took my hand but left his other on my leg. "I'm nervous about that, yeah. But we don't have to talk about it now, right?"

I shrugged. "Maybe we should? We can't keep... ignoring the subject." I held his gaze and said the words I'd been scripting in my head. "I don't want being with you like that to be an accident. I want it to be on purpose."

He nodded. "Me, too. Are you ready for that?"

"Are you?"

"I asked you first." He grinned.

I shrugged. "Yeah? But no. I don't know how to explain it. I love kissing you. I love touching you and letting you touch me. I want more. But that…going all way is…it's a big deal, isn't it?"

He nodded. "Yeah, it is, I suppose. And that's pretty much how I feel." He smirked slyly at me. "Maybe we should just…push the boundaries a little, and see how we feel?"

I snorted, and then giggled. "That is such a guy thing to suggest."

"Well, I *am* a guy." He glanced at his hand, which had inched up my thigh. "Am I wrong, though?"

Damn him, he knew me. That was *exactly* what I wanted, to ease into the idea. Get used to it, some. Part of me was full of warning, however, insinuating that just maybe it wasn't such a good idea.

I ignored the voice and waited for Jason to kiss me. Oh, boy, did he kiss me. His tongue assaulted me, and I loved it. I pulled him closer, and he complied, crushing me perfectly against him, and I wanted to be closer still. Usually I ended up straddling his lap in the driver's seat, but this time, that didn't happen. I felt myself falling backward until my back was pressed into the cloth of the seat and Jason's hot hard huge body was above me, and god...I wanted more. His mouth was on mine, but his hands...god, his hands. They teased and tantalized me. One played on my thighs, touching, tracing, carving, sliding up and down my thighs, but never pushing up under my dress. His other was on my face, at my cheek, curving down my neck to my side, arcing along the outside swell of my breast.

I let go, just a little at first. I pushed his blazer off, and then his tie, tugging down on the knot until it was loose. And then his shirt...yes, I unbuttoned his shirt. That felt so adult, so daring. So like the movies I'd watched with Nell. That, unbuttoning his shirt, I think that was my undoing. It seemed like such a...such a seductive act. His breathing was ragged as we kissed, as I bared his torso, as I played with the now-familiar fields of his pectorals and his abs.

More. I wanted more from him.

I spread my thighs apart a little and scooted down closer to the driver's side so the hem of my dress hiked up. It was a cowardly move, manipulative, rather than just boldly asking him to touch me. He broke apart from my lips and gazed down at me.

"You are so...so beautiful, Becca." His breath caught, and, licked his lips. "I...I love you."

My breath left me in a whoosh. I hadn't expected that. I closed my eyes and swallowed hard, repeated the words in my head, so they'd come out smoothly. "I l-ll-love you…t-t-t-too." I closed my eyes in mortification, because even scripting it out hadn't been enough. I'd never been so embarrassed. The one time in my life I wanted to not stutter, and I'd ruined the moment.

I felt something hot run down my cheek.

"Hey, why are you crying?" Jason's voice was soft, and his weight shifted off me slightly. I felt his hand move, and the radio cut off.

I opened my eyes, and his form was blurred by tears. "I…I just wanted to be able to say that back to you without messing it up. But I couldn't." I breathed deeply and tried to will away the tears, but they wouldn't cooperate. "I'm—I'm so-sss-sorry."

I felt his lips on my cheek, kissing away my tears, literally, and my heart squeezed with emotion for him. With love for him.

"Hey, Becca, look at me." He kissed my chin, the side of my nose, my lips. "Look at me."

I forced my eyes open and wiped them with one hand, knowing I was smudging and smearing my makeup and not caring.

"I don't mind. I don't care." His gaze was serious and compassionate and so, so tender. "Hear me? I mean it. You don't ever have to apologize. You stutter sometimes. So what? I've known you since we were little kids, and it's never bothered me. Remember when I punched Danny for making fun of you? I'll do that to anyone else who gives you a hard time."

I breathed hard, trying for composure and not quite succeeding. "Jason...I just..." Another deep breath, and I started again. "I just know that it was a big moment, you telling me you love me. I just—I wanted to be able to say it back without ruining it with my stupid, embarrassing sss-stutter."

Jason brushed his fingers into my hair next to my ear and kissed me, soft and sweet. "It's not embarrassing. Not to me. You didn't ruin anything." He brushed a thumb over my cheekbone. "Did you mean it less because you stuttered a little bit?"

I shook my head adamantly. "No! I mean it, so much." I hesitated, forming the words mentally. "I love you, Jason."

He smiled at me, and then kissed my worries away. His hand moved back to my thigh and I lifted my leg into his touch, tacitly encouraging him. Now his hand dared up more, to mid-thigh, stopping at the edge of my dress. With one hand, I pushed his face away from mine so he'd look at me. While he gazed down at me, I covered his hand with mine and guided him higher. His eyes widened, and he licked his lips. I put my hands on his arm, his nape, and watched him as he dared farther. Oh...he was nearly to my hip, inches away from my most private center. My entire body was humming, thrumming with anticipation and desire. I could communicate what I felt for him without speaking—I could tell him with my hands, with my lips, with my legs and hips.

"M-more." I didn't even care about the slight block in my voice. "Please."

I pushed and tugged at his shirt sleeves until his upper body was naked, and I let my hands roam his skin, barely breathing as he familiarized himself with my thighs, my bare hips. His mouth touched mine, backed away, then dipped to kiss me again. I didn't know how far this was going to go, but I knew I didn't want it to stop. I was afraid, yes, I felt that in me coiled around the desire. We couldn't take back this pushing of lines. Now that I knew how his naked skin felt beneath my hands, I'd never be able to go without it. Kissing would lead here now. It was like falling over an edge; once you lost your balance and began the tumble, you couldn't stop your descent.

I knew this, yet still I reached up with one hand and, as Jason watched with wide eyes, slid one sleeve off my arm, and then the other. One slight tug would be all it took for me to bare my breasts to him. He swallowed, and my eyes followed the bobbing of his adam's apple. I caressed the hard line of his jaw with one hand, and with the other I bared myself to his gaze.

Oh god, I wanted to cover myself. My skin tightened, my heart galloped, and I blinked hard against the nerves and embarrassment. His nostrils flared and his eyes went saucer-wide, and his fingers clawed into my hipbones. I could only lie there and wait for his reaction, for what he'd do, what he'd say.

"God... Becca." His voice was thick, low, rough. "How am I supposed to be able to breathe when you're so beautiful?" He claimed to be bad with words, but for all that he could be poetic when he wanted.

I could have wept with relief. I wanted to be beautiful for him. I wanted him to like how I looked, to love my body, even if I didn't all the time.

His hand retreated from my hips and skimmed up my stomach, over my ribs, and paused at the bunched fabric of my dress beneath my breasts. His eyes swept over my body and then met mine, searching me for visible hesitation or regrets. I arched my back and scratched my fingers over the back of his head, tugging him down to my lips. I needed to kiss him. His kisses took away my fear, my worry that this was too much, too soon. His palm rose up the underside of my breast, and my breath stopped mid-exhale. Then...

oh, god, oh, god. His thumb brushed across my nipple, and I felt it tighten, swell, harden, and I could have sworn I felt each individual molecule of air, each cell of his skin as it passed over my breast. His palm cupped my breast, and my flesh spilled out over his hand, the heel of his hand scraping over and pressing in against my nipple. I moaned, electrified, and sucked his tongue into my mouth.

I wanted to touch him, to push the boundaries further. I'd never been so daring, so bold in all my life. I slid my hand down his back—my spine still arched up into his hand as he explored my breasts with increasing confidence—and traced the horizontal boundary of his suit pants waistband. He had a belt on, a thin, shiny black strip of leather, but it was loosely buckled. My hand slipped easily under the pants, beneath the soft cotton of underwear, and I cupped the cool, hard swell of his ass. His breathing hitched in my ear as he kissed my jaw and then resumed in a quick, shallow pant when I crossed the gap to caress the other cheek.

I couldn't stop a smile from spreading over my face as I touched him so daringly, my lips curving against the stubble of his jaw and the soft skin of his neck.

"What?" he asked, his voice a low murmur against my clavicle.

"I like your butt." I giggled as I said it.

I felt him smile. "Good. I like yours, too."

"You haven't even really touched it yet," I pointed out.

He nodded seriously. "Very true. How am I supposed to be able to when you're lying down, though?"

I shrugged, pretending insouciance. "I'm sure you'll figure something out." My voice cracked as his lips dared down my chest, hot and moist on my flesh, nearing the swell of my left breast, stealing my thoughts and my breath. "God...keep doing that."

His mouth drew nearer and nearer my nipple, and the closer he got, the deeper I drew in my breath, until his lips were a hair's breadth away from the taut peak and I was holding a lungful of air. I waited, he hesitated, and I caressed the back of his head with my fingers, subtly urging him to continue. His lips closed around my nipple, and my breath rushed out in a long moan. I felt a tugging deep inside me, low in my belly, a tightness, a kind of heated, urgent longing, both physical and emotional.

I withdrew my hand from his backside and carved a line up his spine, clutching the back of his head with both hands as he moved his mouth to my right breast. My awareness of our bodies burgeoned, and I felt his arm like an iron bar next to my face, holding his weight with one hand as his other traced along the outside of my thigh and hip. Then I felt *it*. A hard length against my thigh. I knew what it was. I'd watched *True Blood* with Jill and Nell. I knew, mentally, how things worked and what was what. Knowing intellectually didn't prepare you for the reality of it against your leg.

Should I touch him there? *Could* I? Dare I? I knew, again as an intellectual fact, what happened when you touched a guy there in the right way.

I pushed gently on Jason's chest, and he lifted up, kneeling over me with one foot on the floor of the cab, the other knee between my thighs. I felt my breasts tugged to each side by gravity as I lay mostly naked to his gaze. My dress was bunched up above my hips and down beneath my ribs, my red boy-short panties exposed. I felt an embarrassing dampness down there, and I knew the cotton of my panties was soaking it up. I wondered, with a slight sense of mortification, if he could see that wetness, and what he thought of it.

Then I saw the front of his pants, a thick bulge at the zipper. Jason was blushing as I looked at him, and I realized he probably felt the same way about that obvious bulge. It was easy to tell myself that this was natural and normal, but it wasn't so easy to erase the sense of embarrassment at another person seeing you like that. I felt vulnerable, so nearly naked in front of another person. Suddenly, the reality of what we were doing crashed down around me.

Should we stop?

But still, the part of me that was caught up in the daring, exhilarating rush didn't want to. The part of me that liked Jason's body, liked seeing his naked skin, liked *touching* his body and feeling him react—that part of me didn't want to stop. I wanted to unbuckle his belt, like I'd seen on TV, and unzip his pants, flick open the button. I wanted to see all of him. I even wanted to touch him there. I wanted to. I wanted to see what it looked like when I kept touching him.

I wanted to go all the way with him.

But then my vulnerability kicked in, and the knowledge of what my parents would do if they knew what I was doing. Desire fought with vulnerability and a tortured sense of right and wrong. Was this wrong? How could it be? I knew I loved Jason. I was sure people would tell me I couldn't understand what love really was since I was only sixteen, but I knew the feelings in my heart. I was attracted to the person inside Jason's mind and heart, not just his body. I was in love with who he was. I wanted to be with him all the time. I wanted to help him, I hurt when he hurt, I was happy when he was happy.

Wasn't that love?

And then, almost accidentally, Jason's fingers brushed over my thigh and across the joining of my thighs, over my core, over my privates. I felt a bolt of lightning strike me at that grazing touch, and my breath caught, a thick lump in my throat and fire in my veins.

And then, not accidentally, he kissed me, and I was lost once again, all thoughts gone and wars of reason erased. His hand stopped on my stomach, low, just at the elastic of my low-cut panties. My fingernails traced down his chest and caught at the buckle of his belt. I felt his stomach retract from my touch, as if to make room for me touch him more.

His tongue scraping against my teeth and searching my mouth blasted away hesitation. Oh, god, I was going to touch him, and he was going to touch me. Oh, god.

This was okay. We were in love, and this was part of falling in love.

I tugged the end of the belt out of the loop on his pants and out of the buckle, flicked the prong away from the hole in the leather, and then loosened the belt entirely. He wasn't breathing, wasn't moving, his mouth next to my ear, his breathing harsh. His arm shook, and he switched hands, supporting himself with his other palm now. His fingers rested curled against the hot skin of my belly, his thumb brushing tiny circles on the cotton of my panties an inch above my privates. So close, yet so far.

Oh, god. I wanted this. I wanted to touch him more. I wanted more from him. This was so addicting, unstoppable.

The button popped open, and my thumb and forefinger tugged down the zipper. My gaze descended to the open fly of his pants, and I saw the tenting of his boxers, and a dot of dampness on the blue cotton. The wetness of desire, something we both had.

He was stone-still, his eyes on me, glancing at my breasts, then to my thighs and my panties and finally up to my eyes. He wanted this just as much as I did, but I also saw my own doubts reflected in his eyes. He shifted his weight slightly, and his pants drooped around his hips. I touched his waist near his stomach, meeting his eyes. My fingers curled under the gray elastic band, hesitated. My heart was a wild, tribal drum in my chest.

Jason's fingers moved to one thigh, midway between hip and knee, and then journeyed slowly upward. I relaxed my legs, let my thighs spread apart a bit farther, and then his palm was against the soft, sensitive skin of my inner thigh, curling around the muscle there, his fingers pointing down. So close. I trembled all over, and as his hand moved ever closer to my core, I shivered harder, felt the dampness of desire grower wetter.

Our eyes were locked, exchanging permission, communicating need and desire and doubts.

"You want this?" he asked, his voice a whisper in the silence of the truck cab.

I nodded. "Yes. Do you?"

"Yes. But do think we should stop?"

"Why?"

He didn't answer right away. "I don't know. Where do we stop? Where is too far? I don't want to. I want to keep going. But I don't...I don't want us to regret going past a line we can't take back."

I didn't let myself think about what I was going to say. I just blurted it out, stutters and all. "If w-we went all-all the way t-t-to-together...would you rrr-r-rr-regret it?"

My fingers were still curled around the elastic of his underwear, and his were flush against the hot, trembling skin of my thigh, not even half an inch from my wet center.

He shook his head. "I know I love you. I know I want to be with you, only you. I wouldn't regret it. Would you?"

I shook my head. "No. No way." I was so sure, I didn't even stutter. "I know I love you, too."

His hand dared closer, and now the tip of his thumb was exploring the crease of my privates through the damp cotton of my panties. I couldn't breathe when he did that.

Then he stopped, and his eyes locked on mine. "We can't go that far tonight, though," he said. "We don't have enough time, and I don't want our first time to be in my truck."

"Why n-not?" I tugged on his underwear, just a little. "It's where we spend a lot of our time together, isn't it?"

"Yeah, but…" He seemed uncomfortable talking about it. "It should be special. In a bed, somewhere nice. And plus…we don't have any…you know… things. Protection." He whispered the last word in a barely audible voice.

I sighed. "Yeah, I know. You're right. We should plan it out, then. Make it perfect."

He nodded his agreement. "So what about this? Tonight?"

I swallowed hard. "Well, we're not doing *that*, but we can…we can just spend more time together until I have to go, right?"

He seemed relieved, and glad. "Right. I mean, it's not like it can accidentally just *happen*, right?"

I shook my head. "No. We're making choices, together." I felt grown-up, talking things through and making decisions about sex with my boyfriend.

He bent low to kiss me, and my knuckles pressed into the divot of his hips, where his muscles did that crazy V-cut thing. I kissed him with all I had, eyes closed, heart full. I loved Jason, I really did. It was an exciting thing to admit, to say, to feel, to know.

When we'd kissed each other breathless, Jason pulled away slightly, and his wide green eyes and parted lips drove me wild. He was so beautiful, so handsome, and I just loved him. I met his eyes as I pulled his boxer-briefs away from his body and slid them down his hips. His eyes went wide, and even his breathing stopped as he was bared to me.

Oh. Oh, holy shit.

I caught my lip between my teeth and drew my gaze away from his...I couldn't even think of what word to use in my own mind...and met his gaze. He was nervous, slightly embarrassed. I wasn't sure what to do next. Was there a right way to touch him?

His chest swelled with an indrawn breath as I curled my fingers around him. Wow. Just...whoa. Such a complex mess of contradictions. Hard, soft, thick, springy under my fingers in places, taut skin in others. My hand was a dark tan against the pale almost-pink of his flesh there. I moved my fist down, and then back up, just wanting to touch all of him, and he gasped, jerked in my grip.

His eyes closed tight, and he tried to pull away from me. "Becca, oh, god. I'm—you should let go now."

I was confused. "Why? Don't—don't you want me to touch you?"

He tried to laugh, but it came out strangled. "Yeah, I do. More than you know. But...if you don't stop, I'll...I'm gonna—I mean, I'll make a mess."

I blushed hard and nearly bit through my lip. Curiosity was a big part of my emotions at that point, along with wonder, amazement, nerves...too many things to name, all mixed up together. I liked touching him. I liked the way he seemed barely able to contain himself. Me touching him drove him crazy. I liked that.

I touched the top of him with my fingertip, and he groaned. Every muscle in his body was tensed, I could see that. I didn't want to let go. I liked this. It was daring, it was unlike me, usually so careful and good and calm and reserved and following every little rule.

I closed my fingers around him again and slid my hand down his length, feeling every ridge and ripple of skin, watching his face contort and the veins in his forehead and neck and arms tense, feeling his abs tighten into rock. His arm gave out and he collapsed partially on top of me, and I didn't mind at all. In fact, I really liked the way his weight felt on top of me. He was turned on his side, wedged between me and the seat back. His hips were level with mine, and he was gripping my hip, fingers curled into my flesh, his forehead against my shoulder. I waited until he was still, and then slid my hand up and back down. That motion seemed to drive him the most wild, his body bucking into my grip. And then he tensed even more, going entirely rigid.

"God, Becca. You don't know—what you're doing to me. How good that feels. You should stop before I—"

I shook my head, the only response I could make. I wasn't going to stop. We'd gone too far to stop now. I wanted to see what would happen, and I wanted to make him feel good, as good as I'd felt when he kissed my breasts.

He lunged over me, grabbed a T-shirt that had been abandoned on the floor of the truck, a sweat-stained sleeveless black shirt. He shoved it between himself and my skin, my dress, and then groaned deep in his chest as I slowly plunged my fist around him. He jerked in my grip, shoved his hips up toward my hand. I slid my palm up his length, up around the top part of him.

"Oh…*shit*…" he breathed.

And then I felt him jerk, tremble, and spasm. Something hot and wet spilled over my fingers and onto the shirt, and I slid my hand around him, and his body clenched again, and another stream of white liquid left him. It was amazing to watch. His whole body reacted, and a look of utter ecstasy crossed his face as he moved into my touch, slick and wet now.

"Oh." I heard the wonder in my voice. "That is messy."

He laughed, his eyes closed and his face buried against the slope of my breast. "I told you. I'm sorry, I didn't get it on your dress, did I?"

"Why are you sorry? I liked watching that happen. And no, I don't think you did. It's all over your shirt, though."

He breathed, and his breath was hot against my skin. I ached somehow. Deep inside me, I felt a need I couldn't express and didn't understand. I'd touched myself down there, of course, but hadn't ever really felt anything earthshaking like I'd heard the girls at school talking about.

He took the shirt, turned it inside out to wrap up the mess, then wiped himself and my fingers. He lifted up on his elbow, and his hand grazed along the elastic of my panties. I met his eyes and breathed out a long breath, as still now as he'd been. His eyes roamed over my breasts as he slid his fingers under the leg-band, and fire shot through me in anticipation as he moved over my skin and the soft patch of curls. I was embarrassed all over again. Would he mind the curls there? Should I—

All thoughts left me when his finger traced my opening. It was an awkward angle, and he slid his hand out. I nearly whimpered at the loss of his touch. It felt so good, just that little bit of contact. I wanted more. He slipped his fingers over my belly and under the waistband, and I lifted my hips into his touch. Oh, god. My underpants were stretched tight around his hand, tugging uncomfortably in certain places. I pushed at them, rolling them down my body, and Jason seemed to get the idea, helping me push them down and away. When they were near my knees, I had enough movement to spread my legs wider, feeling naughty for doing so, for wanting more of his touch on me...*in* me.

"Oh...god..." I could barely breathe when he touched me, feeling shivery and hot all over, but yet pulled taut and stretched like a wire about to snap. And he'd only brushed his finger down me. I arched my back and spread my knees, stretching my underwear and not caring. His fingers touched me, brushed, stroked, and I couldn't even get enough air to gasp in surprise at how sensitive I was. It hadn't felt this way when I touched myself. Something inside me felt huge and full of pressure, like a balloon about to pop.

The tip of one his fingers moved inward, and I actually moaned out loud, louder than when he'd touched my breast. He slid up a little, and I forced my eyes open, watching his finger white against my dusky skin as he touched me. It was his middle finger, long and delving farther in. Then he found the hard, sensitive nub of skin near the top of my privates—I was too embarrassed even mentally to think of sexual terms explicitly. I wasn't sure if he knew it was there and how sensitive it was, or if he figured it out by my sharply indrawn breath and the sudden shift of my hips into his touch, but he focused his touch there.

He rubbed it, and I began to move with his touch. His finger brushed and moved, and then swiped a little too hard, and I gasped. "Not so rough," I whispered.

"Sorry," he said, and started to withdraw his hand.

"No, don't stop," I said. "Just...be gentle."

He feathered his finger against the nub, and I gasped, moaned, and moved again. I sounded like a woman to my own ears. Like Sookie in *True Blood* when she was with Eric. A word from some book I read floated through my mind: *wanton*. I sounded wanton, dirty. I giggled at the thought, but the laughter evaporated when he moved his finger in a tight circle and all I could do was moan again. His movements were slow and slightly clumsy, but I didn't care. A little rough, but that was fine. The balloon inside me was burgeoning, stretched to a fullness that couldn't be contained.

"Kiss me," I whispered. He moved his mouth toward my lips, and I grinned, laughing breathlessly. "Not...there." I pushed his head toward my breast. "Kiss me there again."

He complied willingly, and I felt that tugging inside me, like there was a string connecting my breasts to my core, and his moving mouth and licking tongue and tugging lips were pulling at the string, unravelling something inside me. He was moving slowly, consistently, and I needed more.

"Faster." I barely heard myself, and I don't think he did at all. I said it louder, bolder. "Faster. P-please."

His finger sped up, and I gasped, heard a whimper escape from my throat, and I felt my spine arch off the seat, heat flushing my body, sweat beading on my skin, my heart hammering. I couldn't stop another moan from getting past my lips, and then faster wasn't enough, more wasn't enough, and I was thoughtlessly moving against his touch, gyrating hopelessly, lost in the moment.

Heat, pressure, lightning, motion, expansion... I didn't have the right words for what swept through me. All thoughts stopped, and I was arched almost completely off the seat, trying to get closer, more,

more, and I didn't care how I sounded or how I looked or anything. There was no room for anything but the bomb going off inside me, like a star going nova low in my belly.

I think I might have made a really loud noise, and then I was limp and breathless, staring up at Jason, his vivid green eyes piercing me hot and sensual.

"God…that was…am-mmm-m-amazing," I stammered, smiling up at him.

"Now you know what you did to me."

I glanced at the clock on the dash.

1:48 a.m.

"Shit, you have to take me home," I said, sitting up shakily, my every muscle still trembling.

He had me home by 1:59, and my father was waiting. Father had left most of the lights off, thankfully, so he didn't seem to notice the brightness of my eyes, or the glow of my skin, or the mussed mess of my hair. Those are things I saw at least as I undressed for bed. I stared at myself in the mirror before I slipped a long T-shirt on over my naked body. I turned to one side, and then the other, posing, examining myself, trying to see what Jason saw.

I just saw me: five-foot-four, fluctuating between one hundred twenty pounds and one-twenty-five. Large breasts with wide, dark arolae and thick, pink nipples. Wide, curving hips and strong thighs, a flat midsection, dark, caramel-colored skin. Hair so black it was nearly blue, hanging past my shoulders in thick strands of coil-tight springs, impossible to manage. Eyes nearly the same color as my hair, a brown so dark they appeared black, my pupils all but indistinguishable from my irises. I had a bit of a sway to my back, making my ass look bigger than it really was.

Normally, when I looked at myself, I saw the sum of my flaws; now I saw myself a little differently. Now I saw my flaws as the sum of my beauty.

I slept deeply, and dreamed of Jason's touch.

Seven: Falling Into Us
Jason
Two weeks later, the end of January

I was perched on the edge of the couch in Kyle's basement, the wireless white Xbox controller slick in my grip from the last four hours of *Madden*, *Halo 3*, and *Call of Duty: Black Ops*. The girls were out doing their weekly manicure-pedicure-shopping-milkshakes thing, leaving Kyle and me alone on a cold, snowy Saturday afternoon with nothing to do but play video games.

I was in the process of whooping Kyle's ass in *Madden*, my Chargers crushing his Vikings 48-14, when he glanced at me with an odd look in his eye.

"So...you and Becca."

I shot him a "yeah...and...?" look.

"What about us?" I asked.

"Have you guys, like, hooked up yet?" He didn't look at me as he asked, his tongue sticking out the side of his mouth.

I cursed as he made a touchdown, bringing it to 48-21. "Have you and Nell?" I shot back.

"Asked you first, dickhead."

I didn't answer until after I'd chosen my play. "Depends on what you mean by 'hook up.'"

He smirked at me. "All the way. Hook up, not mess around."

"Then no."

"But you've messed around with her?" He was inching forward on the couch, then shot to his feet as my quarterback threw an interception, resulting in another Vikings TD, bringing him to 28 points.

I wiped my palms on the knees of my jeans and glanced at him. "Yeah, we've messed around a bit."

He paused the game, and I knew the conversation was about to get serious. "Will you?"

"Will I what?"

He punched my bicep hard enough to make it sting. "Hook up with her?"

I set the controller on the coffee table in front of me and leaned back to put my feet up, thinking about how to answer Kyle's question. "I don't know. Possibly?"

He just laughed. "C'mon, Jase. This is me you're talking to. Don't bullshit me. Are you gonna sleep with her or not?"

I frowned at him. "Dude, don't be an asshole. This is Becca, not some chick. *If* we do, I wouldn't call it hooking up. That just sounds…I don't know…cheap, I guess. Becca's not cheap."

He raised his hands in front of himself. "I wasn't trying to say she was, man. I'm just curious, I guess."

"What about you and Nell?"

It was his turn to shift on the couch, considering his answer. "We mess around, like, a lot. And at some point, I'm thinking we have to just make the decision to do it."

"How do you feel about her?"

He snorted. "What, we're gonna talk about our feelings now? Should we paint each other's nails, too?"

I kicked his ankle. "Don't be a dick. This isn't the locker room, this is a private conversation. We've known each other almost as long as you've known Nell."

He sighed. "I think I'm in love with her." He pulled at a loose thread on a hole in the knees of his designer jeans. "If you laugh or make fun of me, I'll kick your ass." He glared at me in warning.

"I wouldn't have asked if I was gonna give you shit about it, dude." I dug my phone out of my hip pocket and checked for texts. "Have you told her how you feel?"

He shook his head. "Nope. Why is it I can say that shit to you, but if I think about saying it to her, I freeze?"

I laughed. "It's scary, that's for damn sure. Girls can get you all messed up. You know I'm gonna either understand or I'll laugh at your sissy ass, in which case you'd try to kick my ass—"

"I wouldn't have to try, I *would*," he cut in.

"Yeah, whatever, pussy. You'd be crying like a baby by the time I was done with you." I kicked out with my heel, knocking his feet off the coffee table. "My point is, with Nell you can only hope you know she feels the same way. There's just no telling how she'll react. I think that's what makes it harder to talk about with her than with me. My heart was beating so hard I was sure she could hear it when I told Becca I loved her."

"You told her?"

I nodded, feeling stupidly smug about it. "Yeah, man. Right after Winter Formal."

"Did she say it back?"

I grinned. "Yeah."

I think he must have caught the hints in the way I grinned. "What were you two doing when you said it to her?"

"You know that spot, up on the hill beneath the big oak, where we go to plink cans with my .22?" He nodded. "We were up there after everybody left Ram's Horn."

He lifted an eyebrow. "And?"

"It's *real* nice having a truck with a bench seat." I knew I had a shit-eating grin on my face.

"Come on, man. Don't hold out on me."

"This stays between you and me, Kyle. I'm serious."

"No shit."

"Remember the dress she was wearing for Winter Formal?"

He grinned and nodded. "She looked hot."

"Well, I discovered she wasn't wearing a bra beneath it." My mind brought up the mental image of Becca beneath me, and I resisted the urge to shift positions. "She *was* wearing underwear, though."

The silly grin on Kyle's face told me he'd had a similar experience with Nell at some point. "I love those kinds of dresses."

"Almost as much as I love yoga pants."

"Whoever invented yoga pants *had* to have been a guy," Kyle said.

"No shit. So you and Nell…?"

He shook his head. "Same as you. We've messed around, gotten pretty close, but we haven't had sex yet."

"But you're going to."

He nodded without looking at me. "Yeah, we will. Not sure when or where yet, but yeah. I know she wants to, and I know I do, obviously."

"Obviously." I smirked at him. "Have you gotten *all* her clothes off?"

He shook his head. "Not all of them all at once, no. I've seen all of her at one point or another, but it's always been with other clothes on."

"Have you made her…you know…" I trailed off, not sure how to put it without sounding either stupid or like a tool.

Kyle wasn't going to let me off that easy, though. He wanted to see me squirm. "Have I made her what?"

"Have you made her come?" I said it in a rush, staring at my thumbnail, knowing I was blushing like a little boy.

Kyle's grin was equal parts shit-eating and embarrassed. "No, we haven't gone quite that far yet. I think we're both kind of afraid if we let it go that far, we won't stop." He gave me a curious look. "Why, have you?"

I nodded, looking down at my feet. "Yeah."

"What was it like?" He sat forward.

"It was fucking awesome," I said, laughing. "It was like watching her just…lose it. It was cool."

"How'd you…you know…get her to…make her—" He obviously couldn't say it, which made me laugh.

"I honestly don't know. You just touch her in the right place, and you can tell she likes it. Keep doing that, and eventually she'll just…" I shrugged, grinning awkwardly.

"Touch her…down there?" He seemed eager and awkward. I felt odd talking about, explaining it, telling him about something I'd done and he hadn't.

I nodded. "Yeah." I laughed with self-deprecation. "I honestly had no fucking clue what I was doing. I was just…trying to figure out what she liked, and then she was going crazy."

"Did she scream?" Kyle asked.

I could only nod, remembering. "Yeah. Pretty loud. I don't think she meant to. Good thing we were in the middle of nowhere."

He lifted an eyebrow. "What about you?"

"What about me?" I asked, even though I knew exactly what Kyle was asking.

"Has she…have you—" He cut himself off and grabbed a coaster off the coffee table and hurled it at my head. "You know what I'm asking, you fucker."

I laughed and swatted the coaster away. "Yeah, I know. And yeah." That was as much as I'd say.

"But you haven't actually done it, though?"

I shook my head. "No."

"Aren't you guys worried you'll go too far?"

I frowned at him. "Dude, it's...it's not like that. It's not something that you can just go 'whoops, I slipped!' You get carried away, yeah, but you can't, like, *accidentally* take off all your clothes and *accidentally* have sex. I mean, once you start crossing physical lines, in terms of how far you go, it's pretty much impossible to go back, though. I'll tell you that much." I cracked my knuckles, and then tossed my phone in the air and caught it. "I mean, at first, just holding her hand and kissing her was exciting, right? And then once you know how awesome kissing is, you want to keep doing that. Then, once she lets you touch her a little bit, then you want to kiss her *and* touch her. Outside the clothes at first, right? And then once you feel her skin, it's... touching her on the bra isn't enough."

Kyle nodded his understanding. "That's what I'm saying. You just want to keep going further."

"Yeah, but going from making out and, like, groping or whatever, to actually having sex? I personally don't think you can just 'end up' doing that. Just my opinion."

The conversation drifted after that, but I could see the wheels in Kyle's head whirling, much as they were in my own. For all that what I'd said to Kyle was true, Becca and I had been skirting the fine line between "messing around" and "having sex," and I knew we had to either slow down or go all the way. We couldn't keep up the balancing act much longer.

The fact was, I'd imagined what sex with Becca would be like, and I wanted it. Badly. And I was pretty damn sure she felt the same way.

Becca

I stared at the foil packet of pills in my hand, my emotions a roller-coaster within me. I'd had my cousin Maria take me to a clinic to get birth control, which was, honestly, one of the most frightening experiences of my life. Sitting in that waiting room, then sitting on the crinkly-paper-covered table/chair, getting examined...ugh. All of it taken individually wasn't too bad, but knowing I was doing it with the intention of having sex with Jason, and knowing the doctor knew? I was so nervous I could barely breathe, barely swallow my own saliva.

Maria was a comfort, explaining what was going on, what would happen, all that—it was helpful. She was several years older than me, and was willing to take me to the clinic in secret. She told me it was best to wait till I was older, and that even birth control wasn't one-hundred-percent effective, but she'd rather I be on the pill knowing I probably would be active anyway. She also told me not to let Jason pressure me into anything, and to come to her if I had any questions about anything.

I couldn't tell Maria that I was putting more pressure on myself than Jason was. I knew he wanted to have sex, and I did, too. Even in my own mind it was hard to explain the way I felt about having sex with Jason. I wanted it, badly. I knew how it felt to touch him, to be touched. I knew what it felt like to have an orgasm, what it looked like when he did. I knew all this. We'd crossed every line there was, pretty much, except actual intercourse. I could easily imagine what that would be like, and I had, in fact, fantasized about it all too often. I'd even touched myself, imagining Jason above me.

We both knew where our physical relationship was going, that it was only a matter of time. So why wait? Why keep putting it off? Why keep torturing ourselves? Jason kept telling me not to feel like we had to until we were both ready. Which…felt like pressure, to me. Unintentional pressure, but there nonetheless. And I didn't know what to do about it. I didn't want to disappoint him. I didn't want him to feel like I didn't want to be with him, but there was a sense of fear surrounding the whole thing. I was sixteen and a virgin; once I crossed that line, I couldn't go back. It felt like the last step to growing up, to being a woman in truth. I knew I'd still be me, essentially. But how would it change me? I already felt different just from what he and I had done together.

I pushed the first pill through the thin layer of foil and held it in the palm of my hand, a tiny yellow circle of chemicals that meant so, so much. According to the doctor at the clinic, since I'd started my period on Wednesday, I could take the pill today, Monday, and be protected right away. The doctor had given me a long, involved explanation as to why that was necessary, and how estrogen pills were different from progestin-only pills, but most of that had gone straight past me. I'd absorbed the strict warning about how important the timing was, but that was it.

I popped the pill into my mouth, washed it down with a sip of water from the bottle of Fiji on my nightstand. There, I was officially on birth control. I slid the packet of pills into the pink plastic makeup case, which was basically a compact but fit the circular packet of pills perfectly. I'd Googled how to hide birth control from your parents, and the compact case was the best solution I'd found. I tucked the compact into an inside zipper pocket of my purse and tried to calm my inner panic. I hadn't told Jason I was getting birth control, but only because I hadn't seen him since I'd gone. It had been a kind of last-minute trip. Maria had come over unannounced for a weekend away from college, and we'd gone shopping. Gossip about boys had turned into my relationship with Jason, which had turned into her pestering me about whether we were "active" or not. All of which led to her dragging me out of the mall and to the nearest clinic. She hadn't taken no for an answer.

"Becca, you don't want to be stupid about this, okay? Maybe you're not sleeping with him yet, but you will. This way, if anything happens, you're protected." Maria was very practical and matter-of-fact. "You're only sixteen, and shouldn't be having sex, but I was when I was your age, so I can't talk."

I put in my earbuds and scrolled through my playlist on my iPod until I found something that seemed to speak to me: "First Day of My Life" by Bright Eyes. I had my notebook open, a pen in my hand, waiting. I knew the feeling by now, the swelling in my heart and mind, the flux and flow of disconnected words inside me. I put the iPod on shuffle, closed my eyes, and waited, just listened. "We're Going to Be Friends" by The White Stripes came on next, and god, did I love that song. I'd heard the Jack Johnson version first, and then The White Stripes version had come up on Pandora, and I'd been hooked. I still wasn't sure who'd recorded the song first, and I didn't care. "Falling Slowly" by Glen Hansard and Marketa Irglova started, and I nearly cried. I wasn't sure why, what the rush of emotions was about, but something about that song brought everything I'd been dealing with to the fore.

My pen started moving, and I let the well of words open.

FALLING INTO US
How do I resist the gentle need in your eyes?
I don't
I can't
Not when that same heartdeep, soulspearing desperation is rooted within me
Tendrils of sunhot want wrapping around my soul
Like ivy up a brick wall
God, your eyes
Greener than summer grass
Greener than moss and sunlit jade
Sharper than obsidian
Gentler than clouds and feathertouch
They burn into me when we kiss
They scorch me when I score your skin with trembling fingernails
And I know, I know, I know

All too well
Where all this is going
I've seen it happen in my dreams
I've seen it play out in the steam-wreathed privacy of
my shower
Where I touch my hot, shivering flesh
And imagine it's you
Wish it was you
It's been you
But not like we both want
And that's where it's going
We're dancing on the edge of a knife
And I want to fall over
With you
But I can't help being a little afraid
Of the adulthood lying on the other side
I'm afraid of what we can't take back
Of giving away that last piece of my girlhood
Even to you
And yeah, I know, I love you
And yeah, I know, you love me
But yeah, I know, we're still just kids
We're as close to junior high as we are college
As close to twelve as we are twenty
And I don't want to regret a thing
God, I'm so confused

And the only time I'm sure of anything

Is when you're kissing me

And then it's all too easy to forget

Everything but the way I feel

The way you feel so close to me

And I can't help wondering

If that's the smartest time to make such decisions

Exactly because I get so lost

Because it feels so much like falling

Into love

Into you and me

Being in love is scary

So much like falling

A frightening descent into

Beautiful madness

Yes, you and me

We're

Falling into Us

And I don't dare stop the fall

Because I need it far too much

I put the pen down and leaned back in my desk chair, staring out the window at the thick fog of skirling snow, letting the surge of words subside. "Comes and Goes (In Waves)" by Greg Laswell played in my ears, and I was grateful that the words didn't apply, didn't seem to be tailored to my emotions. So often, the music I listened to fit into my life, seeming like a soundtrack to my soul. I usually loved that, chose songs and artists for that reason, but with the poetry still juddering in my veins, I needed music that was just music, just sonic beauty for its own sake.

A knock on the door startled me out of my thoughts. "Who is it?"

"Ben."

"It's not locked." I closed the notebook and stuffed it into my purse.

Ben came in and flopped onto my bed like he so often did. He didn't light up this time, thankfully. "So what's up with you, Becca?"

I shrugged. "Homework, school, Jason."

Ben grinned. "So what's up with you and Mr. Football?"

I shot Ben a look. "We're good. I like him."

"You got Mom and Dad to let you see him openly, huh?"

I smiled. "Yeah, that was all him, honestly. We got caught, so Jason basically confronted Father and made him realize if he let us see each other, he'd have more semblance of control."

"Pretty badass. Dad can be scary."

I nodded. "Not much scares Jason."

Ben eyed me quizzically. "You seem…better. Happy. You're not stuttering at all."

I shrugged, hiding a grin. "I am. I'm happy. Jason is awesome."

"So he's to thank, then?" Ben dug in his pocket and pulled out a cell phone and flipped it between his fingers. "He's taking care of my baby sister? He's not pressuring you into anything, is he? I'll kick his ass if I have to."

I laughed. "I love you, Benny, but you couldn't kick his ass. And yes, he's great. He's not pressuring me into anything, I promise." I gave my brother a stern glare. "And that's all I'm saying to you. I'm *not* having that conversation with you."

Ben tapped his phone, and I heard the telltale sounds of *Angry Birds*. "Believe me, I don't want to have that conversation, either, but you're my baby sister, and I know Mom and Dad wouldn't be open to talking about reality with you. All I'll say is, be careful, okay? Please? I don't want to see you on *Teen Mom* or some shit." He didn't look up from his game, but I knew he was being as serious as my brother could be, in the only way he knew how.

I left my chair and slid into my customary place on my bed, against the wall with Ben on the outside. I smelled cigarettes on his shirt, but no pot or any other chemicals. I loved these moments, when Ben was happy, lucid, and sober. This was how we spent time together, how it had been since we were kids. He'd come into my room unannounced at random intervals, and we'd talk, just hang out. He'd lie on my bed and I'd lie next to him, and we'd just hang out. He only did it when he was in a good mood, though. If he was on a downswing, he'd be gone for days at a time, and when he was around, he was closed off, silent, hiding in his room with rap thumping.

I watched Ben play *Angry Birds* for a while before saying what was on my mind. "You don't seem high."

He didn't react right away. "I'm not," he said.

"At all?"

He shrugged. "I'm trying to learn how to just deal with the mood swings on my own, no drugs, no meds."

"Do you think you'll ever go back to college?"

He shrugged. "Maybe. Probably not. I hate school, always have. I'm working at Belle Tire for right now. Changing oil and tires. It sucks, but it's work, and it keeps me out of trouble."

"I'm glad you're working."

Ben glanced at me as the next level loaded. "Why?"

"Well, like you said, it keeps you out of trouble. You know how I feel about you smoking pot. You should be on your meds, Ben. I know you don't like them, but they do help."

"Are you my little sister or my mom?" He sounded disgusted.

"I just care about you. I worry about you. Sometimes…" I struggled with how to say it without insulting him. "Sometimes I feel like you don't…care. About your future. About yourself."

"Sometimes I don't. I'll never amount to anything, Beck." He sounded so matter of fact, it hurt.

"Don't say that, Ben. It's not true."

"What am I good at, then? What can I do that's worthwhile?"

I didn't have an answer. He didn't really have any hobbies that I knew of. "You're a good person, Ben. You have talents. Everyone does. You just have to find yours."

"You sound like a goddamn guidance counselor. I *don't* have any, Becca. I'm good at smoking pot. I'm good at selling it. I'm good at being a bipolar fucking mess, that's what I'm good at." He clicked the top button to put the phone to sleep and shoved it angrily in his pocket.

I sighed. "I'm sorry, Ben, I didn't mean to upset you. I just meant to point out how glad I am that you're not smoking pot."

"Well…I'm trying, okay? That's the best I got." He stood up and took three angry steps across the room.

"Ben, wait. Don't be mad. I-I'm sorry."

His shoulders slumped, and he turned back around to crouch next to the bed, his face level with mine. "I'm not mad, sis. I know you care." He smiled gently at me. "But you shouldn't waste your time worrying about me. I'll be fine. I can take care of myself. You worry about you, huh?"

I frowned at him. "You're my brother. I love you. Of course I'm gonna worry about you. I can't help it."

He shook his head at me. "You don't need the weight of your messed-up brother on your shoulders, Beck." He put his hand on my shoulder and wiggled it. "I'm *fine*, okay? I'm in a good place. I'm working, I'm sober, I've even got a girlfriend. She's good for me, like Jason is for you. Kate doesn't let me smoke anything but cigarettes, so that's good motivation. She holds out on me if she finds out I've gotten high."

"Holds out on you?" I wrinkled my nose in confusion.

Ben quirked an eyebrow at me. "You know—she won't put out."

I squealed in mortification and buried my face in my quilt. "Eeew, Ben! I didn't need to know that."

He laughed at me and smacked my shoulder before standing up. "Hey, it works, doesn't it?"

"I guess so. I just didn't need need to know."

Ben left then, and I turned my attention to my AP bio homework. Jason was picking me up at seven-thirty, so I had to be done by then, which only left me three hours to finish four hours' worth of homework.

Eight: The First Night of Forever
Jason
Two days later

I FINGERED THE KEYCARD IN MY POCKET as I sat in my truck, waiting for Becca. We'd planned this out, and now we were going through with it. My nerves were jangling, and I wondered if Becca felt the same way. I was sure she did. I had a CD player plugged into the lighter outlet and the tape deck, an old-school arrangement that I only used when I was in the mood for something specific. Today it was Johnny Cash, and currently playing was "God Is Gonna Cut You Down," which seemed unfortunately ironic given the circumstances, but it was still a kick-ass song.

Becca came out just as the song was ending, and I clicked the radio off. She hopped into the cab and closed the door behind her, letting in a cold blast of frozen air. It was a bitterly cold day, the sky clear blue, the sun distant and watery, the air so still and so cold each breath hurt. She smiled at me, and I was struck by how beautiful she was. Her hair was loose, a white knit cap pulled low on her head, a stark contrast to her tan skin and blue-black hair. She had on a black pea coat that came to mid-thigh, and a pair of tight gray yoga pants.

"Ready?" I asked.

She gave me a small nod and reached for my hand. I twined our fingers together, hers icy from the walk from house to vehicle. "Yeah, let's go."

"Where'd you tell your dad we were going?"

"Great Lakes Crossing."

"So should we go there first?"

She nodded. "Yeah. I do actually have a few things I want to get." She gave me a cryptic smile.

When we got the mall, we strolled around for a while, chatting and browsing, but then we passed a store and Becca split away from me, telling me to meet her at the food court in half an hour. I knew she was up to something, but I went along with it, spending most of the time in the athletics store. I ended up with a new pair of cross trainers for the spring, and was waiting by Aunt Annie's with five minutes to spare. She showed up with a wide grin on her face but no shopping bag.

"Didn't get anything?" I asked.

She shrugged. "No, I did."

I frowned. "What was it, then?"

She wrapped her arm around my waist, fitting herself against me. "You'll see. You'll like it…I hope." When my confused look didn't go away, she just smirked at me. "Here's a hint: I'm wearing it."

I started to get an inkling then. I gulped a little, wondering how I could ever have mistaken Becca for shy.

"What are you grinning about?" she asked as we drove to the hotel where I'd rented a room.

"Just that I used to think you were shy."

She laughed. "I *am* shy, just not with you."

"So…what color?"

She ducked her head, and her cheeks darkened a little. "Not telling. You'll have to find out."

We reached the hotel after a short drive, but we sat in the car in tense silence before getting out.

Becca wasn't looking at me, scratching at her knee intently.

"I don't want you to think…" I sighed and started over. "I mean, we don't have to do this now. We can go back to the mall, or a movie. Or just home."

She shook her head but still didn't meet my eyes. "No, I want to. I'm just…nervous."

I expelled a breath of relief. "Me, too, Beck. Me, too."

"Do you think that means we're not ready?" she asked, finally lifting her dark eyes to mine.

I shook my head. "I think we'd be nervous no matter how long we waited. I think it'd be weird if we weren't nervous."

She nodded. "Let's go in. We'll just…take it one step at a time."

I got out and circled around to open her door while she was still unbuckling. She took my hand, cold fingers slipping neatly into my palm. Her teeth were white as she smiled at me, a private, brilliant, beautiful smile just for me. The concierge, a dour older man, gave us a hard, disapproving stare as we strolled past him to the elevators. We stood outside room 425, the keycard held in my suddenly sweating and slightly shaking hand, my eyes on hers, asking her silently if she still wanted this. She leaned into me, her arm going around my waist, low, her hand on my hipbone.

I slid the card into the lock and pulled it out, shoving the door open when the green light flashed. The room was dark, shadowed by the drawn curtains, a gleaming crack of light showing. I fumbled in the darkness, finding a switch and illuminating the room. A single bed, king-sized and enormous, took up most of the room; I'd splurged on a fairly nice hotel and an upgraded room.

I turned around from switching on the light to find Becca peeling her coat off, revealing a tight white V-neck T-shirt that clung to her curves, the "V" dipping low enough to show me a mouthwatering glimpse of her cleavage. Yoga pants, tight T-shirt? Oh, god. She noticed my gaze raking over her body and gave me a surprisingly shy smile, then turned around, posing for me. She clenched her gluteus muscles, the yoga pants clinging like a second skin to her generous hips and ass, and all I wanted to do was run my hands over her. I stifled the urge for about six seconds before remembering why we were there, alone in a hotel room on a Saturday evening.

I crossed the space between us to stand a few inches away from Becca. She started to turn around, but I stopped her with gentle hands on her shoulders. She turned her head to watch me, her chin on her shoulder. I slid my palms down her sides, feeling her breath catch as I carved my hands along the bell-curve of her hips, then slid them around to cup her backside. She released her breath, her eyes sliding shut briefly.

"I love your ass. Especially in yoga pants," I murmured.

Her brown-black eyes flicked up to mine. "I know. That's why I wore these. I had to kind of sneak past my dad before he saw how tight they are."

My hands explored the taut, supple curves of her ass, down her thighs, up her hips. I grew a little daring and slid my middle finger up the crease where the stretchy fabric clung between her cheeks. She gasped when I did that, so I did it again, letting my finger drive a little deeper, until she pulled away with a breathy laugh.

She stepped away from me and turned around, sliding her knit cap off her head and shaking her curls. "Sit down on the bed, Jason." Her voice held an odd note of command, and I couldn't help but obey.

"Don't interrupt, and don't laugh," she said. "I want to do this for you, but I know I'm going to feel silly."

"Do what?" I kicked off my ADIDAS cross trainers, and then peeled away my socks.

She tilted her head back, eyes closing, hands pushing up through her springy mass of hair. "This." She let her hair fall and slid her hands down her waist, much as I'd done, and then crossed her hands in front of her body to grip the hem of her shirt.

I swallowed hard, and felt the blood rush out of my brain to pool in other areas of my body. Noticeably so, I was sure.

And then, oh, lord god, she glanced at me with heavy-lidded eyes, and slowly peeled her shirt upward.

When she reached the underside of her breasts, she paused, drawing out the moment. She wasn't dancing, wasn't trying to do a striptease, she was just being... naturally sexy. Giving me a show. And oh, god, what a show. I could see her hands trembling on the hem of her shirt; I could see her knees shaking, just a little.

She tugged the shirt up farther, and the white fabric was so tight against her skin that her breasts were drawn up and pressed against her chest, only to fall free with a luxurious bounce. I hardened even further at that bounce. I stopped breathing once I registered what she was wearing. It was strapless and pink with black lace curling around the bottom edge, the cups split apart between her breasts, her tan flesh barely contained. I struggled to swallow past the lump in my throat, to breathe at all at the sight of Becca in nothing but a bra and yoga pants. She stood with her hands at her sides, taking long pulls of air, each breath swelling her breasts even larger. I couldn't help but adjust myself, and her eyes followed my hands.

"Want to see the rest?" she asked.

I nodded. "Y-yes."

She smirked at me. "Now who's the one stuttering?"

"Me. God, Becca. What are you trying to do to me?" I meant it as a rhetorical question, but she answered anyway.

"I'm trying to turn you on." She pivoted on her heel, presenting me with a fine view of her ass and her back with the slight sway inward, the strap of the bra dimpling her supple skin.

"All you have to do to turn me on is be you," I said. "I'm turned on every time you so much as take a breath. This? What you're doing? You're killing me. I'm going to explode. You're too fucking sexy for me to be able to take it."

"Well, I'm not done yet." She ran her hands over the curve of her backside, then hooked her thumbs in the waistband of her yoga pants. "Do you want to see the panties I got to go with it?"

"God, do I ever."

"You're not gonna pass out on me, are you?"

I almost didn't recognize this Becca. She was... confident, sexy, alluring...nothing at all like the girl I'd first met. I wondered, briefly, if she was overcompensating for her nerves, her fears, her doubts. I knew I should question why she was doing this, taking off her clothes for me like this, but I didn't. I felt like a bit of tool for not saying anything, but I just...I couldn't bear to stop her.

She faced away from me, head turned to watch my reaction. She slowly slid her yoga pants down to her knees, although the pants were so tight it was more like peeling herself out of them. My zipper got even more strained at the sight greeting me underneath the pants: they were cut so that the back hem sliced across the middle of her ass cheeks, disappearing between her thighs. They had black lace at the top and bottom, with vertical pink and white stripes in between.

I couldn't take it anymore. She was standing in front of me in nothing but a bra and panties, facing away, still and watching me. I rose off the bed, shaking all over, unable to believe I was so lucky. I stood behind her, strangling on my own breath, mouth dry.

"Jesus, Becca." I barely heard myself, but I knew she did. "You…you're the most amazing thing I've ever seen."

Her cheeks pinked, and she ducked her head. "Thank you, Jason." She turned in place and pressed up against me, lifting her lips to mine. "Your turn."

"My turn?"

She nodded, unzipping the leather jacket I'd forgotten I was still wearing. "I want to see you, too." Becca spun us in place so I was facing the bed, then backed up and sat down, crossing her legs demurely, her hands folded on top of her thighs.

I couldn't and didn't try to stop staring at her, soaking in her beauty. I'd never known a girl could be so beautiful. I mean, yeah, I'd seen shit on TV and movies, I'd flipped through Victoria's Secret catalogues. But that had nothing at all on the reality of my girlfriend in real life, real flesh for me to touch, to kiss, to hold.

I was nowhere near as confident as Becca seemed to be. I had no idea how to take off my clothes for her and look cool doing it. I would sure as hell try my best, though.

Becca

I sat perched on the edge of the bed, fear, embarrassment, worry, and excitement shivering through me. I had no idea how Jason didn't see that I was shaking from head to foot. I couldn't believe I was here doing this. I couldn't believe I'd just done that, just stripped out of my clothes like a harlot. I felt so stupid doing it, like a poser, an ugly girl trying too hard to be a sexy woman. My knees had knocked together the entire time, and my hands had shaken so bad I'd been almost unable to get my shirt over my own head. I'd actually gotten it stuck on my breasts, which were turned into giant balloons by this bra I'd bought at Victoria's Secret and put on in the mall bathroom, stuffing my old bra and panties in my purse. I think Jason appreciated the way my tits had bounced when I'd finally been able to get the shirt over them, though.

Each breath was shaky, my skin tingling, hot and then cold. Jason stood in front of me, wearing a pair of faded, tight-fitting jeans, black athletic shoes with red trim around the bottom, and a black long-sleeve henley shirt, the buttons undone to show a sliver of bronze skin. I let myself stare at him, waiting for him to take his clothes off.

God, the boy was hot. I'd always had a crush on him, and now it was turning into all-out true love, and he was sexier than he'd ever been, just standing there with his weight slightly to one side, his biceps straining the fabric of his sleeves, his shoulders broad and strong. His eyes raked over me, chips of green set deep in his chiseled face. I watched his adam's apple bob in his throat, watched his powerful hands curl into loose fists and release. He was barefoot, and I remembered reading in some novel that there was nothing sexier than a man barefoot in blue jeans. Seeing Jason in that moment, I had to agree.

He finally summoned a smile and tore his eyes away from my assets to meet my gaze. I lifted an eyebrow in a *get on with it* smirk that I didn't entirely feel. I was acting to cover my fear. I wasn't sure I was ready for this, but I knew I couldn't and wouldn't back out now. Well, no, that wasn't true. I *could* back out. Jason would be totally understanding—he'd take me anywhere I wanted to go without complaining if I said I wasn't ready. The problem was, I *wanted* to be ready. I wanted this with him; I just couldn't seem to rid myself of the shakes, of my fear that I'd do something wrong, that someone would find out, that I'd messed up my birth control and I'd get pregnant...

Then Jason grabbed his shirt by the hem and lifted it up, stretching his abs taut as he peeled the shirt away in one smooth motion. I licked my lips at the sight of him. Yes, I actually licked my lips. He was a god, it seemed to me, an ancient Grecian athlete, blond and hard-muscled and perfect. He stood shirtless in blue jeans, a rim of cotton elastic peeking over the waistline of his pants. I had my legs crossed, and I had to press my thighs tighter together to keep from lunging off the couch and wrapping my legs around him. Desire raged, at war with the ever-present fear.

He reached slowly down and flicked open his jeans, then stopped.

"Flex for me," I whispered. "Show me your muscles."

He shook his head and laughed. "Flex? Like a bodybuilder?" He acted like that was the most absurd notion he'd ever heard, but he wasn't me, looking at him.

Even at rest he was glorious, just standing with one hand in his pocket, the other reaching behind his head to scratch the back of his opposite shoulder. His arms were long and thick, biceps bulging and lined with veins, but his chest and stomach were my favorite places. He had broad, heavy pectoral muscles that bulged out from his chest, a fine line chiseled between them, pointing down to the rippling wonderland of his abs. He didn't have the ultra-defined kind of abs that Kyle did. Jason's stomach was hard, and definitely ripped, just toned in a different way than Kyle's. Not that I was trying to compare the two, but more as a matter of differentiation. I'd seen both boys shirtless before on numerous occasions, swimming at the beach in the summer, after football practice…Kyle had the honed definition look that I thought of as "cut," whereas Jason's build was more heavy muscle, thicker, harder, less defined but with more bulk.

He made a face at me, then assumed an overtly ridiculous flexing pose, and I laughed so hard I snorted, even as I appreciated the view. He was being silly, I knew, bending forward with his hands clasped in front of himself, but the pose worked to flex every muscle in his upper body to incredible effect.

A thought struck me, and I acted on it before I could lose my nerve. I stood up in front of him, then reached for his zipper, feeling the springy hardness of him behind his boxers. I was shaking again, shivering all over, suddenly cold and terrified of what I was about to, but determined to go through with it. I unzipped him, shoved his jeans down, crouching down with them to help him lift his feet out of them, one at a time. I was kneeling in front of him then, eye level with his privates. I could see him bulging against the tight cotton of his gray boxer-briefs. Still kneeling, I curled my fingers between his skin and the elastic, then, looking up to watch him, I pulled his underwear down, baring him completely.

I sucked in a breath, seeing him again. Oh, god. Oh, god. So much. Could I do this?

I leaned forward, parting my mouth, felt him against my lips, tasted salt and musk, and then I was being lifted up.

"No, Becca. No." He held my face in his hands, forcing my eyes to his. "Not that, not now, not like this."

I wasn't sure whether to be relieved or upset that he'd stopped me, especially after psyching myself up to do it for him. "You don't want that?"

He frowned, clearly struggling with his answer. "I don't think any guy could say 'no, I don't want that.' But not...not in this situation. That's not why we're here. We're here to share something together." He searched my eyes. "Are you afraid?"

I looked down, away from his eyes, and was greeted by his manhood in all its glory, tall and thick. I looked back up to his eyes and nodded. "Yes," I whispered. "I'm terrified."

He pulled me against him, and I suddenly felt vulnerable and naked, even though I was still in my bra and underwear and he was completely bare. "We don't have to do this. You didn't...you didn't have to do that. Buy new lingerie and do the whole stripping thing."

"You didn't like it?" I felt my nerves overtaking me, my false confidence leaving me.

He laughed. "Becca, baby. I *loved* it. But...I'm worried you were doing it because you thought I'd...I don't know, expect it, maybe? Or maybe that I wouldn't want you if you didn't? Either that, or you were...overcompensating for being afraid."

"Aren't you afraid?"

He nodded. "Hell, yes. I have no problem admitting I'm afraid. I'm nervous. I don't know what we're doing...what to do. I've heard it might hurt you, and I don't want that. I just...I want it to be perfect, since it's our first time, for both of us and as a couple. And I just...I love you, and I don't want to mess anything up."

I rested my head against his chest, feeling his hands caress my shoulders, my back. I liked having his

hands on my skin; it was soothing, relaxing, calming...
and erotic. He had full access to all of me like this. A
flick of his hands, and I'd be naked. His hands made
me forget my fears and accentuated them all at once.
So confusing.

He just held me, smoothing his palms over my
spine, my shoulder blades, my arms. I breathed, forcing myself to relax.

"Do you want to leave, Becca?" His voice was soft,
concerned.

I shook my head against his chest. "No. I don't."

"You're sure?" I nodded again. "Then kiss me," he
said, touching my chin.

I tilted my face up to his, lightly pressed my lips
to kiss him. It was gentle, hesitant, almost chaste at
first. Then his hands skated over my back, traced the
line of my bra strap, descended lower to the small of
my back. I gasped into his mouth at his increasingly
hungry touch. I pressed closer to him, feeling myself
squish against his chest. His hands arced into the sway
of my back and over my ass, cupping, holding, and
god...so perfect. I felt a hesitation in his kiss, and then
he slipped his fingers under the fabric of my underwear, against my skin, skimming over my hips first and
pushing my panties down. I stopped kissing him but
left my lips against his, opened my eyes and gazed into
his bright green stare.

He pushed my panties farther down, then slid his palms around to touch my bare flesh, and I closed my eyes in a drawn-out blink. My hands were on his shoulders, where they always seemed to gravitate during a kiss. I matched his action, carving my hands down his arms to his waist, his hips, then to the cool hardness of his backside and clutched it, kneaded it, explored it while he did the same to me.

We were acclimating to each other's touch, the feel of naked skin. It was a slow introduction to completed nakedness. I'd only touched his man part—I nearly snorted out loud as I thought that silly, girly phrase in my own head. I wondered what to call it. I backed away from him and put my hand on his chest and drew a line downward, stopping just above it.

Then I grasped it, bold and sudden, and met his startled gaze. "What do you call this?"

"What?" He was confused by the question.

I slid my palm down him a bit and then back up. "This...what word do you use?"

He shrugged. "I don't really refer to it much." He glanced up and to the left as he thought, then flicked his gaze back to me. "If I have to use a word for it, I usually use the word 'cock,' I guess. Why?"

I lifted my shoulder a little. "Just curious. I couldn't decide. I don't like most of the words for it."

He laughed. "I don't, either. Usually, to be honest, it's just 'it.'" He took my hand and drew it away from him, from his "it." "You gotta let go, or this will be over before it starts."

I went back to caressing his buttocks. "I can touch you here, right?"

He blushed, and it was adorable. "Yeah, if you want. I like it."

"You do?"

He shrugged, his hands resting on my hips. "Yeah." He slid his palms around to my backside. "Do you like this?"

I nodded, never taking my gaze from his. "Yes, I do. A lot." I still had my underwear partially on, which felt silly, so I wiggled out of them. "Now what?"

"The bed?"

I let him guide me backward until my knees hit the edge of the bed, and I sat down, letting his body wedge my knees apart. His green gaze never wavered from mine as I scooted backward across the mattress, Jason following me. He reached past me and jerked the blankets and sheet away, and then I was on my back against the pile of pillows, Jason above me, my heart pounding, my nerves racing and my pulse thrumming and my skin singing and his hands sliding up my thighs.

I swallowed hard as he hovered above me. Everything inside me was at war. I wanted this so badly. I was terrified, I was eager, I was feeling sexy and desired, yet awkward and unsure. Jason paused, then swore under his breath. He was off the bed before I could ask him what the problem was, digging into the pocket of his jeans and pulling out a string of condoms.

Oh. Oh, god. That made it all the more real. It was really going to happen, if I didn't chicken out first.

He set them on the nightstand and slid onto the bed next to me, rather than above me. I traced the curve of his pectoral muscle. "I started birth control," I said.

He seemed shocked. "You did?"

I nodded. "Yeah. My cousin Maria took me to a clinic last week. So…I'm protected, even without those."

"Should we use them anyway?"

I shrugged. "I don't know. Probably? Just to be… extra sure?"

He nodded, and his fingers slid along my hipbone, over my stomach and up between my breasts. "Before this goes any further, I just wanted to tell you…I love you."

I smiled, the wall of nerves and fear melting a bit. "I love you, too. How'd you know I needed to hear that?"

His index finger followed the swell of my breast. "I guess I just wanted you to hear it, to know how I felt before we got...involved in things, so you'd know I wasn't just saying it in the heat of things, you know? That I really feel it. I really love you."

I tipped my body closer to his, trying desperately to mimic his sense of comfort with his own nudity. I wanted to cover up, to pull the blankets over my body, to cross my arms over my breasts and my legs over my privates. I didn't, though. I summoned all my courage and let him see all of me. His gaze raked down over my body, over my breasts and hips, my legs, and then to the "V" between my thighs.

I called up the memory of how it had felt to have him touch me there, how the detonation within me had felt. It would be worth all this awkwardness to feel that again. There was no question of that.

"Kiss me, Jason."

He leaned into me, his lips gently settling on mine, tenderly seeking out my response. I opened my mouth to his, let my tongue explore his lips, his teeth, letting my own hunger overtake me. It wasn't enough to erase my doubts and fears, but it was enough to let me go on despite them. His palm cupped my hipbone, tilted my body so I was flat against the bed and he hovered over me from the side, his mouth never leaving mine.

My thighs were pressed tight together, and when his fingers trailed over the hollow of leg and hip, I unconsciously clamped them tighter together. His hand slid down my thigh, over the quadricep and to my knee, dipped down between my legs and began a slow path upward, trailing fire along my skin. I forced my thighs to loosen as his touch rose upward, closer and closer. I called the memory of his touch into my mind, pushed out the doubt. I made myself touch him, and then let myself get lost in the heat of his skin, the hardness of his muscles, let myself enjoy the feel of his body under my hand. I touched him everywhere I could reach, except *there*. Lying down in a bed, his body bare against mine…the reality of imminent sex was overwhelming, and I wasn't sure I was ready suddenly. I didn't want to stop his touch, though. The callused pads of his index and middle fingers were at the juncture of my thighs, and I was shaking all over, panting, our kiss broken. I felt his eyes on me, and I knew I was still clamped down too hard for him to touch me properly. I had to loosen up or put a stop to the whole thing.

"Are you sure about this, Becca? We can stop." His voice was low, close to my ear.

Somehow his words, so concerned, so genuine, made me determined to experience this. I didn't want to let him down. I didn't want him to think I didn't want this. I wasn't sure, not one hundred percent; I was *mostly* sure, and that had to be enough.

I relaxed my knees first, then my thighs. I met his gaze, his green eyes soft and so full of so much love. I forced my muscles to go slack, and I realized as I did so that my whole body was tensed and taut, even the hand wedged between our bodies curled into a fist.

"I'm sure. I'm just…nervous," I said.

"So am I."

"You don't seem like it."

He traced a line down my thigh, then back up the other one, each touch making me alternately tense and relax. "I am, though. I'm trying to play it cool, but…I'm nervous, too."

"Scared, or nervous?"

"Both? I don't want to stop, though. I don't want to you to feel pressured."

"But you want this?"

"Absolutely." There was no hesitation in his voice at all.

I moved my legs apart, and his touch skated into the gap, a single finger tracing my opening, an almost-tickling brush along the sensitive skin. I breathed out with the fire of his finger's grazing up and down, let my legs fall farther apart. I realized my eyes were closed again and forced them open, met his eyes. His gaze searched me for demurral as he slipped the tip of his finger into me, and I gasped, letting my hips lift a bit. It was enough of an encouragement for him.

Oh...he'd found the perfect place to touch me, and I couldn't help but gasp again, breathe in and tilt my head back, raise my hips, widen my thighs, and silently urge him onward. How did he know exactly what I needed? How did he know that felt so good? Was he lying about having never done this before me? No, I knew he wasn't, but the thought crossed my mind, because his finger at my clitoris was so perfect, exactly what I needed to let desire sweep over me.

Within seconds I was at the edge of explosion, a few circles of his fingers enough to have me writhing. It didn't take much, I realized. I'd heard other girls talking about how they couldn't make it happen, that they'd faked it with their boyfriends, or exaggerated their reactions. I couldn't fathom that. All it took was his touch, his fingers just there touching me, and I was lost, unable to hold back the whimpers escaping me. How could anyone fake it? How could you fake such glorious rapture? I was moaning as I came apart, my breathing ragged and my body trembling, not from nerves now but with tremors of ecstasy.

I heard something crinkle and then he was kneeling over me, his hands beside my head. I opened my eyes just in time to see his mouth descend to my breast, and he took a nipple in his mouth, drawing a groan from me. And then I felt it, a gentle pressure between my thighs. His hands were visible on either side of my face, so I knew what it was.

His eyes sought mine. "Becca? Is this okay? Are you ready?"

All the world fell away, and all that remained was Jason's eyes on mine, his breathing slow and his lips close to mine...and the hot, hard presence between my legs. I hesitated, suddenly unsure all over again. He felt my hesitation and began to pull away, so sweet, so considerate, and that decided me. I reached between us, my heart hammering in my chest so hard I was sure he could see the pounding against my ribs. I grasped him in my fist, so soft and warm yet iron hard. He gasped at my touch, his eyes going hooded. I nestled him between the damp lips of my privates and drew in a long breath.

"I'm r-rrr-ready." It was the first time I'd stuttered in weeks. He caught it, of course, and hesitated. I slid my palms down his back and pulled him closer to me. "I promise—I'm ready." I made sure my voice was strong, sure, and confident.

All things I didn't entirely feel. Oh, god. Only the very tip of him was inside me, and it was so much *more* than his fingers had been. I refused to think about the stories I'd heard of other girls' first time. This was all that mattered. I wanted this. I was only partially convincing myself.

I kept my eyes on his, let them close and leaned up to kiss him. He slid forward a tiny bit, and I gasped into his mouth as he filled me slowly. It hurt. I couldn't stop my eyes from flying open and my body from tensing. It felt like an invasion. I was so, so stretched. Jason had frozen stone-still.

"Are you okay?" He sounded worried.

I nodded. "Yeah, just…wait a moment." He was tense; I felt his muscles knotting and going rock hard under my hands. Slowly, my body became used to his presence, and then I nodded. "I'm okay. A little more."

"Does it hurt?" he asked.

"Yes," I said, knowing he'd want the truth. "But it's okay. It's not too bad. It's getting better. Go a little deeper."

He adjusted his weight and moved his hips toward mine, sliding himself deeper. That's when I felt the pressure of blockage, and I knew what was coming next. I don't know if he felt it, but I knew there was nothing for it but to let him push past it. I held onto him, one arm around his neck, the other around his waist, and I pulled him by his buttocks against me.

There was a short, sharp pinch, and I couldn't keep the gasp of pain from escaping. The sense of fullness, of being stretched out, increased as he moved deeper, and now that feeling was moving from discomfort to something like pleasure. The pain was lessening, and his hips were flush against mine. I pressed my lips to his shoulder and focused on my physical feelings. Now that the worst part was over, the fullness wasn't so alien a sensation. It felt…right, and more so with every passing moment. He was still against me, trembling. I realized this wasn't going to last much longer, and I wanted it to. I said nothing, but placed my palm on his cheek and rocked my hips against his, meaning just to encourage him, but when I did so, that tiny motion of rolling my body against him…a rocket of heat shot through me, a lightning bolt striking me low in my belly.

"Oh," I gasped, my mouth going wide. I did it again, rocking my hips against his, but harder this time. "Oh…oh, god."

Jason's body was rock-hard, every muscle flexed. He was holding back, trying to last. "This is…amazing," he said, his voice a ragged murmur.

"Move with me," I whispered.

He breathed a sigh of relief and drew back, only to plunge forward again, and I whimpered at the way that felt. It sent a different kind of thrill through me than when I'd rolled my core against him, but both felt amazing. He drew back, and this time I moved to meet him, thrusting against him, and we both groaned, almost in unison.

"I'm not gonna—I can't stop…" Jason's voice was a low whisper against my ear.

I knew what he was saying. "It's fine," I whispered back to him, whispering low as though speaking out loud would break the moment. "Don't…don't stop yourself."

He was moving in a rhythm now, each motion growing more desperate. "I couldn't if I tried," he murmured.

I was on fire all over, and even though I hadn't expected to orgasm again, I was close. I moved with him, seeking my own release, knowing he was feeling pleasure and letting myself seek my own. I crushed my body against him, wanting to get closer, needing more, more, more. I remembered something I'd seen on *True Blood*, and lifted my legs to wrap them around his waist.

"Shit…that feels good," Jason said.

"So good," was all I could manage.

I used my legs to pull him against me, and the pressure built higher, the heat inside me billowing to nearly unbearable proportions. He was moving fast, and I'd have thought it would hurt to have him slam against me like he was, but it didn't. I liked it. Each thrust sent me higher, and I knew he was about to lose it, and I wanted him to.

My fingers clawed into his shoulders, and I gripped him close as if to make sure he didn't stop.

Then the earth fell apart beneath me. My body shuddered, tensed, and exploded. What I'd felt before was barely a tremor in the ground compared to the juddering earthquake shaking through me now. I whimpered, and then he crashed against me, crying out, and I felt the explosion cut loose inside me and heard an actual scream leave my mouth as I came moments after he did.

We both moved together in sync, breathing hard and gasping and moaning.

"Oh, f-fuck," I said. "I didn't know it would feel l-like th-that."

He laughed at my uncharacteristic use of the F-bomb. "Me, neither," he said, stilling above me.

And then it was over. The whole thing had lasted less than five minutes, but it was a life-changing, earth-shaking five minutes.

Jason slid off me and went into the bathroom. I giggled at the sight of his naked backside as he walked away. Then he came back to me and slid into the bed beside me. "Did you bleed?"

I pushed the sheets away and sat up. The sight of the bright red spot on the bed brought reality crashing down around me. I wasn't a virgin anymore. Something about that blood opened the floodgates. I felt my eyes burn, and I didn't want to cry, but I was just so overwhelmed that I couldn't stop it.

Jason had me against his chest before the first tear had fallen. "Becca? Why are you crying?" He sounded afraid, and I knew he had to be assuming the worst, but I was in the process of completely losing it and couldn't speak as shuddering overtook me, tears sluicing down my face. "Oh, god, Becca. I'm sorry. I shouldn't have—"

I shook my head against his naked chest. "No," I choked out. "I'm just…just over-overwhelmed. N-not upset."

He sighed in relief. "You're not mad at me?"

I giggled through my tears. "Mad? Why would I be mad?"

He shrugged. "I don't know. You saw the blood and started crying, and I thought…I don't know. I thought maybe you regretted doing this…with me."

I wrapped my arms around him, sitting on his lap and still crying. "No, Jason. No. I don't. I'm overwhelmed is all. It was so much better than I'd ever thought it could be, better than I'd heard some girls talk about their first time having been."

"Really?" He sounded hopeful.

I nodded. "Yeah. I don't think most girls have an… an orgasm their first time." I tilted my head back to meet his eyes. "You gave me that."

He blushed but looked pleased. "I'm glad. Did it hurt bad?"

I shook my head. "A little at first, and then it pinched when…you know. But then it didn't hurt at all after that, and it started to feel good. Really good."

There was still so much going on inside me that I couldn't express. I didn't regret what we'd just done, but I knew I was different. That was a moment that could never be experienced again. I wasn't a virgin any longer, I wasn't a girl anymore; I was a woman now.

I came again the second time, even harder than the first, and Jason lasted even longer, bringing us both to rapture and trembling ecstasy. I knew, as I drifted sleepily in his arms after the second time, that I'd never be able to get enough of this. I wanted more even as I felt the aftershocks still shaking me.

Jason brought me home five minutes before my 1 a.m. weekend curfew, and we kissed slowly and tenderly in the warmth of his truck's cab before I got out.

We kissed differently, I realized. We were aware now of what came after kissing.

I waved to him from my front door and went to my room, flopping on my bed with a crazy grin on my face, thoughts floating around my head as I fell asleep. I was a little sore between my legs, and I knew I would be tomorrow, too. It was worth it, even though I wondered, at the bottom of my heart, if it had been too soon, if we were too young, if I'd been totally ready.

Nine: A Tree Falls
Jason
August, two years later

I LOUNGED ON MY COUCH, expecting a call from Becca. My phone was on my thigh, the TV on, tuned to Sports Center. It was odd to be graduated, at loose ends. I had acceptance letters from the University of Nebraska and the University of Michigan, full-ride scholarship offers to both on the merits of football and grades. I needed the scholarships, especially since I'd stopped accepting any money from Dad for anything. I'd broken the national records I had my sights on by the middle of my senior-year season, and Dad had tried to give me something like two thousand dollars for each record broken. I refused it, he got pissed, we fought, and I put him in the hospital. He hadn't even looked at me since.

Becca was supposed to call me when she was done with her hair appointment, and we were going to go out for a late lunch to discuss university options. She was set on U of M, to the point that she'd only applied to there. Of course, she'd gotten in with a huge grades scholarship on top of all the other grants and scholarships she'd applied for. She was the valedictorian of our graduating class with a 4.26 final GPA. Yeah, she was that kid. Her speech was moving and fluent, not one stutter. She'd even gone down to one ST session a month from twice weekly. She had so many scholarships her entire BS degree was going to be totally paid for, and I wasn't quite sure how she'd done it. Well, I did, actually. She spent hours every day her entire senior year applying for them, writing essays, mailing them out, hunting for more scholarships. Her parents could afford to pay for her education, I was fairly sure, since they were pretty loaded—although they were quiet about that fact—but Becca refused to accept their help since it came with conditions. Namely, that she and I couldn't live together. A deal-breaker for my girl, god bless her.

I glanced at my phone: 3:52 p.m. She was supposed to call me at 3:30. I wasn't worried or mad, just curious. She was punctual to a fault, so her being this late was unusual.

I flicked off the TV and went to the dining room table, where the bills and mail were piled up. I lifted the two acceptance letters and stared at them, unsure of what to do. I really liked Nebraska's football team, plus they had a great architecture program that I was interested in. Nebraska was Dad's first choice for me, which sort of worked against it, in my book. The big issue with the University of Nebraska, of course, was the fact that it was in Nebraska. Fucking Nebraska. Six hundred and ninety-five miles from Ann Arbor, where Becca would be.

Hell, no.

U of M, of course, meant living with Becca. It had a couple of academic programs I was interested in besides their football team, which had improved over the last few years. Their starting quarterback was promising, and I was pretty sure his style would mesh with mine. Kyle and I had talked about going to the same college just so we could play together, but we had different careers in mind, and it just wouldn't work. He didn't really plan on trying to go pro, I didn't think. He liked football, and he was damn good, but… it wasn't his focus. He wanted to be a trainer, I think. I wasn't sure. Me? I wanted to go pro, but I also wanted to have a degree to fall back on, a secondary career in mind. I'd learned something from Dad after all.

He'd never planned on anything but playing ball. He'd floated through school, had a degree in English that wasn't good for shit when it came down to jobs, since all his life was focused on ball.

I didn't want that for myself. I knew I was smart; I knew I had potential beyond football. I hadn't spoken to another living person about this, yet, not even Becca, but I'd been browsing degree programs on the U of M website, and the one that had jumped out to me was their art and design department. Photography.

I had a huge portfolio of photographs put together. Becca had helped me with it, claiming it was for herself so she could leaf through my photos in physical form. I knew better. She loved my photography. She was always encouraging me to pursue it. She'd be over the moon if she knew I was even considering a degree in photography.

As stupid as it seemed, the biggest reason keeping me from it was my father. He'd disown me. Photography was art, and art was for sissies. I'd play ball, and that was it. As much as I hated my dad, deep down I knew I still wanted his approval.

An engine in my driveway had my attention immediately. It wasn't my dad's diesel F-350, that was for sure. I went to the window and nearly passed out when I saw Becca getting out of a sleek, black, brand-new VW Jetta. Her parents had refused to buy her a car, especially since I was always driving her everywhere, and they also refused to let her get a job to buy her own. That had been a point of contention in her relationship with her parents, which had improved over the last two years somewhat.

I pushed through the screen door to greet her. She jumped up into my arms, wrapping her legs around my waist, a huge grin on her beautiful face.

"They bought me a car!" She kissed me hard, holding the back of my head with both hands; I loved when she did that. "Isn't it gorgeous? They said I needed a car to get back and forth from school." She wiggled out of my arms and ran to her car, running her hands over the hood.

I laughed at her excitement, happy for her. "It's awesome, baby. I'm so happy for you!"

She straightened, bouncing up and down on her toes and clapping, acting more girly than I'd ever seen her. "I c-can't believe it! I have a car!" I couldn't keep myself from watching her boobs jiggle as she bounced on her feet. She caught me staring and gave me a wry glare. "Eyes on me, hon."

I grinned sheepishly. "Sorry. I can't help it if you've got a rack I can't take my eyes off."

She slid into my arms. "Haven't you gotten enough of my *rack* by now?" She grimaced at the term

I'd used. "Our two-year anniversary is next month. You'd think you'd be used to them by now." She smiled up at me, knowing the truth.

I shook my head. "That's impossible. I'm a guy. You can never get too much of a good thing. And, baby, your boobs are a *great* thing."

She smacked my arm, but it was an empty protest. "You're such a pig."

"Yep. Oink oink."

She just giggled, and god, did I love her cute little laugh. "Get in, hot stuff. This time *I'm* gonna take *you* for a ride."

"I love it when you take me for rides." I grinned as I slid into the passenger seat.

Becca ignored my not-so-subtle innuendo. "It's a hybrid, sss-so it gets forty-two miles per g-g-gallon city, and forty-eight highway…" She backed out of my driveway, rattling off all the various specs of her new car. It made me seriously happy to see her so excited that she didn't even notice her own stutters, which only happened when she was super nervous or excited. Or during the throes of passion, you might say. She tended to stutter a little as she came, and that always put a smile on my face. It was adorable, to me. A part of who she was, and knowing she felt comfortable enough with me that she didn't even get embarrassed when she stuttered meant a lot to me.

We passed my dad pulling into the driveway, and he gave us a cursory glare, lifting his eyes derisively at Becca's *foreign* car. Buying foreign was a sin in his book; the fact that Becca was half-Arabic bugged him to no end, and we'd actually gotten in one of our worst fist-fights over that very fact. He'd used a derogatory slur about her during my junior year, and I'd flattened him without hesitation. We'd gone three rounds right there in the kitchen until we were both bloody and needing stitches. Neither of us got them, though, and damn it if we weren't alike in that way. I'd left in a red rage, still bleeding, and Becca had met me at our tree with a first aid kit. She hadn't asked what the fight was about, thank god. I don't think I could have told her without losing my shit all over again.

I forcibly moved my thoughts away from my dad and listened to Becca chatter happily. I'd tuned out and had no clue what she was talking about, so I had to play catch-up, realizing she was talking about having already started on the required reading list for her classes at U of M.

Of course Becca would be already registered and have the books and reading, and I wasn't even sure which school I was going to. Becca refused to weigh in on my decision. She never brought it up, ever. She said she wanted me to make my own decision. She loved me; she'd support whatever I chose. I knew deep down she wanted me to go U of M with her, but she'd never say that. She'd said we'd make our relationship work even if I chose Nebraska, and I knew she meant it.

I held her hand as she drove, listening to her talk, letting her words wash over me. It wasn't that I wasn't paying attention—I just knew that sometimes she needed to just talk, get out all the words she'd held back throughout the day. It was one of the ways she coped with stuttering, I'd discovered. She kept quiet during the day, only saying what she was sure she could get out fluently, and then when we were alone, she'd just ramble without expecting me to respond, and she'd let herself stutter, let it happen as it would, knowing I didn't care.

I tuned back in as she made a left turn onto the main road through town. "S-so anyway, I'm pretty excited about this lit class I'm in. It's err-early eighteenth-century British literature. We're f-focusing on Defoe, Jonathan Swift, and Galland's translation of *One Thousand and One Nights*, which is really unusual. It's a higher-level class, since I've taken most of the freshman-level classes already." I'd only heard of Defoe, but wouldn't have admitted that except under duress. "My major coursework classes are the ones I'm most excited about. It's all undergrad stuff, of course, but

U of M is a respected university, ee-even if they're not really ranked in the speech-language pathology field. My graduate work will probably be at somewhere like the University of Iowa. They're the b-best, I've heard. I c-can't say I'm excited at the idea of living in Iowa, but...it's far enough away that I don't have to decide n-now."

I laughed. "But you're already thinking about it?"

She grinned at me. "Yeah, you know how I am."

I snorted. "Yeah, you're a career overachiever."

She frowned at me. "What's that supposed to mean?"

Uh-oh. "It's a good thing, Beck. You're just always prepared, and you're fucking amazing at everything. Like, I don't think you could fail at anything, even if you tried."

She rolled her eyes at me. "I got a D on a test once."

I stared at her, unsure if she was kidding. "Dear Lord, a D? When was this? Second grade?" I teased.

She didn't look at me as she answered. "It was the end of the year, last year. This year, whatever. Senior year. In my stupid research paper writing class. I mean, the whole point of the thing was learning to write for research, going past the block-outline method. There aren't supposed to be any tests other than the papers themselves. So then she springs this idiotic mu-mu-multiple choice test on us, no rubric, no warning. No one got better than a C because no one had studied for it or even had any c-clue what the questions were talking about." She was getting worked up just thinking about it. "God! That one test, that D-plus? It took me down four-tenths of a percent! I would have graduated with an even four point three if it wasn't for that stupid f-fucking teacher!"

Damn, she used the F-word.

I couldn't help laughing a little. "A whole four-tenths of a percent? That bitch." There might have been just a little sarcasm in my voice.

Becca's head swiveled slowly toward me, her eyes narrowed, her jaw set. "It's a b-b-big d-deal…to m-mmm-me."

I sighed. "I'm sorry, babe. That was a dick thing to say." She snatched her hand away and drove in silence until I couldn't take it anymore. "Becca, I'm sorry. I wasn't making fun of you. I'm just saying, you still graduated with one of the highest GPAs in the entire *state*. I know it was a big deal for you, though. I'm sorry."

"And that four-tenths of a percent could have been the difference between *one* of the highest and *the* highest." She glanced at me. "Like how if you'd missed even one catch, it might have made the difference between breaking the record or not."

I nodded. "I know, Becca. I was just being stupid."

"Well, you *are* a guy." She smirked, and I knew she'd forgiven me.

"Yeah, and guys are idiots. I don't know why you put up with me." I really didn't, in truth, but I let it sit as a joke, knowing Becca would have a field day if she sensed that insecurity in me.

"It might have to do with what you did last night." She licked her lips and winked salaciously at me.

"Which part?" I asked, deadpan.

She pretended to consider. "Hmm. Probably that thing you did with your tongue."

I nodded seriously. "Oh, that. Well, I'll have to make sure to do it again, if that's why you put up with me."

"You'd better, farm boy." Ever since we watched *The Princess Bride* together last year, she'd taken to calling me "farm boy," which she found cute for some reason. I let it go, because arguing was futile.

I slid my hand onto her thigh and cupped her sex. "Pull over, and I'll do it right now."

She clamped her thighs around my fingers, feigning horrified shock. "No! It's broad daylight!"

"That didn't stop you from letting me go down on you in the bed of my truck yesterday. It was daylight then, too."

"Barely. The sun was going down. And that was at our tree. There was no one to see. This is a busy road."

"So let's skip dinner and head to the tree," I suggested.

"I would, but I'm hungry. I never ate lunch." She grinned at me. "We'll go after dinner."

She was as eager as I was, as insatiable. More so, if anything. I'd heard other guys complaining that their girlfriends never wanted it as much as they did, but I didn't seem to have that problem. She was often the one trying to get me up for round two...and three. I couldn't stop her some days.

Then her phone rang. There wasn't anyone but me and her parents who would ever call her. Nell and Kyle were up north together, so it wasn't Nell, and her mom and dad were at some fundraiser gala weekend in Washington, D.C., so it wouldn't be them.

Becca stared at the screen of her phone. "Hmm. It's Mrs. Hawthorne. I wonder why she's calling me?" Becca fumbled a Bluetooth earpiece out of the center console, fit it into her ear, and touched a button to answer the call. "Hello? Hi, Mrs. Hawthorne, how are—*what*?" Becca's face paled. "Are you fucking kidding me? He's—what? No. Please, no."

She hit the brakes and skidded off the road on the shoulder, her hand over her mouth, eyes wide, tears flowing, shaking her head in denial.

"Becca?" I shoved the shifter into park for her and touched her shoulder. "What is it?"

She didn't answer me. "No. No. It's not true." She turned to look at me with horror in her eyes. "And Nell? Is she okay? Oh, god. Oh, god. Okay, we'll be there. Yes, he's with me, I'll—I'll tell him. Sh-shit. *SHIT!*" She ripped the earpiece out of her ear and threw it so hard it smashed against the dashboard.

"Becca? What *happened*?" Something bad was going on, and my stomach was flipping. "Why wouldn't Nell be okay? Talk to me!"

Becca was sobbing, her head against the steering wheel. I lunged out of the car and circled around to the driver's side, tugging open the door. Becca fell against me, and I had to hold her with one arm and unbuckle her with the other. I gathered her limp form in my arms and carried her around into the grass at the side of the road, kicking her car door closed behind me. I sat down with her on my lap and held her.

"Becca, you have to tell me what's going on."

She sniffed and choked on her breath. She looked up at me, and I could see the tragedy in her expression. "There was an accident. Up north. It-it's Kyle. He's— he's—h-h-he's d-dead."

I didn't hear her right; that was my first thought. I misheard what she said. "What? What do you mean? Kyle? Kyle Calloway?"

"Yes, Kyle! Our Kyle. He—he's dead. A t-tree fell on him. Nell's parents are on the way back from Traverse City with Nell. She's got a broken arm, and she's...she's not talking."

"How...I don't understand. How can Kyle be..." I was unable to process what I was being told.

"I don't *know*! All I know is what Mrs. Hawthorne just said. There was a bad storm, a tree fell and hit Kyle, and now he's dead." She struggled in my arms, squirming to stand up. "We have to go. We have to meet them at their house in half an hour."

I was frozen. It wasn't real. It wasn't possible. He'd...he'd told me he was going to propose to Nell. Just this past Thursday he'd told me. I'd told him he was crazy-train, he was barely eighteen, but he'd insisted that he knew he loved Nell enough that he didn't want to wait till they were older.

It was all a joke, that was it.

I fumbled my cell phone out of my pocket and dialed his number, listened to it ring and ring and ring...it went to voicemail. "Hey, this is Kyle. I'm probably out being awesome somewhere, so leave a message and I'll get back to you. If I feel like it." The snorts of laughter in the background as he recorded the message were mine.

I felt a small, cold hand take the phone from me. I let her. She tugged me up to my feet, hauling me bodily up. "Come on, baby. Nell needs us."

I stumbled, and she caught me with her shoulder under my arm. I stared down into her wet black eyes, and I saw a compassion there, a love, an understanding. Her own sadness was taking a back seat to her sadness for me. I didn't know what to say, what to do. All I knew was I needed Becca to get through this, and I could only hope she'd stay with me, keep loving me through it.

I found myself in the leather seat of Becca's Jetta, the new car smell almost cloying now. Becca's iPhone was plugged into the auxiliary jack, and when she started the engine, a song came on: "Your Long Journey" by Robert Plant and Alison Krauss. My eyes burned, and my throat closed. Becca went to turn it off, but I stopped her. She took my hand in hers and drove, letting the music play. A song I didn't know came on, and I picked up her phone to check the Pandora display: "Been a Long Day" by Rosi Golan. It was a quiet, beautiful song, piano providing a backdrop to a sweet female voice.

We pulled into the Hawthornes' driveway, gravel crunching under our tires. There were several cars in the driveway already. Becca tangled her fingers in mine as soon as I was upright and out of the car; she basically had to drag me into the house. I didn't want to go in. I didn't want to see the grief of other people. That would make it real. If I kept pretending it wasn't, maybe it wouldn't be.

Mrs. Hawthorne opened the door, her eyes red but dry. "Jason, Becca. Thanks for coming. Nell is in her room."

"How is she?" Becca asked.

Mrs. Hawthorne squeezed my hand, touching Becca's forehead with her own. "Not good. She...she watched him...go. She's totally unresponsive."

Becca sniffed softly, and I watched her literally square her shoulders and push her own emotions down. She tugged me by the hand up the stairs, stopping at Nell's bedroom door. Becca tried the knob, found it unlocked, and went in, with me trailing behind her.

Nell was lying on her side in her bed, eyes dry, a note clutched in her hand. A cast covered one entire arm. She stared into middle distance, not even registering our arrival. I didn't know what to do, where to look. She was clothed in an old hoodie of Kyle's and a pair of black underwear, lying on top of the blankets. I focused my gaze on the Avett Brothers poster on the wall as I drew a blanket up to her waist. I sat in Nell's desk chair while Becca climbed onto Nell's bed behind her, brushing a lock of hair out of her face.

"Nell?" Becca's voice was hesitant. Obviously, she didn't know what to say. "What—what ha-happened?"

Nell didn't answer for a long time. When she did, her voice was a raw, barely audible whisper. "He… died." Her eyes flicked up to me. "He's gone."

I choked, shaking my head. "I—fuck. How?"

She visibly withdrew into herself. "We were… arguing. A storm, crazy wind. It…blew a tree down. It was supposed to be me, but he…saved me. Pushed me out of the way. Saved me. It should have been me, but it's him."

Neither Becca nor I knew what to say to that.

"It wasn't your fault," Becca finally ventured.

Nell physically flinched, but she didn't respond. I watched her nails claw into her palm, digging in so hard I was sure I'd see blood trickle down her hand.

We sat in horrible, heavy silence until it became clear Nell wasn't going to say or do anything else.

"We're here for you, Nell. *I'm* here for you. I love you."

Nell's teeth clamped down on her lower lip when Becca said those last three words, biting so hard her pink lip turned white.

Becca led me out of the room, leaving Nell in the same position she'd been in when we arrived, eyes open and staring into nothing, a white scrap of paper clutched in her hand.

Mrs. Hawthorne pulled us into the kitchen. "How is she?"

Becca shook her head. "She s-said, like, three sentences. I don't know, Mrs. Hawthorne. I'm ww-worried about her. She's nearly catatonic."

"Maybe she just needs time." Mrs. Hawthorne was staring out the kitchen window.

"Maybe," Becca agreed, but an odd note in her voice told me she didn't exactly agree, although Mrs. Hawthorne didn't seem to catch it.

"The funeral is Wednesday." People were coming and going, bringing in dishes of food. I saw Mr. and Mrs. Calloway sitting on the couch, his arm around her thin, trembling shoulders. Mr. Hawthorne sat on the couch next to Mr. Calloway, offering a stony, stoic silence as comfort.

Becca took me home and slid into my bed next to me. I'd never been in my room with her before. We never came here because I knew my dad would be a dick and make a scene, and I didn't want Becca to have see that. In this moment, though, I couldn't summon the energy to care about my father. I just knew I needed her beside me.

I wasn't sure how long we lay there in silence, Becca's arm curled around my chest, her face pressed to my back. I felt wetness seeping into my thin cotton T-shirt, but she never made a sound.

My door banged open, slamming violently into the wall. "Who's fucking foreign piece of shit car is parked in my goddamn spot?" He filled the doorway, huge, wild-eyed, not swaying but clearly intoxicated.

Becca shrank behind me. "It's mine, Mr. Dorsey. I'm sorry. I'll move it."

"Fuckin' right you'll move it," he snarled. "Get your car out, and stay out."

"She's not going anywhere," I said, not looking at my dad. "Neither is her car."

"Why the hell is she in your bed, boy? Don't you know any better?"

"Kyle Calloway died." I said it, and it broke me.

A tear fell from my eye, just one, and I couldn't stop.

"Are you fucking *crying*?"

Becca rose to a sitting position behind me. "Kyle was his b-best friend, you know. His best friend is *dead*." Her voice was hard and quiet, but I heard the tremor of fear. She was terrified of my dad, for good reason. "Give him a break."

"Wasn't talking to you, girl." I saw the derisive curl of his lip as he glared at her, and it pissed me off.

Normally, I'd have been up in his face about it, but I didn't want Becca to see us fight. "Please just leave us alone, Dad. Don't do this. Not today." I'd never, ever asked him for anything before.

"Shut the fuck up, boy. Don't tell me what to do in my own home." He took a step toward me, and I was instantly on my feet, fists curled, ready. He stopped, though, and gave me a long, hard look. "You know how many friends I lost? How many buddies I watched die? You think I ever fuckin' cried like a pussy about it? I don't think so. People die, and it fuckin' sucks. Man up and deal with it."

"This wasn't a war. I'm not a soldier. I'm not you. I'm allowed to be upset about my best friend getting killed. I've known him since fucking *kinder*garten. So how about you just shut the fuck up and leave me alone."

I heard Becca's harsh, terrified breathing. If she didn't have to go past my asshole old man, I'd tell her to go.

"I ain't leavin' till she does."

I stepped closer to him, staring up at him, fearless and ready to snap. "I don't want to do this in front of my girlfriend, but I will. Fucking *leave*. Just leave my room. That's all I'm asking."

His nostrils flared. "Yeah, you don't want your little friend seeing you get your ass beat, that's what."

"Why are you s-s-such a bastard?" This was Becca, and my dad and I both stopped and stared at her.

"What have I ever done to you, except love your son? Do you know how many times I've fixed up his bleeding face after you beat him up? What is your p-problem? Wh-why do you hate your oh-own son so-so m-much?"

My dad gave me an incredulous look. "You're actually dating this stuttering Ay-rab bitch?"

Becca hiccuped in shock, and then sobbed when I hit him. I saw white, blinding rage. He didn't have a chance. He got some hard knocks in, but I was unstoppable. I hit him, and I hit him, and I hit him until he stopped moving, and then I kept hitting him. I felt a hand on my arm pulling at me.

"Jason, stop! Stop!" She was hysterical, nearly unintelligible. "P-please! Please just *stop!*" She screamed the last word in my ear, and it finally broke through the wall of rage.

I came back to myself, shaking, feeling wetness covering me. Warm, sticky wetness. My hands were coated in blood. I was sitting on Dad's chest, his face a wreck. I felt blood sluicing down my face, felt my jaw aching, my ribs protesting, bruised. Becca pulled me away, choking on sobs.

I lunged to my feet, grabbed her by the shoulders, and pushed her out of my room. "I'm sorry you saw that. I'm so sorry I let you come here." As I spoke, a glob of bloody saliva dripped out of my mouth, and I spat it onto the carpet, beyond caring. "I'm so, so sorry, Becca. You need to go. I have to deal with this."

"I'm not leaving you, Jason." She jerked out of my grip and spun around to face me. "What are you going to do?"

"Call an ambulance."

"Won't they ask questions?"

I shook my head. "They know better. This won't be the first time."

She didn't get it. "But...don't they *have* to report domestic violence?"

"Report it to who?" I gestured at the badge on the table, the formal picture of my father in his captain's uniform. "He is the police. He can have the report buried. Besides, I'd be the one arrested in this case, which would lead to questions neither of us want answered."

"But, Jason—"

"NO!" I hated that I was yelling at her. I forced myself into calm. "I'm sorry, but no. There's nothing to do. I'm leaving today anyway. I'm done with his bullshit."

"Where will you l-live?"

"I don't fucking *know*, Becca! My truck? A hotel? I don't fucking know. I don't care right now. I just can't stay here another day."

She nodded her understanding, knowing I just wanted her to drop it. "Let me get you cleaned up." She turned away and ripped the hand towel angrily from where it hung off the microwave door handle.

She dabbed it gently on my lip, wiping away the blood, folding it and wiping again, then wetting it under the faucet and scrubbing at my chin. She hiccuped, sniffed, blinked hard, and licked the tear away from the corner of her mouth. I sighed, angry with myself for losing it at her.

I wiped at her face with my thumb, and she flinched away. "Beck, I'm sorry. I know you don't get it. I *should* report this. But if I was going to, I would have, should have, years ago. It's too late now. I'm eighteen, I'm legally an adult, and I'm moving out. I'll never see him again after today. You'll never have to see this again, okay?" She nodded, but didn't answer, scrubbing at the blood crusting on my cheek. "Talk to me, please."

I tried to wipe a tear away again, and she flinched. As if...as if afraid of me now. "And s-say what? I was so scared. For you. *Of* you. You weren't...you w-weren't *you*. You were...so violent. You were hitting him and he wasn't fighting back, and you were still fighting him. It was so-so terrifying."

"You heard what he said."

She shook her head. "He can say what he wants about me. He's a monster, and I don't care what he thinks of me."

"I won't let him talk about you like that. He's got no right. The last time you saw me like this? He'd said something just like that."

The first thing Dad did every day when he came in from work was click on the radio, tuned to 99.5 FM, the country radio station. "Please Remember Me" by Tim McGraw was playing, and I was reminded all over again that Kyle was dead. I'd almost managed to forget for a moment.

It hit me in the gut harder than my father's fist ever had. Kyle was dead.

I collapsed onto my hands and knees, sobbing. I'd never cried, not ever. Not since I was a baby, not for anything. I couldn't have stopped it, even if I'd tried. I don't know how long I cried, but I felt Becca beside me, still with me, touching my shoulder, letting me cry.

I heard a wet, choked coughing from my bedroom, forced myself to my feet. "Shit, he's gonna choke on his own blood." I stumbled into my room and shoved my father onto his stomach, and he sputtered, vomited, and coughed again. I dragged him away from the mess and left him on the floor, half in my room, half in the hallway. I noticed shattered picture frames, broken trophies, my desk cracked in half. I had no memory of the fight itself, and I hadn't realized how bad it must have been. There was a huge hole in the drywall next to the door, another in the wall kitty-corner. My desk chair was tipped on its side, one of the casters snapped off.

"Jesus," I whispered. I turned to glance over my shoulder at Becca, who was standing in the hall, staring down at Dad's bleeding form. "I didn't know it had gotten this bad."

"I thought you were going to k-kill each other." Her voice was tiny. "Should you do something for him?"

I glanced at him, moaning now. "Fuck him. Let him bleed. He'll live." Becca stared at me like she didn't know me. "You know how many times he's left me on the floor just like that? Let me pack some shit, and we'll go. I'll call someone when we leave."

She just stood there, watching me pack. I stuffed clothes into an empty football gear bag, as much as would fit. I stuffed my laptop, charger cords for that and my phone, my prized leather jacket, and a football into the bag. I tossed a few toiletries into a gallon-size Ziploc bag, then dug my stash of cash out from under my mattress. Everything else I left. Books, trophies, my football card collection from grade school, posters of Jerry Rice and Barry Sanders and OJ Simpson and Emmett Smith, everything. None of it mattered. My camera was in my truck, and Becca was waiting for me. That was all that mattered.

I slung the bag onto my shoulder and stepped over my dad. He stirred and then rolled to his back, groaned, and sat up as I stood at the front door, about to leave. He wiped his face, peering blearily at me.

"I'm leaving," I said, not looking at him. He just nodded, not answering. "I'm not coming back."

He spat blood. "Fine."

"You need an ambulance?"

"No. Fuck you." He struggled to his feet, clutching the doorframe for balance, wiping at his mouth with his arm.

"Yeah, fuck you, too." I slammed the door behind me.

Becca was standing on the sidewalk, waiting for me. "Aren't you going to call an ambulance?"

I spat blood into the grass. "No. He doesn't want one."

"But does he need one?"

I shrugged. "Fuck if I care. That's his problem."

Becca opened her car door but didn't get in. "He's your father. What if he bleeds to death?"

"He won't. He was on his feet when I left." I probed my swollen lip and a loose tooth with my tongue.

She closed the door and stood behind me as I tossed my bag into the bed of my truck and bungeed it in place. "I don't understand how you two can be so blasé about this. You're hurt. He's hurt. You both need medial attention."

I whirled in place. "Two things," I said, my voice calm, but my eyes blazing. "One, don't ever lump me in with that fucking bastard piece of shit useless goddamn waste of humanity. I'm *not like him.* And two, I've been hurt far worse than this. I was hurt worse than this when I broke the state record for most receptions in a single game. I'm fine. I don't need your goddamn concern."

She cringed. "I'm—I'm sorry, Jason. I just—I—I—" The worry and fear and sadness and exhaustion in her eyes threatened to break me all over again.

I slumped forward, my hands on my knees, doubled over, sick with myself. "Fuck, Becca. I'm sorry. I'm sorry. I don't know what's come over me. I shouldn't have talked to you like that. You don't need to know that shit." I straightened, disgusted with myself. "God, Becca. I'm such an asshole. You deserve better than this. Better than me."

I turned away from her, fidgeting with already taut bungee cords, just for something to do other than look at the stricken expression on her face. "Just go home, Beck. Find someone else, someone worthy of being with you."

"You're...breaking up with me? Just like that?" She whispered it, her voice broken. "I...don't want to find someone more *worthy*. I want you. I want you to love me. I want you to let me worry about you."

"I'm not—god. I'm not breaking up with you. I'm setting you free of my bullshit. You don't have to be with me. I don't—I don't deserve you. I yelled at you. You could have gotten hurt in there." I pointed at the house, choking on the hot lump in my throat, terrified of her doing exactly what I was telling her she should do. "I let that happen. What if...what if I turn into him? What if I *am* like him?" I whispered the last, finally admitting out loud the deepest, darkest fear inside me, the terror that kept me awake at nights, that gave me nightmares. I shook my head, finally looking at her. "Becca, I love you. But you shouldn't be with someone you're afraid of."

She stepped closer to me and I backed away, but she followed me. "No, Jason. Stop. Just...j-just s-sss-stop. I love you. I'm not letting you push me away because you're hurrr-hurting. You're afraid. I n-n-know that. But I believe in you, okay? I th-think you're better than that, s-s-stronger than that." She took another step, and her heat and softness washed over me, her scent enveloped me, her liquid black eyes wrapped me up in love. I could see her formulating her words before she spoke. "I don't *want* to be free of your bullshit. Where is this coming from? How long have you thought this way?"

I shrugged. "Off and on since forever."

She reached up hesitantly to touch my cheekbone, as if not sure I'd let her touch me. "Well...don't. You're not him, Jason. You're not. I'm choosing to be with you, knowing you come from...that." She gestured at the house with her other hand. "Now quit trying to be macho and come home with me."

"I'm fine in my truck."

She glared at me. "You're such a stubborn idiot. You're not sleeping in your truck. I'll get Father to let you stay on our hide-a-bed in the basement."

I followed her home, and she followed through on her promise. She even sneaked down the stairs in the middle of the night to cuddle against me for a few hours before creeping back up the stairs before her parents woke up.

I registered for classes at U of M the next day and, while Becca watched, added a photography class to the list.

She drove me out to our tree that afternoon and rode me in the back seat of her Jetta, her hair a loose cloud of black curls around her bare, dark skin.

The following day, we dressed in our best black clothes and went to bury our friend.

Ten: Scratching Arms and Locked Doors
Becca
November

NELL SAT ACROSS FROM ME, her hands drawn into the sleeves of her coat. She didn't meet my eyes, just like she hadn't the last several times I'd seen her since Kyle's funeral.

She'd bolted in the middle of a speech, and then when I'd seen her again at the burial, she'd been with Kyle's older brother. At least, that's who I thought it was. I wasn't sure, as I hadn't seen him since I was ten or eleven. He was older than us by five years or so, I thought, and he looked it. He was hard and rough-looking, even in a suit, although I had to admit he was gorgeous. Dark hair, long and a bit shaggy around his collar, and piercing blue eyes darkened by an edge of maturity and the shadows of something deep.

I'd only heard Kyle talk about him a few times growing up. He was reclusive, I remember. Spent most of his time locked away in his room or in the old barn that served as a garage. He spent a lot of time in trouble in high school, I remember that much. Or rather, I'd heard the gossip. He'd left Michigan the day he graduated, leaving behind everything. I remember Kyle talking about it, sounding hurt and confused even as an eleven-year-old. He just left, and that was it.

Then he'd shown up at the burial, and Nell had gotten out of his huge pick-up truck. What was she doing with him? I couldn't figure it out, standing at the awning-covered gravesite with Jason's hand in mine. Why had he come back at all? He'd abandoned his family, his little brother, and as far as I knew, hadn't so much as called. And now Nell was hanging out with him the day of her boyfriend's funeral? I tried not to feel betrayed somehow. She didn't look at me, at anyone. She just stood in front of the cherrywood casket with the brass railings around the outside, the wet grass around the hole covered by the fake-grass-turf sort of carpeting. She looked as if she was about to jump into the deep dark hole and stay there with Kyle.

When Nell stumbled on the grass, Colton's hand steadied her. I didn't want him to touch her. She belonged to Kyle. I felt anger radiating from Jason beside me, and I knew he was feeling a similar conflicted confusion.

Nell sat down on a chair and stared listlessly into space as a minister spoke meaningless words. I cried softly, like Kyle's mother, like Mrs. Hawthorne, like so many people...except Nell. Nell wasn't crying, hadn't cried that I saw.

When the words were spoken, she had tossed a flower into the grave, then turned and ran, stumbling on her high heels, kicking them off, her cast cradled against her side. Who followed her? Colton. I heard whispers, people asking the same questions I was thinking.

Now she sat with a cup of coffee in front of her, stirring it idly with a battered spoon. We were in a diner in Ann Arbor. She'd come out to see me since I was inundated with classes and homework. When I called her this morning to see if she could come hang out for a few hours, she'd agreed, but her voice had sounded apathetic and resigned.

I sipped my coffee and watched Nell stare into the swirling caramel-colored depths of her coffee. "Nell? Have you...seen anyone?"

"Seen who?" She glanced at me briefly, but then went back to staring into her coffee, just the tips of her fingers peeking out from the sleeves of her dove-gray North Face fleece.

I shrugged. "Someone. A…therapist. About what happened."

She shook her head, the tip of her loosely braided hair shaking over her shoulder. "No. I'm fine."

"I don't think you are."

She finally met my eyes, her gaze almost angry. "Okay, well, am I supposed to be? He died barely three months ago. I loved him. What's a therapist going to do? Tell me it's not my fault? Talk to me about acceptance and the stages of grief? I don't need that *bull*shit, Becca." She looked away, out the window to the cool, overcast October afternoon. "I just want him back."

"I know."

"No…you *don't*." The last word was uttered in an intense whisper, and the utter anguish I saw in her eyes tore into me.

"Nell…" I wanted to help her, to get her to talk about it.

She wouldn't. She hadn't said one word about the accident since that first day in her room. She'd stayed home with her parents rather than go to any of the universities to which she'd been accepted. She was going to Oakland Community College and working with her father in his office. Basically, she was going through the motions, but it seemed to me she'd just stopped living.

"I have to go," Nell said, finishing her coffee and standing up.

"You just got here."

"I'm sorry, I just...I need to go."

I tossed money on the table for the coffee, my stomach rumbling since I'd foregone breakfast to have an early lunch with Nell. "Okay, then."

Nell must have heard the irritation in my voice. "Beck, I'm sorry. I just...I can't be a good friend right now."

"It's not that, Nell." I followed her out into the cool fall air, buttoning my pea coat part way up. "I'm worried about you."

She stopped and turned to look at me. "I know. Everyone is. I don't know what to say. I just have to get through this, but I don't know how and no one can help me do it. I just need to go home. I need to be alone." She was scratching at her right forearm over the fleece, almost as a nervous habit.

I stared at her scratching hand. "Nell, you're not... you're not doing drugs, are you?"

She flinched and dropped her hand. "No! Of course I'm not."

"Show me your arm. The one you were scratching."

Nell folded her arms under her breasts. "No. Stop worrying about me. I swear to you on Kyle's grave I'm not doing drugs."

I heard the sincerity in her voice and had no choice but to believe her. I leaned in for a hug and smelled alcohol on her breath. "But you've been drinking." I squeezed her tight, refusing to let go.

She looked down at me. "A little, here and there. It helps, okay? It helps me cope, and it's under control." My concern must have shown on my face. "I'm an adult, Becca. I can drink if I want."

I narrowed my eyes at her. "You're underage."

She huffed. "Stop being such a stickler, Beck. If this hadn't happened, I'd be drinking at college anyway. This is just under different circumstances." She dug in her purse for her keys. "I'll see you later, okay?"

"Are you safe to drive?" I asked.

"God, Rebecca! Yes! I'm fine! Geez. You're worse than my parents. At least they leave me the hell alone!"

"Well, maybe they shouldn't, Nell!" I snapped back. "Maybe they should be worried about you. I know I am. You're scaring me."

"You're my friend. You're supposed to understand and support me."

"I do. I am. But that doesn't mean I have to sit by and let you s-sink." I ground my teeth together at the stuttered last word, squeezing my eyes shut and focusing. I never stuttered anymore, especially not in public. "I know it's only been a couple months, but you seem…worse, not better."

She shrugged. "I don't know what you want from me. He wasn't just my boyfriend, he was my best friend. I knew him my entire life. I saw him every single day for eighteen years." Her hand trembled and she squeezed it into a fist, her unpainted nails digging into her palm. "He was *every*thing. And he's gone. How am I ever supposed to be better?"

"I don't know, Nell. I don't. I know I can't understand what you're going through."

"So stop trying."

"But I—"

Nell leaned in and kissed my cheek. "I'm going. Thanks for the coffee. I'll see you later." She turned and left without a backward glance, slipping into the driver's seat of her mother's Lexus SUV.

I watched her drive away, heart burdened by worry for my friend. She didn't seem drunk, but I worried I was being a bad friend by letting her drive when I'd smelled alcohol on her breath. And the scratching of her arm? I'd seen Ben do that before, and I knew for a fact he'd tried hard drugs. She wouldn't lie to me and swear on Kyle's grave about it. I knew Nell well enough to know that.

Right?

I found Jason in the gym reserved for the football team, using a weight machine to lift what looked to be an enormous amount of weight with his legs. He was shirtless, his body glistening with sweat, the muscles swollen from exercise. Even though I was upset, I couldn't help the low growl of desire from rippling through me. I watched him lower the weight until his knees were bent to his chest, and then he blew out a slow breath and pushed to straighten his legs, visibly straining.

He was alone in the room, so I crossed behind him, unseen, the clink of the machine and the huffing of his breathing covering my presence. I waited until he had the weights resting before sliding my palms across his sweaty chest.

"Hi, baby."

He tilted his head back to look at me upside down. "Hey, beautiful. What are you doing here? I thought you were hanging out with Nell?" I leaned down to kiss him, tasting sweat on his lips and Gatorade on his tongue. "I'm all sweaty. Isn't that gross?"

"Have I ever been grossed out by you sweaty?" I brushed my fingers along his jaw. "It's sexy. Watching you work out turns me on." Even though we were alone, I whispered it.

He grinned at me, but he must have seen the troubled look in my eyes. "What is it, Beck? Where's Nell?" He swiveled off the bench and stood up.

I didn't let him wrap me in his arms, though; just because I liked the way he looked all sweaty and didn't mind kissing him that way didn't mean I wanted his sweat all over my clothes. Apparently he knew this, though, because he just held me by the arms.

"She left."

"Already?" He unbuttoned my pea coat, one button at a time.

I nodded. "Yeah. I'm really worried about her, Jase. She showed up half an hour late, stayed for one cup of coffee, and then left." I let him push the coat off my shoulders and set it across a rack of free weights. "We argued. We *never* argue. She was so closed off, so defensive."

"She's going through hell, Beck. You know that." He grabbed a towel out of his gym bag on the floor and wiped his face, neck, and chest with it, after which I let him pull me into his arms.

I sighed against his skin. "Yeah, I do know. But… she was acting…off. Scratching her arm constantly, plus she smelled like she'd been drinking."

That surprised Jason. "Drinking? At one o'clock on a Saturday afternoon?"

"Exactly. The way she was scratching her arm bothered me. Ben used to do that when he was on drugs. Like, bad drugs."

Jason's eyes narrowed. "Your brother shoots up?"

I shook my head. "Not anymore. He went through outpatient drug counseling last year, and he's been clean since. He did that voluntarily, too. But Nell? I wouldn't have thought she'd even know what drugs were, much less that she'd do them."

"Did you ask her about it?" Jason's lips touched my hair, my temple, the tip of my ear.

"Yeah, of course. She swore on Kyle's grave that she wasn't."

He thought for a minute. "I don't know, then. Maybe it was just a rash."

I shook my head. "She had her sleeves pulled down over her hands the whole time. She wouldn't show me her arm."

"Well, what can you do? Tell her parents? She's eighteen—they can't force her into anything."

"I know," I said. "I just worry. She's not herself anymore. She's changed. I mean, yeah, I know she's going through a lot, having lost Kyle, but...so have we all. We're all coping with his loss."

"Think she'd go to a therapist?" His hands massaged my shoulders, and then slid down my back, kneading as he went. "I did, and I know it helped me. And you know how I feel about shrinks."

I'd had to badger him and threaten to refuse to have sex with him until he went to an on-campus therapist with me about Kyle's death. He still went once a month, and it had turned into a healing process for him regarding his relationship with his father.

"I know. And yeah, I asked her about that, too. She said it wouldn't do her any good. All she wanted was Kyle back."

Jason just sighed. "I don't know what to tell you. It all sounds worrisome. But…what can we do except keep trying to help her and be there for her if she needs us?" I nodded and tilted my chin up for a kiss. "I'm gonna rinse off real quick, and then what say we go have some lunch? I hear your stomach growling."

"Now that I've been snuggling up against you, Mr. Sweaty Muscles, I'm gonna need a shower, too."

His eyes heated up, and his fingers dug into the small of my back. "My roommate is gone for the weekend."

"So's mine," I said, shrugging back into my coat.

"My dorm is closer," he pointed out, winning the discussion.

He threw a hoodie on over his bare torso and caught up his bag in one hand, pulling me along beside him with the other. His dorm room was a ten-minute walk through the campus normally, but we made it in nearly five. Jason had his arm wrapped low around my waist, propelling me forward. I pressed my face into his shoulder to hide my grinning giggle. He was in a hurry, and so was I.

My arm mirrored his, slipping low around his waist, and I felt his muscles shifting under my hand as I walked. I had an image of him as he'd be as soon as we closed the door to his dorm room: shirtless, his heavy, swollen muscles tantalizing me, spiked blond hair messy and wet with sweat, gym shorts riding low around his hips to show his V-cut.

I pushed him through his door as he opened it, then put my back to the door as soon as it latched. I twisted the lock and stood with my feet together, hands pressed against the door behind me, head tilted back slightly. I was waiting.

Jason made a game of it then, once we were locked in his room. He set his bag gently down on the floor beside his bed, then dug his keys, phone, and wallet out of the side pocket and set them on his desk. He hadn't looked at me, hadn't so much as turned around. He was moving as slowly as he could, just to see how long I would let it play out until I jumped him.

Over the last two years, we'd discovered that I was often the aggressor in our sexual relationship. He liked it that way, and so did I.

He flipped open the top of his laptop, logged in, and checked his email, typing a quick response to a classmate. Then, with agonizing slowness, he peeled his shirt off, and I was treated to a view of his ridiculously muscled back, the huge deltoids, lats, and traps rippling deliciously as he wadded up the shirt and tossed it into the hamper in the corner. Then, just to tease me, he stretched and tensed his arms; he knew all too well how I felt about his back. Then he turned slowly around, and I could tell he was flexing his abs because he knew how I felt about them.

Yeah, I was a lucky girl.

He lifted an eyebrow at me, and I just lifted mine back. I unbuttoned my pea coat, slipped it off my shoulders, and let it fall to the ground. Then, in a private joke, I bit the corner of my lip and shook my hair like a model in a shampoo commercial. Jason tried not to laugh at me, and marginally succeeded, the corners of his mouth quirking up in a constrained smile.

We each kicked off our socks and shoes, then stood a foot apart, staring at each other, daring the other to move first. I broke; my fingers grasped the edge of my T-shirt and peeled it off slowly. Jason's gaze locked immediately onto my breasts, pushed up by a basic red front-clasp bra. I teased him again, brushing one strap off my shoulder, then the other. I hesitated at the clasp, pinching the edges together so only my hands held it closed. I held the edges with one hand, slipped my arm out of the strap, then switched; in one quick motion I dropped the bra and covered my breasts with my hands, and Jason groaned out loud.

"You're killing me, Smalls." He stepped closer to me, staring hungrily at the swell of skin spilling out from behind my hands.

I stood in place, tilting my head up as he drew closer. "I'll drop my hands when you drop your pants."

"But then I'll be naked, and you'll still be in your pants."

I lifted a shoulder in an insouciant shrug. "I'm sure you could help me out with that."

He stepped out of his shorts to stand in front me in a pair of tight boxer-briefs, blue and green plaid cotton darkened by sweat. I compromised with him and moved my hands so all that covered my nipples were my two middle fingers. He drew in a deep breath, then closed the last few inches between us, slid slowly to his knees in front of me, his hands on the flesh of my hips above my skinny jeans. He kept his eyes on mine as he released the button and slid the zipper down, then pushed them down around my thighs, where they stuck.

He frowned at the pants, then up at me. "Damn, baby, these are tight. How the hell did you get into them?"

"Generous use of Crisco and a long running start," I said.

He laughed hard, his face resting against my belly. "God, that was funny. Seriously, though. How do you get them off?"

"Pull them by the cuff."

He lifted my foot and tugged the jeans off one leg, then the other, and I was naked in front of him except a V-string thong.

"Holy shit, when'd you get those underwear?" He took me by the hips and turned me in place so I faced the door. "Damn, Beck. That's like dental floss and a Band-aid." His hands slid over the sides of my buttocks, then curved inward to cup the swell, kneading the flesh and muscle greedily.

I laughed breathlessly. "I bought them yesterday. Victoria's Secret was having a sale, so I actually got a few pairs." I arched my back, pushing my chest forward and my backside out, drawing one leg forward and stretching the other, a pose that felt silly to me but clearly drove Jason wild, judging by the growl in his chest and the way his hands palmed my thighs and ass. "They don't cover much, do they?"

"Cover *much*? They don't cover *anything*. Your entire ass is completely bare."

"Good thing only you will ever see them, then, huh? Well, except my roommate."

"She's not a lesbian, is she?"

I quirked an eyebrow at him in question. "Would it bother you if she was?"

"Not in general, no. But as it concerns you, yes. You're mine. Man, woman, it doesn't matter. No one else can have you."

I sighed at him. "No, she's not. She's kind of a skank, actually. She brings guys back to our room almost every night, and they have sex whether I'm in the room or not. Like, they don't always even bother to pull the blanket over themselves. It's gross." I tilted my head as a thought struck me. "I thought guys were supposed to be turned on by the idea of two girls going at it?"

Jason hooked his index fingers into the string of my thong and drew it slowly down, pulled it off, then held it to his nose and sniffed, much to my mortification. "It's more of a visual thing, I think," he said, sliding up my body so his erection nestled between the cheeks of my ass, his hands slipping around my waist to cup my hipbones. "I'm pretty sure for most guys it's not really the idea of two women having sex that turns them on, in a homosexual sense. It's more the visual of two naked women together, all those curves, you know? And no, watching you with another woman would not turn me on. I'd be just as possessive and jealous over that as you with another guy."

"Good to know," I breathed.

His fingers were inching toward the joining of my thighs, and I was struggling to hold out, to not spread my legs for him and beg him to touch me. Instead, I ground my backside against him, sliding up and down his rock-hard length. I wanted it, but I wouldn't give in. He had to break first, or I'd never hear the end of it.

I was still covering my nipples with my hands, and Jason tried to nudge my hands out of the way. "Uh-uh, buster. You know the rules. Underwear, then you get to touch."

"Oh, that's the rules, huh? Since when?"

"Since right now."

He pressed his lips to my shoulder in a kiss, then across to my spine and down, down, each kiss sending trembles through my body, shivers along my skin. He was kissing my spine as he slid out of his underwear, and then I felt them settle on my head. I squealed and brushed them off.

"Gross! I don't want your sweaty boxers on my head, you jerk!" I spun in place, glaring at him.

He was laughing, and he used my momentary distraction to reach up and cup my breasts, which I'd released as I planted my hands on my hips to accentuate my irritation.

"I win," he said.

I tried not to gasp when his thumbs brushed over my nipples. "No...you...don't," I moaned. "I let you..."

"Let me what?" He had the hard-beaded peaks pinched between his thumbs and forefingers, rolling them until I was unable to think.

"Let you...win." I had to take the control back, I knew I did, but his hands knew all too well how to keep me distracted, and then his mouth descended to my breasts and laved hot kisses over my skin, and I was gone, unable to prevent myself from arching into his mouth. "Oh, god, don't stop."

"No? You like that?" He paused his oral attention to smile up at me, smirking, knowing I'd given in.

"Yeah, you know I do."

"You want more?" I could only nod and remind myself to breathe.

We'd both been so buried in schoolwork that this was the first chance we'd had to make love in over a week, and we were both desperate. I needed more, and he knew it, but he wanted to hear me say it.

"Yes, I need more," I whispered, holding his head against me, fingers tangled in his hair.

"What else do you want?"

I sucked in a breath as he pinched my nipple in his lips and stretched it away from my breast, releasing it with a pop. I had to take back some kind of control. I racked my brain, and then smiled to myself as I came up with a plan.

"Take me," I murmured.

He slid up my body, his erection stuttering against my thigh and resting hot and hard against my belly. He pulled me against him, kissed me, and bent to lift me in his arms, intent on carrying me to the bed.

I pushed him away. "No, not there."

He frowned in confusion. "Then where?"

I turned away from him, facing the door once again, and stood with my palms flat on the door, feet wide, bent slightly at the waist, head turned to watch him through a curtain of black curls. "Like this."

"Oh, fuck. Are you serious?" His hands gripped my hips, paused, and then curved over my backside.

"Like this, right now."

He reached between my legs to trace a finger through my damp folds, dipping his middle finger into me, sliding up to circle my clit. "I lied," he whispered, taking his erection in his hand and guiding himself to my entrance. "You win."

"Don't you forget it," I said, and then lost capacity for speech as he slid slowly into me, burying himself deep and deeper, until his hips were flush against my ass.

One hand on my hip, the other sliding up my back, he drew slowly out, then pushed back in, groaning. He thrust twice, then three times, and I nearly lost it right then, nearly fell over the edge just from the bliss of him inside me, but I struggled to hold it back. I wanted to go with him, wanted to feel my walls clench around him as he released.

He started to move faster, and even though that was exactly what I needed in that moment, I slowed him with a whisper. "Not so fast, Jason. Slow down. As slow as possible."

He halted mid-plunge, sliding in the rest of the way in a glacially slow thrust. "Like this?" He pulled back at the same pace, so slow it was barely movement.

"Yes," I gasped. "Just like that. So slow."

"Why?"

I tweaked my nipple with one hand, sending a bolt of lightning shooting through my body as he slid back in. "So I can feel every inch of you as long as possible."

He reached up to cup my breast, rolling my nipple between his middle fingers, pinching almost too hard at the same moment that he impaled himself in me. I gasped, ducking my head as the impending climax washed over me, built up within me. I felt his orgasm nearing as well, evidenced by the shuddering, spasmodic slide of his shaft into me.

He began to lose control of his pace, gripping both hips in his hands and driving himself in, jerking out and groaning as he slid in again. I loved it when he lost control. I loved being able to do that to him, make him feel so good he couldn't hold back. I had to move then, lifting up on my toes and driving down to meet his thrusts, bending lower and pushing away from the door with my hands, letting him drive me forward with increasingly powerful thrusts. Soon the room was filled with the slap of flesh against flesh and our joined sighs and moans, and then I felt my body clamp and spasm, a hot judder of pressure unleashing inside me, climax detonating within me. I bit my arm and screamed into my flesh as I came, and I felt him tense behind me, his fingers digging into my hips.

"God, Beck, you feel so good like this," he growled.

I couldn't respond—I could only whimper and shove myself against him as he slammed into me, frenzied now and thrusting harder than he'd ever done before. I heard him growl, and then he pulled back, paused, and thrust, the hardest yet, and I couldn't stop a cry from escaping me as he buried himself in me, slapping against me almost painfully, but not quite. It never took much to set me off, but feeling him lose control completely then, slamming into me again and again, groaning with each thrust, taking me for his own...that set me off a second time. The slap of flesh, the way he buried deep, stroking against me just right, his fingers in the hollow of my hips, pulling me against him...I came again, unable to stifle my cry this time.

"Oh god, oh Jesus," I whimpered, going limp and boneless, only his body and hands holding me upright, but still fluttering my backside against Jason's hips as he continued to thrust, lost in his own impending climax. "Are you gonna come now?"

"God, yes. Right now," he groaned.

He thrust home one last time, and then I felt the hot gush of his release inside me and I cried out as he pressed himself deeper and deeper, not thrusting but crushing himself against me as he came, gasping my name over and over again.

When he was still, I pulled away from him and stumbled to the bed, collapsing onto it and pulling him with me. He fell in next to me, burying his face against my breasts and sighing. I held him there, feeling his scratchy stubble brush the soft skin, feeling our pulses hammer in tandem.

"You really liked it like that, didn't you?" I asked, after several minutes of restful silence.

He nodded. "God, yes. I kind of lost it there at the end, didn't I?"

I giggled. "Yeah, you kind of did."

He twisted to peer up at me, concern on his features. "I didn't hurt you, did I?"

I shook my head. "No, baby. You can fuck me hard anytime you want."

He laughed and rolled over on top of me. "I can? Really? I knew I was being too rough, but I couldn't stop. I'm s—"

"Don't apologize. I said you didn't hurt me. I liked it. I'm serious." I scratched his back and rubbed his backside with my feet, pulling him closer.

"Next time I want you on your hands and knees," he said.

I quirked an eyebrow at him. "You do, do you? Doggy style, huh?"

He ducked his head. "I hate that term. It sounds degrading."

I shrugged. "I don't care what you call it, but yeah, we'll do that next."

He grinned and slid against me. I felt him hardening already, and I reached down between us, taking him in my hand and stroking him into a full erection. He tried to push into me, but I shook my head, grinning at him. I pressed the tip of him to my clit and circled it, using his thick, warm flesh to stimulate myself, slowly at first but with increasing fervency, until I was arching my back and moaning. Through slitted eyes I watched him tense, holding back, the motion of my hand on him as I pleasured myself with his cock bringing him to desperation.

I came hard, biting his shoulder to quiet my breathless shriek of climax. When the initial wave had rolled over me, I crammed his hot flesh into my opening and clenched my legs around his waist so tightly he couldn't move. I rolled my hips, grinding mine against his, clamping down with my vaginal muscles as hard as I could, my body slick against his, my sweat mingling with his, my mouth seeking his lips and whispering "I love you" into his groan, milking my orgasm. When the shudders had slowed, I relaxed my hold on him and let him pull out partway, and then held him in place, smiling into our kiss. He was close, too, but I wasn't ready for him to release yet. I was greedy for another orgasm, determined to milk it from him before I let him come. He knew what I wanted by now, and instead of merely plunging deep immediately, he thrust shallowly, lifting his hips to slide his length downward into me, his hardness pressing against my clit with each slight motion. I moaned into his mouth, feeling a second climax coiling inside me."

"I thought you said I could have you the other way next time?" he murmured, grinning.

I shrugged, smirking saucily at him. "I lied. You'll have to wait."

"Not nice."

"I'm nice all the rest of the time," I told him. "I don't have to be nice in bed with you. This is when I get to be bad."

He pushed in against me, but I moved away from his thrust to keep him from thrusting deep. "What are you doing?" he asked.

"Keeping it shallow."

"Why?"

I shrugged. "I don't know. Just doing what feels good. Making you wait."

He slid his arms beneath my head, supporting his weight on his elbows. "Then I'll have to wait, I guess." His playful grin went serious. "I want to do whatever makes you feel good. Whatever you want, baby."

I clutched his hard ass and urged him to move. "And that's why I love you. Well, one of the reasons." We found a rhythm together, meeting in the middle of each shallow thrust, teasing both of us.

"What are the other reasons?"

"Fishing for compliments, are you?"

He smirked, his face tensed, betraying his concentration. "Yep. Shamelessly."

"Well, I love you for the way you make love to me. I love you for your body. I love you for being possessive of me and taking care of me." I paused to slide my eyes closed as he adjusted his weight and inadvertently found my sweet spot with the gently thrusting tip of his erection. "Oh, god yeah, just like that, right there. Don't stop…oh, shit that feels good."

He moved into me in a series of quick, shallow thrusts that had me arching desperately against him, fingers clawing into his lat muscles. "Any other reasons?"

I laughed breathlessly. "Hmm. I might love you for your talent with a camera. I especially love you for what you do with your tongue. I definitely love you for loving me despite my speech impediment."

"Which is pretty much gone now."

I nodded, unable to speak as my body began to be rocked by earthquake shudders. He didn't increase his pace or his depth, though, and I loved him for that, although I couldn't summon the words to say so. He stayed shallow and quick, driving the waves of climax up into sharp peaks of ecstatic bliss, not breaking over me yet, but still building with each slight push of his erection against that wonderful spot he'd found. I felt my chest tighten, felt my heart swell, and I met his eyes, seeing a depth of love in his vibrant jade gaze that brought me out of mere physical orgasm and into the desperate, weeping clinging of overwhelmed love.

Long moments passed, and the climax continued to build, and I grew frantic for the break of the orgasm, gasping against his arm, whimpering when he dipped his head to suckle one of my breasts. That was all it took, the hot wet pull of his mouth over my taut nipple. I cried out, uncaring now who heard.

"Now, Jason. I n-need it, n-now!" I stammered, panting against his ear.

He groaned in relief and thrust deep, hard, letting his weight settle on my body and crashing deep into me. "Oh, god, Becca, oh…I'm gonna come so hard…"

"G-g-ood…give it all to m-me." The only time I ever stuttered anymore was when I climaxed with Jason, and he seemed to make it his personal goal to make me come so hard I lost my fluency.

He kept his mouth on my breast, teething my nipple gently and pushing deep, but softly, lovingly, moving sinuously in long, perfect strokes.

I came, and let myself fall into it, a tear sliding down my cheek and my body freeing itself of my control, writhing against Jason as he unleashed inside me, whispering my name over and over again in a chant of release.

We held each other, letting school and away games and everything vanish for a while as we drowsed together. My last thought, though, before I fell asleep with Jason's heartbeat in my ear, was of Nell, and how to help her.

Eleven: Calm Before the Storm
Jason
April

I SCRIBBLED THE LAST FEW PARAGRAPHS of my essay test into the booklet, closed it, checked for my name at the top, and then gathered my backpack over my shoulder. I dropped the test on the professor's desk, returning her nod as I left. That was my last final for the spring semester, and I knew I'd killed it. Of course, Becca had been instrumental in helping me study for it, as she was instrumental in every aspect of my life. She was still taking hers, I knew, since she was the kind of test taker who would finish first but would go over every answer one by one before she turned it in. I never had that kind of patience. I'd answer the last question and turn that bitch in, while Becca would usually be the last person in the classroom. I stopped by my dorm room to drop off my backpack, grabbed the duffel bag I'd already packed, and hopped in my truck. I sat in the parking lot closest to Becca's last final exam location, my iPhone plugged into the aftermarket stereo Becca had given me for Christmas. "Ten Cent Pistol" by The Black Keys came on, and I jammed out to it, followed by one of Becca's songs, "The Blower's Daughter" by Damien Rice. I didn't like a lot of Becca's acoustic, folksy, artsy-fartsy music, but there were a few songs I liked, and most of Damien Rice's music met my approval, this song in particular, especially when Becca sang it. She tended to get lost in it, eyes closing and the words sounding so sweet in her lovely voice. She claimed she wasn't very good at singing, and she'd never sing for me intentionally, but I'd turn on songs I knew she liked and listen to her surreptitiously.

I saw her then, an old hoodie of mine with a "V" cut into the neckline showing a sliver of dark skin, her hair bound loosely at the nape of her neck, tight black yoga pants making me horny just by the way she walked and the sight of the tiny keyhole gap between the swell of her thighs. She wasn't looking yet, her attention on the phone in her hands, making plans with Nell, most likely. I snatched my camera out of the bag, flicked it on, and zoomed in on her, catching her in a perfect candid moment. My breath caught when I saw the picture I'd taken of her: Her face was framed by a loose lock of springy black hair, a tiny smile on her face as she laughed at some secret thought. The sun was behind her to the left, rays slicing past her and bathing her in late afternoon gold. My hoodie was loose around her, but her breasts still pressed against the gray fabric, and the curve of one hip was popped out as she took a swaying step. The lighting of the photograph lent it a washed-out look, and I could already see what filters I'd apply in Photoshop to make it look even more vintage.

I put the camera away as she approached, since I knew she hated pictures of herself, for some stupid reason. I knew it, and I generally respected her dislike of photos of herself, but every so often I snapped some in secret, just because I couldn't help myself. I actually had an entire album in my closet dedicated to stolen pictures of her. No one but me had ever seen them, and I planned to keep it that way. Especially the one I'd snapped of her getting out of the shower. That was probably my favorite photograph ever. She had a white towel pressed against her chest, draping down to barely cover her front. The generous swell of her ass was in profile as she leaned back, her chest pushed out, her free hand slicking her hair back. She had her weight on one leg, the other slightly bent in a classic pose. Her throat was bared, her spine arched, and her eyes shut, and I don't think she'd ever looked so beautiful as in that single moment.

She hopped into my truck and leaned over to kiss me before even saying hello.

"How'd your exam go, babe?" I asked.

She shrugged. "Good, I guess. It was for my anatomy class, which I've already taken, but the credits didn't transfer. Glad to be done. You?"

"Aced it, thanks to you."

She shoved her backpack on the floor at her feet and buckled up. "Nah, I just helped you study. You already knew your shit."

I backed out of the parking spot and navigated out of the campus into Ann Arbor, stopping at her dorm so she could grab her duffel bag and bungee it in the bed of the truck next to mine. "Why do we always take my truck when your car is so much nicer than this old piece of shit?" I asked, apropos of nothing.

Becca just shrugged. "Habit, I guess? I love your truck. I have so many memories in this thing that I'll probably actually cry when you finally replace it."

"I'm with you on that. The first glimpse of your body I got was in this truck."

She snorted. "Is that all you ever think of?"

"You know you're just as bad, Beck, and don't even try to deny it." I twined our fingers together and squeezed her hand. "What memories were you thinking of, then?"

She didn't answer right away. "You're right, damn it." She smirked at me. "I was thinking of making out with you by the tree. All the conversations we had in this truck? We made all the biggest decisions of our lives in this thing."

She glanced sideways at me, and I knew something dirty was coming.

"What else?" I prompted.

Her eyes flicked down to my zipper and back up. "I was thinking of Winter Formal, sophomore year? How we were messing around and you ended up coming into a T-shirt?"

I leaned back in the seat and laughed, remembering. "You looked so hot in that dress, Becca. I literally had a hard-on the entire night."

"What'd you end up doing with that shirt?"

I grinned sheepishly. "I actually stopped at a McDonalds and threw it away."

She giggled. "I wondered about that, since I never saw that shirt again."

We chatted aimlessly until we were pulling off the freeway and onto the highway that led to our hometown. "Do we have plans?" I asked.

She shrugged. "Nell is being difficult again. I want to get together with her, but she's...she's just not cooperating. We're having lunch with Ben and Kate tomorrow."

"Kate?"

"His girlfriend."

I nodded. "So how is Nell not cooperating?"

Becca answered in a calm enough voice, but she spoke facing the window, and she spoke slowly and enunciated the words carefully, which was a pretty good indicator as to how upset she was. "She just doesn't seem to want to hang out. Every time I text her, she's 'busy.'" Becca made air quotes with her fingers. "The last time I saw her, she was definitely drunk."

"When was this?" I asked.

"Over the holidays? You were at the gym, and I got her to stop by my parents' house. She was so drunk, Jason. She stank of whiskey so bad it made me sick. She was s-scratching at her wrists again, too."

"Was she driving?"

Becca shook her head. "No, her mom dropped her off."

"Her mom didn't notice?"

Becca had her hand over her mouth. "I guess n-not." The stammers were a precursor to tears, I was pretty sure; I pulled into the parking lot of a dive bar not yet open at 3 p.m. "I don't know h-how she couldn't tell, though. Like, I smelled it on her as soon as Nell walked in my room. I don't know what her parents are d-doing, Jason. She's getting worse every t-time I see her. It's like she's fading away or something. She's going deeper and deeper into her s-self, and her parents aren't doing a fucking th-thing to stop it! I love Mr. and Mrs. Hawthorne, I do, you know I do. They were there for me when I was mad at my parents, but now Nell needs them and they're...they're burying their heads in the sand. And I just—I don't know what to do."

I unbuckled my seatbelt and slid across the bench to put my arms around her. "I don't know either, Beck. She's their daughter, and you'd think they'd do something. But...she's eighteen, you know? What are they going to do? Ground her? Take away her car? From what you tell me, she barely leaves the house. If she's refusing to see a therapist, how can they make her?"

Becca nodded, sniffling. "I know, I know. I mean, unless she does something drastic like tries to kill herself, they can't really forcibly admit her to a psych ward or something, and I'm not sure that wouldn't do more harm than good." She was trying so hard to keep it together, and it hurt me to watch her hurting. "She's my oldest friend, Jase. I love her, and I'm so worried about her. The arm-scratching thing really scares me."

"What do you think it is?"

I held her against my chest as she quietly cried. Eventually, she straightened up and sniffled, wiping underneath her eyes with a finger. "I don't know. The obvious thing is drugs, but she's not, like, twitchy or moody or anything. I saw that with Ben, so I kind of know what to look for. She's not scary skinny like Ben got, either, so I don't think it's drugs. I just don't know, but it scares me."

"Well, maybe we can get to the bottom of it this summer," I suggested.

"Maybe. I hope so." Becca took a deep breath and let it out. "Okay, I'm okay. So where are you going to stay over the summer?"

I'd stayed with her family over the Christmas holiday, sleeping in their basement on the most uncomfortable pull-out bed in the known universe. I wasn't eager to repeat that experience. "I don't know," I said. "Maybe I can find a summer job or something and get a short-term lease on an apartment."

Becca glanced up at me. "I don't know how you'd feel about this, but Ben has an apartment with his girlfriend Kate. I know they have a two-bedroom, but they're only using one room. One of Kate's friends was staying with them, but she moved out. If you got a job, they'd probably let you stay there if you helped with rent. It'd be better than my parents' basement, that's for sure."

Her parents had warmed up to me a good bit, since it was clear I was responsible and loved their daughter. It didn't hurt that her dad was a U of M fan and I could get him tickets for home games at a discount. They still didn't entirely approve of me, or of her dating in general, I didn't think, but they'd smartened up enough to know they couldn't stop us from being together, and to try would be to alienate Becca. They'd let me stay at their house whenever we came back for weekend trips or holidays, but I had to stay in the basement, two full floors away from Becca. I think they knew I had a bad home life, and finally over the past Christmas holiday I'd explained that I wouldn't be going back to my parents' house ever again, due to "differences with my dad." I left it at that, and I was pretty sure Mr. de Rosa understood the context of what I wasn't saying.

I considered living with Ben and Kate over the summer, and the idea did hold certain merit. Becca could come over, and we could do what we wanted in relative freedom, whereas there was little to no opportunity for much of anything at her parents' house. I didn't know Ben all that well, but he seemed like a decent guy. I knew he was severely bipolar and had a history of drug abuse, but was currently going on a year sober and had worked at the same job for nearly two years, so he was doing better.

"If Ben and Kate would let me stay with them, I'd stay there. It'd save my back some pain."

Becca grinned. "You know you just want to be able to sleep with me without worrying about my parents."

I nodded seriously. "Absolutely. That's my top priority. I'm thoroughly addicted to you, Becca. If I don't get a regular fix of your body, I might go into withdrawal."

She didn't bat an eyelash. "That's a very serious condition. Maybe we should wean you off that addiction."

I shook my head. "Oh, no. I'm happily addicted. I don't have many vices, you know. I don't really drink, don't smoke, I'm not into partying or anything like that. But you? I'm very much into you. I wouldn't give you up for anything."

Becca nodded, touching her chin as if in thought. "Well, in that case, we'd better make sure you get your fix, Mr. Dorsey. I wouldn't want you to go into withdrawal."

I traced a line up her thigh, the supple flesh giving easily under my touch. "No, we wouldn't want that. It'd be bad."

She turned on the seat slightly. "What are the symptoms of withdrawal, just so I know what to look for?"

I turned my hand to face palm up, following the seam of her yoga pants up her groin. The pants were so tight I could feel the lips of her privates through the thin cotton. She stifled a gasp as I found the spot I was looking for and massaged it through her pants.

"Well," I said, "I tend to get cranky, that's the first thing. I get really horny, and it's hard for me to concentrate."

She let her thighs fall apart a bit, eyes hooded and back pressed against the door. "I see. And what's the best method of giving you a fix?"

"I'm not particular."

"So if you touched me, right here in this parking lot, that would help you?"

I tilted my head back and forth in a "yes and no" kind of gesture. "Well, temporarily, it would. I mean, it's been, what, three days since I had you last? We've been so busy studying there just hasn't been time. And now I've got you where I want you. I might need more than that."

"But it would be a start, wouldn't it?" She took my hand, twisted on the seat so her back was nestled against my side, and slid my palm down her belly,

under the elastic of her yoga pants. "What if I promised to return the favor however you wanted later?"

"However I want?"

She pushed my hand closer to her core, and I
obliged her by slipping a finger into her.

"Yes, yes. Anything. Name it."

I sucked in a breath, finding her already wet. "God,
Beck. You're all ready for me, aren't you?"

She licked her lips and arched her back as I curled
my two long middle fingers into her, finding her sweet
spot, using the side of my thumb to massage her
clit in a somewhat awkward but effective maneuver.
"Yeah, I am. I was thinking about this all morning. I
couldn't concentrate on my last final because I kept
thinking about that thing you did with your tongue on
Wednesday."

"You liked that, didn't you?" In the two years we'd
been together, we'd somehow never experimented
with oral sex until fairly recently. When I first went
down on her, it had been a little uncomfortable, but
I'd gotten the hang of it and had gotten her to scream
so loud my upstairs neighbor banged on the walls to
shut us up. Becca had been mortified at herself, but I'd
felt proud of myself for getting that kind of a reaction
from her.

Yeah, my baby was a screamer. I loved it. It was so
unlike her, unlike the way she was all the rest of the

time. She was normally demure and quiet and with-drawn, but once I got her clothes off and her juices flowing, she lost all her inhibitions. She had a hair trig-ger when it came to orgasms, and there didn't seem to be any limit to how many times she could come, if only I had the stamina, self-control, and patience to keep all the attention on her. You'd never think it, but my quiet, hyper-intelligent, overachieving, rule-fol-lowing girlfriend was a voracious, insatiable lover. I couldn't keep up with her sometimes, it seemed.

It was a good problem to have.

Now, in a public parking lot at five o'clock on a Friday afternoon, I had her writhing in desperation as I slowly fingered her closer to climax. Within minutes, my fingers were coated in her slick, warm juices and she was breathless, clinging to my arm and gyrating her hips into my touch.

She was biting her lip in an attempt to keep quiet, but I knew that wouldn't last long. Her curls were coming loose from the ponytail, beads of sweat dot-ting her forehead. I slipped my hand down her neck, over her clavicle and under the hoodie. I tucked my fin-gers into her bra and tugged her breast free of the silk cup, twiddling her nipple into a diamond hardness. She shrieked then, and I tilted her face to mine, swallowing her screams of climax.

My erection was hard against her back, and I knew she felt it, but she didn't let on as she got her breathing under control.

"God, Jason. That was intense." She righted herself, tucking the loose strands of hair back behind her ear.

"Yeah, it was," I agreed. "There's not much I love more than watching you come. You know that?"

She ducked her head, glancing around the empty parking lot, belatedly looking to see if anyone had seen us. "I've gathered that. You do it enough you'd think it would get old."

I shook my head. "No. Never. It couldn't ever get old. It's hot as hell every time. It turns me on."

She twisted in the seat, and a sly look floated into her eyes. "Oh, yeah? You're horny now, aren't you?"

"Oh, yeah." I adjusted myself in my pants. "I'm aching for you."

"Well, how about you drive, and I'll return the favor."

I wasn't sure exactly what she had in mind, but I had an inkling. I put the truck in drive and put us on the road, then peeled away from the main highway onto a dirt back road that led in a wide curve. Sure enough, Becca unbuckled my seatbelt, unfastened my jeans, and pushed them down around my thighs, along with my boxers. I lifted up on the seat to allow them past my ass, and then Becca's hands were around me and I had to put both hands on the wheel to keep it straight, slowing down to barely thirty miles per hour. She stroked me slowly, watching as I hardened even further under her touch, and then slicked her thumb over the tip as drops of clear liquid escaped. She slid one fist around me, up and then down, up and then down, switching hands as she adjusted her rhythm, slowing down and massaging my base, then squeezing the tip in her hand. Soon I was bucking my hips uncontrollably, wondering if she was going to let me make a mess all over the place or if she was going to do what I'd never dare ask her.

"God...*damn*, Becca. I'm—I'm close."

She smiled up at me, sank her fist around me down to the base, and then slid back on the bench and bent over me. "Then I suppose I'd better do something about that, shouldn't I?"

"Yeah, maybe you...maybe you should." I touched her cheek to stop her. "Only if you want to."

She gave me a look of love and nudged her face into my hand. "I want to. I promise. I wouldn't if I didn't." And then she wrapped her sweet mouth around me, and I groaned.

"Jesus, that feels incredible," I murmured.

She pumped at my base with one hand and ran her tongue around the tip, then sucked me deeper, backed away, and bobbed down again. I had my hand tangled in her hair, and I made sure to keep my touch light, pressure free, so she'd know this was all about what she wanted to do. She bobbed on me, taking me deeper into her mouth with every motion, and it was all I could do to hold back, to keep from thrusting against her. I leaned back in the seat, clutching the steering wheel with desperate strength as she slowed on me, leaving only the tip in her mouth and sucking hard, massaging the base.

"Oh, god," I murmured. "I'm—I'm right there... please don't stop. I'm coming...oh Jesus..." I had to stop driving then.

When I told her I was coming, she slid her lips around me and took me deeper than ever, so deep I felt her throat muscles clench around me and I wasn't sure why she wasn't gagging, and I then I felt myself release in a rush of heat and throbbing wonder. She took it all, and her throat muscles moved in a swallowing motion, drawing me to even harder spastic shudders. I came so hard it felt like a nuclear explosion inside me, and she milked it all from me, sucking and moving on me until all the juddering, wracking shivers had stopped.

She straightened and wiped her mouth with her palm, smiling shyly at me. I leaned over and kissed her so hard we both pulled away a couple minutes later panting and breathless.

"Does that mean you liked it?"

I wasn't even sure how to respond. "Liked it? God, Becca, that was…amazing. Beyond amazing. I can't believe you did that."

"I didn't know what I was doing, so I was just hoping it was okay for you."

I laughed at the idea that she could doubt herself. "Baby, it was the best thing ever. Seriously. Thank you."

"The best thing ever?" She frowned at me, a cute pout on her lips. "Better than making love to me?"

"No, god no. Just…different." I brushed her cheekbone with my thumb. "Anything you do is the best. Anything with you. Did you mind doing that? Did it, like, make you gag?"

She ducked her head, embarrassed. "A little. Not enough to really bother me. I liked how much you seemed to enjoy it." She buckled up, and I started driving again. "Maybe I'll do that the next time I'm on my period and we can't have sex."

"That would be awesome, but it's up to you."

"What do you mean?"

I shrugged. "I'd just feel weird asking you to do that."

She tilted her head and smiled at me. "Why? If I don't mind doing it and like making you feel good, why should you feel bad asking me to do something for you? If I don't want to, I'll just say no, that's all. I have no compunction about asking you to go down on me, believe me. If you want me to go down on you, just ask. I liked doing that to you. For real."

I stared at her. "How can you be this awesome? Seriously. I'm pretty sure there's never been any guy as lucky as me."

"I'm the lucky one," she said, her voice quiet.

I shook my head, knowing better than to argue with her.

For some reason, that Beyonce song about "if you liked it, you should've put a ring on it" floated through my head. I knew we weren't ready for that yet, but the seed was planted. I knew I was the most fortunate man in the human species. There wasn't another woman like Rebecca de Rosa anywhere in the world, and I sure as hell didn't want to take a chance on her getting away from me. It wasn't just how eager and willing she was sexually, though. It was that she loved me, supported me, encouraged me. She got down on me when I wanted to slack off, refused to let me give up. My motivation in life was to be a good enough man for her, worthy of her awesomeness.

Becca

Jason was moved into my brother's apartment, which was weird but convenient. My parents had clearly known exactly why Jason hadn't wanted to stay in their basement, but there wasn't much they could do about it. I planned to be careful about it, though, because they were still providing me with a budget for living expenses and were paying for my car. I could do without those things if I had to, but they were great to have. I didn't want to damage my still-fragile relationship with my parents, so I knew I had to tread a fine line when it came to flaunting my relationship with Jason in front of them. Things had gotten better with them as of late, in part because Ben seemed to be doing a lot better. Kate really was good for him, it seemed. They liked Jason as much as they'd ever like anyone. I don't think they were capable of just being happy for me, but at least they didn't openly disapprove or try to force us apart. They still thought I should focus on my studies rather than "fooling around with a boy," as my father had once put it, earning a snicker from me and a hard glare from him. I knew they wanted the best for me, but what they didn't seem to understand was that what they wanted for me wasn't the same as what *I* wanted for me.

Jason was at the local Powerhouse Gym, which was the first place he'd gone after dropping off his bag of clothes. He'd almost immediately scored a job as a trainer, so he could spend most of the summer at the gym working out *and* earning money. Since the gym was only a couple miles from Ben's apartment, Jason decided to walk, run, or bike there, which meant I had his truck. I knew it was big deal for him to let me drive his truck. It wasn't much, that old truck, but it was the only thing he owned, really, aside from his camera.

I pulled into the Hawthornes' driveway and sat for a moment, hoping Nell would be receptive to me this time around. Over the holidays, she'd been silent and withdrawn, and had gotten defensive when I'd tried to bring up Kyle's death or the way she was coping with it. I don't think she even really registered my words, just my tone of voice, which had triggered an automatic reaction calculated to push me away. It had worked, and that had been the last time I'd seen her. I had taken six classes in the spring semester, and I'd barely had time to see Jason, much less drive home to see Nell.

I felt guilty for not making more of an effort, but I knew, too, that nothing I did would make much difference.

I knocked on the thick brown French doors, which were promptly opened by Mrs. Hawthorne. She had on a black-and-white paisley apron spattered with flour, and the kitchen smelled like oatmeal raisin cookies.

"Hi, Becca! You're back for the summer?" She greeted me with a one-armed hug, holding the other away from our bodies as if she still had dough on it.

I hugged her back and took a whiff of the air. "Yeah, Jason and I just got in. It smells awesome in here."

Mrs. Hawthorne smiled warmly at me. "Thanks, I'm just making some cookies. I've got a batch cooling on the counter. Want one?"

"Do you even have to ask?" I grabbed a huge, soft, perfect cookie from the newspaper on the marble counter and bit into it. "Oh, my god, Mrs. Hawthorne, you make the best cookies."

She waved at me. "Oatmeal raisin cookies are my weakness." She ate one herself and then gestured at me with it. "And you know, Becca, you're an adult now, so you might as well call me Rachel."

I grinned at her, speaking through a mouthful. "I'll try, but it's pretty ingrained in me to call you 'Mrs. Hawthorne.'"

"Well, you'll learn," she said. "So, how's Jason?"

"He's great. He's the starting wide receiver next season." I decided to fish a little. "So Jason and I are both seeing a school counselor from health services at the university. You know, about everything that happened with Kyle."

Her smile faded a bit, and a haunted look entered her eyes. "I'm so glad to hear that. We worried about all of you."

"It took some convincing to get Jason to go," I admitted, "but he's going once a month now. He says it helps."

"With other things, too, I'm sure," she said.

I nodded. "It helps him deal with…the way he grew up," I hedged, knowing Rachel—it was weird to think of her like that, as an adult and another person rather than my friend's mother—knew at least a little bit about Jason's history, but not exactly what. He was very closed off about that topic in general, so I wasn't sure how much to say to her.

"He had a very difficult upbringing, I know that much," she said. "He never spoke of it to us, certainly not to me, but, well, this is a small town, and you hear things. And I saw things myself. I'm glad to hear he's finding help with it."

"Me, too." If Jason hadn't told her about it directly, I certainly wasn't about to tell her anything. "How about Nell? Is she…how is she doing?"

Rachel turned away from me, taking tiny nibbles from her cookie and staring out the glass patio door. "I can't get through to her, Becca. I've tried. Her father has tried. She won't talk to us. She just shuts down and walks away. She's upset enough, and we don't want to make it worse by forcing a confrontation, but…I don't think she's doing well. But we don't know how to help her. She won't let anyone close." She glanced at me hopefully. "Has she talked to you at all?"

I shook my head. "No. She won't let me in, either."

"She's drinking," Rachel said, almost blurting it out. "I know she is. I smell it on her. But I never catch her with it, and I've never found it in her room. I'm not sure where she's getting it, where she drinks or when. But what can I do? She denies it and gets mad when I ask her about it, and she goes to work with her father on time, does her job…"

"I smelled it on her when I was down here for the holidays." I always referred to going home as "down," even though I knew logically that Ann Arbor wasn't in any way "up" from home. "I wondered if you knew."

"I know." She looked at me then, and I saw a fleeting expression cross her face, something desperate and almost pleading. "Don't think we're in denial, Becca. We're not. We know she's…not okay. But I don't know what we can do. How do you force a legally independent child to see a therapist? She could run off to college whenever she wanted. She has several offers from universities still on the table, you know. If we push her away, she might run, and then we wouldn't even be close enough to help her if something goes wrong. At least this way we're here, you know? If something happens, we're close. If she's in California or New York, we'd be thousands of miles away if something happened." Rachel stood up and drew me into a gentle hug. "If she'll let anyone in, it'd be you, Becca. But you need to take care of yourself first and foremost."

I nodded. "I'll try. I've been trying. Kyle's death was hard on Jason and me, too. Jason especially. He was depressed for weeks. The only thing that really seemed to help was football and, well—me." I blushed, embarrassed to be referring to sex in front of Nell's mom. "Once I got him to go see Dr. Malmstein with me, he got better. He dealt with it, and so did I. The hardest part of Kyle dying, honestly—aside from losing him, obviously—has been seeing Nell deteriorate. She's not herself. She's not my best friend anymore. She's just...gone."

Rachel sniffed and blinked hard, turning away to open the oven and pull out a sheet of cookies with an oven mitt. "I know, believe me, I know. We all miss Kyle. He had so much potential. He was so young, too young to die so tragically. But for Nell, I think he was everything. And now, she's lost."

I stood up from where I'd been sitting at the island counter. "Is she here? I'd like to go see her."

Rachel nodded. "Yeah, she's in her room."

I went up the back stairs and found Nell's door closed, but I heard music playing. The knob twisted in my hands, unlocked, and I pushed it open.

The sight that greeted froze me in place.

Nell was sitting on her bed, cross-legged. She had a long-sleeve T-shirt on, with one sleeve pushed up past her elbow. She had a razor blade in one hand, and I found her in the act of dragging the blade across her wrist. I stood, halted in stark terror, watching as the thin white line she'd carved in her skin welled up with crimson blood.

Twelve: A Thin Red Line
Becca

A TEAR TRICKLED DOWN MY CHEEK. I couldn't move, couldn't breathe. "Nell? What—w-what are you doing?"

She leaped up, clapping a wad of paper towel against her wrist. She stormed past me and closed the door, locking it, and returning to her place on the bed. She didn't look at me as she held the paper towel to the line of blood.

I sat beside her on the bed. She had a kit. An empty tampon box held a packet of razors, antiseptic wipes, Band-aids. She took the box from me, ripped open a wipe, and slid the razor through it, folded the wipe, and rubbed it over her arm, then fitted a Band-aid over the small incision she'd made. She hadn't looked at me, hadn't spoken to me. She tossed the wipe, the empty packet, and the Band-aid wrapper into a plastic Meijer bag from underneath her bed, filled with these same discarded items. She tied up the bag and stuffed it deep into her purse, clearly planning to throw it away someplace where it wouldn't draw notice.

"Nell?"

She sighed. "What, Becca?"

"What…what is this? What are you doing?"

"You're smart, Beck. You tell me." She got up and scooped her iPhone from the desk and plugged it into the speaker dock. Eddie Vedder's "Longing to Belong" came on, the unexpectedly amazing pairing of Eddie Vedder's voice and a ukelele filling the room.

I spent a quiet moment listening to the song, fighting my anger and my tears. "It looks like you're cutting yourself."

"Bingo." Nell sat at her desk, browsing through pages of what looked like guitar chord progressions in a thick book.

"Why?"

She gave me a look of disbelief. "Why? Really? Why the hell do you think?"

"I don't *know*, Nell!" I had to fight to keep my voice down. "I have no clue why you would cut yourself open with a razor blade."

She huffed and shook her head. "You wouldn't understand."

"Try to explain it, then."

"It helps, okay?" She slammed the book shut and skipped a song so "City" by Sarah Bareilles came on. "I don't expect you to get it. But it helps. I don't want to hurt anymore. I'm tired of hurting, and this—" she held up her left arm, the sleeve now pulled down, "this helps me feel something besides missing him."

I sniffed, knowing if I cried it would only piss her off. "But...isn't there...isn't there a better way? That's not healthy, Nell. You n-n-know it's not. You have to stop, please."

She shook her head. "Beck, listen. This is my life. This is how I'm dealing with it. You didn't see what I saw. You didn't lose....Look. I know—I know he was your friend, too, but he was the man I loved, and he's gone. It hurts so much, every day, and you can't—you don't understand. No one does. I'm not trying to kill myself. I promise. And I will stop someday."

"How can I just sit aside and let you do that to yourself?"

She picked at a thread in a hole of her jeans. "You don't have a choice." She glanced up at me, her eyes challenging. "What are you going to do? Tell my parents?"

"If I have to. You can't keep doing that. It—it's wrong."

"Which makes me feel *so* much better about it, Beck. Thanks." She snapped at me, pissed off. "If you tell my parents, I swear I'll never speak to you again, Rebecca. I'm dead serious. They don't get it any more than you do, *ob*viously. No one can help me. I'm not in danger of killing myself. I'm not suicidal. It's not like that. So just...just keep it to yourself, if you're my friend."

I couldn't stop myself from crying. "That's not fair, Nell. You know I'm your friend. You know I love you, and I'm just—I'm so scared and confused."

"I know, okay? I know." She moved to sit beside me and put an arm around me, as if to comfort me. "I'm sorry. I'm not trying to act like you don't care. But this is my thing to deal with. It hurts so bad, Beck. You don't even know. I hope you never know. And the cutting...it...distracts me, just for a moment."

She withdrew her arm, her voice shaking. I watched as she wrapped her fingers around her left wrist, her thumb pressing into the spot where she'd cut herself. She went pale with pain, but somehow she seemed to steady herself emotionally.

"I promise you, I'll stop, Becca, I will. Just...keep my secret, okay? For now? I'll deal with it on my own."

I nodded, sniffling back the tears. "I promise, for *now*." I trembled all over. "I hate myself for this. It feels wrong. You need *help*, Nell, professional help."

Nell hugged me. "I don't want help. They can't bring him back, and they can't make it hurt less."

"Jason and I both are seeing a therapist. It *does* help."

"I'm not going. Just drop it."

We sat in silence until it grew awkward. "I should go," I said.

"Let's hang out this weekend, okay? Saturday?" Nell said.

I nodded. "Sounds good. Get mani-pedis like we used to." I glanced at her, but I couldn't see anything except the image of her with a blade to her wrist. "I feel guilty, promising you I won't tell."

"But you shouldn't. I'll be fine, okay?"

"Just promise me one thing, okay?"

She gave me a hesitant look. "If I can."

"Call me or text me when you feel like cutting. I'm your friend. I won't tell if you promise me this is all it is, that you're not suicidal—"

"I swear I'm not, Becca. I told you that already. I don't want to die—I need to not miss him so much, just for a second."

"Okay, and I believe you. But talk to me about this, okay? I don't care when it is, what time, where I am. I'll leave class in a heartbeat."

Nell nodded. "I will."

I nodded, unable to believe her, but not sure what else to say or do. I left then, shrugging noncommittally when Rachel asked how it had gone. The truth was burning my lips: *Nell is a cutter.* Someone should know. What if she accidentally cut too deep and something happened? Wouldn't it be my fault for keeping her secret? Wouldn't I be a better friend by getting her help when I knew she needed it?

But Nell said it herself—she wouldn't accept help. To tell would be to lose Nell forever, and I did believe her when she claimed to not be suicidal. I watched her calm down visibly when she pressed her thumb to the cut on her wrist, as if the pain had centered her, pushed away the emotional heartache. I didn't get it, but I saw it work.

I hated secrets. I hated being the guardian of dark truths. I'd kept Jason's secret for two years when I knew he was suffering every day. I woke up at night ridden with guilt, wondering if my silence was deepening his pain. Now I had an added burden. I felt like I would literally have Nell's blood on my hands.

I sat in Jason's truck listening to "Dream" by Priscilla Ahn, and I wondered if that's how Nell felt, if she was willing to leave this life, feeling old and gray. I drove to my brother's apartment and lay down in

Jason's untouched bed, crying quietly. I saw, as I drifted in the afternoon glow, the thin red line on her wrist brightening scarlet.

I woke up with words bubbling in my head. It was early evening, and I had a text from Jason from ten minutes earlier saying he'd be home soon. I dug my notebook from my purse and let the thoughts flow.

A THIN RED LINE
You looked so guilty
When I walked in
Your eyes were haunted
Your hands trembling
And I watched a thin red line blossom on your wrist
An evil scarlet flower
Trailing skeins of leaked pain down your arm
So easily wiped away
Covered over
Hidden
By bandages and lies and shirtsleeves
Glossed over by blasé reassurances
That it helped
Somehow
As if gashes gouged in your skin
Could take away the grief
You looked so guilty
When I walked in

Jumping up from giving yourself scars
And I wonder
If my bought silence
Will be your death
And I wonder
If the vault of my soul
Can hold any more secrets
Any more hidden sins
All this wells up on your skin
Bleeds out from
A thin red line
Cut into your wrist

Jason walked in as I closed the notebook. He took one look at me and dropped his bag in the doorway, slid onto the bed next to me, and pulled me against his chest. He didn't have to ask what was wrong; he knew I'd gone to see Nell.

"It's bad, Jason."

"Yeah?"

"She's cutting herself."

Jason leaned away from me, eyes wide in disbelief. "She's *what*?"

"I surprised her in her room. She was cutting her arm with a razor blade. She said it wasn't about trying to kill herself, just…like it was something to manage the pain." I buried my face in his shirt, smelling the dried sweat on him layered over Old Spice deodorant. "She made me swear to not tell anyone. She promised she'd get it under control."

"God. Poor Nell. I can't believe she'd do that."

"Her mom knows she's drinking, but since she's never actually caught Nell drinking and hasn't found anything in her room, she says there's not much she can do. What do I do, Jason? How do I keep this to myself?"

"I don't even know."

"She said she'd never talk to me again if I told anyone. And if I felt like she was suicidal, I'd risk that to help her."

"But you don't think she is?"

"No, I really don't. When I walked in, she acted more like I'd caught her smoking pot or something. It's so f-fucked up, Jason. What if I'm wrong? What if I don't know her as well as I think I do, and she does something to hurt herself, or worse? What if she does something by accident?" I shuddered in his arms.

He tightened his hold on me, then scooped me up so I was curled on his lap. "I'm not trying to excuse what she's doing, but I think I can sort of understand it." Jason let out a long breath and tucked a stray wisp of hair down, then continued. "When Dad would fuck me up, I would spend all day in pain, you know? I'd be pissing blood or something, but I couldn't let on. And then I'd have to play ball with bruised ribs or whatever. And after a while, the pain sort of...becomes its own thing. Like, it's a separate—I don't know—a whole beast of its own. It's not about the fact that you got beat up by your father, it's pain, and you can rely on the pain to be there. It's there, and it's not going away. When you hurt for long enough, it becomes familiar. After a while, you get to need the pain because it's what you know. For me, I can play ball and work out. I can shred my muscles until I'm shaky, and then I'm okay. It's not about the pain for me so much, though. Not anymore. Now I guess I'm kind of addicted to the rush of working out, the endorphins or whatever. My point is, I can understand how Nell would turn to physical pain to escape the emotional. Doesn't make it right, though."

"But what d-d-do I *do?*"

"There may not be anything you can do, honey. I don't know. If she doesn't want help, then we can't help her. Who do you tell? Her parents are aware she's not okay, apparently, but unless she does something drastic, they can't force her into anything. Do you tell the police? She's not breaking any laws. If you really think she's suicidal, you have to do something drastic, no matter the consequences to your friendship if it means saving her life. But if you're convinced she's not suicidal...I don't know. Just be there if she needs you."

The next day was Saturday, and I left my parents' house as soon as I'd showered and changed. I was out the door before anyone was awake, and knocking on Ben's apartment door at seven in the morning. Jason answered in his boxers, hair messy, eyes squinting.

"Jesus, babe, it's the asscrack of dawn on a Saturday, first day of summer vacation. Can't you sleep in past six in the fucking morning?" He let me in and shut the front door behind me, then shuffled back to his bedroom, shoving the bedroom door closed behind us.

I laughed as I set my purse down on the floor and crawled into bed with him, snuggling up behind him and pulling the covers over us. "No, I really can't. I've been waking up at six since my freshman year of high school, and now I just wake up at six regardless. I figured if I was up, I might as well come see you."

"Can I go back to sleep?" he mumbled, already halfway there.

"Sure you can, love. But what if I had something else in mind?" I let my hand roam across his chest and belly, dipping lower suggestively.

He didn't respond for a long moment, and I thought he'd fallen asleep, but then he rolled in my arms so our faces were millimeters apart, his green eyes hooded with sleep but sparking with desire and amusement. "Ah, now I know the real reason why you're here so early."

"You're not the only one with an addiction, you know." That was the raw truth; I was totally addicted to Jason's body, to his love, to the heat of our bodies merging.

There was more to it, though, and I wasn't about to admit the rest out loud. I needed Jason for the same reason he needed to lift weights and Nell needed to cut. I needed a distraction. I needed something other than the worry for Nell and the weight of the secrets and my parents' disapproval. When I'd gone home the night before, it had been well before midnight, but my parents had acted like I'd been out past curfew, despite the fact that I was in college. They wanted to know what I was doing and if it would be a habit for me to stay out that late. When I'd told them I wasn't going to be treated like a child anymore, it had led to a fight. It didn't matter that I was valedictorian of my high school, or that I'd completed sixty-four credits in three semesters with a 4.0 GPA at one of the top universities in the country.

I knew, logically, that my overprotective but loving parents were a minor blip on the life-problems scale.

But personal problems were a relative thing. I hated feeling their distrust. I hated the disapproval in their eyes when I told them I'd been at home with Jason last night.

Jason distracted me from these thoughts by slipping his fingers under the hem of my shirt to touch my bare back. I shivered and leaned in to bite his lower lip.

"Out with it," he said, deftly removing my shirt.

"Out with what?" I pretended ignorance, hoping to keep the conversation light.

"Whatever's bugging you."

I wiggled out of my skirt and threw my leg over Jason's, sighing in pleasure as he stroked my leg from knee to thigh. "Just my parents. They still want me home by 1 a.m. and expect me to check in with them and tell them where I am."

"And they still don't approve of you spending all your time with me." He had my bra off in seconds and was pushing my underwear down past my knees and hooking them off the rest of the way with his toes.

I shook my head. "No. I'm wondering if they ever will."

"Probably not."

"So should I even bother trying to follow their rules?"

Jason paused, his mouth between my breasts. "That's gotta be your call, honey. The last thing I want is to be a problem between you and your parents. I can't tell you what to do with them. I want them to accept that we're adults, young adults, sure, but still adults. But whether you toe their line is up to you."

"I don't expect them to like the fact that we're together, like...well, like this. And I'm not going to flaunt it in their face, but I'm also not going to let them dictate my life. If I want to stay here with you till four in the morning, I'm going to."

"What if you just stayed here?"

"Like, didn't live with my parents over the summer?"

He nodded. "Yeah. Why not? They're going to have to get used to it sometime, right?"

"They'd cut me off. They'd take my car and my monthly allowance."

Jason didn't answer right away, and I knew his answer would be something I might not like by the fact that he slid back up my body and met my eyes, all playful touching stopped. "Don't—don't take this the wrong way, baby, but maybe it's time you let that happen."

I frowned at him. "What's that mean?"

He sighed. "I—just that maybe you should get that stuff on your own."

"Because I don't know what work is? Because I've always had things given to me?"

"Sort of? Look, I know you're gonna get pissed off at this, but I'm never gonna sugarcoat things for you." He wrapped his hand around my nape and brushed a ringlet of hair away from my eyes. "You need to get a job. You've never had one. If you let them pay for everything, they'll always have leverage over you. If you earn things yourself, they'll be forced to see that you're capable of making your own decisions."

"How many jobs have you had?"

He frowned at me. "I'm not trying to...belittle you, or say I'm better. But I stopped taking Dad's money—"

"When it was convenient for you to do so. *After* you had a car and an expensive camera and money saved up." I poked him in the chest. "You don't have a job, either. You have a full ride that includes room and board and books as well as tuition and a dispensation for living expenses."

He grimaced; his full-ride offer from U of M was generous, to say the least. "I'm not—look, baby. I'm just saying maybe it's time you cut the strings a little, okay? Not that there's anything wrong with the way things are, but...your parents will still love you, right? If you stay here with me full-time, will they disown you and refuse to speak to you ever again?"

I shook my head, seeing his point. "No. They won't like it one bit, but they won't do that. They'll be pissed off for a long time, but they'll come around. Eventually. I hope."

"You don't need their money or their car, not if it comes with conditions. You can take my truck whenever you want, and you know it. Your scholarships cover tuition and room and board, too, so all you need money for is books and other shit, right? So we'll find jobs. Both of us. You can cut back to four or five classes next semester and work part-time. I'll get a job, too, and we'll pool our resources. If you come to a point where you need your own car, we'll get you one." He kissed me on the cheek, then just beneath my eye, then the corner of my mouth. "Don't be mad, please. I just don't want you to have this issue with your parents every time we come back."

I sighed, covering my eyes with one hand, thinking. "No, you're right. I'm not mad. I just hate conflict. I hate confrontations. We argued last night, and they just...they had the gall to look disappointed in me, like I'd let them down by coming home at eleven-thirty without checking in. What do they think is going on at school? They think I'm in my dorm by nine every night? That I'm some innocent virgin?"

"I think they want you to be their little girl forever. Just be glad they care as much as they do." The wistful tone in his voice brought everything back into perspective.

I pushed him onto his back and moved to sit astride him. "You're right. Of course you're right. I'm just being silly and selfish."

He caressed my hips and shook his head lovingly. "No, baby. You're the least selfish person I know."

"But I'm worried about my stupid little problems when you and Nell are—"

He touched my lips with a finger, silencing me. "It's not a competition." He massaged the hollow of my hips with his thumbs, and I unconsciously shifted my weight to allow him access where I most wanted his touch. "I'll support whatever you decide. I'll help you any way I can. What's mine is yours, okay? If you need something, I'll make sure you have it, however I have to get it."

I melted at his words. "You're not responsible for me. We're in this together."

He laughed. "You're my woman. Of course I'm responsible for you. It's my highest duty in life to take care of you, protect you."

"Old-fashioned much? I can take care of myself."

He sighed dramatically. "I *know* that. That's not the point. I'm not saying sit back and be Susie Homemaker here. I'm just saying you're not in this alone."

I giggled and leaned over him, silencing him with a kiss. "I know that, Jason. Shut up and distract me already. I need my fix."

He grinned then, and palmed my breasts, and I felt the heat in my belly turn to dampness between my thighs. He slid one hand between our bodies and slipped a finger into me. I shifted forward to deepen the kiss, my weight on my knees and shins. He tugged me forward and slipped my nipple into his mouth, and I gasped, arching my back toward his mouth, feeling the first wave crash over me.

He circled my clit as I came, drawing the orgasm out until I was writhing above him. I felt his erection at my core, but he still had his underwear on. I lifted up and tugged at them frantically, fumbling with them until he managed to help me get them off. I threw them across the room, my thighs trembling as I hovered over him, hair falling in a curtain around his face. I wiggled my hips downward, nudging the tip of him into my folds, guiding him into my opening with a shift of my hips. I hesitated, sitting upright on my knees, hovering with trembling muscles, relishing this moment, the pause before I sank down with him deep inside me. He held onto my hips, eyes locked on mine, his breath bated. I took his hands in mine, tangled our fingers, and then fell forward, pinning his hands above his head. He let me pin him, a grin on his face. I knew he loved it when I took control.

I drew the moment out, lifting my hips slightly so he nearly slipped out, neither of us breathing, letting the contents of our hearts exchange silently between our eyes. I sank down with a whimper, resting my forehead against his, mouth wide in a breathless scream. I curled my fingers into fists around his, squeezing as hard as I could, setting an immediately frantic rhythm above him. He met me stroke for stroke, never taking his eyes off mine, breathing with me, sighing with me, giving me exactly what I needed.

When the second wave came, I fell onto him, clinging to his neck with both arms, my lips at his ear, our hips crushing together as we climaxed in unison.

"God, Jason...I love you. S-so, *so* much." I was nearly weeping with the intensity of the love rippling between us.

I felt, in that moment, that our souls had crashed together and merged, like every aspect of our minds, hearts, bodies, and souls were bleeding together. I knew I'd never love anyone the way I loved Jason, and I knew I'd never try.

"I love you, too, Beck."

I took his face in my hands. "Promise me you'll love me forever. No matter what."

He caught the desperation in my eyes, my voice, and he didn't question it, didn't hesitate for a split second. "I can't promise you forever, Beck." Tears started in my eyes at what sounded like a rejection, but he kissed them away, silencing me by speaking over my protest. "I can't promise you forever, because that's not long enough."

I laughed into his mouth, giggling and sniffling against him, clinging to his neck with all my weight resting on his strong, hard body. "Good. Longer than forever I can work with."

He laughed and held me tight, his arms around my back and across my backside. With a tug, he tossed the blankets over us, and I turned my face to the side, his chest my pillow. I fell asleep like that, and knew then that I'd never want to fall asleep any other way.

Thirteen: When the Bough Breaks
Becca
February, two years later

TIME PASSED IN A BLUR. That first summer home from college, I did end up moving in with Jason in my brother's somewhat dingy two-bedroom apartment. My parents, as predicted, lost their shit completely, but when I still came home to do laundry and spend time with them, making sure to include Jason in all family get-togethers, they eventually came around. It turned into a "don't ask don't tell" sort of situation, and it worked. We went back to U of M in the fall and lived in separate dorm rooms for that first semester of our sophomore year. Jason got a part-time job as a janitor at a local high school, and I ended up in the tutoring center.

We went home for holidays and stayed with Ben and Kate, who managed to hang on to the apartment through the school year just so we'd have somewhere stress-free to stay. My brother was doing better than I'd ever seen him. He was an assistant manager at the Belle Tire, sober, and managing his mood swings with only occasional use of prescribed medication in extenuating circumstances. Kate really was a miracle worker when it came to Ben, and I loved her like a sister. She was one of the tallest girls I'd ever met, standing over six feet. She was willowy, slim with long auburn hair, pretty gray eyes, and a wide, always-smiling mouth. She never had an unkind word for anyone, and seemed totally devoted to my brother. She was one of those people who never bought anything that isn't 100-percent organic, supplementing a vegetarian diet with a plethora of vitamins and shakes. She did yoga religiously, and got me hooked on it. She had a way of defusing even the worst of Ben's manic rages, and she could lift him out of the worst depressions with a few whispered words. She never lost patience with him, never took his snapped insults to heart when he was in the grip of a mood swing. The only time I ever saw her lose her temper was when she caught Ben with a joint in his cigarette pack. She wigged the hell out, packed a bag, and walked out without so much as a backward glance. She didn't actually go anywhere, though. She hopped in her car and drove around the block a few times, and then sat in the apartment parking lot, waiting for Ben to apologize. Which he did, abjectly, begging Kate to come home and never leave him again.

The worrier in me saw an element of codependency in their relationship, because I didn't think Ben could maintain his lifestyle without Kate at his side. But she was always there for him, so it worked, I supposed. If she ever got tired of Ben's bipolar mess, though, I worried he'd regress to his days as a stoned-out drug addict.

As for Nell? She seemed to improve with time. She finished a basic liberal arts associates degree from OCC, worked her way up to a mid-level manager's position within her father's company on her own merits, and seemed to be doing okay. She never reached out to me about cutting, and I never caught her doing it again, even when I surprise-visited her every once in a while. I saw scars on her wrists sometimes, and every once in a while she'd have a Band-aid on her forearm, but she claimed it was a slip, that she'd stopped cutting for the most part.

At the start of our senior year, Jason and I decided to move out of campus housing. We found a one-bedroom apartment a few miles from campus but not too far from the high school where Jason worked. My job was on campus and our schedules tended to coincide for the most part, so we got along with just Jason's truck, which now had almost two hundred thousand miles on it. Those first months together in our apartment were the happiest of my life. I went to bed in his arms, and woke up in them. I was an early riser, whereas I discovered Jason hated mornings with a passion, unable to so much as hold a conversation until he'd had at least two cups of coffee. I always considered myself a neat person, but it turned out Jason was the one who did most of the cleaning. He claimed it was because if he didn't clean his house growing up, it wouldn't get done, since his mom didn't care and his dad was a drunk.

I had a straight 4.0 GPA at the start of the spring semester, and I had applications out to a dozen of the best universities for post-graduate work in speech-language pathology research. Jason was still breaking football records, and had scouts for half a dozen NFL teams watching every game he played.

If I had to pick a word for our lives, up until February of our junior year at U of M, I'd have called it idyllic. I filled thirty-six composition books with poetry during those years, and Jason had a portfolio of breathtaking photography and was warming up to my suggestions that he think about trying to sell a few of them. Football was his passion, but to me photography was his true talent. He could capture so much in a single photograph. He focused on macroscopic shots primarily, closeups of everyday objects, especially insects and flowers. He had a few closeups of flowers that reminded me eerily of some of Georgia O'Keefe's paintings, which he said was his intention. His photography major included a heavy dose of art and art history, and he seemed to absorb it all like a sponge.

Then, one Sunday morning in mid-February, Kate called me.

"Becca? I'm worried about Ben." Her soft, quiet voice sounded panicked.

"Why? What's going on?" I set aside my textbook and sat up on the couch where I'd been studying.

"He's not answering my phone calls. We...we had an argument, a bad one. He left, and I thought...I thought he was just going out to cool down, but it's been three hours and he's not back, not answering my calls or texts. He knows that worries me, and he always texts me back right away."

"Was it bad enough that he'd...regress? Like, relapse?" I asked.

"I don't know. I hope not, but I'm worried. Is there anywhere he'd go that you know of?"

I racked my brain. "I don't know. I'm sorry, I can't think of anything." I sighed, worrying at my lip, trying to think of something I'd know that Kate wouldn't. "If I think of anything, I'll let you know. Are you worried enough that you want me to come down and help you look for him?"

She hedged. "I don't want to worry you, and I know you're busy getting ready for finals, but…no. Not yet. If I don't hear from him soon, I'll let you know."

"Ben used to disappear for days at a time," I told her. "I never knew where he went, honestly. I guess I assumed he had, like, secret druggie hang-outs or something. Since he's been with you, that stuff has stopped. But if he was mad enough to have a relapse, he might go back to one of his old hangouts. I just don't know where that is or who to ask. I stayed out of his life, in that sense."

Kate moaned. "He hasn't seen anybody he used to party with in, god, a year and a half. Aside from the time I found that pinner in his Pall Malls, the only really big fight we've ever gotten in was a few months after I started dating him. He'd been sober for a while, and we'd talked about his drug problem, and I told him if he really wanted to stop the temptation to do drugs, he had to cut off his association with people who did them. So he stopped hanging out with his party friends. Then he hung out with an old friend who I knew for a fact was a hard-core stoner, and I got mad at him. He said he hadn't smoked, but that wasn't the point—it was just being around people who smoked. Eventually he'd relapse."

"Well, you might want to check with someone like that." I hesitated, then blurted, "What were you fighting about?"

"His cigarettes. I asked him if he'd ever quit those, too, and he got mad. He said he'd given up everything else for me, so why should he give up those, too? He stormed out when I reminded him that he had quit drugs for him, not me."

"That's it?"

She sniffed. "That's the Cliff's Notes version. There was a lot more to it." Kate sighed. "He'll come back. I know he will."

"Keep me updated, okay?"

"Okay, I will. 'Bye, Becca."

"'Bye." I hung up and set the phone on the coffee table, but I didn't go back to studying.

I was worried now. The longer I thought about it, the harder the knot of fear in my stomach became. Eventually I got back to studying, but my mind wasn't totally in it.

Later that day, during dinner with Jason, Kate texted me: He's back now. Stoned. Says it was only a little pot to calm him down. Im so mad but dont know what to do.

I sighed and showed the message to Jason. I'd explained the phone call to him after he'd gotten back from his run, and he'd agreed that if we hadn't heard from Kate by tonight, we'd have to think about going down to look for Ben.

I texted back: At least he's back and it wasn't hard drugs.

Yeah, but for him weed really is a gateway drug to worse things.

I know, I responded, but I also know he loves you, and he won't want to risk losing you. Maybe remind him of that, without making it a threat?

After a pause, Kate responded: Good point. I'll try that. Thanks.

A few weeks passed and things seemed to have settled a bit, as I hadn't heard anything else from Kate. Jason and I decided to head down for the weekend to check on them. Both Ben and Kate were at work when we got in, so we unpacked some of our clothes and went for a drive, ending up at the old oak tree, where we made love in the cab of his truck for old time's sake. When we got back, Ben was home, sitting on the front step of the apartment building, smoking a cigarette, smoke mixing with the steam from his breath.

I nodded for Jason to go on in and sat down next to Ben. He looked pale, thinner than I'd last seen him, and his eyes held the old glint of tamped-down anger.

"Hey, you," I said, bumping him with my shoulder.

"'Sup, Beck." He didn't look at me, flicking the filter of his cigarette with his thumb so a chunk of ash fell between his feet.

"So, how are you?" I wasn't sure how to broach the conversation now that I was here. He looked like shit, but I'd never say so outright.

"Kate send you?" He sounded petulant, morose.

"No, I haven't seen Kate. She's still at work, isn't she?"

"Fuck if I know. She left."

I was stunned. I thought Kate would have told me if she was leaving Ben. "Why? When? Why would she leave?"

"Stupid shit. She never understood how smoking helps me. I tried, Beck. I really did. But it was just never good enough for her. No matter what I did, it wasn't good enough for Miss Perfect Kate Yearling."

"So you're smoking again?"

He shot a *well, duh* glance at me, lifting his cigarette in gesture. "I never quit, thus Kate moving out."

"No, I meant…I meant pot."

"Oh. No…well, yeah, but that started after she left."

I frowned in confusion. "She moved out and broke up with you over cigarettes? You were clean otherwise?"

"It's fucking complicated, okay? I don't need you breathing down my neck, too."

"I'm not…I'm sorry, I'm not trying to breathe down your neck. I'm just confused."

"What's confusing to you? I'm a bipolar fucking mess. She got sick of my bullshit, just like I knew she would." He finished his cigarette and lit another with the butt of the first.

"But…that doesn't make sense. She loves you."

"Loved. Emphasis on past tense, sis. It's over. I haven't seen her in two weeks. I'm losing the apartment because my stupid job at Belle Tire isn't enough for a two-bedroom, and they don't have any one-bedrooms left. I don't know where I'm gonna go. I'll live in my car, I guess. Won't be the first fucking time. So yeah, sorry, but you and Jason will have find somewhere else to crash."

I sensed there was more to the story, and I had to find it. "Ben, please. Talk to me. There has to more to this than you're saying."

He flinched visibly when I touched his arm. "Yeah, well…there's no point, okay? More to the story or not, it's over. She's not coming back, and I'm fucking lost without her." He shot to his feet and walked away, long black hair loose around his shoulder, obviously unwashed. He was wearing a Belle Tire mechanic's jumpsuit, stained with grease. Which was odd, since last I heard he was an assistant manager.

I called Kate, who picked up on the fourth ring. "Hey, Kate. I…I came down for the weekend, and Ben says you left."

She laughed, but it was bitter and mirthless. "Is that what he says? What else does our dear Benjamin say?"

I was confused as hell at this point and just trying to make sense of it all. "That it was about cigarettes. He said you're gone and he's lost without you. He said he was clean when you left him."

She made a sound that was part sob and part laugh. "That's the bullshit lie he's feeding you, huh? Don't you know any better than to believe an addict, Becca? He's *using*."

"Using? What is he on?"

"I found cocaine in his car. But of course it wasn't his, oh no, he was holding it for a friend." She was clearly devastated. "I begged him to just tell me the truth and we'd get through it. But…it's not enough that he quits for me. He has to quit for himself, or it'll never work, no matter how much I love him."

"He's a mess, Kate."

"I know!" she wailed. "Don't you think I know that? I watched my father do this same exact fucking thing ten years ago. He OD'd on coke. He died right in front of me. Ben *knows* this. He knows I cannot and *will* not watch anyone else die because of drugs. *I* was hooked on coke. I nearly died, okay? For three years after my dad died, I was hooked on that shit. I OD'd just like him, but I didn't die. I got help, and I haven't gone back. I *won't*. Not for anyone. I thought...I thought if I did what he did, I'd understand why Daddy left me. I'd understand why he couldn't stay alive for me, why he abandoned me."

"God, Kate. I never knew."

"Of course not. You think I tell people this shit? No, it's depressing. I'm alive. God gave me a second chance at life, and I'm not gonna waste it this time. I won't watch Ben kill himself, no matter how much I love him." She sobbed again, then composed herself with a few deep breaths. "Sorry, Becca, but I have to go. My shift at the hospital is starting."

The line went dead, and I was left staring at the cracked concrete and the smoldering butt of Ben's cigarette.

"Babe? What's going on? Where's Kate?" Jason plopped down on the step next to me, then saw the tear on my cheek. "What's up? What's wrong?"

"Kate's gone. She left Ben…because he's back on drugs."

"Shit." Jason scrubbed his hand over his face. "That's not good."

"No." I leaned against him for support. "Ben says he's losing the apartment. I'm—I'm worried about him. I've never seen him look so depressed as he was just now. He's angry. I don't know. I have—I have a really bad feeling, Jason."

Jason didn't offer empty reassurances; he just sat with me until I felt ready to figure things out.

We stayed in the apartment that weekend, but Ben only came back once in the three days we were there, and he stayed in his room the whole time, filling the apartment with the acrid stench of marijuana. I tried to get him to come out and talk to me before we left, but he cracked the door enough to hug me good-bye and that was it.

I grabbed lunch with Nell before we left town for Ann Arbor, and that at least was an uplifting moment in the weekend. She seemed stable, if not happy, and she willingly showed me both forearms. She was wearing a dress with short sleeves, her wrists not covered, all the scars old and white.

"I haven't cut in a long time," she told me, sipping on a milkshake. "It's not something that ever just goes away, and I can't promise I won't cut again, but I'm doing better."

"I'm so glad, Nell," I said. "You don't even know how happy that makes me."

She smiled at me, stirring her milkshake with her straw. "So, I'm moving to New York in a few weeks."

I coughed, choking on my Coke in surprise. "You're—you're what?"

"I'm finally moving on with my life. I'm going to NYU. I'm going to try and get into their college of performing arts."

I wiped my lips with a napkin, then dabbed at the droplets of soda that had stained my T-shirt. "The college of performing arts? What? I mean…what do you perform?"

"Guitar. Singing." She shrugged, as if this thing I didn't know about my best friend was no big deal.

"You play the guitar? Since when?"

"Actually, you inspired me to try it. You said there had to be a better way to cope, and so I found one. I've been taking guitar lessons from a guy in town for almost two years now. I play and I sing. Just for myself, so far, but I'm going to try busking in New York."

"Busking? What's that?"

"Those guys who sit on the street and play with their guitar cases open? That's busking."

I frowned. "Oh, okay. But...okay." I was stunned; I hadn't seen this coming. "So you're going to New York? In, like, a couple weeks?"

She nodded, and I could sense real excitement in her, subdued, but still there. "Yeah. I won't just get into the college of performing arts, though. You have to audition and stuff, and it's competitive. If I don't get in, I'll try other stuff. Music management maybe. I don't know. I just know I wanted to move to New York a long time ago, and now I'm going to. I'm feeling like I finally might be able to live on more than a day-by-day basis."

"So you're...like, okay?"

She shrugged. "I don't know. I guess? As much as I'll ever be, I think. It still hurts, every single day. I think about...about him every day. I miss him. So much. But...I'm tired of being here. Maybe a change of scenery will help. Like, if I'm someplace where no one knows me, knows what I've been through, I can sort of start over, you know? Be someone new."

I wanted to tell her that your problems tended to follow you, because they were inside you, but I held my tongue. I'd be a stutterer no matter where I lived, and all I could do was accept that fact and be content with who I was despite it. Jason had helped me with that, although I'd never told him so. He'd accepted me, loved me despite my stutter, and hadn't minded when I stumbled over my words, or hit blocks because I was nervous or excited. Knowing he loved me regardless of my speech impediment was a huge part of my ability to speak fluently now. I was confident in who I was, and I knew that my impediment didn't define me. If I stuttered, I slowed down, moved past it, and kept going, and didn't let myself get embarrassed about it. That was the thing, I'd realized: When I got embarrassed over a stammer or block, it turned into vicious cycle. I'd be embarrassed, which would make me stutter, which would upset me, and make me stutter worse.

"I can't believe you're moving to New York," I said. "I'm going to miss you so much!"

She smiled at me, equal parts happiness, sadness, and affection. "Oh, Beck. Me too. You've always been there, even when I wasn't a very good friend. It's not like I'm leaving forever, though. I'll be back for holidays, just like you. We'll see each other again soon. It really won't be much different than now, except you can't just pop down for the weekend and see me."

We'd finished our lunches by this time, so we paid the bill and left, standing in front of our cars, which were parked side by side.

She smacked the side of Jason's truck above the wheel well. "Jason is still driving this thing? He's had it forever, hasn't he? It's got to be about dead."

I laughed and rubbed the truck where she'd hit it. "Be nice to his truck. I love this thing. He's had it since he was sixteen. I told him I'd cry when he replaced it. But yeah, it is dying. He just replaced the brakes, and now the snake belt is going, or something like that. Snake belt? Serpentine? Something. I don't know. Another part needs fixing. At some point, it won't be worth the money to fix it."

"It's the serpentine belt. I watched…" She paled and blinked hard, then forced the words out. "I watched Kyle replace a serpentine belt once. On the Camaro."

"Well, whatever the hell it's called, he's gonna spend more money to fix that part, and then I'm guessing something else will break. We're gonna have to buy a newer car soon, I'm thinking."

"We." Nell said it with a sigh and a wistful lift of her lips, not quite a smile.

"What do you mean?"

"You. You and Jason. You've been together for how long now?"

I grinned. "More than four years."

"You have a 'we,' that's all. I'm happy for you."

I shrugged. "Yeah. I'm pretty lucky, I guess. I mean, I *know* I am. I've been so fortunate. He's awesome."

"Are you guys living together?"

I jangled my keys, shaking the ignition key loose. "Yeah. Since August. It's…well, it's great."

"I bet. What's it like? What do your parents think?"

"My parents hate it. They think we're rushing it. But they've learned to accept it, as much as they ever will." I shrugged again, knowing I was making her think of all she was missing out on. "It's great. It's an adjustment, in some ways. It's really, like…it makes you realize you're an adult. Living in a dorm is just fun, you know? You don't have to worry about bills or rent or whatever, and there's always people around, all the time. People you know, who you're in classes with or see at football games. In an apartment, you're responsible for it. Jason and I have to pay rent and utilities and keep food in the house and all that. Plus, it's not right there on campus. If you're late, you're extra late. You can't just rush out in your comfy clothes and slip into class—you have to drive there and find a spot to park…. Plus, living with a guy is…different. The whole leaving-the-seat-up-thing? It's real. I fell into the toilet just the other day."

"Eeew!" Nell laughed. "But you're with him all the time. You can do whatever you want with him, whenever."

I giggled. "That's the best part. Even just going to sleep with him and waking up with him…I don't think I'll ever be able to sleep alone again."

Nell ducked her head. "Think you'll get married?"

I swallowed hard. I'd had those same thoughts myself. "Probably, eventually. I don't know. We haven't talked about it."

"Do you want to? Marry Jason, I mean?"

"Well, yeah. I mean, I want to be with him forever, so I'm guessing we'll get married someday, but it's just not come up."

Nell smirked at me. "But you've thought about it, haven't you? Of course you have. You've been with him since you were sixteen."

I nodded. "Well, yeah. Of course I have. But I want to graduate first. We're together, and there's no rush to change things, you know? We just turned twenty-one. Maybe once I'm working on my graduate degree we'll talk about it."

"What's Jason going to do after he graduates?"

"Play pro. He's got scouts from New Orleans, San Francisco, New York, Kansas City, and Dallas looking at him." I frowned, knowing there was one more he'd told me about. "Oh, and the Patriots, that's the other one. New England."

Nell seemed shocked. "He's really getting scouted by the NFL?"

I blinked at her. "Nell, he holds national receiving records on both the high school and university level. He's one of the best players in the NCAA, and

he thinks he's got a chance at a first-round draft pick."
I'd learned a lot about football over the years I'd been
with Jason.

Nell, not so much. "Is that good? The first-round
thing?"

I snickered. "Yeah, it's good. It means he'd be one
of the first people chosen to play for their team. The
draft thing is complicated, and I really don't get it all,
but being first-round draft pick is a big deal."

"So he's really good."

"He's fucking *amazing*." I was proud of my man.

Nell laughed at my vehemence. "Well, then." She
sighed and leaned in for a hug. "I should go, Becks."

I pulled her against me, holding her hard. "I'll miss
you. Even if you're all the way in New York performing, you can still call your BFF, right?" I shook her playfully. "We're kind of fighting, you know. I can't believe
you play the guitar and I didn't know."

She shook me back. "Nobody knows. It's not a
secret—it's just something I do for me, because it helps
me cope. I can play and sing and not think and put
all my emotions into that instead of needing to get it
out…some other way."

I hugged her and watched her drive away, knowing it would be months before I saw her again.

Becca
April 9th

I yelled a hello into my parents' house and received silence in reply.

Since Jason and I lived in an apartment now, we weren't going home for the summer after finals but were finding jobs to supplement our savings for our senior year. For Jason, it was a second job, and for me, it was something other than tutoring, since the program wouldn't really need me in the summer. I'd settled on answering phones at a local law office, which was boring as hell but paid enough to be worth it. Jason was still looking, but had a line on a position with a landscaping company.

I poked my head into Father's office, found it empty, and Mom's as well. This wasn't surprising, since they both often worked late. Ben should be home, though; his car was in the driveway. He'd moved back in with our parents after he'd lost the apartment, and I'd heard from Kate that they'd been trying to work things out, but it wasn't going so well. She was worried about him again, since she hadn't heard from him in several hours. He was still working at Belle Tire, but he'd resigned his position as assistant manager, going back to changing oil since it was less responsibility. A wise decision, I thought. The problem was, I had called Belle Tire before swinging by the house. He hadn't shown up for his shift at nine that morning, and it was three in the afternoon. Kate had sent me a text asking me to look at my parents' house for him

Cool conditioned air washed over me, and I heard the faint *tick-tock-tick-tock* of the grandfather clock in the den. My skin crawled, but I couldn't identify the reason. Nothing was out of place. The kitchen was spotless, nothing was missing, the front door had been locked, and the patio and garage doors were locked as well. I licked my lips and tried to calm my breathing as I searched the main floor, finding everything in place. I made my way up the stairs, avoiding the creaking tenth step by habit. The door to my old bedroom was closed, and I went in. My old bed was there, made, an old quilt laid across it since I'd taken my favorite set of sheets and blankets with me to college. My dresser, now bare of knickknacks, and the desk, empty but for a Starbucks mug full of pencils and pens. The closet was closed, empty upon checking. No posters anymore, no pictures, nothing. No Ben, either.

I checked my parents' room, which felt odd. I'd only been in there a handful of times in my life; their bedroom was a sanctuary, by unspoken rule. You just stayed out. My father's slippers were, ridiculously enough, in the classic TV dad position at the side of the bed, neatly aligned. My mom's blue terrycloth robe was slung over the back of her antique rocking chair. The rocker was a family heirloom shipped over from Lebanon for my mother's fortieth birthday a few years ago.

The last place to check, of course, was Ben's room. My dread increased to a palpable sense of stomach-knotting fear, my heart hammering, my hands trembling, my breathing coming in ragged gasps. I put my hand on the cold silver knob, twisted, and pushed…

The room was empty. It was also spotless, the bed neatly made, nothing out place, which was unlike Ben, who was a bit of slob. I don't think his room had ever been this clean. Posters of rappers papered the walls, along with *Sports Illustrated* and *Playboy* centerfolds. A rack of CDs covered one entire wall, each jewel case aligned the same way, writing facing the left. It even smelled clean, and Ben's room had always smelled, even through a closed door, of patchouli incense, which he used to cover the stench of his pot. The only sign of life was the open window I'd once escaped through to see Jason. A warm breeze blew, rippling the curtains.

There was a single sheet of notebook paper aligned square on the top of his dresser. I shook my head at the paper, denying even before I'd read it.

Becca,

I'm guessing you're the one who'll find this. I'm sorry. You're honestly the only reason I didn't do this a long time ago. I didn't want to let you down. You always believed in me when no else did. It's just not enough anymore. I don't have much to say to Mom and Dad, except I wish you'd tried harder with me. Loved me as I was, instead of judging me and trying to fix me, and then just giving up on me. I'm sorry to everyone. I'm sorry, most of all, to Kate. I don't deserve her, I never did and never could. I let her down, time and again, and I just can't keep failing her. She needs someone better than me. Now she can find him. I do love her, but it's not enough.

Goodbye.

Benjamin

P.S. Becca, you remember the tree? That's where I'll be.

I touched the paper, and the ink smeared on my fingers. I felt a bolt of hope at the sight of the smeared ink. If the ink wasn't dry yet, maybe there was still time. The tree. God, the tree. Our house was at the far edge of the subdivision and backed up to acres of open land, part forest, part scrub, part endless grass fields. About a mile from our back door was a mammoth pine tree with straight, low-hanging branches, the lowest one just out of reach. We used to play beneath that tree for hours. Then, when Ben got older and his bipolar mood swings took hold, he would go out to the tree and get away from everything. He claimed he could feel whatever he wanted beneath that tree, instead of feeling like his moods needed adjustment. That's where he'd go when he wanted to get stoned, too, until he realized our parents were either oblivious or were playing blind.

I didn't even think. I swung my legs out the window and scaled down to the ground at record speed. I stumbled through the bushes and into the scrub-covered hillside, fumbling my phone from my purse. I called Jason, because I was too overcome by panic to even think of anyone else.

"What's up, baby?" He sounded out of breath, and I heard the clink and rattle of weights in the background.

"It's b-Ben. I th-think he's…he left a note, a suic—s-s-s—ide note." I couldn't breathe, couldn't speak.

"What? Are you serious? Did you find him?"

"No, n-not y-yet. There's a tree, be-h-hind our h-house. I think that's w-where he is."

"That huge granddaddy pine tree, I know it. Baby, listen, don't go there by yourself. I'm less than five minutes away, okay? I'll be there, wait for me, okay?"

He was too late. I was already there. The tree was up a rise and down the other side. I could see the top of

the pine tree swaying in the wind. Birds chirped cheer-
ily, a harsh contrast to the terror in my gut. I was running as fast as I could, the phone forgotten, clutched
in my hand. I could hear the tinny, distant sound of
Jason's voice calling my name. I crested the rise, stumbled, and fell, skidding down the steep, gravelly incline
on my backside. I felt rocks gouging and scraping my
bare thighs, my shorts too short to protect my legs.

I righted myself and tripped around to the other
side of the tree, where the lowest branch was. My eyes
were closed, as if to block out what I feared I'd see if I
opened them. Tears were already streaming down my
face, and I heard Jason's voice in the phone, or maybe
it was in the distance. I forced my eyes open.

I screamed.

Ben hung from the lowest branch, swinging, legs
kicking still. An orange Home Depot bucket was over-
turned beneath him, still rolling in circles. His eyes
showed white in his face, his mouth wide, face going
purple.

I smelled shit.

I lunged forward, screaming his name over and
over again. I grabbed his legs in my arms and lifted
with all my strength, sobbing. I got him lifted high
enough that the tension was eased, and I heard a faint
raspy choking noise, and then my legs gave out and his

ankles slid out of my grasp. I fell to the ground beneath him. His toes drooped earthward, limp, swinging in tiny circles, no longer twitching.

"BEN!" I heard my voice shrieking, shrill. "No, Ben, no, no *no.*"

I scrambled out from beneath him, struggled to my feet, and tried to lift him up, knowing he was gone, knowing it was too late. I felt something hot and sticky and putrid on my hands from where they grasped the back of his legs, and I knew what that was, too. I knew what happened to the bowels when someone was hung.

I looked up at his body, twisting in my grip. His head was craned at an unnatural angle, his eyes rolled back, tongue lolling out.

"Oh...fuck." I heard a voice behind me. Jason.

I felt his arms around me, pulling me away. I fought him. I needed to help Ben. He was hurt. He needed me. He'd always needed me, and I wasn't there. I was too late. I had to help him. I fought the pinioning arms, heard screaming go hoarse as vocal chords gave out, heard broken whispers in my ear, Jason begging me to turn away.

Don't look anymore, baby. He's gone. He's gone.

NO! HE ISN'T GONE! My brother, my brother, my Ben. I fought even when my strength gave out and

Jason was holding me. I wasn't speaking anymore, I wasn't intelligible, I was sobbing and gasping and babbling, straining for Benny. He twisted in the breeze, rope creaking.

A crow cawed somewhere, announcing the arrival of Death. The ink-black creature hopped on a branch on a nearby tree, head tilted, eye glinting. It ruffled its wings, cocked its head to the other side and cawed again, directly at me.

"*NO!* You can't have him!" Those were the last words I would speak fluently for a very long time.

I ripped free from Jason's arms and scooped a rock from the ground at my feet, hurled it at the crow, who only ducked and cawed again, twice, harsh and mocking. Then, with a ruffle of feathers and a snap of wings, the crow was gone, and I fell, boneless, to the earth.

I felt myself scooped up into strong arms, and I clawed helplessly at the iron chest, Jason's sweat-scent in my nostrils all that kept me from dying in that moment. I clawed at him, scraping his chest with my fingernails. I'd just had a manicure the day before, and my nails were bright purple, perfectly painted and shaped. I watched with disconnected horror as my purple fingernails curled into Jason's shirts and ripped it, then clawed again at the bare skin, dragging pink lines down his flesh. I couldn't draw breath, felt stars speck in front of my eyes, my lungs burning. I couldn't draw breath, because I was caught in an endless looping scream, soundless, shuddering.

I was being carried away. I felt the hill beneath us. I fought, gasped, fought.

"B-Ben! N-no! T-take me b-back! He-he-he needs m-m-me…plea-please!"

Jason didn't answer. He didn't have to. I heard voices pass me, radios crackling, sirens in the distance. Red and blue lights bathed my eyelids. A door opened, closed. Stairs creaked. Another door opened. I felt cool porcelain beneath my thighs. Water sputtered and rushed, and soon steam enveloped me. Shit stank in my nostrils. One of my hands stung, and I glanced apathetically at the middle finger on my left hand, missing a fingernail and bleeding.

Jason's hands peeled away my shirt, unclasped my bra, lifted me to my feet, pushed away my shorts and panties. I felt his skin against me, and I wanted to burrow into his heat and forget everything. But he wouldn't let me. I was so cold. He helped me over the wall of the tub and into the shower. Curtain rungs rasped against the metal rod, and then I was doused in scalding water, quickly adjusted to a more tolerable temperature. I didn't care. The burn was fine.

A pink and orange poofy loofah sponge crossed my shoulder, down my back, over my arm. He scrubbed me diligently, gently. He let me rest against his chest, my back to his front. He lathered my hair, rinsed it, massaged conditioner into it. Washed me again, rinsed my hair. I felt a brush scrape through the wet, tangled curls, gently, over and over again, tugging through knots until my hair was smooth.

The water ran lukewarm, and he shut it off. Wrapped a towel around me, rubbed me dry, then wrung my hair out, dabbed it dry, brushed it again. I shivered against him. He scooped me in his arms and carried me to my room, laid me on my bed, tugged the sheets and quilt from beneath me and covered me with them. I felt his absence for the briefest moment, and panic shot through me.

"No! C-come b-back!" I grasped air and twisted in the bed.

He was there instantly, still naked, still wet. He slid into the bed with me and wrapped himself around me. "I'm here, my love. I'm here. I'm not leaving you. I'm here."

"B-Ben…" I turned in his arms and pressed my face to his chest. "W-why? God, b-Benny…"

"I don't know, honey. I wish I knew." He smoothed my hair against my scalp, and his breath was on my ear.

"Ben-Benny…" I sobbed, and couldn't stop once I'd started. I heard hinges creak, and Jason's weight shifted, then returned. A thought struck me. "K-Kate? I have to tell Kate."

"She knows. She's been told." He held me against him. "I'm so sorry, Becca. I'm so sorry."

I sobbed until I slept, and then when I woke, I sobbed again until I passed out once more. I'd been dressed at some point, and Jason was gone when I woke a second time. Full dark hung thick beyond my window, sliced by a sliver of moon. I found him in the kitchen talking to my parents, a cup of coffee in his hands, dressed in track pants and a gray hoodie with his last name across the back.

Father was the first to see me. He crossed the kitchen in two strides and clutched me against his chest. "Rebecca, I'm so sorry you saw that. God, *figlia*. I'm so sorry." His voice broke. "I failed him. I failed…"

I couldn't take the cloying scent of his cologne, the unfamiliar feel of his embrace. I pushed away from him and found Jason. He pulled me into his arms, and I broke down again. He sat down on the high bar chair and lifted me onto his lap, smoothed my hair away, held me.

Mother was silent, but I felt her sorrow. I peered at her, saw her face streaked with tears, eyes red.

I felt Father behind me. "Rebecca, I—"

I didn't blame him, wasn't angry at him, but I couldn't take his presence. I writhed away from his touch and twisted to look up at Jason. "I-I-I c-can't be h-here. Take mmm-mmm—me away. Take me s-somew-w-w-where else. Anyw-w-w-where."

He stood up with me in a fireman's hold and carried me away. I heard a door open, and I smelled my mother's scent. Cold, small fingers touched my forehead. I opened my eyes to see her brown eyes shimmering above me. She didn't speak, just brushed my forehead, her lips pressed into a thin, hard line.

"He-he's gone, M-mmm-Mom." I fisted Jason's hoodie in my hand as I locked eyes with her. "He killed hims-s-self. Hung himself from a f-f-f-fucking t-t-t-tree!"

"I know, I know." It was all she said.

"W-w-why?"

She shrugged, shaking her head. "I have not...any answers."

Jason carried me out into the warm summer night, a gentle breeze riffling my hair, smelling of flowers and cut grass and nighttime. A frog croaked somewhere, and a cricket sang a shrill song. He set me on my feet, and I heard the creak of his truck door opening, the pale, dim yellow glow of the cab light familiar, the *ding-ding-ding* of the open-door alert chiming. I climbed into the truck, grateful for something familiar. He started the truck with a grumbling roar, and music began immediately: "To Travels and Trunks" by Hey Marseilles. My music, rather than Jason's country.

I felt Jason watching me, and he knew me well enough to leave the music on. "Rhythm of Love" by Plain White T's came on next, and I let my eyes close. I could almost forget, nestled in the warm familiarity of Jason's truck.

"Where do you want to go, baby?" I felt the right turn out of the subdivision, and then the left onto the main road.

"Anywhere. Just…drive."

The Civil Wars played next, "Kingdom Come," and I laid my head on Jason's lap as he drove. I felt dirt and gravel rumble and plink under us, and Jason's hand rested on my side.

We drove, and we drove. I slept, and woke in Jason's arms, my head against his chest, early morning cold frosting me, sunlight gleaming golden-red through the windshield. I saw the branches of our oak tree, each one familiar. I knew how many branches the tree had, knew the scar of an ax or saw on one side, the knot near the joining of the trunk and a low branch, the place where birds liked to nest near the top.

I had a moment of peace, just the cold and Jason's arms and the truck and the tree and the sun. And then I remembered, a waking nightmare flashing through my mind. I shuddered, choking back tears. Jason's arms clutched me, and I knew he was awake.

"I love you," he whispered. "I love you so much, and I'll be here with you every single moment."

I nodded against his chest. "I l-love you, t-too." I cringed at the stutter. "I'm s-sorry."

"Sorry? For what?"

"I k-keep…keep stutter…r-r-ring." Mid-word stutters were the worst. I hadn't stuttered in the middle of a word since junior high.

He made a sound almost like a sob. "Never apologize. You know that. I love you. Always, forever, no matter what."

"P-p-prom—promise?" I clutched him desperately.

"On my soul. On my life."

I needed him. I wasn't afraid of admitting that, not ever. Especially then. I knew he was the only thing that would get me through this crushing sorrow, this haunting vision of Ben swinging and twisting in the air above me.

He held me, and he didn't let go.

Fourteen: Elegy
Jason
Two days later

I HAD TO LITERALLY HOLD BECCA UPRIGHT as we entered the viewing room at the funeral parlor.

Why is it a "parlor"? It seems like such a flighty, frivolous word. Parlors are for sipping tea and laughing at flat jokes, not mourning the loss of a loved one.

I'd tried to call Nell to tell her, but she never answered, never returned my call. I didn't leave a message, because how can you pass news like this via voicemail?

Becca was…just broken. It crushed me to see her like this. She was always such a bright person, lively and lovely. Quiet in public, but still vibrant. Now? The sunlight had been leached from her smile, the sap sucked from her eyes. I held her against my side, pinning her there with my arm. She clutched my ribs tight enough to restrict my breathing. I half-carried her across the same carpeting with the fleur-de-lis pattern, past the same out-of-place paintings of old English fox-hunt scenes as when Kyle died. Not the same room, thank god. I don't think I could have taken that. This one was subdued, with wood-paneled walls and pale charcoal carpeting and brass lamps, some ubiquitous hunt scene artwork and three rows of folding chairs.

And the casket. Mahogany or some other nut-brown wood, brass handles around the edges. The top half of the lid was open, and as I escorted Becca closer to it, I saw first Ben's hair, black and shiny. Becca hiccuped as we approached and clung to me. I steeled myself as we took the last step. Then we were standing in front of the casket, and Becca had her face buried in my suit coat.

"I d-d-don't want to l-look," she mumbled.

"Then don't," I said. "You know who he was."

She shuddered in my arms, and then slowly turned her face away from me, straightened, stood on her own. Her hands smoothed her shin-length black dress over her hips, and I watched her visibly steel herself. Her back went ramrod straight, her head tilted back, her hands clutched into fists, and her breathing went long and deep and fast. I stood beside her and forced my fingers into hers, and she grabbed at me as if for a lifeline, gripping hard enough to cause pain.

I watched her. She opened her eyes and stared into the middle distance over the casket, and then, nearly hyperventilating, she forced her gaze down to the body of her brother. He was dressed in a plain black suit, white shirt, black tie. His hair was slicked back, and makeup had been so artfully applied that you could barely see the dark black bruise ringing his neck.

"God, he w-w-would have hay-hated that s-s-suit," she murmured, then covered her mouth with her hand. "Why do w-we d-d-do th-this? Why do we t-t-t-torture oursel—selves like-like this? That's n-nnn-not Ben."

I had no answer for that question. I just held her, my arm high around her waist.

Mr. de Rosa came up beside Becca and rested his hand on her shoulder. She'd told me she didn't blame him, late last night, but now she shook his hand off, moaning low in her throat.

"D-d-don't, Father." She pushed away from me, stumbling and almost knocking over the framed collage of photographs of Ben standing on an easel near the casket.

He watched her go, sadness in his eyes. His gaze flickered to me and held a hint of accusation, as if I'd done something to alienate them. She said she didn't blame Enzio de Rosa for her brother's death, but her actions said otherwise. It was none of my business, so I did the only thing I could: I followed her, wrapped my arm around her waist, and pulled her to a chair near the back, by the door. She'd bolt again, I knew.

A priest came and stood in front of the crowd. "Dearly beloved," he began, his voice throaty and phlegmy, "we are gathered here to mourn the passage of Benjamin Aziz de Rosa. His life ended far too soon, we would all agree. We'll probably never know why Benjamin chose to take his own life, but nonetheless, we mourn his death and choose to celebrate his life—"

Becca choked on a sob, coughed, and stumbled to her feet. I chased after her as she righted herself and stepped in front of the priest, who cut short and stared at Becca in shock and confusion. She met my eyes and shook her head, and I knew she was fully aware of what she was doing, so I stood with my back to the wall and my arms crossed over my chest, daring anyone to try to stop her.

"Th-this isn't what my brother would have wanted." She spoke slowly, an artificial, scripted quality to her words. "H-he would have hated that s-stupid suit. He would have hated those stupid pictures of him, and these stupid flowers. He would have hated the fake words this preacher is saying—no offense, sir. He-he-he—would have wanted us to get sss-stoned for him. We w-won't do that, ah-ah-obviously. We know *exactly* why he hu-hung himsel—self. He was troubled. He was depressed. He was angry. He did-didn't th-think he ha-had any-anything t-t-to off-off-offer." She paused, closed her eyes, and gathered herself.

I noticed Kate then for the first time, wearing, instead of black, a deep emerald dress that hung at her knees and clung to her svelte frame. Her hair was twisted up into a complicated braid, and she had thick makeup on. She'd dressed for Ben, I realized, not everyone else. Her eyes were red-rimmed, tear-stained, and angry.

Becca saw her, too, and she spoke to Kate.

"I knew him best, except for Kate. I loved him, and I hated to see him…s-struggle…with himself." Becca was pausing frequently, forcing words out, forcing fluency on herself. No one was breathing. "His n-n-note said he was sorry. That he'd failed…Kate, and everyone. He didn't fail. He did-did…*didn't*. Not once. W-*we* failed *him*. We all did." Her eyes flicked her father then, and he visibly flinched, eyes screwing tight and a single tear slipping down his cheek. "We all…judged… hi—him. We tried to fi-fix…him. Only Kate just *loved* him. Let him feel what he felt and…accepted…

him-him-him." Her eyes ticked with the last three stuttered syllables.

At that, Kate broke, standing up suddenly in a
crash of metal folding chairs, and ran. Becca watched
her, and then moved her gaze back to the podium,
staring at the wood. She glanced at me, then gestured
to her purse on the chair where she'd been sitting.
I snagged it and handed it to her. She pulled out a
piece of lined paper folded into eighths, unfolded it,
smoothed it against the wood surface.

She breathed deeply, her mouth moving as she
read the words in preparation to speak them aloud.

"I wrote this. For Ben." I knew how hard it was for
Becca to share her poetry. This was the only thing, the
best thing she could give him.

"I don't mourn you,
Brother.
I don't grieve for you.
If there is thought
Or grief
Or love
After this life,
Then you're watching,
And you're mad at us.
You're angry,
But you're at peace.

I don't mourn you,
Brother.
But I miss you.
I wish you hadn't left,
Hadn't removed yourself
So violently
From us all.
From me.
I miss you.
I love you,
Brother.
And I'm sorry.
I'm sorry I didn't love you
More.
I can't say if you're in a better place.
Maybe that's a myth we tell
To comfort ourselves.
There's too much to say,
And not enough words
For me to say it all.
If you're here,
If you're listening,
Then I hope you find,
In whatever place you're in,
What you were looking for."

She crushed the paper in her fist, slumping forward onto the podium as if the effort to say all that so fluently had used up all her strength. I moved to her, pulled her against my chest, and moved backward, away. She hung from my embrace, and I lifted her into my arms, careful to keep her dress smoothed modestly over her legs. I carried her out of the viewing room, out of the parlor, and to the tree, the same tree where I'd seen Nell run from Kyle's funeral. I think that's where she'd first met Colton, or, well, met him again, really, since we'd all sort of known him before he'd left.

Kate was there, beneath the tree, the branches casting a broad shadow in the bright, hot June sunlight. Becca set her feet down and moved to sit beside Kate, and I plopped down in front of them.

"I'm not—I didn't love him, like you said," Kate blurted. "I didn't. I was always trying to fix him. Make him better."

"But you accepted him any-anyway. You l-l-lo-loved him, even though he was so messed up."

"He wasn't messed up. He was just Ben."

"See?" Becca smiled, a tiny, sad smile. "That's w-w-what I mean."

A long silence ensued. Kate sat Indian-style and stared at the grass between her legs, plucking blades of grass and shredding them. I moved to sit next to Becca, since the way Kate was sitting left her open so I could that she wasn't wearing anything under the dress, and I didn't need to see that.

"I'm pregnant." Kate whispered the words.

Becca's head snapped up. "What?"

"That's why Ben killed himself. He couldn't take it. He thought he'd ruined my life, our lives. The kid would be like him, he said. He said...he wasn't capable of being a father. He...I found out the day before he...the day before. I told him, and he just...he flipped out. He got so mad, worse than I've ever seen him. At himself, though. Not at me. He smashed the apartment, and almost hit me. It was so scary. He wasn't himself, he was just...crazy." She was still whispering so low I could barely hear her. "When he realized he was so close to hurting me, he stopped. That was the next morning. Then he left, and I didn't know where he'd gone. I was so sick, I was puking so hard I couldn't breathe. I couldn't get off the bathroom floor for hours. So I sent you that text asking you to look for him. God, Becca, I never thought...I didn't think he'd—he'd do this..." She sobbed and fell sideways, burying her face in her hands, slipping down so her head rested on Becca's lap.

Becca stroked her hair away from her forehead and wept with her, sniffling quietly, letting her tears fall. I felt my chest clench, my stomach twist. Watching Becca cry so hopelessly was the hardest thing I'd ever done. Knowing I couldn't help her, couldn't comfort her was even worse.

Kate stopped after a while and wiped her eyes with her hands, and her nose on her forearm, leaving a clear trail across her pale skin. "What do I do? How do I...how do I do this?" Kate asked.

Becca stared at me, pleading with me silently to have some kind of answer.

"I—you just...live. One day at a time. That's all any of us can ever do, isn't it?" I hated how trite my words sounded. "You're family, now, Kate. You won't be alone. We'll...we'll help you any way we can."

"I...I thought about having an abortion. That's all I can think about. Do I have this baby? Do I not?" Her voice cracked and she cleared her throat, continued in a broken murmur. "But...I *have* to have the baby. He... or she...is all I'll ever have of Ben. God...he's gone, and I have to do this alone." She curled her fists in the grass, ripped hunks of grass loose, speaking through clenched teeth. "I'm so *mad* at him. So angry. He *left* me. He didn't die on accident, he wasn't taken from me...he *left* me...on purpose. And I...I *fucking hate* him for that. Does that make me an awful person? I'm so angry at him for leaving me that I could just...I can't take it."

"I-I'm mad at him, too," Becca whispered. "I n-n-know what I s-sss-said in there, but...I'm angry, t-too, Kate. He took the coward's way out. I h-hate mys-ss—self for ee-eev-even thinking that about him, b-but it's t-tr-true."

"You're allowed to feel whatever you want," I said to both of them, again feeling like I was spouting cliches.

Another long silence, and then Kate stood up shakily, brushing her hands off and smoothing her dress, slipping her feet back into her black heels and re-tying her auburn hair into a sleek ponytail. And just like that, she was back together again, eyes dry but full of sadness. "I have to go. Thanks, both of you."

I stood up and leaned in to give her a quick, chaste hug. "Call us, okay? Anytime, for anything."

She nodded. "I will." And then she was gone, long legs striding across the grass.

Becca held her hands out to me, and I lifted her to her feet. She clung to me, drawing in a lungful of air with her face against my chest. "Take me home."

An hour later, we were back in our apartment. I had my shoes kicked off, the stupid, slippery dress socks making my feet slide on the cracked white laminate stick-on of the kitchen floor. I shucked my coat and pulled on my tie to loosen it, and then I felt a hand on my arm, turning me.

I spun in place, and Becca's hands were on my tie, pulling it free, her eyes fierce and determined, mouth open slightly. She fumbled with a button, then another, and then she growled and yanked it open. The first few buttons popped open, and then the rest tore free and clicked onto floor.

"Beck? What—?" I didn't get a chance to speak.

She attacked me, kissing me a desperation I'd never felt from her before. My ruined dress shirt hit the floor, and then my wife-beater tank top was flying across the kitchen and my belt was snapping free and my pants were around my ankles.

"Make me feel s-sss-something." She whispered it, her voice harsh and ragged in my ear. "Any-anything else. *Please.*"

I had no chance to reply. She had her dress off and then the rest of her undergarments before I could register what was happening, and then we were naked together and I was stumbling across the kitchen with Becca's weight on me. She hung from my neck, her legs around my waist, her lips locked on mine. I groaned as she devoured me, biting my tongue, nipping my lips. Her fingers dug into my skin so ferociously I knew I'd have marks, and then she was reaching between us and guiding me into her, rising up with her thigh muscles leveraged on my hips, and then slamming down so hard the slap of flesh echoed in the tiny apartment. I stumbled again, and then spun in place to set her on the counter with her back against the peeling white paint of a cabinet.

"No, no. More. Need…more." She thrust against me, and I pulled her airborne, staggering across the kitchen, and we slammed into the hallway wall. "Yes. Like-like this."

I pushed gently against her, holding her against the wall and kissing her tenderly, trying to slow her. She growled in frustration, locked her arms around my neck, and lifted up, then slammed down with a satisfied moan, her lips leaving my mouth and stuttering across my cheek.

"Bed. P-please." She was lifting up and lowering herself frantically, setting an impossible pace for me to keep while standing.

I carried us into our room and fell back against the bed. I didn't have a chance to even straighten myself on the bed before she had her fingers twined in mine above my head, her hips sliding over mine. She rested her forehead against mine in a kind of desperate relief as she resumed her frantic grinding pace on top of me. Her breasts bounced against my skin, and her thighs whispered soft as silk against mine. She was gasping into my mouth, riding me with a furious, wild abandonment. This was both hot and kind of scary, because her eyes weren't entirely her own. She was possessed, in a way. She was wild-eyed, ferocious, leaning back on me to sit up straight, lifting up with her thighs and sinking down on me relentlessly, her hands buried in her hair, breasts swaying and bouncing with each lift and fall of her body. God, she was so gloriously beautiful, and this angry goddess mood was something new, something I'd never seen in her before. She gave nothing to me. She took. I held her hips and let her ride me, gave her everything I had, not daring to speak, to whisper, to even breathe. She took all of me for her own, driving herself into an orgasmic frenzy, screaming through clenched teeth and then spitting an ululating moan with her head thrown back and her spine arched and her fucking glorious tits bouncing, and finally I lost myself in it, giving her more and more, harder and harder until she came a second time, and a third, because my baby could just keep coming and coming until she was too exhausted to move, and I think that was what she needed. I clenched my muscles and closed my eyes to block out the erotic sight of her body above me and focused on holding back even as I drove into her as hard as I could. She fell forward, planting her palms on my chest and grinding onto me in a new rhythm, not pulling out at all but grinding her clit against me and pushing herself over the edge yet again, mouth wide in a gasping shriek, eyes closed, brows raised, and yeah, I was watching her because I couldn't help it, because Becca, such a giver in all things, was finally taking all of this for herself, because for some reason I couldn't entirely fathom, she needed this, and so I would give it to her again and again until she was sated.

She rolled off me and onto her back, scrabbling at my arms and back to jerk me into place, grasping my ass and pulling me forward, shoving me into her and coiling her powerful legs around my backside and clenching me, pulling, pulling, thrusting with every muscle in her body against me. Her arms wrapped around my neck and she refused to let go, so I pressed my lips to her shoulder and planted my hands next to her ear and settled into a driving, almost punishing rhythm, hard and dirty and relentless, and she only cried out for more.

She took it, and clawed gouges into my shoulder when she came again, climaxing with a deafening scream. I'd held back for so long at this point that I ached for release, but she wasn't done with me.

She pushed me away and turned onto her hands and knees, presenting her ass to me. God...damn. I didn't know what it was about seeing her like that, but it was always my undoing. Something about her beautiful, taut ass presented to me, her sex-slick folds wet from our lovemaking, our fucking...it drove me wild. I plunged into her and she stuffed a pillow under her stomach, clutching the other pillow in her fists and rocking back into my every thrust, the slap of flesh a rhythmic echo in our apartment, and then she came again, and this time she clenched down extra hard with her vaginal muscles and I was buried deep and something in the way she moaned, something in the way she ground her ass against me and whispered my name was my undoing. I couldn't hold back any longer then. I lost it, growling and pulling back and fucking into her so hard she whimpered, but it was a breath-less *"yes!"* from her lips, and she rocked forward and crashed back into my next thrust, and then again, and then I was unleashing inside her, flood after flood, and she was clamped around me and spasming and crying out hoarsely and pressing her soft dark skin into me, not minding at all the way my hands clutched her hips with bruising power and jerked her against me with every spasmodic thrust of release.

She fell forward away from me with a sigh, rolling to her back, reaching up and jerking me roughly down to the bed. She found her spot, nestling in the crook of my left arm, her right leg thrown over mine, her hand resting low on my belly, her breathing whisking hot across my clavicle.

"Thank you, baby," she whispered. "I n-n-needed it, just like that. I know it was...rough, but I nee-needed it."

I chuckled. "Honey, I'm pretty sure that was the hottest sex we've ever had."

She nodded. "I think s-so, t-too. I think I mi-might be able to slee—sleep now. I hope." She was exhausted, wrung dry.

I held her tight and whispered to her over and over again how much I loved her. Eventually her breathing changed, and she was asleep.

She did dream, though. I held her through that, too.

Fifteen: The Aftermath
Jason
One month later

BECCA WASN'T OKAY. For a while, I thought she was getting better. I thought she was coping. But then, about two weeks after Ben's death—after his suicide—she seemed to start regressing. She never really got her fluency back entirely, but she was beginning the process of recovering it. She'd stutter less, block less, although she had gone back to sounding as if she was reading from a script.

Her entire family had basically shut down. Her mother and father had both taken extended leaves of absence from work, which, from what I'd learned about Mr. and Mrs. de Rosa over the years, was akin to the apocalypse. Ben's death had rocked everyone, really. The entire community had been shocked. Ben was a fixture in the town, always around, always up to no good but nice to everyone. He'd kept the depths of his struggles secret from everyone, it seemed, and so his suicide had taken the community by storm. People who hadn't really known or even liked Ben all that much were going to grief counseling. Parents had started taking a deeper interest in the mental and emotional health of their kids. Gradually, however, as weeks passed, things returned to normal. Her parents went back to work, and Kate continued at the hospital, seeing an OB/GYN regularly.

Except for Becca. She gradually began to speak less and less. It started with shortened responses, going from stutter-broken sentences to three- and four-word answers, and eventually to one-word answers. She was...listless. I would find her in bed at eight in the morning, a Kleenex crumpled in her fist, eyes open and staring into the middle distance. Becca hadn't stayed in bed past 6 a.m. even once in the two years we'd been living together, whether it was Wednesday or Saturday, February or July. She'd been in the process of deciding on a school for after graduation when Ben killed himself. Now? She'd stopped cold. Stacks of acceptance letters sat unopened on her desk. Books for her senior-year classes were still stacked, unread, on her bookshelf. She was showing up for work, but that was it. She'd requested and gotten a change in position at the law firm, and was now filing paperwork and other duties that required little to no interaction with others.

I caught her on the way out the door once, her blouse mis-buttoned so drastically that two buttons showed at the bottom.

The following day, I got back from an early morning workout to find her still in bed, a half-hour late for work. She'd never, in the nearly five years we'd been together, ever once been late for anything.

She wasn't speaking at all by that point.

I would speak to her, some normal interaction such as asking her if she knew where my watch was; she would walk away silently and return with the watch rather than telling me. "Yes" or "no" questions would be answered with a shake or nod of her head. Sometimes she would simply not answer. She would stare at me almost blankly, as if she hadn't heard me.

I never once found her writing in her journal.

Eventually, I couldn't take it anymore. I found her sitting on our bed, knees drawn up, Kleenex in one hand, her phone in the other. She was scrolling through her pictures frantically, her thumb swiping across the screen over and over again, and with each photograph she bypassed, her features grew more and more panicked.

I sank onto the bed beside her, sitting cross-legged with my hands on her knees. "Becca? Are you looking for a specific picture?" She nodded without looking at me. "Which one?"

She then did something I'd never seen her do: She signed. I'd heard her say once that when she was really young she used sign language if she couldn't express herself in verbal speech, but she'd abandoned the use of sign language by fourth grade.

I didn't know sign language, not even the alphabet. She'd formed an "L" with her right hand, starting near her forehead and drawing it downward to her right hand, which was held as if pointing at me, or a number one.

"I don't...I don't know sign language, baby."

She just shook her head and kept scrolling. I tried to take the phone from her, but she jerked away from me, turning in place so she was facing away. I watched over her shoulder as she scrolled, picture after picture blurring past on the screen, snapped selfies, pics of her and me, her and Nell, random things. Then she reached the end of her photo album on the cell phone, the image bouncing but not swiping. She swiped at it repeatedly, as if unable to comprehend that it was the last picture. She moaned, a high-pitched whine in her throat, and slammed the phone down on the bed, but then immediately picked it up and tapped the blue and white Facebook icon, brought up her photo album in the Facebook app and began the process of frantically swiping through the pictures.

"Becca, honey, talk to me. What are you looking for?" She made the same sign, over and over again, L-shaped right hand brought down from her forehead to her pointing left hand. "I don't know what that means, Beck. Please, talk to me. *Please*."

She shook her head and kept going through her Facebook pictures. When she reached the end of those, she whimpered through clenched teeth and pressed the phone screen to her face, shoulders shaking. Then, with a burst of inspiration, she logged back into Facebook and brought up Kate's profile page and found her pictures.

That's when it registered. "Ben? You're looking for pictures of Ben?" She nodded, rocking in place in time with her scrolling thumb.

Kate had taken down every single picture of Ben from her page. There wasn't one, not a single photograph of Ben. Becca screamed out loud and threw the phone across the room, where it smashed against the wall, putting a hole in the drywall and cracking the screen.

I gathered her in my arms and pulled her against my chest. She thrashed in my grip, screaming, pounding on my chest hard enough to cause pain.

"I-I-I-I doh-don't-don't n-n-n-nnnn…don't remem-mem-mem…remember what he luh-luh-luh-looks like. I don't r-r-r-rem-rem-remember!" She shook in my arms, trembling violently.

That was the most she'd spoken in more than a week.

"We'll find you a picture of him, okay? I'm sure your parents have one. We'll get one. I'll go there right now, if you want."

"Everyone's forgotten hi-hi-him," she whispered. "Eev-eev-even Kate…and m-m-mmmm-me. Everyone. He's guh-guh-gone, like he never w-w-wwww-wuh-was."

"You remember him, honey. You do. You remember what he was like. You remember who he was." I had her wrapped tightly in my arms, and she'd stilled, barely breathing now. "When my grandpa died, I had this same fear. I loved Grandpa so much. He was Mom's dad, and he was my favorite person in the whole world. He lived up north, between Grayling and the Mackinaw Bridge. He had, like, twenty acres. He had horses and dirt bikes and all this awesome stuff. I'd go up there for weeks at a time during the summers, and he'd let me do whatever I wanted. We'd go hunting and fishing and four-wheeling, and I'd stay up till midnight every night. Then one day he died. All of a sudden, just gone. He had a heart attack and died, just like that. I cried for days. Dad kicked the shit out of me for crying, but I didn't care. I loved Grandpa, and he was gone. Then, like a month after he'd died, I had this panic attack. I couldn't remember what he looked like. I thought it meant I didn't love him, or that I'd forgotten about him. It was the only time Dad was anything like helpful. He told me you have to forget what they look like. Otherwise, you can't learn to live without them. Forgetting is your brain's way of telling you it's time to try and move on. Not forget who they were, just…keep living."

Becca seemed to shrink even further. "Why did he lee-l-l-l-leave me? *Why*, Jason?"

How did you answer that? Telling her that I thought he'd taken the coward's way out probably wasn't a good idea. His suicide was confusing and tragic, and it had fucked up so much for so many people. Like both Becca and Kate, I was angry at Ben. It felt wrong to feel that way, like I wasn't being compassionate enough, but it was the raw truth of how I felt. Times like this, when Becca was falling apart, I *hated* Ben for killing himself.

"I don't know, Beck. I wish I did."

She lapsed back into silence then, and eventually fell asleep in my arms. I laid her down on the bed and covered her with the blankets. She stayed asleep all that day. The next day was Monday, and when she showed no signs of stirring from bed by eight in the morning, I called the law office and told them she was sick and couldn't come in. I think they understood what I meant when I said "sick," because they didn't argue or ask any questions.

I left her in bed to work out, hoping when I got back she'd be up and doing something, but she wasn't. She was still in bed, but awake, staring at the ceiling. I stood in the doorway, watching her, unnoticed, for a long time. My heart was breaking for her, for us. She'd completely stopped living.

"I think you need to start seeing Dr. Malmstein again," I said.

Becca glanced at me, furrowed her brow, and then shook her head dismissively.

"You made me go when Kyle died. Remember that? Do you remember what you said? Do you remember

what Nell went through because she wouldn't let anyone help her?"

"Leave me alone, Jason." She said it clearly, bitterness lending her fluency.

"No, Beck. I can't do that. You know I can't, and
you know I won't."

"Going to drag me in?" she asked.

"If I have to." I sat on the bed in front of her, and
let her roll away from me. "I love you too much to let
you do this, Rebecca."

She glared at me, then; she hated being called
Rebecca. "Just s-s-stop."

"No. I'm sorry." I tossed the covers away from her,
scooped her up in my arms, and carried her into the
bathroom.

She didn't fight as I set her on the toilet lid, but
she watched me warily. I reached into the shower and
turned it on, let the water run hot, and then adjusted
it.

"W-w-w-what are you…" She trailed off as I closed
the shower curtain and then shied away from me as
I tugged up the T-shirt she'd slept in. "No! J-Jason,
s-s-sss-stop!"

I lifted an eyebrow as she jerked away from me,
crossing her arms over her chest. "Becca, either get in
the shower, or we're going to do this the hard way."

She lifted her chin and pressed her lips together. "Leave me *alone.*"

I sighed. "I love you, Rebecca Noura de Rosa. I will not let you stop living."

She wavered then, her chin quivering, her eyes shimmering, but she tightened her arms over herself and shrank into the corner of the bathroom. I grabbed her by the hips and pulled her against me, wrapping my arm around her waist and pressing my lips to her cheek, whispering.

"Last chance, babe. You're going in, like it or not."

She rested her forehead against me. "P-please, Jason. Just give me some time."

"If I saw you making an effort, I would. But you've just shut down. I don't know what else to do."

"So you're going to f-f-force me to t-t-take a sh-sh-shower?"

"I'm taking you to see Dr. Malmstein. She has an opening in one hour. I checked."

"And ih-ih-ih-if I refuse to go?"

"I'll carry you. I'll sit with you in that office for an hour at a time for as long as it takes. You know Dr. Malmstein helped both of us. You're the one who said we needed to talk about it. Now you need it. You need to tell someone who knows what to say. You have to deal with it. Please, baby? For me, if not for yourself?"

"Would you break up with me if I didn't go?" She whispered the words into my tank top.

"Nothing you could ever do would make me break up with you. Except cheat on me, maybe, but you wouldn't do that."

"Never. *Never.*" She finally turned her face up to mine. "I love y-y-you. More th-th-than anyth-th-thing."

"Then get help. Please, Becca."

"I'm scared."

I frowned in confusion. "About what?"

"Of being told it's wrong to hate him. To be so *fucking* angry at him." She spoke through clenched teeth, scripting her words with care. "I'm afraid that I'll...end up like Nell. Hurting myself just to feel anything else. I *want* that, sometimes. I get why she did it now, Jason. I do."

My heart constricted, and my stomach twisted. "Have you? Cut yourself?"

She shook her head, meeting my eyes so I'd see she was telling the truth. "No, I s-s-s-swear. But I-I've thought about it."

"All the more reason to go see Dr. Malmstein."

The bathroom was wreathed in steam by that point, and it skirled between us, fogged the mirror, and dampening our clothing. Becca hesitated, then pushed away from me and peeled her shirt off, then her underwear, and stepped into the shower. I sighed in relief as she started washing her hair.

Maybe she would be okay. Maybe.

Jason
July

She made slow progress. She saw Dr. Malmstein once a week, and I was pretty sure she did most of her talking there, because she still rarely spoke to me, or to anyone else. When she did, she was fluent, but that was little comfort. She was writing again, which was a relief. At least she was expressing herself. We'd started our senior year, and she was pushing herself at her usual pace, but it seemed automatic, out of habit.

We hadn't had sex since the day of Ben's funeral. I hadn't wanted to push her, pressure her, rush her. I was going crazy from need, but I knew she was hurting and I was trying to be understanding. I didn't say anything, didn't try to instigate it. She was still very much in her own headspace most of the time, and when I did engage her, she responded only as necessary.

I woke up one morning well before dawn. Gray light filtered in through the open blinds facing the street. Becca slept beside me, hair spread in dark waves on the white pillow, her features at peace for once. She lay on her back, face turned to me, breathing slowly and evenly, chest rising and falling. I rolled to the side, facing her, and rested my hand on her belly briefly, then traced her jawline. She stirred but didn't wake. I sidled closer to her so my legs brushed hers under the blankets, and let my hand roam her arm beneath the sleeve of her T-shirt, then to her thigh. I brushed the shirt up a little, needing to just feel her skin, feel her warmth. I caressed her hip, then moved up her side, across her ribs.

I heard her breathing shift, and turned my eyes to hers.

"Don't stop," she murmured.

"Sorry, I didn't mean to wake you up." My hand was frozen on her hipbone.

"It's okay. Keep…keep touching me. L-l-like you were. Please." She rolled so she was angled toward me.

"I'm not trying to…start anything you're not ready for."

She placed her hand over mine, and I saw tears in her eyes. "I thought…I thought you didn't w-w-w-want m-me…anymore. Because I'm too fuh-fuh-fucked up. In my heh-heh-head."

I felt salty heat burn my eyes. A lifetime of conditioning kept the tears from falling. "Baby. No…no. I haven't….I thought you didn't want…" I took a deep breath and focused. "You've been hurting. I didn't think you wanted to."

"I don't—I don't know. I haven't, I guess." She tangled her fingers in mine and slid our joined palms across her belly. "But now I need you. I need to n-n-know you still want mmm-me."

Usually she would take over at that point. I loved it when she did that, when she showed me with such fiery domination how much she wanted me, how much she loved me. She was so demure, so quiet and proper in most other situations, that when she cut loose in the bedroom, it drove me wild.

Now I realized she needed something else, something different. She needed me to show her the way back.

I started with a kiss. I moved closer, my front to hers. Not over her, but face to face, on our sides. I slid my lips across her cheekbone, ghosted down to the corner of her mouth, kissed her there first. She gasped gently and held her breath, her hand resting on my ribs, the other tucked up between us. I grazed her lips, her silk merging with my chapped ridges, rough against soft. Heat and moisture met my mouth, and I ever so hesitantly moved our lips together, sealing our mouths.

She didn't return the kiss; she lay frozen beside me and let me kiss her, let me probe her slightly parted lips with my tongue. I pulled away, cupped her face in my palms, and kissed her again, deeper this time, more confidently. Her fingers curled against my skin, and now she finally moved her lips against mine, opened to my kiss and began to return it.

I pushed her slowly to her back and followed so I was leaning over her. She splayed her palm on my shoulder, the other on the nape of my neck, and she kissed me back.

Desperation built inside me, but I pushed it down, kept it bay. Gray blushed into hazy pink, and still we kissed, making out like we did in the days before the lines were crossed. I kissed her, and put all my love into that kiss, all my need. I kissed her to show her how much I missed her. She'd been there physically, but had been absent emotionally. Now she was coming back to me, and I kissed her in welcome.

Her fingers clutched my hair, clawed against my spine. Then her calf snaked around mine, and it was time to push the lines again. I slid her shirt up, up, parted the kiss to pass the cotton between us and over her head, set it aside. Nothing beneath but taut, firm, dusky flesh. Peaked nipples and the inward curve from breast to hip, breasts pulled to either side by gravity, heavy, areolae wide circles darker than her flesh. She held the back of my head with both hands as I pressed a kiss to her shoulder, slid my lips across her skin to the rise of one breast. Her breathing caught, and I kept going. I dragged my tongue across her pebbled nipple and felt it rise beneath my lips, going erect under my breath. I thumbed her other nipple erect, circled it with the pad of my thumb, then scraped my fingernail across it gently as I pinched the other with my lips and teeth.

"Jason..." she breathed.

I wasn't sure what she was begging me to do. "Tell me what you want, baby."

"Give me...m-m-more." She rubbed my calves with hers. "Give me...sh-show me...more."

I slid my mouth to lave kisses on her other breast, rolling her nipple between my lips. Then lower. I kissed between her breasts, the undersides, then lower. I kissed her belly, over her navel, each hip. And then lower.

I knew the moment when she realized my intentions when she drew her knees up to either side of me, framing me in the "V" of her thighs. She spread herself open to me, eager for anything I could give her. She wanted to feel, to escape, to be lifted away from the earth for a while, to lose herself in the waves of ecstasy.

So that's exactly what I planned to give her. Wave after wave of escape, until she begged me stop.

I trailed feathery kisses along her thigh, up to her knee, crossed empty space and kissed her other knee, ran my tongue down the inside of her leg to the hollow between hip and folds. She arched her back slightly, a silent encouragement. I kissed her lower lips, spreading them with my mouth and driving my tongue inside her. She moaned in relief, clutching my head in her hands. I kissed her there slowly, sucking her clit into my mouth and flicking it with my tongue, licking upward and circling. When she began to buck beneath me, I slowed to soft, fat swipes of my tongue up her folds, and then gradually increased my pace until she was desperate beneath me once again.

And then I slowed.

She tangled her fingers in my hair and pulled me against her. "Please, Jason. Please."

I gave it to her. I let my mouth and tongue match her wild thrashing pace, her hips lifting off the bed, her moans turning to ululating screams as she came. When she crushed my head with her thighs, I slid my fingers between our bodies and searched her opening, finding wet warmth.

The warmth resisted, though, and I pushed gently inward.

"Wrong...wrong place," she murmured, gasping in shock, almost laughing.

"Oh...oh, my god, I'm sorry—"

"Don't...don't stop. It's...I l-like it."

I froze in surprise. This was something we'd never discussed, never tried. "Are you sure?"

"God, yes. Just don't stop. More. Every—everything. More."

I flicked her clit with my tongue, and she arched off the bed, whimpering. Gently, hesitantly, I let my longest middle finger probe her tight opening. Becca moaned and shifted her hips, pushing downward. An encouragement. I pulsed my finger slightly, not pushing in, but testing her resistance. She whimpered and then gasped with her mouth open wide as I gradually insinuated my finger into her rear opening. My mouth worked on her clit, slowing and speeding as she bucked against me, driving my finger deeper into her. I felt her muscles constrict around my middle finger, rippling in tightening waves, and then she cried out in a breathless scream that turned to a full-voiced shriek as the orgasm washed over her. She came, and she came, and she came. Every contraction of her muscles worked my finger deeper, and with every inserted centimeter she widened her legs and shifted her hips lower. I laved her folds with relentless hunger, not letting her down from the second orgasm. Becca's rocking hips and whimpering screams slowed slightly as the orgasm retreated, and then increased again as a third climax took hold. She was panting and barely able to moan by the time the third round of waves ended.

"I need...y-you." Becca pulled me up to her level, crushed her mouth to mine.

"Do you taste yourself?"

"Yes..."

"I like the way you taste."

"In..." Becca fumbled with my underwear, pushing at it until we got it off together. "I need...you. Ins-s-sss-side me."

I slid against her, hovering above her, poised at her entrance. "I love you." I locked my eyes on her black gaze.

"P-p-promise?" She caught my lower lip between her teeth and pulled it away. "For-for-forever?"

"And then some." I slid into her tight wet heat as I spoke, and she gasped, her mouth wide in a silent scream.

She held still, trembling, eyes searching mine, breath stopped in her lungs. "Again...I'm ab-about to come already...again."

"Good. Let go, baby."

She moved against me, lifting her hips to mine, fingernails clawing into my shoulders, scratching down my back to my ass and pulling me harder and harder into her. I resisted her efforts to speed my pace, slipping in slowly, withdrawing more slowly, moving softly, each motion, each gentle thrust a declaration of love.

Our eyes never wavered from each other's.

She wrapped her legs around my waist and moved frantically against me, finally breaking gazes to bury her face in my shoulder as she shattered beneath me. She wept as she came, thrusting against me and sobbing, smiling through her tears—her first smile in days—pulling at me and clutching me and chanting my name without stuttering.

Limp beneath me, Becca sniffed and caressed my face with the back of her fingers. "Your turn."

I let go then. She matched me thrust for thrust, clinging to my neck and letting our hips crash together, our flesh slapping, our mouths bumping in clumsy, panting kisses. I fell over the edge helplessly, and she came with me. I unleashed inside her, gush after gush filling her, and then I let my weight go against hers; I knew she liked that, after.

We drifted, and her fingers feathered in my hair.

"I love you, Jason." She whispered it softly into the silence, sounding more like my Becca from before the events of that April day.

Becca

Jason's weight pressed wonderfully against me, kept me grounded in the present. His breathing began to shift, and we rolled together in a familiar habit. He tucked me into the nook of his arm, his warm flesh and hard muscle perfectly caging me.

I was, for the first time in weeks, feeling lucid and something like okay.

And that's when it hit me: I hadn't taken my birth control since April ninth, the day I found Ben.

Sixteen: Secrets & Revelations
Becca
September

I WAS PREGNANT. I KNEW I WAS. I hadn't taken a test or seen a doctor, but I knew. I was seven weeks late for my period, my breasts were tender, and I'd been sick in the mornings. Jason had been giving me odd looks when I'd rush to the bathroom, but I didn't think he knew, or even really suspected.

I had panic attacks every day. In private, in the bathroom at school, in the tutoring center between students, silently shaking and unable to breathe.

Pregnant?

Like, with a baby? A little human? No. No.

I didn't know how to do that.

What if Jason couldn't handle it, handle me being pregnant? What if he left me? I was still in therapy over Ben's death…his suicide. I was better about that every day, less fragile. I'd stopped needing escape, started talking more. I still stuttered when I spoke, which drove me nuts. I was back to high school, basically, back to before Jason.

He was on fire on the football field. I went to every game and sat on the sidelines with the other players' girlfriends, cheering on the boys in blue and yellow. The pro scouts were sniffing around him, primarily New Orleans and Dallas. I'd seen the same scout from New Orleans at every game Jason played, and he and Jason had spoken a few times. I knew Jason was geeked at the prospect of playing with Drew Brees more than any other QB in the NFL.

I had to tell him. I had to. But first I had to be sure. After my last class, I bought four different kind of pee tests, took them home, and sat on the toilet, staring at the first one. Finally, I sucked in a deep breath, lowered my pants and peed on the end, set the test aside, and washed my hands.

I stared in the mirror at my pale reflection, waiting. I picked up the test and stared at the box.

Pleaseletmenotbepregnant…pleaseletmenotbe pregnant…

Blue cross: pregnant.

Shit. Fuck. Shit.

I felt my lungs contracting and expanding rapidly, sucking in air and expelling it far too quickly. I was hyperventilating. I smacked clumsily at the toilet lid, knocking it down so I could slump onto it, ducking my head between my knees. Slowly, after long minutes of forced deep breathing, I managed to calm myself down.

Then my phone rang. "Hello?" I still sounded out of breath.

"Hi, Becca? This is Rachel Hawthorne."

"Hi, Mrs....I mean, Rachel. How are you?" I tried not to panic, but I didn't see why she would call me if it wasn't bad news.

"I'm okay. Has Nell called you recently?"

My heart rate and breathing ratcheted into hyper-ventilation territory all over again. "N-no. I haven't heard from her in months. I called her, but it went to voicemail and she never got ba-back to me." I tried a deep breath but couldn't make it slow down. "Why? What's...what's going on?"

"Well, she came back suddenly. She showed up this morning without warning. She's...I don't know, Becca. I'm worried about her, but she says she's okay. I was wondering if you could come down and talk to her. See if you can get her to tell you what's going on."

"What do y-you th-think is wrong?"

"I'm not sure, honestly," Rachel said. "I just...she wouldn't just come back out of the blue like this for no reason."

"I have a couple big tests tom-mmm-morrow morning," I said, "but I c-c-can head down and s-s-see her afterward, okay?"

"Okay, that sounds good, thanks, Becca."

"Let me know if any-th-thing comes uh-uh-up?"

"I will. I'll see you tomorrow, then."

"Okay, 'bye, Rachel." I hung up and set the phone aside, worried about Nell now.

And pregnant.

I hid the extra tests, not ready for Jason to see them, and then threw the used one away, burying it in the kitchen trash and covering it. Then, driven by a sudden rush of hope that the first one had been wrong, I dug them back out and took a second test, washed my hands, and waited.

Two pink lines: pregnant.

Third test...pregnant.

Fourth test...pregnant.

I threw them all away and then took the bag to the dumpster. Intellectually, I knew Jason wouldn't leave me, especially if I was pregnant. But...knowing in my head wasn't the same as knowing in my heart. Fear was fear, and fear had me paralyzed, unable to tell him.

I half-heartedly attempted to study until Jason came home from work. He walked in wearing khaki cut-off shorts, battered and grass-stained Timberland boots, and a neon-green *Bob's Quality Landscaping and Snow Removal* T-shirt with the sleeves cut off. He had a blue U of M ball cap on backward, with his jersey number stitched in yellow thread on the back, and his earbuds trailed down the front of his shirt where he'd strung them underneath to his shorts pocket. He stank of grass, sweat, gasoline, and oil, and he was filthy from head to toe. He had dirt smudged on his forehead and right cheek, his hands were nearly black with dirt and grease and bits of grass, and his shirt was sopping wet with sweat. He was gloriously sexy.

The euphoria of seeing my man all nasty from a day of hard work only lasted a moment, and the weight of reality set in.

Jason must've seen the crash on my features. "Hey, baby. What's up?"

I went for the easy answer. "Nell came home s-ssss-suddenly. Rachel is worried about her."

Jason frowned. "That's all she said, though?" He set his iPhone and earbuds on the table along with his wallet and hat.

"Yeah, basically." I set my books aside, stood up, and kissed him, tasting the sweat on his upper lip. "I'm going to d-d-drive d-d-down tomorrow after my tests." I felt the weight of my secret in my chest, but I couldn't get the words out.

"I'll drive down with you, then," Jason said from the bathroom, stripping off his clothes.

I stood in the doorway, watching him undress, admiring the way his darkly tanned skin slid over his rippling muscles. "You have class and you work two jobs, don't you?"

"Yeah, but this is more important, isn't it?"

I shrugged. "Maybe. All I know is that Nell showed up out of b-b-bl-blue and Rachel is worried something is wrong. I don't know for a f-f-fa-fa-fact that anything is wrong."

Jason stepped under the steaming spray, and immediately the water around the drain turned brown. "True enough. Take my truck from school, then. I can get rides to and from work."

A sudden burst of need shot through me, need for his hands on me and his mouth on me and his heat on me; for the first time in our relationship, I squashed the need. I pushed it down and walked away, leaving him to his shower. If I gave in to that need, I knew what would happen. I would get sucked in to the emotional whirlpool of the afterglow, and I'd tell him.

For now, this was my secret. I needed time to figure out how I felt, aside from the sheer blind panic.

Was I glad? Was I upset? Did I want, even deep down, to be a mother? Was I in any way ready?

There was only one question that never crossed my mind: not keeping it was never an option. Regardless of my feelings, regardless of Jason's reaction, I was keeping it.

Him. Her. Not *it*.

Him or her.

My tests flew by. I knew the material to the point where part of my mind was whirling with a thousand thoughts and questions, and only part of me was tuned in to the tests. I left the lecture hall and headed to the Hawthorne home, driving almost absently, the radio off, my body and brain driving on autopilot, the rest of me dizzy with rumination.

An hour and a half later, I pulled in to the Hawthornes' circle drive, which was empty. The front door was locked, and no one answered my repeated knocks and rings of the bell. I circled around to the back, knowing Rachel often had music on while she baked and didn't hear the door. When I reached the back of the house, I stopped in shock. A piece of plywood covered the sliding glass patio door, or where the glass had been, rather. What I could see of the house was dark and empty. As I turned away from the house, I happened to glance down at the cobblestone patio, and my heart shuddered to a stop. Dark brown splotches led in a trail to the house, disappearing into the grass beyond the patio.

The Hawthornes and the Calloways lived on a private lake, beyond which was an expanse of grass field, and beyond that a forest. A county line road arced through the forest, and I knew Nell used to run from her house to the county road, then follow that for a few miles to where Mr. Farrell's corn field began, at which point she would cut through the thin strip of forest and into the acres of knee-high wild grass behind her house.

The brown spots were dried blood. Who had bled? Why? Where was everyone?

Had something happened to Nell? Had she...had she done something to herself? I wasn't sure I could handle finding out.

I fumbled my phone from my purse and scrolled through my contacts until I found **Rachel Hawthorne cell**. I dialed it, held the phone to my ear with trembling hands as I made my way back around to the driveway.

"Hello?" Mr. Hawthorne's voice on Rachel's cell phone. He sounded...broken.

"Mr. Hawthorne? It's b-b-Becca."

"Becca?" He sounded confused, lost.

"Becca de Rosa. Nell's friend?"

"Oh. Of course. Yes, of course…sorry. I'm—we're…Nell's in the hospital, Becca." I heard the distant garble of a hospital PA.

"What—what happened?"

"She…" He trailed off and seemed to be listening to a voice in the background. "Yeah, you're right, Rach. Becca? Just come to the hospital. We'll—I'll—we'll explain when you get here. The ICU, she's in room one-four-one. We're in the waiting room right now."

"I'll be-be th-there s-s-s-soon." I hung up then, abruptly, not bothering with the formality of a goodbye.

I was in Jason's truck and peeling out, driving recklessly, tears stinging my eyes and hot on my cheeks. I felt myself cracking. I called Jason.

Mowers blasted deafeningly in the background, blowers, weed-whips. "Hey, Beck," Jason said, shouting over the noise. "Talk to Nell?"

"She-she's in the hah-hah-hos-hospital. I don't n-n-n-know why. Someth-thing happened. Something b-b-bad." I was choking on my half-hysterical sobs, and I could barely understand myself.

Jason had no problem, though. "Shit. *Fuck*! Okay, I'll meet you there. Wait, which hospital?"

I hadn't asked. "I d-d-don't n-n-know. I don't—"

Jason interrupted. "If it happened at their house, then the closest would probably be Genesee Regional."

I heard my phone ding in my ear, signaling a text message. I held the phone away from my ear, seeing a message from Rachel verifying Jason's guess. "Rachel j-j-j-just t-t-texted me. She's at Gen-Genes-s-sss-s—*d-d-damn* it!" I hissed in frustration; the last thing I needed right then was to stutter myself incohorent. "What... you...said." I forced the words out slowly and clearly.

"I got you, babe. It's okay. Breathe, all right?"

"I'm...trying." It took every ounce of focus to get those two words out fluently.

"I love you. I'll be with you, no matter what. It's going to be okay."

"'Kay." One syllable, such a lie. It wasn't going to be okay.

I set the phone aside and focused on driving, focused on keeping my breathing slow and deep.

Arriving at the hospital, I found Jim and Rachel Hawthorne sitting side by side, and across from them Mr. and Mrs. Calloway, Robert and Theresa. Why were they here?

Rachel saw me first, then rushed over and wrapped me in a hug. She pulled away, and must have seen the fear in my eyes. "It's not that, Becca. It's not...

she didn't…she didn't do anything to herself. Not like your…like Ben." I hiccuped in relief. "She's going to be okay."

"Wha-what happened? Why is your doorwall broken?"

"Come sit over here," Rachel said, gently but firmly ushering me to a chair. My flip-flops squeaked on the tile; the plastic chair was hard and cold under my legs. Rachel took my hands in hers, and I knew whatever had happened was going to be awful to hear.

"Just t-t-tell me."

"She had a miscarriage last night."

I didn't respond, didn't react. I'd heard her wrong, clearly. "She…what? She had a what?"

Rachel sniffed, and Jim Hawthorne reached over from her other side to rest his hand on her shoulder. "She was pregnant," Rachel said. "She was out running, and she…she lost the baby. She lost a lot of blood, too much blood. She's going to be okay, but if Colton hadn't found her when he did, she might have…oh, *god*…"

Shock hit me so hard I would have fallen over had I not been sitting down. "*Colton*? Colton Calloway?"

Why would Colton have found her? He lived in New York…and then the penny dropped.

"Wait…he-he's the father?" I asked.

"Yes." Rachel nodded, her fine blonde hair bouncing and glinting in the harsh fluorescent lighting.

Robert and Theresa sat on the row of chairs opposite us, their faces showing concern, confusion, worry, fear. I glanced at them; I didn't know them at all. Robert Calloway was a congressman, so he spent a lot of time in Washington, D.C. I didn't know what Theresa did, but she was gone a lot, too. Even as kids we rarely spent time at the Calloway house. When Nell and I had played with Kyle as young children, it was always at Nell's house, so Robert and Theresa were basically strangers to me. Robert was tall, broad-chested with a bit of roundness to his belly, strongly built and rugged of feature, dark salt-and-pepper hair and bright blue eyes, where Colton had gotten his from, clearly. Theresa was more like Kyle, lean, trim, classically beautiful features and dark brown eyes like Kyle's had been.

"Colton and Nell…" I began, hoping the rest would be filled in.

"Ran into each other in New York, I guess," Rachel said. "I don't really know much more than that. It all happened so fast. Nell came back yesterday morning, early. She must've caught a red-eye out of New York, because she was walking through our door by seven in the morning. She looked…tired. Not sleepy, I mean…

emotionally exhausted. Burnt out, worried. She said she just wanted to come home for a bit, and that everything was fine. I didn't believe her, because I know Nell. I know when she's hiding something. I watched her hide *everything* for so long…but she wouldn't talk to me. She spent most of yesterday in her room, playing her guitar. Then—late, like nine o'clock or so—she came down and said she was going for a run. She'd only been gone for maybe twenty minutes when our front door slammed open. It startled me so bad I dropped a glass. It was Colton. He was…he was acting crazy. Upset, demanding to know where Nell had gone, like he'd been looking for her. I told him she'd gone running out to the Ennis farm, and he took off after her. Then he…he came back…carrying her. God, she was…so bloody. He had blood running down his shirt from her. It was all coming from between her legs. I knew…I knew. I had two miscarriages before I had Nell. Mine were…they weren't as bad as Nell's. God…my baby girl." Rachel shuddered and turned away from me into her husband's arms.

Was that going to happen to me? That was my first thought when Rachel finished her story.

"Can I…can I s-s-see her?" I asked.

"You'll have to ask a nurse," Jim answered. "I don't know if she's awake yet."

The nurse behind the desk informed me that Nell was awake, and I could see her if Nell permitted it. I followed the long hallway, watching the room numbers count up closer to 141. A crowd of people surrounded a doorway, clustered and silent. They were around Nell's room, I realized. As I got closer, I heard why.

A guitar played, and a deep, rich male voice sang. I couldn't make out the words yet, but the tune was haunting, like a raw and ragged lullaby, simple chords repeated in a soul-searing refrain. I pressed into the crowd of nurses and doctors and patients until I could see into the room. Colton sat beside Nell's bed, a guitar in his hands, head turned to one side, eyes squeezed tight, neck muscles tensing as he sang, massive biceps rippling as he strummed and picked the simple melody. His voice was so hypnotic, so full of raw grief, that the potency of his song was a palpable force washing over my skin as I listened.

> *"...Did you dream?*
> *Did you have a soul?*
> *Who could you have been?*
> *You've never known my arms,*
> *You've never known your mother's arms,*
> *My child, child, child.*
> *I'll dream for you,*

I'll breathe for you,

I'll question God for you,

I'll shake my fists and scream and cry for you.

This song is for you,

It's all I've got.

It doesn't give you a name.

It doesn't give you a face.

But it's all I've got to give.

All my love is in these words I sing,

In each haunted note from my guitar,

My child, child, child.

You're not gone,

Because you never were.

But that doesn't mean

You passed unloved.

It doesn't mean you're forgotten,

Unborn child, child, child.

I bury you

With this song.

I mourn you

With this song."

He strummed the last chord and let the notes hang, his head ducked, shoulders shaking. The song reminded me of what was growing within me, the very thing that Nell just lost, that Colton just lost. I choked on a sob, coughing. Colt turned and opened his eyes, seeming surprised to see the crowd around the door. He didn't see me, or didn't recognize me. He turned back to Nell, who scrambled stiffly out of the bed, trailing tubes and wires and monitor leads. She climbed onto Colt's lap, wrapping her arms around his neck and clinging to him, sobbing so brokenly it was painful to hear, to watch. Her entire body quaked uncontrollably, and her sobs were loud, hoarse, choking screams in the small room, laced with the constant *beep-beep-beep* of the heart monitor.

I recognized the way she clung to Colt, as if he was the only thing keeping her from flying apart, from becoming nothing more than the sum of her grief. He held her gently, stroking her back with familiarity and aching tenderness. I could see his love for her in the way his finger brushed her hair away from her eyes, the way he didn't speak words of empty consolation, the way he merely held her and let his love speak silent volumes. I turned away from the door, put my back to the wall just out of sight.

I listened to her cry, listened to him sniff quietly. They grieved together for a long time, and I waited. Eventually, I felt Jason join me. My eyes were closed, and I was listening to Nell and Colt murmuring to each other, their words indistinct, speaking in the familiar mumble of lovers.

I was still floored by the fact of Nell and Colton being romantically involved.

I pulled Jason away, farther down the hallway. As I passed the doorway, I glanced in to see Nell back in the hospital bed, holding Colt's hand. She saw me, then looked away.

"What happened?" Jason asked.

"Did you see who was in the r-r-room with Nell?" Jason shook his head. "Colton Calloway."

"What? What's he doing back in Michigan?"

I sucked in a deep breath. "They're together. Nell and Colton, I mean. Like, *together*. Sh-she…they…Nell had a m-mmm-miscarriage." I let that sink in.

Jason's mouth dropped open, and he closed it, then turned back to look at the doorway to room 141, as if some kind of answer was visible there. "She…you mean she was pregnant?" I nodded, and he tilted his head back, blowing out a surprised breath. "Holy shit. That was the last thing I expected."

"M-me too. I thought—I was afraid she'd—"

Jason cut me off by pulling me against his chest. "That was my first thought, too. I'm glad it wasn't that."

"Yeah." I pressed my forehead to his chest; my secret was a hot, hard, heavy ball in my gut.

There was no way I could tell him here, now, in this situation.

Jason's fingers tilted my chin up, and his jade eyes bored into me. I realized then that he knew I was keeping something from him. "Becca...what's going on with you?"

I shook my head. "Not-not here, okay? P-please?"

"I'm not crazy, though, right? There's something you're not telling me?"

I shuddered, sucking in a harsh breath. "Yes. But this...here, this isn't the time or the-the place f-for it."

"God, I'm gonna go fucking crazy." I heard the anger and worry in his voice.

I palmed his cheeks and brought his mouth to mine in a brief but deep kiss. "I love you. Always and forever, okay?"

He let out a gusting sigh. "So you're not leaving me or anything, right?"

I had to laugh at that. "Never. Not...not ever." I pushed away from his embrace and led him to Nell's room.

She took a deep breath as we came in. Colton stood up and faced us, seeming unsure if he should shake our hands or hug us or do nothing. I waved awkwardly at him, hesitated, and then stepped past him to hug Nell, cradling her shoulders gently.

She pulled away slightly, and her gray-green eyes searched mine. "Becca, I—"

"How did this happen?" I asked.

"Well, see, when a man and woman love each other," she started, then broke off into laughter.

I smacked her arm lightly. "D-don't be a bitch. You n-n-know what I m-m-mmm-mean."

She frowned at my stutter. The last time we'd seen each other I hadn't stuttered at all. "It's...complicated."

I turned to glance at Colton, who was standing next to Jason, looking uncomfortable. "Un-un-uncomplicate it, then."

She shot a look at Colt and Jason. "Can you guys give us a few minutes? Please?"

Colt slid next to me and bent over her, kissed her. "I'll go get some coffee." He pressed his lips to her ear, but I heard the words he whispered. "I love you."

"I love you, too, Colton." She said it out loud, not bothering to whisper.

Jason hugged me briefly, kissed the corner of my mouth. "You want coffee?"

"Sure. Thanks, baby." When they were gone, I sat in the chair Colt had abandoned and turned to Nell. "Spill."

She stared past me, as if seeing Colt still standing there, or as if she could see him through the walls. "He's...everything I never knew I needed. I know it doesn't make any sense, Becks. It doesn't. He's...he's

Kyle's older brother. He's rough around the edges. But...god, how do I even explain this? He's so talented. You heard him, I saw you. He's...he's showing me how to heal. How to let go. I was never okay, Becca. Even when I left for New York, I know how it seemed. Like I was finally starting to make progress. I wasn't, though. I was just better at hiding the fact that I hurt, every single day. That I missed him, every single fucking day." She glanced at me, assessing the effect of her words. "He saw through that. He saw through it at the funeral years ago. He knew I wasn't letting myself feel it. Feel anything."

I ducked my head, the pain of reliving those days too much to bear. "Doesn't...doesn't he remind you of...of Kyle?"

"Yes. A lot. But...he's not him. He's so, *so* different. We never knew Colt, you know? Back when we were kids, we never even remotely understood what he was going through. He's so strong, Becca. You can't know how strong he is. What he's endured and come through still able to love me, to smile and be okay every day." She rubbed a thumb over her wrist, and I saw a recent scar, deep and thick and jagged. She saw me see it. "That will never happen again. The cutting is over. It's like an addiction, though, you know. I'll always be a cutter—I'll just...refuse to do it."

I met her eyes. "I think I unders-sss-s-stand, now."

She heard something in my voice. "What do you mean?" It was a fearful whisper.

I showed her my arms. "I thought about cutting, a couple times. I never did, but I thought about it."

"Why?"

"Ben...hung himself on...April...April ninth." I was forcing myself to slow down, going back to my fluency shaping lessons.

Nell covered her mouth with her hand, eyes wide and tortured. "He *hung* himself? Ohmigod...Becca, I'm so sorry."

"I tried to call you, but you never answered. Never called me back. Jason called, too." I tried to keep the bitterness out, but I couldn't, quite.

"I know. I'm sorry. I just...it was all I could do to stay sane, to survive one day at a time. Things between Colton and me were...tumultuous, at best." She took my hand. "I'm sorry, Becca. I'm sorry I'm such a shitty friend. I wasn't there for you when you needed me, and you've always been there for me."

I shrugged. "You had your own...business to take care of. I understand that."

"What happened? Why did he do that?"

I shook my head. "It's a long story. He was never well, you know that. Things just...life...it all became

too much for him. It was the only way he could...
could cope, I guess."

"Is that why you're stuttering again? You were
doing a lot better for a while, weren't you?"

I nodded. "Yeah." I stared at the floor between my
feet. "I found him. He left a note, and I found him.
He'd...he'd just done it. He was still...still twitching,
when I found him. I have...nightmares abou—about
it. I always will, I think."

"God, Becca. I don't—I don't know what to say."

"I'm doing better now. I've been seeing Dr.
Malmstein again."

"That's your therapist? The one you saw after Kyle
died?" She said it so smoothly, so calmly. I admired her
for it.

"Yeah. I wasn't going to go, for a while. I sort of
shut down for a few months."

I wasn't stuttering. I still spoke in the stilted,
scripted way I used to, but it was an improvement. It
was almost like having Nell here needing me as her
friend had given me a purpose for fluency even Jason
couldn't provide.

"Shut down?" Nell asked.

"Yeah. I basically stopped talking. For, like, two
months. Jason made me start going to therapy."

"Well, I'm glad he did. I'm glad you didn't cut."

I breathed out slowly. "Me, too." I peered at Nell. "How are you, Nell? Really."

She leaned back and burrowed deeper into the bed and the nest of thin pillows. "I don't know yet. I lost the baby. I was pregnant, and I was afraid. I couldn't tell him. I should've. I just…I couldn't. I kept worrying what he would say, how he would react. If he would still love me, if he would hate me for tying him down with a child. Now…I know I should've known better. I should have told him, should have trusted him."

I couldn't breathe. Could she know? She wasn't looking at me; she was picking a loose thread of the scratchy, loosely woven white hospital blanket. "What—what's going to happen? With you and Colton?"

"He doesn't like being called 'Colton,' you know. Well, by anyone except me. He goes by 'Colt.'" She combed her fingers through her hair, wincing at the way her muscles stretched, still feeling pain. "I don't know what's going to happen. We'll be together. I'll probably stay here for a while, a few weeks at least, until I heal. Physically heal. I'll probably end up seeing a therapist myself. God knows it's long past due. Colton and I…we love each other. He gets me. I know lots of people aren't going to understand, though. How can I be in love with him when he's Kyle's older brother? I struggled with that for weeks. I fought it so hard. I didn't want to. I didn't want to let go—I didn't want to accept love or let him in. I knew somehow that he'd force me to open up."

She pinched the bridge of her nose and breathed out, then met my gaze. "You know I never cried for Kyle? Not once. I refused to let myself feel anything, refused to grieve. That's why I cut. It…it let out the pain, gave me something else to think about, something else to feel besides the ache for him." She breathed deep, let it out, repeated the process. I saw her pain in the furrow of her brow, the contained quiver of her chin. "It still hurts. I still think about him…I still see him die in my dreams. But I know—I *know*—I can't keep living stuck in that loop. The only way out is through. As for this, losing—losing the…the baby? Same thing. The only way past the pain is through it. You can't escape it. You can't ignore it. Pain, grief, anger, misery…they don't go away—they just increase and compound and get worse. You have to live through them, acknowledge them. You have to give your pain its due."

"Listen to you, sounding so wise." I tried to laugh, lighten the mood with a joke, but it fell flat.

She winced. "I'm not. God, I'm *so* not wise at all. I just know pain. That, what I just said, it's what Colton's been showing me. He's been through it himself, through so much. We're going through this together."

"I'm glad you have someone to go through it with."

She turned her eyes to mine. "I'm pretty sure I'd be dead without him."

"Do you need him to be okay?"

She shrugged. "Yes and no. I know what you're worried about. It's not a codependency thing, I promise. I need him, yes, because he's…just everything. But I know now that I have to keep living, regardless of what happens in life. I'd be a mess without him, but I would like to think I'd cope as best I could."

"But you don't have to be without me," Colt said from behind us. "I'm not going anywhere."

I moved out of the way, felt Jason's arm come around my waist. He held a Styrofoam cup of burnt coffee in each hand, and I took one from him. The coffee was really, really burnt, but I sipped it anyway.

Nell glanced at me. "I'm really tired. I'm gonna sleep now. Come back tomorrow?"

"We'll be here," I said.

As we left, Colt's broad, muscular form was bent over Nell, kissing her, brushing her hair away and tugging the blankets around her. He turned to glance at me, his blue eyes piercing mine. I smiled at him, trying to let him know I supported them. I didn't totally understand how they'd gotten together, how it had happened, but it didn't matter. I'd heard the love in her voice when she spoke of him, and I'd seen it in the way they looked at each other, in the way he kissed her.

We were halfway home when a thought struck me. "How'd you get here? I have your truck."

"Now she wonders." Jason laughed. "Bob drove me. I told him it was a family emergency."

"Thanks for coming."

He glanced at me as he shifted lanes around a slow-moving semi. "It's Nell. Of course I'd come." Silence for a moment, and then he broached the subject. "Are you going to tell me what's been eating at you for the last two months?"

I felt my heart start to hammer out of my chest. I tried to calm myself with forced deep breathing, but I only succeeded in making myself hyperventilate. I felt Jason's hand on my back as I leaned forward to put my head between my knees, my head bumping against the glove box.

"Breathe, baby. It's okay. Breathe. Deep breaths, okay? Slow down." His voice washed over me, soothing murmurs.

I sat up and shook my hair out of my face, focused on breathing and scripting out what I was about to say.

When I was under some kind of control, I turned to Jason. "Maybe you should pull over."

Jason lifted an eyebrow in question but did as I said, swerving across two lanes of traffic to the exit ramp. He pulled into a McDonalds parking lot, put the truck in park, and then turned to me. "What the hell is going on, Beck?"

I took several deep breaths, forced my eyes to his. "I…I'm…I'm pregnant."

He blinked at me several times, his expression not altering for the space of several seconds. "You're pregnant?"

I nodded. "Yes. I took four tests."

"How long have you known?" His voice was carefully calm, precisely modulated.

"I've only known for sure since yesterday."

"But you suspected before that?"

I nodded. "When we had sex, that first time after so long without it? I realized just before I fell asleep that I'd…I'd forgotten to take my birth control since… since Ben's death. I just…forgot." I couldn't look at him. I stared at the dashboard, the specks of shadow cast by the sun through the windshield. "I'm sorry," I whispered.

"Why are you apologizing?" He touched my chin, tried to turn my eyes to his, but I pulled away. I didn't want to cry, but I was going to. He seemed mad, and I was so afraid. "Hey…look at me, please."

I wanted to throw open the truck door and run, but instead I focused my tear-blurred gaze on his too-green eyes. "I'm scared, Jason. I'm so scared." My voice shook, shuddered, cracked. "You seem mad. I don't want you to…to leave me. I know we didn't t-talk about th-this. We—we're not r-r-ready f-for this. I know we-we-we aren't. I'm sorry I didn't tell you sooner, but I—I was scared."

I heard the *click-zip* of his seatbelt unlatching and sliding away, felt his hand drift up my arm to my cheek. He pulled me toward him, and I lunged into his arms. "Baby," he whispered, his voice a fierce but tender rasp in my ear. "Becca, baby, I'm not mad. I'm not. I'm surprised, yeah. I had no idea. You've been acting…odd lately. Getting sick and stuff. I was worried you were gonna tell me you had cancer or something. Don't apologize."

"And then…I found out about n-n-Nell, and I got even more afraid. What if…what if that happens to me?"

"It won't."

"I couldn't…I couldn't handle losing anyone else, Jason. I feel like I'm barely hanging on as it is."

"This is us, okay?" Jason tilted my chin up and kissed me softly. "I love you. This is a surprise, yes, but

I'm not mad. I'm not sure what all exactly I'm feeling, but mad isn't any part of it."

Scant centimeters separated our lips. I felt so vulnerable, so needy. "Promise? I just…I was so scared you'd be upset that I let this happen."

He nuzzled my cheek with his. "No, baby. No. You were so messed up after everything happened with Ben. It's not your fault. It's not…this isn't a 'fault' thing. It happened, and that's how it is. We'll deal with it one day at a time together, okay?"

"I just…you should know now that I'm keeping it. No matter what."

"Of course. I wouldn't want it any other way."

He stank of sweat and cut grass and gasoline, and his lips smeared sweat on mine when he kissed me, grease on my skin from his hands, but I wouldn't have pulled away from him for anything. I clung to him with every fiber of my being, needing his reassurance.

We were having a baby.

Seventeen: Breaking the News; Competing Voices
Jason
Two months later

I SAT ON THE EDGE OF THE COUCH, my palms sweating. Becca sat next to me, her fingers tangled in mine, squeezing hard, telling me she was just as nervous as I was. This, telling her parents she was pregnant…it was terrifying.

By contrast, the NFL Scout Combine earlier in the year had been a cakewalk. My performance at the Combine plus my record made me an easy shoe-in for a first-round pick. I'd been talking to agents for a while and had one lined up, paperwork in order and terms set. Now I just had to wait for the draft next year in

April, but it was looking like the New Orleans Saints were the most likely team.

I shook my head to clear it of football thoughts. Enzio and Leena de Rosa sat on the love seat opposite us, Enzio's arm around his wife's shoulders, his thick fingers tapping an idle rhythm on the cushion.

"Mom...Father," Becca started. She glanced at me, then her father. "Dad, I mean. I...Jason and I have something to tell you."

Enzio and Leena glanced at each other, exchanging some kind of silent communication. Their eyes contained the shadows of long-term sadness. In the months since Ben's suicide, they'd changed. They'd invited Becca and me over for dinner on numerous occasions, and seemed to be genuinely taking an interest in us, and in me. Becca had seen this change in them and had consequently been making an effort to repair the strain on her relationship with them. She'd even gone so far as to start calling her father "Dad" instead of "Father" as she had for so long.

Becca dug a small envelope out of her purse and handed it to Leena, whose eyes widened as she withdrew the ultrasound pictures. "I'm pregnant," Becca said.

"How long are you?" Leena asked in her thick accent, then cleared her throat. "I mean, how far along are you?"

"Four months." Becca's eyes were shifting from her mother to her father and back, assessing. "I won't find out the gender for another few weeks, though." She said the last part for her father's benefit, I figured, since her mother, as a pediatrician, would know that.

Enzio cleared his throat, sitting forward. "This was...unplanned, *sì*?"

"Yes, sir, it was," I answered.

"And what are your thoughts regarding this... unforeseen development?" he asked me.

I drew a deep breath, choosing my words with care. "It may have been unforeseen, sir, but it's not unwelcome. I love your daughter with all my heart. I think you know that by now. I will be with her every step of the way. I will take care of her and our child."

Enzio nodded. "Perhaps once I would have demanded you wed her *immediatamente*, right away, yes? But...now? She is happy with you. This I have seen. She has never been without. You do love her, I have witnessed this. She is...my only child, now. I only want to see her happy." His voice broke and he looked away, clearing his throat again and blinking hard. "I worry, of course, that this will interfere with her plans for a career, but that is her choice."

"Mr. de Rosa...Enzio, sir, that is completely her choice. I want her to do what makes her happy. I will do everything in my power to make sure she finishes her degrees and has a career, if that's what she wants." I paused, then continued, "I don't know how much you know about my plans for after college, but I've been scouted by the NFL for the last few seasons, and there's no question of my going pro. I will take care of your daughter, and I'll do it well. Money won't…won't be an object."

He nodded and glanced at his wife, then back to both of us. "And marriage? Have you discussed that?"

Becca spoke up, answering for us. "Yes, we have. We're not officially engaged, but we are getting married. I hope you'll approve, and that you'll be a part of the wedding and our lives."

"Of course we will, *figlia*," Enzio said. "I know…I know I was often very strict with you, but it…I only wanted the best for you. I am only sorry for it taking the…the death of your brother for us to—for *me* to realize…" He seemed to run out of words then, and he trailed off awkwardly.

"What your father is trying to say is that we are all of us family." Leena rose and glided to the couch where Becca and I sat, drawing her daughter into her arms. "I love you, Rebecca. I can't believe I will be a grandmother!"

Enzio sat back against the cushions, looking stunned. "And I…I will be a *nonno*. Amazing."

We discussed, or rather Leena and Becca discussed, plans for baby showers and wedding location ideas. No one brought up my parents, which was fine by me. I hadn't spoken to them since the day I left with Becca, and I had no intention of that ever changing. I wouldn't reach out to them, either of them, ever. I hadn't thought of them in a very long time, but all of this talk of weddings and babies somehow brought Mom and Dad to mind. I wondered what they would think of me being a father. I wondered if Dad would approve of me playing for the Saints. Probably not. Whichever team I chose wouldn't be the right one, most likely, and I wasn't fool enough to seek his approval anymore.

By the time Becca and I were on the way home late that evening, she was chattering a mile a minute about all the plans she and her mother had made. Apparently, we were having a small spring wedding, around March. We were inviting only those closest to us, mainly Enzio and Leena, Nell and Colt and their parents, a few of Becca's friends from the university, Coach Hoke and few of my closest buddies from the team. Becca would be about ready to pop by that point, as she was due at the end of April. Apparently, unbeknownst to me, Becca had already been looking at wedding dresses and had found one online that would be perfect for her to wear eight months pregnant. I wasn't quite sure why we didn't just get married sooner, like in December or January, but when I suggested that, Leena and Becca both just gave me matching *what are you, stupid?* kind of looks.

"I'm not getting married in the winter," Becca had declared, and that was that.

Enzio had smirked at me, drawing me into his study, where he poured me a glass of thick amber scotch. I almost never drank, so the scotch burned all the way down and settled in my stomach like a ton of bricks, but after the first few sips I'd started to like the heat of it.

"It's best to let the women have their way with these things," Enzio had told me, clapping me on the shoulder. "They will ask your opinion, perhaps, but it doesn't really matter, unless you are fool enough to say you don't care, which is the wrong answer. I remember when my niece was married, I saw this whole thing play out. The poor boy Maria married was hopelessly confused, always not understanding when they asked which napkin he preferred, or which flower arrangement was best, and they would never pick the one he liked. 'Why ask me if you aren't going to listen?' he wanted to know all the time. It is women, I told him. You cannot understand their ways, especially as it comes to weddings and parties."

I nodded at his words and sipped the scotch, feeling a warm buzz settle over me as I finished the tumbler of fiery alcohol. Becca drove us home when she realized how buzzed I was, and giggled at me whenever I spoke, the words slurring slightly.

"You're funny when you're drunk," she said, pushing me into our apartment and guiding me to our bedroom.

"It's weird. I don't like it," I told her. "I feel disconnected."

"Well, maybe you should just lie down and let me have my way with you, then." Becca shoved me backward so I stumbled and fell onto the bed, then caught my foot in her hand, unlaced my sneakers and drew them off, then my socks.

"Sounds good to me," I mumbled, watching her as she reached for the button of my shorts.

When I was naked, she stepped away from me and kicked off her flats, then reached behind her to unzip her skirt and let it fall to the floor. I felt myself hardening at the sight of her thighs and muscular legs, the lacy red "V" of her panties. She unbuttoned her shirt slowly from the bottom upward, gradually revealing a bra that matched her underwear. I swallowed hard at the sight of her standing in her bra and panties, skin dark and firm, black eyes roving my body. I lay still and waited, licked my lips, and shifted back on the bed, pillowing my head on my crossed forearms. She unhooked her bra and tossed it aside, her heavy breasts swaying as she moved. Her panties went next, and then she was naked and crawling over the bed toward me, pressing a kiss here and there as she climbed over me, a predatory gleam in her eyes. Her knees settled on either side of my ribs and she leaned over me, draping the soft, heavy heat of her breasts onto my face and dragging them downward, kissing my chin and my cheek, my shoulder and my chest.. She slid and slid, her body flush against mine, until I pressed against her damp, hot opening and glided in. She never paused in her downward slide, pressing me into her folds until our bodies were joined hip to hip and we were moving together, her forearms on my chest, hands cradling my face and her lips devouring mine, the seal of our kiss shifting with each rock of our bodies.

Soon Becca was moaning in rhythm with our thrusting, her motions growing erratic and frantic, and then she collapsed onto me with all of her weight and gasped a breathless shriek into my shoulder as she shuddered and came apart. She thrust madly against me then, pushing up to sit straight, lifting up with her thigh muscles, and sinking down with violent despera-tion. She held her hair back with her hands, head tilted to the ceiling, balancing effortlessly, riding me hard, her full breasts jiggling with every motion. I cupped them in my hands, leaned forward to suckle a nipple into my mouth, eliciting a whimper from her, and then I fell back as my own climax washed over me. I gripped the curve of her hips in my hands and crushed her down onto me, watching her face contort with her second orgasm, watching her breasts bounce so perfectly, and then I came and came into her, calling her name in a low growl. I sat up as my climax rocked through me, pulling Becca's legs around my waist, cradling the back of her head in a tender kiss, her hand on my neck near my shoulder, the sheet draped around us, our hips moving in perfect synchronicity, our hearts beating together.

We sat like that, breathless as our climax receded, bodies entwined and meshed and merged, eyes locked and searching, exuding love in silent exchange.

"Marry me," I whispered.

Becca froze, staring into my eyes, and then a delirious smile spread across her face. "Yes. Yes! Oh, Jason, yes."

"I know I'm supposed to have a ring and ask you on my knees, but—"

"No, this is perfect. That wouldn't have been you." She pulled my mouth against hers in a fierce kiss, then drew away just enough to speak, her lips whispering against mine. "I love this proposal. It's perfect. It's us."

She tightened the grip of her legs around me, moving slightly as if to test my readiness for round two. I was still buried inside her, and the slick warmth of her body around mine was an intoxicating drug in my system, her scent in my nose an aphrodisiac, her lips on mine and her hands skating over my arms and back and chest sending blood thrumming through me, and then I was ready once more, hardening and lengthening inside her, needing her all over again.

I lifted up onto my knees, Becca's weight held in my arms, then crashed forward on top of her, fitting my hips into the "V" of her thighs. She never unlocked her legs from around me and refused to loosen her hold on my neck, gripping me close and rocking against me, our thrusting bodies grinding together in a wild and reckless pace, each taking what we wanted and giving everything we had, crying out and grunting and sighing and moaning and whispering each other's names. She came first, as she always did. I followed soon after, and then we wrapped each other up in a serpentine tangle of limbs and fell into sleep together.

Jason
September, one year later

I danced along the sideline at a full sprint, the toes of my cleats digging into the turf at the very edge of the white line, arms outstretched, eyes locked behind and above me on the brown and white bullet rifling toward me in a perfect spiral. I felt the defenders in front of and behind me, jostling me, shoving and pulling at me, but I ignored them, bulled my way through them. The ball was a laser, shot from Drew's hand straight where I'd be in about....three seconds. Ten more steps. I strained, feeling my balance wobble as I struggled to stay inside the line, between the defenders, and on pace with the incoming ball. My breathing was ragged inside my helmet, and I barely heard the shouts of fans screaming my name. I liked that part, I had to admit.

Then I heard her, above them all. *"Go, go, go! Get it!"*

Such a sweet voice, shouting loud just for me, a momentary distraction as the ball spun into the waiting cage of my high-stretched fingers. I was airborne, although I didn't remember actually making the leap. The ball slipped through my fingers, and I felt desperation flare inside me. A single-second distraction caused by just the sound of her voice, but it was enough to possibly cost us the game if I didn't make the catch. We were down by a single TD, and this could tie the game, giving us a chance to win my first game as an NFL wide receiver. I was still airborne, coming down on one foot, the ball balanced on one palm. My other foot hit, my breath left me in a *whoof* as gravity took over and tried to crash me through the turf.

I had the ball in both hands now, captured in my gloves.

Wham.

A defender slammed into me from behind, his burly arms around my waist, shoulder in my ribs. I went flying with him, knocked airborne by his brutal tackle. I focused every ounce of strength I possessed into clutching the ball in my hands. Time slowed as I sailed forward, green turf and white lines blurring. I saw an orange cone at the L-intersection of two white lines, and realized I was near the end zone. I extended my body toward the thick boundary line of the end zone, stretching my arms as far as they'd go, willing my momentum to carry me far enough. Time unfroze, and the earth crashed up into me, knocking the breath from me as the defending player landed on top of me. I heard a distant roar, but it could have been the blood in my ears, or the crowd going wild. I struggled for breath, sharp pain shooting though my chest, signaling a bruised or broken rib. The other player, a huge beast of a guy named Nate Johnston, was also a rookie, and I'd played against him in college a few times. Nate rolled off me and scrambled to his feet, then extended his hand toward me, his black skin shining with sweat, teeth showing brilliant white as he grinned at me from inside his helmet.

"That was a fuckin' spectacular catch, Jay," he rumbled, jerking me to my feet.

"Thanks," I gasped.

I leaned forward, still unable to catch my breath. I was bowled forward by my teammates crowding around me, jostling me and slapping me on the back. I realized I'd made the touchdown at that point, and glanced at the sidelines where Becca stood with our son Ben on her hip. I kissed the tips of my index and middle fingers and pointed at them. Becca grinned at me, then lifted Ben higher, taking his little arm in her hand and waving at me.

Benjamin Kyle Dorsey was born on April 19th, and he had his mother's curly ink-black hair, but my green eyes. He was the center of my world, and the highlight of my every day. Becca and I were married on March 20th, on a sunny but chilly Sunday, and everyone we loved was there, except Kyle and Ben. We'd set a place at the head table for them, left empty with cards bearing their names on the stacks of china plates.

I gave Becca one last glance, then turned to celebrate my first career touchdown with the rest of my team, still struggling to fully catch my breath. I followed the offense players off the field for the extra point, slumping onto a bench, pressing a hand to my side, where each breath seemed to stab through me.

Doug, the trainer, came over to me. "Okay, Dorsey?"

I shrugged. "Hard to breathe. Might've dinged a rib on the landing."

Doug knelt in front of me, poking and prodding under the pads, then got up to his feet with a grimace. "I think it might be broken. We should get you to the locker room so I can look at it."

"I'll be fine. Just tape it and get me back out here."

Doug shook his head. "Don't be stupid, Dorsey. If it's broken, you can't play."

"Then it's not broken." I didn't bother telling him how many times I'd played with bruised ribs.

I'd never tried to play with a broken rib before, but I knew I had to do it. I wasn't about to get benched my first game. Each breath, each motion was pure fucking agony, so bad my eyes stung and watered when I stood up. I stretched gingerly, stifling a gasp when the motion sent a lance of pain through me.

Doug was no fool, though. He saw the wince on my face. "You tied us up, Jason. Jarred's got the next drive. Come on back, let me look."

I knew I had to at least let him tape it, so I followed him off the field.

"Jason, what's wrong?" I heard Becca's voice from one side and saw her jostling through the crowd to the edge of the stands, cradling little Ben against her chest.

I moved to stand beneath her. "I'm fine, baby. Nate caught me in the ribs, but it's nothing. Don't worry, okay?"

Becca knew me, though, and she saw the pain in my eyes. "Don't be a tough guy, please? Sit out if you're hurt."

"Fuck that. I'm fine."

"Watch your language around your son, Jason Michael Dorsey."

Doug snickered beside me. "Oh, snap, you got the full name."

I glared at him. "Shut up, Doug." I turned back to Becca. "Sorry, babe. But I'm fine, I promise."

Doug moved away and beckoned to me, glancing back at Becca. "I'll make sure he's really fine, ma'am. Don't worry. He doesn't play unless I give him the okay."

Becca seemed relieved, but the worry never left her eyes. I forced myself to perfect stillness while Doug examined my rib, refusing to so much as wince.

"Well, I don't think it's broken, but it's definitely bruised, if not cracked. I'll have to get some X-rays done to be sure. You're definitely not playing with it like that, though."

"The hell I'm not. Tape it and get me back out there." I stared him down.

"Dude, seriously." Doug was a younger guy, thin and fit, carrying himself with authority despite the newness of his position. "It's not worth it. You don't have anything to prove. You just made a catch that'll be pure gold on the Sports Center highlight reels. Sit it out, take care of yourself. Be smart so you can go back to playing that much sooner. If you play and it gets broken further, you'll be out for weeks."

I hung my head and rubbed the back of my neck. I knew if my dad was standing over me, he'd insist I play. Men play hard, and they don't sit out. Unless you can't move, you play, no questions asked.

I could almost hear his voice: *Don't be a fucking sissy, Jason. Get out there and score. You're my son, and you're a winner. Winners don't quit. If you don't get out there and play, everyone will know what a fragile little fucking bitch you are.*

I'd never backed down, ever. From anything. No matter how hurt I was, I played. That had been drilled into me since I'd heard those words at age eleven, the first time I'd gotten hurt on the field. I'd sprained my wrist, and Dad had knelt in front of me, hissing those words into my face, the smell of whiskey on his breath overpowering me, making my eyes water along with the tears I knew I didn't dare shed. I'd gone out and I'd played, and I'd scored. He'd only nodded at me, hadn't said a kind word.

I gritted my teeth and stood up. "Tape…my *fucking*…ribs." I growled the words at Doug, flexing every muscle in my body, clenching my fists, letting adrenaline surge through me.

I let my anger at my dad take over, brought up every memory of his fist crashing into me, every demeaning word. I felt myself swelling up, heat radiating from my skin, anger from my eyes.

Doug paled. "Okay, man. Okay. It's your career, not mine." He snagged the role of tape from the counter and stuck the end to my sternum and pulled it taut around my body, stretching it so it bound my ribs together.

I ground my teeth and clenched my fists, staring at the wall over his head. He rolled it around my torso again and again, pulling it tight and smoothing the edges together. When he was done, the agony of each breath was intense but more manageable. I donned my gear, slid my gloves onto my hands, and pulled the straps tight.

Doug stopped me with a hand on my shoulder, pale blue eyes on mine. "Jason, I'll say it again: You shouldn't play. I'm gonna tell Coach Payton you're playing against my recommendation. You don't have to prove anything. Whatever's driving you right now, it's gonna get you injured. Season-ending, possibly, or worse. A broken rib can puncture your lung."

I pushed past him, my shoulder jostling his and sending a brief bolt of pain through me. It was going to seriously suck to get tackled.

Becca was waiting for me. She saw me in my gear, saw the expression on my face. I didn't stop for her, though, even when she called my name. Ben's babbling voice stopped me, though. I turned back and glanced at him, his innocent face lit up with excitement as he reached for me, and then I looked up to Becca's eyes, which was my undoing.

I moved back to the stands, and Becca switched Ben to the other hip so she could reach down and take my hand. "Don't let him push you anymore," she murmured to me, barely audible over the noise of the stadium. "He's not here. I'm here, and I'm proud of you."

Her words pierced through my self-induced haze of anger-fueled adrenaline. I kissed her fingers and then continued on to the sidelines, taking my place next to Coach Payton.

"Ready, Dorsey?" he asked without looking at me. "We stopped their drive. You're up. Let's win this."

I glanced back at Becca, who was watching me with a pleading expression on her face. She knew exactly what was driving me, and she hated it.

I'm here, and I'm proud of you.

When Dad had been injured, he'd been warned not to play, but he had anyway. His ankle had been fucked up by a tackle, and if he'd let it heal, he would have gone on to play again. Things could've been different for him, I realized. The trainer who'd been working for the Jets at the time had recognized me at a training camp in Florida a few weeks back, since apparently I looked exactly like my dad had back then. He'd told me the story, shaking his head ruefully and bemoaning the stupid loss of what could have been a damn good career.

All this flashed through my head in the split second that my eyes met Becca's.

Coach's voice shook me out of my thoughts. "Dorsey? You're up."

"No, sir. Put Jarred in." The words tumbled out before I could stop them.

He glanced at me. "Sure, son?"

I nodded. "I'd rather not take the chance. It fucking hurts, man."

He peered sideways at me, glanced at his clipboard, then nodded, clapping Jarred Fayson on the back and pushing him toward the field. "Good choice. Go sit."

Fayson ended up making a game-winning touchdown. I went home with my wife and son rather than party with the rest of the guys. They expected this from me already, though, and a few guys ribbed me about being pussy-whipped, but they all respected me for it.

Becca showed me how proud of me she was that night, using just her sweet mouth and soft hands in ways that had me groaning with pain-tinged bliss.

Eighteen: Our Forever
Becca
November

JASON HAD HIS ARM AROUND ME, and beyond him were six of his teammates and their wives and girlfriends, all of us crammed into a roped-off section of the club. The boys were rowdy and the girls loud, most of them having been drinking in the limo we'd all ridden in together. Jason and I were nursing beers, the first either of us had had since before Ben's birth. My parents had come down to visit us in New Orleans, and they were watching Ben so we could have a night out together. Ben was seventeen months old, walking and talking and charming everyone he encountered. He reminded me all too often of his namesake, my brother, in the way he laughed, in his smile and certain angles of his face.

The stage lights dimmed and the crowd in the bar quieted a bit as an MC strode on stage, a mic in his hand trailing the black thread of a cord. "Hey y'all. Welcome to Circle Bar. I'm Jimmy, and it's my great pleasure to introduce tonight's act. Some'a you may know 'em, but after tonight, you'll all love 'em, I can guaran-damn-tee you that. Please help me welcome... Nell and Colt!"

The entire bar rose to their feet when Nell crossed the stage, a guitar slung over one shoulder to hang at her side. Cheers filled the bar, shaking the floor beneath our feet. Colt was right behind her, his guitar held by the neck in one hand, no strap. They sat side by side on stools, settling their guitars on their laps and adjusting the microphones.

"Hey y'all," Colt said, shifting the mic closer so his voice boomed over the fading applause. "Am I allowed to say that? I'm not from the South, but it's okay, right? Cool. So yeah, I'm Colt, and this is the love of my life, Nell." He turned to face her, keeping his mouth near the mic. "Say hey, babe."

Nell smiled at him, then addressed the crowd. "Hey, guys. Thanks for having us here. I guess we'll get started, huh? This first song is a cover that Colt and

I got permission to rearrange. It's called 'Breathe Me' by an amazing artist named Sia. I hope you like it."

She strummed a few chords, paused to adjust her tuning a bit, and resumed strumming, finding a rhythm. Colt waited a few beats, then began picking a counter-melody, filling in the spaces around her rhythm with a more complex tune. After a few bars, Nell began singing. The song was at the upper end of her register, but it fit their sound perfectly.

I'd never seen Nell perform before, and I was in awe. When she'd mentioned, so long ago, that she was going to a school for the performing arts, I'd been stunned and not a little skeptical. She'd never expressed an interest in music before, never shown any particular talent or enthusiasm for performing. Her declaration then had come out of left field for me. It showed me just how out of touch with my best friend I'd been. When she'd left the hospital after her miscarriage, she'd talked about going back to New York with Colt and playing some gigs with him, but she'd never played anything for me. We'd hung out nearly every day for over a month while she recuperated and took some time to find her equilibrium emotionally. She'd told me more about her relationship with Colt, how they'd met and the integral role music had played for them.

She'd eventually gone back to New York with Colt, and we'd seen little of each other over the next year. She'd come to my wedding, of course, but had to go back pretty much right away for a series of shows she and Colt were playing in the New York area. I'd heard from her off and on since then, and she'd emailed me links to articles written about her and Colt highlighting their rising fame as a singer-songwriter duo. They had a knack for covering songs in a unique and unforgettable way, the articles all said, and they would cover anything from classic jazz and swing numbers to indie folk songs, as well as some of the more popular rock and pop radio-play songs.

Nell and I had made plans over and over again to meet up, but after Jason got drafted by the Saints, our lives had entered a whirlwind period of frenzied activity. We'd moved to New Orleans, and I'd applied to and been accepted into LSU's speech language pathology graduate program. Sports media had followed Jason's every move for the months leading up to his first game, and then he'd made that spectacular catch. The subsequent injury had placed him even more directly in the public's eye. He'd sat out two games and then gone back to playing, and he'd been absolutely on fire, scoring multiple touchdowns in every game, setting a pace which would, by the end of that season, shatter club records for most receptions and most receiving yards in a single season.

Nell and Colt, meanwhile, had been rocketing to fame themselves, issuing a self-produced debut album of original material and a few of their more popular covers. They'd gotten numerous offers from studios, but they'd turned them all down, preferring to stay independent, recording and producing a second album at a friend's studio, issuing that album less than a year after the first.

They'd received more and more press as the months went by, and eventually had been featured on the *Late Late Show with Jimmy Fallon*, a spot which had garnered them national attention.

Now they were at the tail end of a tour of the East Coast and several cities along the Gulf Coast. They'd specifically included a stop in New Orleans so they could see Jason and me, and our son Ben.

I watched Nell perform and found myself quietly crying with pride. She'd come so far, endured so much, and now she was on stage in front of hundreds of people every night, singing in a sweet, clear voice I never knew she had. Nell shone—there was no other word for it. She was captivating, her gray-green eyes sweeping the audience, her voice rolling over us with hypnotic beauty. Colt, too, was stunningly talented. He had a way of weaving his voice around hers, matching her in magnetic harmony that underscored the beauty of Nell's voice. Colt was a truly talented guitar player, and together they had the crowd spell-bound.

Jason held me close and nudged me when he realized I was crying. I smiled at him and shook my head, letting him know they were happy tears.

"They're amazing," he murmured into my ear.

"I know. I'm so proud of her. She's incredible."

Nell and Colt played two sets, coming to have drinks with Jason and me and the others in between, and then, at the end of the set, when Nell would have gotten up to leave, Colt stopped her.

"I've got a little surprise," he said into the mic, turning to the side so he could face Nell, dragging the mic over closer to him. "I've been planning this for a while, but I've never felt it was the right time until now."

"What are you doing, Colt?" Nell was clearly a little panicked, glancing from Colt to the crowd and back, fidgeting with the strings of her guitar. This was obviously not a part of the routine they'd planned.

"Watch and see," Colt said, grinning. He strummed a few chords, tuned a few strings down a bit, and then continued, "This was the first song I wrote about us. Remember when I played this in that little dive bar? I thought about writing a new song, or using a cover, but I realized this one really has the most history. It means…just so much for us. This song has changed a bit since then, but…yeah. Here it is. 'Falling Into You.'"

"All my life it seems
I've been barely keeping
My head above the water
And then I saw you
I saw all the pain
Hiding in your eyes
And I wanted
To take it away

But I had no words to heal
'Cause I had no words to heal myself

I was falling, flailing, falling into you
I can't resist you, baby
I was falling, failing, falling into you
Your love healed me

Fate has intervened
Conspiring to draw us back together
And tangle our lives
The siren of your song
And the music of your heart is calling
Whispering my name

And I have the words to heal you
'Cause I found the words to heal myself

Now I'm falling, flailing, falling into you
I can't resist you, baby
I am falling, flailing, falling into you
And I'm falling still
I'm falling still

Now that fate has intervened
And drawn us back together
Past the years and all the pain
Behind our eyes
Despite the ghosts trailing around us
Like a fog of haunting souls
I'm still trying hard to heal you
To take your pain and make it mine
So your beautiful eyes can smile
Into mine

Now I'm falling, flailing, falling into you
I can't resist you, baby
I am falling, flailing, falling into you
And I'm falling still
I'm falling still
I'm falling still."

The crowd didn't move for several seconds, didn't clap or cheer. They simply sat, spellbound. Before they could start, Colton set his guitar down on the stage floor, dug in his pocket, and pulled out a little black box. Nell gasped, covering her mouth with her hands, her eyes shining.

"Nell, baby." Colton snatched the mic out of the stand holder and slid off the stool to kneel at Nell's feet. "I said it to you a long time ago, before I ever wrote that song: I'm not just falling in love with you, Nell, I'm falling into you. That's what the song means. Well, I've fallen completely. I'm into you now. All the way. I love you so, *so* much. More than I could ever say in words or in a song. More than a thousand years of loving could ever express."

The crowd was dead silent. Colton flipped up the lid of the ring box with his thumb, holding it up toward Nell. Light caught the facets of a diamond, glinting bright in the dim bar. Nell slid off the stool and knelt with Colt.

"You're supposed to stay up there until I say the words, babe," Colt said, laughing.

The crowd laughed with him, but quickly fell silent again.

"Yes!" Nell said, the breathed word caught by the mic.

"I haven't asked yet, babe." Colt took the ring from the box, held Nell's hand in his, and slid the ring onto her finger. "Nell, will you marry me?"

"Yes, yes, yes!" Nell flung herself into Colton's arms, the mic popping deafeningly as their bodies collided.

The mic was caught between their bodies, pressed so close the sound of their heartbeats pounding in overlapping rhythm.

"Now, *that's* a proposal," Jason muttered.

I turned to him and snuggled up against him, nuzzling underneath his jaw with my nose. "Ours was perfect. I would have killed you if you'd proposed in public."

He squeezed my shoulder, and we joined the crowd in whistling and cheering as Nell and Colt stood up and kissed deeply, as if they'd momentarily forgotten they had an audience. After a few minutes, Nell and Colt squeezed through the crowd, responding as they came to the numerous pats on the back and congratulations. We chatted idly with Jason's teammates and then slipped away, leaving Circle Bar and catching the St. Charles streetcar line. We ended up in a tiny cafe far off the beaten path, having left the streetcar and meandered through the city on foot until we found an open doorway and inviting smells.

Over coffee and beignets, Nell and I inevitably turned the discussion to wedding plans while the boys talked cars, football, and the latest developments in some show they both watched.

"You're my maid of honor, obviously," Nell said.

"Obviously. So when is the wedding?"

Nell shrugged, sipping her coffee. "I have no clue. I didn't know he was planning this. I honestly had no idea. I'd been hoping, of course, and I'd dropped a couple conversational hints—"

"Nelly, sweets, your hints are like a bludgeon upside the head." Colt chuckled as he delivered this line. "You worked it into conversation at least six times a day."

She frowned at him. "I was not that bad."

Colt just stared at her. "You've got, like, ten episodes of *Say Yes to the Dress* on DVR."

Nell ducked her head. "So?"

Colt's electric blue eyes softened. "So I took the hint."

Jason snickered. "Got news for ya, buddy. Those episodes of *Say Yes to the Dress*? Only gonna get worse. Believe me. Then there's *Four Weddings*, plus there's bridesmaids' editions of *Say Yes*, and…oh, yeah, don't forget *Say Yes Atlanta*. Can't miss that."

Colt's face visibly paled. "Fuck me," he muttered. "That show makes my balls shrivel. I always feel like I need to, like, take a shit or work out or something just to get my testosterone back after she's done watching that shit."

Jason laughed so hard he almost fell out of his chair. "Trust me, I know all too well. We'd sit down to watch TV, and I'm thinking *Law and Order* or *Dexter* or something, but no, she turns on that bullshit, and my choices are sit and watch it, or go in a different room by myself, or have an argument. But when you've been gone all day and you just wanna chill with your girl, shit...it's not much of a choice, is it? Pussy-whipped isn't holding your wife's purse while she's in the changing room, or going home instead of hanging with the guys. Oh no, pussy-whipped is watching back-to-back episodes of a show about goddamn wedding dresses because it's easier than fighting about it. The worst part is when you start to have actual opinions on the dresses, and liking certain saleswomen in the store more than others. You know you've lost your man-card when that happens." He leaned forward and shoved half a beignet in his mouth, just to prove a point. "Here's the deal, though. Real men watch girly shit with their wives, and they don't bitch about it. Because you know what? When you're done watching that girly shit, your woman is happy. And what do happy women do? They take you to bed and bang your brains out."

Nell snorted, Colt laughed so hard he nearly spat his coffee out, and I turned to Jason and smacked him on the arm. "Well, that was crass," I said.

He shrugged, grinning. "I'm just making a point. Am I wrong?"

I rolled my eyes at him. "As it happens, no. You're not. But you could have made your point with less cursing."

"Where's the fun in that?" Jason grinned. "I like swearing. It makes things more interesting."

"Agreed," Colt said, sticking out his fist, and Jason tapped his knuckles against Colt's.

"So," Nell said, in an effort to change the subject, "when do we get to meet your son?"

"How long are you guys in town for?" Jason asked.

"Till Monday," Colt answered. "We have a show in Biloxi on Tuesday."

"I've got practice most of the day during the week, but we have a shortened practice on Saturday since we're playing Sunday. So maybe y'all can come over for dinner Saturday?"

"Sounds good," Nell said. "That gives us time to explore New Orleans a bit anyway."

Saturday was only two days away, and I had a huge paper due for class that Friday. Mom and Dad were asleep on the couch when Jason and I got home a few hours later, Ben passed out across their laps, sprawled out as only a toddler can do. Jason carried Ben up to his crib while I shook my parents awake so they could go to bed in the guest suite.

In bed, Jason turned to face me, his eyes heavy with sleepiness. "Does Nell know what Benny's middle name is?"

I sighed. "I don't think so. It's never come up, I guess. I just call him Ben, or Benny."

As soon as we'd found out the gender of the baby growing inside me, I'd decided to name him Ben, and Jason had agreed. It seemed only natural, then, to give him Kyle's name as well. I knew Nell was doing worlds better these days, but I also knew reminders were still hard. After all, it was still difficult for me to talk about my brother without getting choked up, so I imagined it must be similar for Nell.

Becca
Two days later

Mom and Dad had gone back to Michigan and Jason was still at practice, so I was home alone with Benny, trying to cook dinner and get the house cleaned before Colt and Nell showed up. Jason's salary even as a rookie was enough that we could have afforded help around the house, but I felt strange about paying someone else to take care of my child or clean my toilet, so I'd put my foot down. Today, however, I found myself halfway wishing I had someone else around to keep Benny out of trouble.

He was a fearless one, my little boy. He had no qualms about climbing on to the back of a couch and throwing himself off, just to see what would happen. He also had a penchant for climbing onto the kitchen table and toppling backward off it. The first few times I heard the *thump* and the subsequent squeal, I felt like the worst mother in the world. Even though I'd only turned my back for five seconds to fill his sippy cup, I still felt as though I should've been watching him more closely. He never hurt himself, I came to realize. His cries after falling off the table were more from fear and embarrassment than actual pain, since he never seemed to learn. He would fall off, crack his head on the floor, scream and kick his feet until I kissed him and hugged him all better, but then he would be right back up on the table five minutes later, giggling and doing the booty-scoot across the table....straight off the edge once more.

Now, with my hands drenched in raw chicken juice as I trimmed the fat off a bag of boneless skinless breasts, I heard the telltale impish giggling of Ben doing something he would regret in about ten seconds. I turned away from the counter with the carving knife held point up, effluvia-coated other hand held away from my body, scanning the open-plan kitchen and living room.

"Benny! God, you little troublemaker!" I huffed.

He was standing on top of the flat-topped, waist-high entertainment center, a red and yellow plastic hammer in one hand and his favorite stuffed giraffe in the other. He was bouncing up and down, the butt end of the hammer shoved into his mouth, muffling his giggles. He was daring me to come and get him, I knew. He'd pushed his miniature folding *Mickey Mouse Clubhouse* camp chair over to the entertainment center so he climb up onto it and was now doing a *come-and-get-me-Mom-I-dare-you* dance, waving Giraffey at me.

I set the knife down and nudged the faucet on with my wrist, washing my hands swiftly while keeping one eye glued to Ben the entire time. I was a good fifteen feet away from him, across the kitchen, so if he started to fall, there wasn't much I could do to stop him. I dried my hands cursorily on the hand towel hanging from the microwave handle and then approached Ben. It was kind of like a lion stalking prey; if I moved too quickly, Benny would bolt in an attempt to get away, so I had to move slowly and non-threateningly until I was close enough to lunge for him. As soon as I got within arm's reach, Benny scrambled onto his belly, searching for the bottom of the chair with his little toes, giggling wildly and watching me over his shoulder. I scooped him up into my arms and rolled him so his tan little belly was exposed. He shrieked and kicked, but he couldn't stop the raspberry. He didn't really want me to stop anyway, but the fight was part of the fun for him.

"You can't be up there, you little monkey," I told him between raspberries. "You gotta stay off the TV stand, silly. No, Benny. No." I pointed at the entertainment center as I said "no," serious now.

Ben caught my stern tone and wiggled to get down. "I do." He scrambled up onto the chair and made to climb back onto the TV stand. He patted the top of the dark-stained wood with his little hand. "I do."

I scooped him up again and crossed the living room, tossing him onto the couch. "You don't. No, Benny. *No*. No climbing."

He made an angry face at me and smacked my arm. "I *do*."

I caught his hand before he could smack me again and gave him a stern glare. "No, sir. No hitting. You don't hit Mommy."

He rubbed his eyes then, toys still firmly gripped in each hand. "Mama." He leaned forward and bumped me with his forehead, pretending to cry now.

I gathered him up and sat him on my lap. "That's right. Be nice to Mommy." I turned his face up to mine. "Kisses?"

He pressed his cheek to my lips so I could kiss him and then scrambled off my lap, running at full-tilt toddler speed, cackling, "I do, I do!"

Right on to the table. I sighed, waited until he was solidly on the tabletop, and then scooped him up and plopped him back on the couch. "How about a show so Mommy can finish dinner before Auntie Nell and Uncle Colt get here?"

He waved his hammer and giraffe at the TV. "House, house, house!" he chanted, meaning he wanted *Mickey Mouse Clubhouse*.

I turned on a DVR'd episode of his favorite show and ruffled his curly dark hair. "Now stay out of trouble for five consecutive minutes, *please.*"

I managed to get dinner made by the time Jason came home, slamming the door to the garage with his foot.

"Where's my little man?" he called, dropping his gear bag on the floor of the laundry room and peeling his sweat-stained tank top off. Jason hated showering at the team gym for some reason, so he always came home sweating and smelly. It may have been because he knew it turned me on, though. I hadn't changed yet, so had no problem with letting him wrap his sweat-slick arms around me and kiss me breathless.

Benny came running around the corner at that moment, show forgotten. He slammed into Jason's legs and clawed at his shorts, trying to get up. Jason scooped him up, tossed him into the air, and caught him, nibbling at his belly until Benny squealed and wiggled free.

"Give Daddy a kiss," Jason said, kneeling down to Benny's level.

Benny threw himself at Jason and gave him a sloppy, open-mouthed kiss on his chin.

I huffed in exasperation. "Ugh. He'll give *you* a kiss, but he won't give *me* one. He'll let me kiss him, but he won't kiss me. No fair."

Jason laughed. "He must just love me best." He clutched Ben against him in mock-possessiveness.

I made a sad face and turned away, pretending to cry. "I want a kiss," I wailed.

I watched out of the corner of my eye as Benny glanced at Jason in consternation, then to me.

"Better give her a kiss," Jason advised. "Mommy gets very sad when she doesn't get kisses."

Benny wiggled out of Jason's grip and toddled over to me, wrapping his arms around one of my legs and peering up at me in concern. "Mama?"

I kneeled down and held him by his shoulders. "Can I have a kiss, just like Daddy?"

Benny smiled at me and gave me a sloppy kiss on my cheek. "I do," he said, which was his phrase for just about every situation.

"I'm gonna shower and change real quick, then I'll finish dinner so you can get ready," Jason said. "What time are they coming?"

"Six-thirty," I said, "and it's already a quarter to six, so hurry up."

By the time I'd finished showering and getting ready, Nell and Colt had already arrived and were on the living room floor playing with Benny while Jason finished the sides and set the table. I stood on the middle stair, unseen as yet, watching Nell help Benny stack blocks while Colt tried to knock them down, much to Benny's delight. As soon as they had four or six colored wooden blocks stacked up, Colt would drive a toy truck through the bottom, making the kind of rumbling, sputtering engine noise only a boy could make. Benny would shriek and laugh when the tower of blocks fell, turning to Nell and handing her an armload of blocks so she could stack them again.

I watched this play out several times, and each time my emotions got further and further out of control. Something about watching Nell play with my son had me in tears. She was so happy, so completely content and in the moment, joy shining from her eyes, totally unreserved. Colt saw it, too, his eyes glued to Nell's face as she played with Benny. I saw the love he had for her, and it only made me sniffle that much more. I remembered all too vividly the day I'd walked into her room as she dragged a razor across her wrist. I remembered smelling alcohol on her breath and seeing the desperation in her eyes, the deeply buried heartache.

I descended the rest of the stairs and sat on the floor next to Nell, helping her stack blocks.

She smiled at me and nodded at Ben. "He's amazing. He's the most adorable thing I've ever seen."

"Thanks. He's a troublemaker extraordinaire, but he makes up for it sheer cuteness."

"He looks so much like both of you," she said. She glanced at me, hesitant. "You named him for your brother?"

I nodded, swallowing hard. "Yeah. We never even considered another name." It was my turn to be hesitant then. "He...his middle name is Kyle."

Nell sucked in a quick breath. Colt tensed but kept playing with Ben, ramming trucks together.

"Benjamin Kyle." Nell stared at the carpeting between her crossed legs. "It's a good name. He even kind of looks like Kyle a little bit."

"It's his eyes, I think. Different color, but they're shaped kind of like Kyle's were."

Nell nodded. "He's a great kid." She obviously wasn't sure what else to say, staring at Benny as if seeing Kyle somehow. She visibly gathered herself, pushing away the memories I could see playing in her eyes. "So, Colt and I discussed potential wedding dates."

"Oh, god," Colt said. "I think I'll go help Jason." He stood up, and Benny followed him, grabbing Colt's thumb and walking with him.

"What is it with men?" Nell asked, laughing. "Why are they so afraid of wedding plans?"

I laughed with her. "I don't know. Jason acted like every little decision was taking years off his life. Either that, or if I gave him a choice between two things, he'd act like he couldn't tell the difference. It's just funny."

We watched as Colt and Benny put silverware on the table, Benny climbing up on each chair in turn to put a fork and spoon on the plates while Colt came behind him with knives and rearranged the silverware to each side of the plate. I thought about saying something, but I decided to let it play out. Sure enough, once Benny did the last plate and saw what Colt was doing, he glared at Colt.

"I do." Benny scrambled off the chair, went to the head of the table, and gathered all three pieces of silverware and put them back on the plate, glancing at Colt to make sure he got the message.

"Benny is kind of particular about certain things," I said to Colt. "Silverware goes *on* the plate in this house."

Colt stared at Benny, then at me, then at the plate, and finally shrugged. "Okay, then, on the plates it is." He then went back around the table, putting silverware on the plates.

Benny watched in satisfaction, then dragged Colt to the fridge and handed him a sippy cup. "Juice."

Nell and I watched Colt with Ben, and then met each other's eyes.

"Is that on the horizon for you two?" I asked, gesturing at Nell's fiancé and my child.

Nell shrugged. "I don't know. It's not come up yet. I have a feeling it's going to after today."

"How do you feel about it?"

Nell was silent for a while, and then shrugged again. "I don't know. Part of me is thrilled at the idea of having a baby. Benny is so cute, so much fun. Colt would be such an amazing father. But…it's scary, too. What if…what if I have another miscarriage? The doctor said it was just one of things that happens sometimes. Like, I didn't do anything wrong, and there's no medical reason I shouldn't be able to carry a baby to term, but…I still worry. Sometimes I still feel…fragile, emotionally. I think I'm gonna be healing for the rest of my life in some ways. Am I even fit to be a mother? I mean, how do I tell a kid how their father and I met? How do you explain that to an adult, much less a child?

What if we have a kid and they ask me about the scars on my wrists? What do I say?"

I thought about my answer for long moments. "I'm not dismissing your concerns, Nell, but I think you're over-thinking it. That's all stuff you'll have to deal with in time. But having a child? As long as you have a good relationship with Colt, it'll all work out. Having a baby…it changes things. It changes you. It changes your relationship. It's hard, I won't deny that. Being a parent is at once the hardest and scariest yet most rewarding thing you'll do." My eyes followed Jason as he pulled the chicken out of the oven and cut into it to check its doneness. "Jason and I weren't ready for a kid, Nell. We weren't. Benny was a total surprise. You know that. And we sometimes wonder what we'll tell him if he were to ever ask why his birthday is less than a month after our anniversary. He'll put that together one day, and we're gonna have to find an answer. But…it doesn't really matter, in the big picture. You and Colt love each other. You're in it for the long haul. Don't hold yourself back from having a child just because you're afraid of all the what-ifs. If you're ready, you're ready. The questions will be answered in their own time. The moment you hold your baby for the first time, you just…you know. Everything is different, and even if you could go back, you wouldn't. I wouldn't change anything in my life, because it's all led me to where I am now. I'm married to the love of my life, my best friend and my…my everything. I've never been with anyone else, and I never will be, no matter what happens in the future. And I have my baby boy, my sweet little Benny. If changing even one thing in my life meant not coming to this place in my life, it's not worth it."

Nell scratched with a fingernail at a juice stain on the carpet. "I know what you mean. I'm so happy in my life now. Most of the time. I have Colton, and I'm touring the country making music. It's a dream come true, a dream I never knew I wanted until I had it. I can't imagine any other life for myself, I really can't. I mean, yeah, sometimes in the middle of the night I lie awake and wonder where I'd be if…if Kyle had lived. I'd have gone to Stanford, and we'd probably have a couple kids by now, and I'd be working in an office, wearing power suits and assembling Powerpoint pre-sentations for execs." She shuddered dramatically. "I'm glad I dodged that career. That's not me. That life… that's all a what-if, and it's a moot point. I wonder, but I don't wish for it, because…god, this is something I struggled with so hard for so long…because as much as I loved Kyle, Colton is perfect for me."

"Well, you and Kyle were so young, you know, so it might be impossible to say what would have hap-pened between you."

"No younger than you and Jason when you two got together. You're the same age as me, twenty-four. But you guys have been together for how long now?"

"Eight years."

"You're twenty-four, but you've been with Jason for *eight years*. That's longer than most relationships ever last."

"And in some ways, it feels like we're just getting started. Benny is almost two already, but it feels like in some ways I just had him. We're talking about having another one, actually. Jason wants a little girl."

Jason announced that dinner was ready, so the conversation was cut short, but I caught Nell watching Benny with a speculative light in her eye. Colton saw it, too, but the same gleam was in his expression whenever he bent to listen to Benny jabber around a mouthful of food.

I had a feeling I'd be hearing some news in a few months.

Becca
The following May

I struggled to hold back tears as I straightened the train of Nell's stunning dress. It was strapless with an empire waist and a sweetheart neckline, tasteful beading on the bodice and a back that plunged daringly low. Her strawberry blonde hair was piled on her head in a complex arrangement of pins and knots, with a few wisps dangling free to frame her beautiful face. Her gray-green eyes gleamed with excitement as she turned in place slowly to give me a chance to rearrange the gown around her feet.

I took her bouquet of white calla lilies with dark purple centers, holding it with my smaller matching bouquet. Colt…well, I was a happily married woman more in love with Jason every day, but Colt was so handsome it almost hurt to look at him. He'd had his usually long and messy hair cut short and neat, and he was shaved clean so his hard, rugged jawline stood out. His eyes were an electric, lightning blue so vivid they mesmerized even as I entered from the back of the chapel. His tux was perfectly creased, black and white and formal, and suiting his muscular frame as if he'd been born in it.

Jason stood two spots away from Colt, and it took every ounce of willpower I had to not drag him into the back of the church and have my way with him. Colt might have been stunningly good-looking, but Jason? He was a dream, a fantasy. His blond hair was freshly cropped and artfully messy and spiked, his green eyes catching the brilliant sun like cut jades. His arms bulged out the sleeves of the tuxedo coat, and his powerful neck strained the collar of his shirt. He was, in a word, statuesque. Michelangelo himself couldn't have sculpted a more perfect specimen of a man. To me, at least.

The doors opened once more as Nell held Colt's hands, and all eyes turned to the back of the chapel. Benny, now just turned two, stood in the doorway wearing his own little tux, shoes tiny and shined to a polish, a clip-on tie at his neck and his hair slicked back. I could feel him psyching himself up as he stood frozen in the doorway, the pillow with the rings held on his outstretched hands. He glanced over at the audience, frowning as he realized how many people were watching.

And then he proved that he was, above all else, his father's son. He straightened his back, held his head high, and marched confidently down the aisle, his gaze never wavering. He fixed his eyes on Nell, whom he had come to absolutely adore. He knew she was his goal, as he'd been told over and over again that his job was to bring the rings safely to Aunt Nelly.

Nell, for her part, doted on Benny to the point of spoiling him. She even went so far as to rearrange the usual order of who came down the aisle when to feature Benny as a highlight, even though weddings were supposed to be all about the bride. Usually the flower girl and ring bearer came after the bridesmaids and groomsmen and before the bride, or something like that, but Nell was adamant that Benny be the last down the aisle, bringing the rings all by himself.

So there he was, marching all by himself down the long aisle, acting oblivious to the whispers and pointing and not-so-subtle accolades of Benny's epic cuteness. I felt my heart squeeze at the sight of Benny in his tux, so grown up, so focused on his job.

Benny ascended the steps carefully, and then, unlike we'd practiced, he stood directly between Colt and Nell, holding the pillow with the rings up as high as he could reach.

"I got rings, Nelly. Here go." He gazed up at her, and the crowd awwww-ed appropriately.

Nell smiled down at him, let go of Colt's hands, and gathered her skirts up to kneel at Benny's level. "Thank you, Benjamin."

"I do good?" he asked her, apprehension in his voice.

Nell kissed him on the forehead, laughing. "You did perfectly, little man."

"I have 'Raffey now?"

Nell glanced at me, not sure what he was asking. Nonno—the Italian word for "grandpa," meaning my dad—came to the rescue, settling Benny onto his lap after the minister took the rings. Benny dug his stuffed giraffe, affectionately known as 'Raffey, out of his Nonno's coat pocket and made a loud animal grunting/barking noise, hopping the stuffed animal across Dad's shoulders. Everyone laughed at Ben's antics, especially Nell. She sobered quickly as she turned back to Colt.

The wedding was beautiful, and Nell glowed with a happiness brighter than I'd ever seen in her. The reception was a huge, lively affair at a banquet hall not far from the wedding chapel. At the end of dinner, Nell seemed to be considering something, sipping idly on a glass of sparkling water with a wedge of lime, glancing at Colt and then away.

I was sitting next to her, with Colt's best man, an attractive but hard-bitten black man named Split, on his right side. Nell sucked in a long breath and let it out, having made a decision. She leaned over to Colt, wrapping her hand around the back of his neck and whispering something in his ear. Whatever she told him had Colt's eyes widening with surprise and then delight.

"You are? You're sure?" he asked, not quite quietly enough.

Nell nodded. Colt glanced down at her belly, then up to her face, and I knew what she'd whispered. "I just found out for sure yesterday, and I wanted a special occasion to tell you."

Colt wrapped his arms around her, hugging her close, whispering under his breath into her ear. I heard Nell sniffle, her arms on Colt's broad shoulders, palms flat and trembling slightly.

"Can I announce it?" he asked.

Nell pulled away. "Right now?"

Colt grinned. "Hell, yeah. I'm ecstatic!"

Nell ducked her head to bump her cheek against his. "You're crazy." She glanced up into his eyes. "What if—"

Colt pressed two fingers over her lips. "No. Just... no."

Nell nodded and opened her mouth to bite Colt's fingers. "If you want to announce it, then go ahead."

Standing at his chair, Colt waved at the DJ, who brought over a cordless mic. "I guess now's as good a time to do speeches as any, right? I've got a captive audience, since most of you are still eating dinner. So, this is the best day of my life. I've had a lot of good days, and a few not so good ones, like everyone has. But today...today's the best of them all. I got to marry Nell, you see. Yeah, you can go ahead and be jealous, fellas, because that beautiful, sexy, talented, amazing woman right there is all mine. I won't bore you with the gory details of how we got together, since most of you know some version of the story by now. The point is, I'm the lucky one. She rescued me, and I'll never be able to love her as much as she deserves, but I'll sure as hell try." He paused, and the crowd filled the space with raucous applause and cheers. "Yeah, thanks. So... this is also the best day ever because Nell just gave me some news. Stand up here with me, baby." He held the mic in his hand and pulled Nell to his side, glancing down at her and grinning. "See, she just told me, just now, that we're gonna have a baby."

The cheers were deafening, but no one clapped harder or cheered louder than I did.

"When are you due, babe, do you know?"

Nell rested her head against Colt's arm. "I'm due in December."

Colt glanced away and toward the ceiling, thinking. "Which means you conceived in...March." A slow grin spread across his face. "I think I know exactly when we—"

"Colton!" Nell shrieked, and snatched the mic from him, smacking him across the shoulder.

"Sorry. I'm just excited."

The crowd was laughing and clapping, and then someone toward the back clinked their spoon against a glass, which was soon caught up by everyone in the room.

Colt handed the mic to his friend Split and turned Nell in his arms. "With pleasure," I heard him murmur to her as he kissed her, long and deep.

After a few moments, Split stood up and held the mic to his mouth. "A'right, a'right. Save it for later, you two." Split turned to face Colt as he and Nell sat down to listen. "I've known my boy Colt here since he was nothin' but a scared little cracker livin' in the 'hood. He's been through more than most of y'all could ever imagine, and he's here because he always was the smartest and the strongest of anyone I know. Now, I ain't gonna lie, I saved his ass a time or two, but he's been there for me more than I have him. He's like a brother to me...a brother, and a *brotha*, if you know what I mean." Split glanced out at the audience sitting rapt at the round tables. "But then, most of y'all are white, so you may not know. Guess that makes me the token black guy at the wedding, huh? It's a'right, it's a'right. Point is, after everything Colt's gone through, there ain't no one in this room happier than me to see him get married, 'specially to a damn good woman like Nell. When I met Nell for the first time, I was skeptical. She was nice, but...well...I didn't see back then how strong she was. She took Colt and she gave him a new lease on life, as stupid as that sounds. She did, though, for real, y'all. She loves him, and she gets him. And that's important. So…Colt, Nell, ya'll two are family to me. You're the family I ain't never had, and that's the truth. I love you both, and I'm happy for you. Congratulations." He lifted his glass of ice water to the ceiling, and then toasted Colt.

It was my turn, I realized. I'd been thinking this through for days. I took the mic from Split and stood up, swallowing hard and focusing on my breathing. "Hi. I'm Becca. Nell has been my best friend since the first—the first day of kindergarten. She stole my glue *and* my glitter. We've been friends ever since." I faced Nell. "I'm going to try to get through this without crying or stuttering, but I'm not making any promises. We've both had some…interesting experiences. I'm going to keep this light, since it's a wedding, but Nell, you know what I mean. There were days I really worried about you. You said once you weren't sure you'd ever be okay. Well, look at you now. You're married to an amazing man, and you're gonna be a mommy soon. I'm proud of you, Nell. You…you've come through s-so much, and you've found your happiness. You've found your way to okay. You're going to be a w-wonderful mother, and Colt, you'll be a wonderful father. I have no doubts in my mind. My son loves you, after all, and he actually listens to you better than he does me some days. Right, Benny?"

Benny was sitting on Jason's lap, a piece of bread in one hand and a fork held awkwardly upside down in the other, mashed potatoes clumped onto the end. He looked at me, hearing his name, and then held out the fork to me. "I gots 'tatos. Want some, Mama? Have some 'tatos?"

I couldn't help laughing. "Thanks, buddy. I had some. Do you love Aunt Nelly and Uncle Colt?"

Benny nodded. "Yep. Colt is a horsey. Gived me ride the horsey."

"What about Nell?"

He glanced at Nell, thinking. "Yep. Nelly, you got more candy? More nem-in-ems?"

Nell laughed and leaned toward him. "That was supposed to be a secret. You weren't supposed to have candy."

I glanced at Nell, who blushed and acted innocent. "It was just a few M&Ms," she admitted.

I shook my head. "So that's why he couldn't sit still yesterday." I grinned at her. "Just remember this when I give you your kid back someday. I'll hop them up full of candy and send 'em home, and we'll see how funny it is then."

I had opened my mouth to resume my speech when a loud fart echoed from Ben's general direction. He looked around in surprise, as if wondering where the sound had come from, then turned to me. "Mama, I go poo-poo."

The audience howled.

I covered my face with my hand, mortified. "It looks my speech has been hijacked by a certain little stinker," I said. "I'll end it with this. Nell, I love you. I'm proud of you, and I'm happy for you. Congratulations."

After changing Ben, I came back to the tail end of Robert Calloway's speech, the last one of the evening. After that, the cake was cut and consumed, and the dancing began. Nell and Colt ended the reception by performing their song "Falling Into You," which had received national radio play since their proposal show in New Orleans.

I danced with Jason and Ben, holding my two men close, and watched as Nell strummed her guitar, her wedding dress pooling on the floor at her feet, her voice capturing the audience, joy on her face.

The newlyweds left soon after, and I hugged Nell just before she got into the limo.

"Thank you, Becca," she whispered to me. "I don't know what I would have done without you, some days. I can't wait to be mommies together."

Jason shook Colt's hand, and then wrapped his arm around me, Ben held on his opposite hip. "So Nell is preggo, huh?" Jason mused. "It's about time. Maybe we should think about number two, what do you say, babe?"

I turned to look up at him, an apprehensive smile on my lips. "I think I'm down with that plan."

Jason's eyes lit up. "So, Benny, what do you think about Mommy having a baby?"

"A baby? I not a baby. I a big boy," Ben declared.

"I know you are, bud," Jason said. "There'd be two kids. You and another baby."

"Two babies?" Benny asked, confused.

"Two babies," Jason answered.

I smiled as I watched Benny try to figure out what "two babies" meant.

"I the baby?" he asked.

Jason tickled his belly. "Nope. You're gonna be a big brother."

Benny frowned, his eyes—so much like Jason's, greenest green and beyond expressive—thoughtful. Then he held up his stuffed animal, the question forgotten. "I got 'Raffey. Have nem-in-ems?" He opened his mouth like a baby bird, waiting for M&Ms to be deposited.

Nonno to the rescue. Paper crinkled and Benny twisted in Jason's grip, his attention laser-focused on the sound of a candy wrapper. My dad plunked M&Ms one by one into Benny's mouth, much to my disgust.

"Dad! It's eleven o'clock at night! He's never going to sleep now!"

Dad just shrugged. "It's a wedding, *figlia*. Rules go out the window."

It was well after midnight before Jason and I got Benny asleep on the cot in our hotel room. We shed our wedding finery and curled up in bed, Jason spooning me.

Jason was silent for a while, drowsing. "I hope it's a girl. We'll name her Bella."

I snorted. "We are *not* naming our daughter after *Twilight*."

"Joking, babe."

"What about Evelyn?"

"Hmm. 'S a possibility." He was drifting off, so I let him go and mused through possible names for boys and girls until I, too, was asleep.

At some point in the night, Benny crawled into bed with us, wedging his warm little body between ours. Jason's arm draped across Benny and over my hip, sliding up to caress my belly in his sleep.

I was half-awake, feeling Benny's breath on my shoulder and Jason's hand on my skin. I was totally content, blissfully happy.

The End

Postscript

COLT HELD HIS DAUGHTER IN HIS ARMS, cradling her tiny body into the crook of his elbow. She was in the twilight between awake and asleep, eyes heavy-lidded, little fingers clutching his thumb. She was swaddled in a soft ivory blanket, cartoonish, wide-eyed green owls gazing wisely in a repeating pattern. Her name, Kylie, was stitched in forest green thread along one corner.

When Kylie stirred in the blanket, fussing and mewling as she fought to stay awake, Colt stood up from the rocking chair and paced the length of the nursery, bouncing her gently. She opened her eyes a little wider, staring cross-eyed at her daddy, mouth working and little whimpers escaping. Colt snagged a pacifier from the crib and stuck it into her mouth, and then hummed a few bars. When the humming caused her eyes to grow heavy, Colt drew a breath and then sang, his voice low and smooth:

"You've got your momma's eyes, you know,
My little baby girl.
You take a breath and you capture my heart.
You've got your momma's nose, you know,
My little baby girl.
You clutch my fingers with all your strength,
And you hold my soul in your tiny hands.
I dreamed of you,
My little baby girl.
I dreamed of you,
Every single night for nine long months.
But I never dreamed
You'd steal me with your eyes
So much like your momma's.
Every father has a ghost, you know,
My little baby girl,
He's haunted by all the things he could do wrong.
So I can only hold you close
And hope I do it right,
Hope I love you enough
Hope I give you everything you deserve.
I dreamed of you, you know,
My little baby girl

With your momma's eyes.
I dream of you still,
I dream of what you'll be
And what you'll do.
I dream of seeing your first steps and
Hearing your first word.
I have another ghost,
Every father's subtle fear,
The day we blink you're behind the wheel,
Blink again and you're on a date
With a boy we can't stand,
Blink again and you're graduating,
Blink again I'm walking you down the aisle.
So don't grow up,
My little baby girl.
Stay small and warm and soft,
And fitting in my arms
Falling asleep to my singing voice.
Don't grow up
My little baby girl.
At least not too fast."

Kylie was fast asleep by the time Colt's voice faded. He settled her in her crib, leaned down, and kissed her softly. Nell stood in the doorway, watching.

She fit herself into Colt's side as they watched their daughter sleep. "Can you believe we made something so perfect?"

Colt smiled down at his wife. "Yes, I can, my love."

In those moments, scars were forgotten, nightmares were banished, and fears were soothed. Each breath, each kiss goodnight, each lullaby sung pushed the past further away, until hidden razorblades and nights of pent-up tears were nothing but old memories from another life.

In those moments, the innocence of a baby healed all the deepest cuts.

In those moments, everything was finally okay.

Featured Music Playlist

"Demons" by Imagine Dragons

"I Drive Your Truck" by Lee Brice

"Sure Be Cool If You Did" by Blake Shelton

"Whatever It Is" by Zac Brown Band

"Flightless Bird" by Iron & Wine

"Singers and the Endless Song" by Iron & Wine

"(Kissed You) Goodnight" by Gloriana

"Must Be Doin' Somethin' Right" by Billy Currington

"First Day of My Life" by Bright Eyes

"We're Going to Be Friends" by The White Stripes

"Falling Slowly" by Glen Hansard & Marketa Irglova

"Come and Goes (In Waves)" by Greg Laswell

"God's Gonna Cut You Down" by Johnny Cash

"Your Long Journey" by Robert Plant & Alison Krauss

"Been a Long Day" by Rosi Golan

"Please Remember Me" by Tim McGraw

"Ten Cent Pistol" by The Black Keys

"The Blower's Daughter" by Damien Rice

"Longing to Belong" by Eddie Vedder

"City" by Sarah Bareilles
"Dream" by Priscilla Ahn
"To Travels & Trunks" by Hey Marseilles
"Rhythm of Love" by Plain White T's
"Kingdom Come" by The Civil Wars
"Sleepless Nights" by Eddie Vedder and Glen Hansard
"Breathe Me" by Sia

As in the previous book, music was the heart-blood of this story. I fell in love with Jason and Becca as I wrote this story, and these songs are the soundtrack to that love. Each song tells its own story, and together they weave a single tapestry. As you support me by buying my books, I urge you to support these amazing musicians by buying their music. Art—any and every kind of art—is the truest expression of our souls. Art is what makes us human. It bind us as a society, as a culture, and as a globe. Support art, any art. Buy it, share it, create it. As Neil Gaiman urged in his now-famous address to Philadelphia's University of the Arts: "Make interesting, amazing, glorious, fantastic mistakes. Break rules. Make good art."

About the Author

New York Times and *USA Today* bestselling author Jasinda Wilder is a Michigan native with a penchant for titillating tales about sexy men and strong women. When she's not writing, she's probably shopping, baking, or reading. She loves to travel, and some of her favorite vacations spots are Las Vegas, New York City, and Toledo, Ohio. You can often find Jasinda drinking sweet red wine with frozen berries.

To find out more about Jasinda and her other titles, visit her website: www.JasindaWilder.com.